Fallen Knight

Ceril N Domace

First Printing: 2024

Print ISBN: 978-0-578-96885-8

Ebook ISBN: 979-8-9914889-0-7

Edited by Chih Wang of CYW Editing

Cover Design by Atlas Theseus Schmidt

Map by Sarah Waites of the Illustrated Page

For information about purchasing and permissions, contact Ceril N Domace at cerilndomace@gmail.com
www.cerilndomace.com

Trigger Warnings: violence, mental control, religious trauma, major character death, body horror, panic attacks, PTSD, and alcoholism.

To my parents, my siblings, my friends, and everyone who supported me throughout my writing journey. Your support means the world to me.

To Sparrow and Ron, who did their absolute best to make make me take breaks by demanding dinner at all hours of the day.

ALSO BY CERIL N DOMACE

The Fae Queen's Court

Haven
Avalon
Hiraeth

The Fae Queen's Court: Collected Edition

The Voyages of the Vulturnous

Fortitude's Prize

TABLE OF CONTENTS

The Knights Vigilant are gone.

The hallowed halls they protected are shattered. The skies

above the city of the gods are empty.

The Knights Vigilant are defeated.

Their city is silent and their fields are fallow. Nothing lives in

the Brother's corrupting light.

The Knights Vigilant are destroyed.

Protectors fallen, warriors slain, watch ended. The bane of gods

and temples will consume all.

The Knights Vigilant are gone.

Chapter 1
The Band of Broken Blades

A deep voice floated above the broken bodies and ruined foliage like a bird flies over the sea, high and without care for whatever chaos might be taking place below.

Leon never sang after battles—or at all, if he could help it. Not even the mourning dirges Kelan offered the dead. It didn't mean he didn't appreciate the music, though. The dead rested easier when mourned, even if their names were unknown. And it made the throat cutting go faster.

"Is that the last of them?" he called over the song. It was rotten work, but once the ones that could be saved were seen by the local healers and taken away, the ones left behind wanted company before they died or release to shorten the wait. It was important to offer both.

Wiping his dagger on a cloth liberated from a corpse, Kelan nodded. His voice dropped from the high tones he favored for singing into his deeper speaking voice. "Aye. Bloody fight, this one."

Leon laughed and sheathed his dagger. "Would you have surrendered if you were in their place?"

The Band had been hired to clear out a bandit den near the border. It was unpleasant, but necessary. The few folks left around here didn't need any more hardship on their shoulders, not with the Fallow Lands creeping closer every day.

The corpses around them had been those folk not too long ago. Desperate people, running from the Fallow Lands and the

Templesbane—or at least, the Sister and her husks. People who needed food and coin before they fled any farther. Pity they turned to banditry instead of honest work. The few that survived would either be branded as thieves and released or be bound in servitude to whatever lord or merchant paid their blood tax until they'd worked their debt off. Neither option lent itself to convincing bandits to surrender.

Their desperation clouded their good sense, and too many had paid for it with their lives. Leon leaned over to close the clouded eyes of a dead woman clutching a bloody satchel and a broken axe, whispering a prayer for Death's sentinels to guide her path to judgment. Kelan must have missed her.

"You head back to camp and let Njeri know we're done," Kelan ordered, shoving Leon toward camp. "I'll go to the keep and let the lord know he can come get the bodies."

Technically, Leon outranked Kelan and should handle that, but he took the order without complaint. He hated dealing with nobility this close to the Fallow Lands. Too many of them had Protector advisers, and he'd rather steer clear of those. He had volunteered to help Kelan with the throat cutting because this particular lord wanted to thank the Band personally. Avoiding people who'd dedicated their lives to slaughtering husks, regardless of the cost, was worth more than any recognition Leon could get for his work here. The Sister and the Brother might be separated, but the Templesbane were just as dangerous when forced apart as they were when they were together.

The lord should be done by now. Or, at least, Leon hoped he was. It was getting late, and he could use food and ale.

He pulled his hood low over his eyes and trudged away from the battlefield, his boots squelching in the mud. Between the fighting and the rain, this portion of the road would be a mud pit for days. With luck, their next job would take them in a different direction.

The lord that hired the Band had set aside a field for camping, which was fortunate, because it was difficult to find space for over a hundred tents and seven supply wagons anywhere close to the road after the autumn rains had delivered their bounty. It almost made up for the lackluster pay.

The Band of Broken Blades consisted of almost two hundred souls, and they did not come cheaply. Between them, there were godsworn who still possessed some sparks of power from their oaths, former guards who'd watched their masters fall to the Templesbane, and knights of various orders fleeing the wreckage of their lives alongside the standard rank-and-file sword arms. They lived by their weapons and asked no questions. If a client didn't mind how rough the Band was around the edges, they'd get one of the best mercenary companies in Hyderia.

Leon had been a member for over a decade. He'd joined up only a year after Njeri formed the Band, literally running into her the day after he left Mezeldwelf for the last time, and he'd stayed at her side ever since. There were only a handful of others who could claim that, and they'd become captains alongside him.

Njeri called out to Leon when he emerged from the trees. "Are we clear?"

He nodded and sat heavily on one of the logs around the fire pit. "Kelan is telling the lord. When he gets back, we can be on our way."

She hummed and poked at the fire with a long stick, sending sparks shooting up into the air. "It'll be too dark to get on the road tonight, so we'll leave first thing in the morning." The flickering light sent shadows dancing across her dark skin, catching on the dozens of metal beads woven into her braids.

Njeri had been a guard before she became a mercenary, and she ran the company like she still was one. If the Templesbane hadn't overrun her family's hold, she'd have taken her father's position as the head of the guard.

Now, as head of a mercenary band, she didn't let her leadership training go to waste. Even if her hard and fast enforcement of the rules was frustrating at times, it brought more comfort to Leon than he'd admit. It reminded him of home.

Leon lowered his eyes and focused on the flame. It wasn't for him to notice the way the firelight played over her skin, catching on the burn scars that covered the left side of her face, dipping below her tunic and expanding over that side of her body. That life was one he'd accepted would never be for him. Njeri and he had tried once, but neither of them could let go of their ghosts for long enough to fully let the other in.

"Good to see you finally made it back." A bowl of stew appeared in front of Leon. The person holding it, a Sihianese man built like a smith and almost as tall as Leon, scowled down at him. "Take it—I was barely able to keep Jackie off it. Kelan will have to find his own dinner."

Leon took it, thanked him, and immediately began eating. There wasn't as much meat as he liked, but between the region's poor harvest and his own tardy arrival to dinner, he was lucky to get even this much. Fighting was hungry work, and he'd take what he could get, even if Shea was stingier with the spices than Kelan was.

Still, it'd be nicer with a mug of beer. Fighting was thirsty work too.

"It's not as good as Kelan's cooking, but it's still pretty good," a small voice piped up from near Leon's elbow, and he brought his bowl closer to his face so the owner of that voice couldn't reach it. There were numerous benefits to being over a foot and a half taller than most men, and one of those was towering over perpetually hungry little girls.

Jackie smiled up at him, her hands already reaching for his bowl. He raised it even higher and made a show of slurping the last of the broth down. He should feel bad about that, but he'd seen her eat more than three grown men combined and still go back for seconds.

Jackie was too young to join the Band—about ten, if Leon had to hazard a guess. The other kids they'd rescued during the raid where they'd found her had all dispersed to the winds and whatever family they had left. Not Jackie, though. She'd stuck to the Band like a spider web clung to a fly, and they hadn't been able to shake her off. Njeri kept her around, partially because the lower ranks had taken a shine to her and partially because she kept herself useful by performing minor tasks around the camp and helping Kelan cook.

Shea snorted and shuffled around the log to sit next to Njeri. Of all the Band, he disliked having Jackie around the most. If he'd had his way, they'd have dropped her off in a village in the Bandarin Mountains or, better yet, in Mezeldwelf at one of the temples. Jackie's stubborn refusal to go anywhere else was the only reason he didn't push the matter further. Despite all that, he pulled a mealy apple from his pocket and tossed it to Jackie. "Here. This should tide you over until Kelan comes back and you can beg for some of his scraps."

Jackie caught the apple with one hand and made a face. "How long has this been in your pocket?"

Njeri raised an eyebrow. "If you don't want it, I'm sure Leon would be happy to take it. You hardly left him any stew at all."

Leon held his hand out for the apple without prompting, and Jackie took a big bite before he could grab it. "No," she snarled through her mouthful, "it's mine, back off."

He pulled his hand back to a chorus of laughter. Jackie stuck out her tongue and went back to eating her apple with a single-minded devotion. Leon ruffled her hair as he set his now-empty bowl on the ground.

"Any chance of some ale?" he asked, standing to grab another log for the fire. He made a mental note to get more wood before they left the area tomorrow. What they had left wouldn't be enough to keep them warm if the weather turned again, and with winter coming on, they needed as much wood as they could get.

Njeri shook her head and jerked a thumb over her shoulder, toward a familiar blond lump that was sleeping underneath one of the supply wagons. "Bettany looked, but the harvest was poor enough that no one is willing to sell us their stock. She wants to keep the rest of our supply for the trip back inland."

"There should be some sleeping tea left if you need it," Shea cut in. He balanced a large washtub on one hip full of the other dishes from dinner. "It's not much, but if you're tired from the fight, it'll knock you out." The unspoken meaning beneath his words was all too clear.

Leon didn't sleep well. Especially not this close to the Fallow Lands. They all knew it, and he'd long since lost the desire to be embarrassed about it. He was far from the only member of the Band that struggled with what they'd seen and done.

He considered the offer, mulling over whether the wine he'd squirreled away the last time they passed through a decent-sized town and the exhaustion of travel would be enough to keep him asleep tonight. He could get by on less sleep than most people, but there was a limit. His limbs ached pleasantly from exertion, but if he pushed them much further, there would be problems.

"Maybe," he finally said. "I'll let you know later."

Ale was best for sleeping, but it would set a poor example for the rest of the Band if he drank himself into a stupor on their stores while they weren't even allowed a mug to keep warm. Of course, that was assuming Bettany let him anywhere near the ale casks to begin with. She was a demon when it came to the supplies and more than capable of handing him his ass if he tried to sneak by her.

Njeri narrowed her eyes but accepted his answer without asking any more questions. "There was a message waiting for me when we got back to camp. We'll need to discuss it when Kelan returns."

The words had scarcely left her lips when Kelan's voice boomed out from the darkening trees. "Anyone there to help with this?"

"Speak of Death and they'll find you," Njeri muttered, shoving herself to her feet. "Shea, Leon, go see what he needs. Jackie, keep the fire up. I'll be right back."

Leon followed Shea toward Kelan's voice, waving off others who offered to help. They passed through the tree line and emerged onto the road, where Kelan waited on a wagon driven by two hooded figures. Two lamps hung on either side of the drivers, illuminating the whole scene in a dim light.

"It's about time," Kelan said, grinning. "Come forth and witness the bounty I have brought for us!"

"Shut it," Shea said with no heat. "What've you brought?"

Kelan smiled and draped an arm over a barrel almost half his height. "A prize from our grateful employer," he said. His cat-like eyes gleamed in the growing darkness, one of the hallmark of those sworn to the Order of the Risen Moon.

Leon snorted. "It must be terrible if they're giving it to us."

Kelan protested, but noticeably, the two people driving the cart didn't.

Shea shoved Leon's shoulder and went to take one of the barrels. "If it's that bad, we'll just drink it all tonight instead of hauling it around." He flashed a grin back at Leon. "I'm sure that will be a terrible burden for you."

Making a rude gesture, Leon stepped forward to take his part of the load.

One of the drivers grabbed Leon's arm before he could take it. "You weren't with the others when my lord came to thank you earlier," he said, pulling his hood down to reveal a Hyderian man with white-blond hair and sun-starved skin. His voice was lyrical and smooth around the words of the trade tongue, a hallmark of Falten birth. "Where were you?"

Leon tugged his arm free and pulled back into the shadows, cursing silently and pulling his hood up. "Working. What's it to you?" Now that he was closer, it was clear that neither driver was wearing the lord's colors, and their clothes were too high quality to belong to servants. It never ended well when unknown but well-dressed people asked after him.

"We're looking for someone," the second figure said, a woman by the sound of it. "A tall mercenary with light eyes." She dropped her hood as well and squinted at Leon. White-blond hair the same shade as her companion's rested in loose waves over her shoulders, and a light not cast by the lamps shimmered in the middle of her forehead, where she had a tattoo of an opening eye. Leon's stomach sank further still.

A seer. By the gods, he hadn't run into one of those in ages. If the seer had seen his face in her visions, he'd need to get out of the area as fast as he could if he wanted to stay out of the Protectors' hopeless war.

Shea stepped between Leon and the drivers, a barrel over one broad shoulder. "And there are hundreds of those around here, myself included." His bulk hid most of Leon from their sight. "So unless you've got something you need to tell this tall man in particular, kindly leave us be."

Leon stepped farther back into the shadows, his eyes fixed firmly on the ground. He'd rather avoid trouble with the Protectors of Hyderia if he could get away with it. Ever since the first of their seers had realized not all of the Knights Vigilant were dead, he'd had to avoid them like a plague. They were persistent and damn near suicidal in their determination to wipe out the husks, hang whoever they'd been before the Templesbane took their souls. He'd seen parents cut down their children rather than leave them to that fate, and he wanted nothing to do with their obsessive devotion to a lost cause.

The woman frowned and grabbed her companion's arm. She pulled him back onto the wagon seat, bowing her head at Leon. "My apologies. We mistook you for someone else."

The blond man made a protesting sound but didn't fight her.

As fast as they could, Leon, Shea, and Kelan unloaded the barrels. Leon's shoulders didn't relax until the blond man cracked a whip and the wagon disappeared into the darkness.

Then the tension in Leon's shoulders unwound a fraction, and he let out a deep sigh.

"Protectors?" Kelan guessed. He shifted the barrel around until he had a hand free to pat Leon's shoulder. "Shit, sorry. I didn't realize. The lord told me they were his guests."

"It's all right," he muttered under his breath, adjusting his grip on the barrel. "Even I didn't figure it out until their hoods came down." Thank the gods that the rest of the Band helped Leon avoid the Protectors, even if they didn't understand why it was so important to Leon.

Hopefully, that was the last he'd seen of those two. The last time he'd gotten too close to Protectors, he'd had to separate from the Band and join up with them a month later. He should be safe this time, since they were leaving in the morning, and no lord with territory this close to the Fallow Lands would let a seer leave.

Not even to chase someone like him.

The journey back to the camp felt much longer now. The barrels weighed as much as a grown man, and Leon's stomach churned with each step, anxiety thrumming through him even as he got farther away from the seer and her bodyguard.

A great cheer went up from the other fires when they emerged from the darkness. The Band gathered around to relieve them of their burden, pulling taps and mugs from wherever they'd been hidden. Few things united folks like the prospect of a free drink.

The next few minutes were the essence of chaos. Bettany emerged from her slumber to bring peace, dispatching the barrels to different parts of the camp and appointing deputies to ensure no one started fights.

One of the barrels found itself by the captains' circle, and Leon didn't hesitate to treat himself to a mug. Contrary to his expectations, the ale was excellent. Either the lord actually wanted to treat them or the Protectors were changing their tactics. Either way, he'd get drunk on someone else's coin.

Njeri waited until Leon was two mugs deep and Jackie had gone to bed to pull out the message she'd wanted to discuss. With the anxiety left by the Protectors drowned beneath a flood of ale, Leon was more than happy to listen.

"One of the merchant princes has offered us a job," Njeri said once she'd quaffed half her mug. "Good pay, but we'd have to go all the way to Mezeldwelf."

Leon almost spat out his ale. "Mezeldwelf?" he asked, coughing. "Why would we go to Mezeldwelf?"

Mezeldwelf was the largest trade city in Hyderia despite its proximity to the Fallow Lands. It was a place of beauty and learning and arts, the gem of the northern coasts. The merchant princes that ran it were wealthier than most kings and bound themselves tighter to contracts than Jackie did to whoever was making dinner each night. Leon hadn't been back there since the merchant princes signed the Great Treaty, and he'd rather not visit if he could avoid it.

Shea sipped his ale and hummed. His fingers tapped an incessant rhythm against his thigh. "That's a three-week trip. Which prince and what do they want?"

Shrugging, Njeri passed the message to Shea. "See for yourself. I already showed Bettany, and she thinks we've got the supplies for it, as long as the Sister hasn't consumed any of the river gods along the way."

Shea read over it carefully, and Kelan peeked over his shoulder. Leon debated looking, too, but he didn't care to stand. Besides, he had ale, and someone would spill the beans soon enough.

Perhaps, if he was lucky, the prince wanted them to take care of something outside Mezeldwelf. The pay was sure to be generous, but he'd pass on the gold if it meant going inside the city.

"She wants us to look into a smuggler?" Kelan asked incredulously, ripping the parchment from Shea's fingers. "Isn't that something for the guard to handle?"

Leon's eyebrows shot up, but Bettany answered before he could say anything.

"Yes. To both." Her mismatched blue and brown eyes narrowed at Kelan, who meekly handed her the parchment.

11

"The prince said it was a delicate matter, which you'd have seen if you read further down."

It must be. The current merchant council and the Mezeldwelf guard had a good relationship. Everyone benefited when smugglers and black-market dealers were shut down. Either the prince was imagining things—in which case the Band would get paid well for doing nothing at all—or they weren't and this job would be more complicated than anyone anticipated.

The circle descended into chatter while Leon debated getting a refill. The ale he'd already consumed swirled uncomfortably in his stomach, but he didn't want to face this conversation sober. He shoved himself up and stumbled over to the barrel.

Shea took the message back to get more details while Kelan interrogated Bettany for the same information and Njeri played peacemaker. The conversation would attract attention from the rest of the Band soon. Maybe he'd have to go steer the others away. He could join another fire.

"Leon, you're from Mezeldwelf," Njeri said over the noise. "What do you think?"

Leon groaned and rubbed his hand over his eyes. He'd nearly managed to get through this without talking. "I haven't been back in years, but if it's a merchant prince, they're good for the gold," he said, breathing deeply through his nose. The world spun at the edges. By the gods, he really hadn't had much for dinner. "But the guard-captain doesn't like mercenaries, so we wouldn't get any help from the city guard."

The guard-captain had a personal vendetta against mercenaries. He'd threatened to lock Leon up when he'd heard Leon wanted to join a mercenary troop instead of the city guard. Just one of many reasons Leon hadn't been home in a while.

Njeri nodded. Her fingers twisted in her hair, playing with the beads in her braids. "I had heard that, but the prince assures me that we won't have an issue with the guard."

Kelan leaned forward, resting his elbows on his knees and his chin on his folded hands. "Have you decided, then?"

Leon finally made it to the barrel and refilled his mug. The fire glinted off the gentle flow of ale, and he swallowed harshly. This was strong stuff.

"I think so," Njeri conceded. "It's a long way, but there's a caravan in Amberbrook that wants an escort to Mezeldwelf, so we could at least earn some money for the trip."

She was chewing on her lips again, Leon noted when he sat. The log shifted under his added weight, and Kelan kicked him without taking his eyes off Njeri.

"We could pick you up after the job's done if you'd rather sit this one out."

It took Leon a moment to realize Njeri was talking to him. He drank deeply from his mug and then nodded. "It's for the best. The old man and I didn't part on good terms. I'll find some work on a farm a day or so outside the city and meet up with you when everything's said and done."

Five years ago, that answer would've been wildly different. Back then, the only way he'd have considered going anywhere within thirty miles of Mezeldwelf was if he wanted to get an up-close look at the city prisons, but it had been long enough that most of the people around Mezeldwelf shouldn't recognize his face anymore. That, and Padraeg didn't know which troop Leon had joined, so it wasn't like he'd be able to track Leon down to drag him home.

Njeri didn't look convinced, but she didn't fight it. "It's settled, then. We'll leave for Amberbrook in the morning."

***

Leon stumbled back to his tent long after the fire died and the rest of the Band had gone to bed, his mind spinning from the ale. He, Kelan, and Bettany had made ample progress on their barrel, but even they had to admit defeat eventually. The edges of his vision swam, yet he could feel the terrible burden of sobriety forcing itself upon him. The drink never lasted as long as he wanted. With luck, it would last long enough tonight that he could get to sleep.

A waxing moon cast its light down on him, and he reveled in it. So much so, he almost missed the ghostly figure walking toward him.

Leon Quinn, uttered the figure, a knight clad in armor that no one else had seen since the Templesbane conquered Dhuitholm. **The time has come.**

"Shove off," he told the apparition. "It's hard enough to sleep when you lot don't decide to have your little meetups by my bedroll." It was time to sleep. Now, before more of them showed up and drove the ale from his blood. He didn't dive for his tent, but it was close.

The figure beat him there, hanging in the air like a marionette on invisible strings. **The Protectors are looking for you. The Watchful Peace stirs from their slumber, so you must gather your allies for what is to come.** Other figures emerged from the mist behind the first. Hundreds, perhaps thousands, all wearing the same crest. An owl with wings spread wide and talons bared, a symbol Leon had yearned to wear as a child. A symbol he hadn't seen in years. **The time has come to stop running.**

Ah, so he was to be treated to a visit from all the Knights Beyond tonight. What a rotten ending to a lovely evening.

"It's been working so far," he shot back at the figures. "The Knights Vigilant are gone. One man does not make an order."

The Templesbane had seen to that. When Dhuitholm fell, trapping the Brother inside and separating him from the Sister, so did the knights that protected it. The officers had been knighting all the squires they could in those final hectic days, and Leon had been the last to take the oath. And now, he was all that was left. One ragged mercenary who got out before the Sister destroyed the city to avenge the Brother. One man who'd spent more of his life running from his past than he'd spent serving the god that took the color from his eyes and left their gray mark behind.

You swore the oaths, the Knights Beyond insisted, their voices ringing as one in his head. Once, he'd wondered how the others slept through such a racket. It hadn't taken long before he'd realized he was the only one who heard their cries. The only one who could. **The Brother stirs in his prison, and the Sister schemes to free him. If they reunite, the Templesbane will bring about the darkening of the world and the death of the gods.**

"So you've said before." And before, and before, and before. They got more insistent with each passing year. At least they'd been useful when he'd been a boy. Now they just reopened wounds he'd closed ages ago. "Get new material."

The Watchful Peace waits for you. You must take up the banner again. Their voices echoed in the darkness, a divine chorus of dead servants to a god no one had heard from in years. **The time has come for barriers to fall and life to touch the city of the gods once more.**

Did anything still grow in Dhuitholm? It couldn't. Not with the Brother and the Sister that close. Any god of the land or water in that area must have been consumed by now. Without them, nothing could thrive. Any people that had survived, that hadn't been corrupted by the Sister, had been cut off from the

15

gods and their gifts for twenty years. Nothing could grow in those conditions.

Everyone knew that. The Sister's gorging on the gods of Dhuitholm was the reason he'd barely survived its fall and why he was so certain that he was the last of the Knights Vigilant. That was why going back there was worse than a suicide mission, yet the Knights Beyond always insisted he needed to prepare for the day he did just that.

"If you're not going to say anything new, I'm going to sleep." Whether from their presence or his body's enhanced defenses filtering out the alcohol, he was approaching sobriety far faster than he'd like.

Pushing through the ghosts, he entered his tent and climbed into his bedroll. Quiet muttering followed him in as the Knights Beyond broke their unified front and each whispered their own desires at him.

Pursue justice, some whispered, their voices sliding over him like a feather. No, he was right to hide, others countered. The Templesbane had ordered the deaths of anyone tied to Dhuitholm. If he emerged now, they'd kill him, and all of this would have been for nothing. Still others encouraged him to join the Protectors, or to beg his foster father for his forgiveness, or to roam on his own, attacking husks and saving gods wherever he found them. To roam, to lead, to return, to survive. Hundreds of thousands of voices, each with their own wants and desires.

And him, stuck in the middle.

Sleep did not come easily that night.

Chapter 2
The Road to Mezeldwelf

The morning was not kind to Leon. He might have been sober by the time the Knights Beyond left him to his rest, but dawn had been closer than dusk. When Kelan sounded the bell, Leon woke feeling like an anvil was on his chest. At least Bettany had been kind enough to prepare a strong black tea for him. It almost made the morning's cheese and bread sit well in his stomach.

By the time they neared Amberbrook, he even almost felt human again.

"Come on, Leon." Jackie's loud voice cut through his thoughts. She smiled at him from her place on the wagon bench. She was one of the lucky few riding today instead of walking, a benefit given to her due to her age. Even the captains had to walk if they weren't driving the supply wagons. If the Band had been wealthy enough for each member to have a horse, they could've sold all their horses and retired. "Kelan says he'll cook tonight if you all stay on topic during lessons today."

Leon chuckled and picked up his pace. His long legs ate up the distance until he was right at Jackie's side. "Is that so? Well, I guess I should make sure my banter is worth losing that."

"It had better be worth it," Bettany shouted from her place on the other side of the horses. The top of her blond head was barely visible, even from his vantage point. Bettany might be as strong as a golem, but she barely came up to Leon's elbows. It wouldn't be long before even Jackie was taller than her. "If the lesson doesn't go well, Njeri's cooking instead."

Leon shuddered in a way that was only half-theatrical. Njeri was a great person to have at your back in a fight, but not so wonderful to have at your cook fire. The things she produced there were edible, but only just. "I'll . . . keep that in mind. Even Jackie's stomach would have issues with that." He bit back a smile when Jackie giggled. "What're you studying today?"

It had been Shea's begrudging idea that Jackie should be educated if she was going to stick around. Or at least, as educated as she could be when her teachers were a handful of mercenaries with varying levels of schooling, and Jackie herself found more worth in scavenging for edible plants while the Band moved than sitting still and listening to lectures. The solution Njeri came up with was to offer bribes and make the others listen too.

"History," Jackie said, bouncing in her seat. Her braids caught on a loose nail, but she didn't seem to notice or care. "Kelan is gonna tell me more about the Great Treaty." Her eyes glinted and her smile turned devious. She loved history, especially the dramatized version favored by Kelan. The discussions that came after, however, were something she'd prefer to skip, if at all possible. "He said you were in Mezeldwelf during the negotiation."

And he'd left when it became clear the merchant princes were more in favor of keeping their own people safe than driving out an unholy evil from the land. "A lot of people were," he said without lifting his eyes from the ground. "I didn't see much."

"But you were there! Did you see the Sister? What was she like?"

Kelan nudged her with his elbow. "Hey now, leave him alone. He doesn't like to talk about it." He sounded apologetic, but whether it was meant for drawing Jackie's attention to Leon or not stopping her before she started to dig was hard to say. "Besides, the Sister didn't come to the negotiations. She can't be that far from the Brother without both losing their abilities, one of the few advantages we have in the fight against the Templesbane."

"Really?" Jackie turned back, Leon forgotten.

He wasn't going to complain about that. He'd only ever seen the Templesbane once before, and the memory still made his legs tremble. The sound of their laughter as the Brother and the Sister cut down knights Leon had known for years haunted him to this day. He'd run as fast and as far as he could. The smoking ruins of Dhuitholm hadn't been far behind him when that sickly green light had flooded from the fortress that had been his home. When the Sister had destroyed the Knights Vigilant as revenge for what they'd done to the Brother.

"Yes, she's been trapped in the Fallow Lands since the Knights Vigilant imprisoned the Brother in Dhuitholm. Whatever magic the knights cast before the city was destroyed keeps him there, so she can't leave either." Nodding, Kelan pulled a canteen from inside the wagon and took a deep drink. "Now, what do you remember from yesterday's lesson?"

Jackie rolled her eyes but sat up straight. "The Great Treaty is a cease-fire between the Sister and the leading rulers of Hyderia," she recited. "It's supposed to keep the husks in the Fallow Lands unless they hear about a Knight Vigilant or the Protectors get too close."

"And?" Kelan prompted, snapping the reins.

Jackie let out a theatrical sigh. "And—" She stopped, brows furrowed, and then threw her hands in the air. "How should I know? All that extra stuff was really boring, and Leon kept making faces at me."

Kelan shot Leon a harsh look, and Leon shrugged. That lecture had been incredibly boring once Kelan got past the story part and into the specifics. Leon hadn't been the only one trying to keep Jackie from falling asleep.

"You still should've been paying attention," Kelan said, turning back to Jackie. "It's important you know this stuff if you're going to be a mercenary one day."

She shrugged and pulled a small bag of nuts from her pocket. "So tell me about it again. I'll try to listen this time."

"I appreciate the vote of confidence," Kelan said, valiantly ignoring the snickering from those around him. "That being said, the treaty *also* forbids any city, village, or farm from harboring a Knight Vigilant or anyone associated with them, even unknowingly. If discovered doing so, the Sister has the right to destroy whoever or wherever is found in violation of the treaty and take the Knight Vigilant."

Leon's smile abruptly fell and his stomach soured. That was another reason he hadn't been home in a while. Bad enough that just being near him could get his friends killed, but going home would risk the people and city that had sheltered him for years. The Sister had sent more than one army of husks to attack people allegedly sheltering surviving Knights Vigilant and Dhuitholm refugees with the bad luck to have worked with them.

Kelan continued, shuffling the reins into one hand so he could gesture animatedly. "Additionally, one of the gods is required to volunteer their altar and high priest to keep the peace."

Shea scoffed and Kelan glared.

"The Sister refused to abide by the treaty unless that was included," he said, a warning edge along each word. "The Templesbane want to wipe the gods out and take their place. In fact, the only reason any gods are still alive—now that the

Knights Vigilant are gone—is that altars and priests need to be brought before her before she can consume them."

Shea snorted again, but this time Jackie interrupted, likely to prevent anything that would keep her from Kelan's cooking. "The gods volunteer?"

To keep the husks—the soulless and empty servants of the Templesbane, the people that hadn't been able to escape them— at bay. Even with their leaders trapped, husks had free rein to travel and couldn't be stopped without wiping out every living person in the world. Hyderia and its peoples would be ruined by endless battle and the corruption that crept out from the Fallow Lands.

"To protect their followers," Shea spat out. "The way the Knights Vigilant should have."

Unbidden, Leon flinched. Fortunately, the others didn't seem to notice.

The Great Treaty was the only one of its kind in all of recorded history. That the gods would willingly give themselves over to a being who wanted to destroy them was unthinkable. That they did it to save humanity, without question and without cost, was a blessing beyond counting. But even that blessing had its consequences. When a god was consumed, the area they held dominion over persisted, but it wasn't *right*.

A smith could still forge, but they lacked the inspiration to truly create. A musician could play, but the words and notes were sluggish and forced. A country could care for poor and disenfranchised refugees, but the people within would grumble and complain that the funds weren't spent on those born there. A lake would persist, but nothing would grow or survive in its depths. Even the gods themselves weren't immune to the effects of consumed siblings. Strength without Compassion too easily became cruelty. Without Control, the Hunt too often forgot all else.

The Protectors—refugees and nobility that had rejected the Great Treaty—were the only ones that fought against the Templesbane these days. By slaughtering husks and removing altars and priests from anywhere west of Falte, they worked to slow the Sister's advance and fill the crumbling hole the Knights Vigilant had left behind in the foundation of society. It was a losing battle though. Without the spells and magic of the long-lost knights, they couldn't hope to hold anything they reclaimed.

Shea continued, his eyes fixed ahead and his knuckles white around the haft of his war hammer. "The gods offer themselves to sate an unholy hunger in the hopes their people will live to find new faith."

It sounded rehearsed. Like something he'd told himself a thousand times before but didn't quite believe yet.

Shea was from Mezeldwelf too. He'd been a Forge priest before the Forge had been consumed. Like Leon and Kelan, Shea had a god's gifts once. His eyes had burned with the fire of the Forge, his hands heated metal and set wood ablaze, and his ears were as pointed as a blade. No more. With his god gone, so was his oath and his order. With his god gone, Shea was no more than a mortal man.

Guilt wound its way through Leon's stomach, churning around the little food he'd managed to eat that morning. He ducked his head and swallowed back bile.

It wasn't his fault the merchant princes had agreed to the Sister's terms. He wouldn't have been able to change anything or save anyone. It wasn't his fault.

They reached Amberbrook before the lesson could continue, and it was for the best. Shea needed time to cool off, and Leon wanted a drink.

Amberbrook had been a good-sized town before Dhuitholm fell; a crossroads between Beldown and the larger cities on the northern coast. It was slowly starving to death now that traders were refusing to pass that close to the Fallow Lands or travel down the Lyrien River. Every year, more people left the houses their great-grandparents had built to find work and food inland, leaving behind rotting homes and graveyards with too many new graves.

The merchant they were escorting was one of the few that still made the long journey out from Mezeldwelf for the sickly vegetables and ratty furs that were the only goods available this close to the Fallow Lands. The gods alone only knew why she made the trip each year, but at least she paid well for the escort on the trip back.

Leon and Bettany shadowed Njeri while she met with the merchant to discuss their pay. Bettany because she had a better head for numbers than anyone in the Band, and Leon because his height intimidated the folks that Bettany's glare couldn't.

Shea and Kelan met with the townsfolk on the other side of the nearly abandoned market square, bartering the leftover ale and weapons for food and fresh water. The weapons were received with grim necessity and the ale with the desperation of those who knew death or worse waited on the horizon. Once they had both in their hands, the few townsfolk disappeared into their battered houses.

The merchant wasn't any more eager to stick around than those that lived here. When the last of the pleasantries and paperwork were handled, she ordered her wagons loaded and asked Njeri to get the Band into place. The sun was high in the sky, and it was best to be as far from the Fallow Lands as possible before dark.

The merchant's wagons didn't dig nearly as deep into the dirt as they should have at the end of a successful trip, or even as deeply as they had at this time last year. The horses that pulled them scarcely seemed to notice anything had been added at all.

This trade route likely wouldn't last much longer, although whatever gods were left in this region were the only ones that could say for certain. The town wouldn't survive once the last of the merchants stopped coming, and the Sister would consume anything and anyone left after that.

That was the deal, after all. Peace for those inland and a slow, creeping death for those on the border.

Gods, it was worse than depressing. Leon shook his head and pulled his hood up. He should spend less time on the borders. It was starting to get to him.

The caravan made good progress out of town. He pulled back, away from Kelan's lessons about the finer points of the treaty that kept the Templesbane from consuming the gods outright, and found a place in the rear guard. Let the others answer Jackie's questions and rib Kelan for his romanticization of the past. Leon hadn't the patience for any of that right now.

Of course, being at the back meant he missed a lot. Like why, exactly, the caravan came to an abrupt halt three hours outside of Amberbrook, near the old crossroads.

Whispers carried back. Dark murmurs barely loud enough to be heard. A shift in the wind sank Leon's stomach, and he pushed forward through the crowd, tugging his hood up farther to hide his face. Fresh blood wasn't a particularly strong smell, which made the heavy way it sat on the wind, even over the ever-increasing smell of smoke, particularly distressing.

His steps quickened as the smell got stronger, and his mind whirled. There wasn't much to burn out here, and fewer things still that even the most reckless bandit would want to burn.

He got his answer when he neared Kelan's wagon and finally passed the last of the trees blocking his view.

The crossroads inn was in flames. Black smoke billowed out of the windows on the second floor, and tongues of fire had long since become raging pillars of flame. Figures in tattered clothes and battered armor gathered in front of the doors, using spears to hold a heavy wagon in front of the doors despite how the flames were beginning to dig into the wagon too. Charred and still hands hung over the top, the wood beneath them defiled with bloody scratches from desperate struggles to escape the flames.

On the far side, where the well had been last time they passed through here, was a gallows. Six bodies hung from it. The innkeeper, her husband and children, the seer and her bodyguard.

A hand grabbed Leon's collar and jerked him back.

"Inside," Shea hissed in Leon's ear, shoving him toward the wagon as only a former blacksmith could. "Kelan says the husks did this."

Leon's stomach dropped and he scrambled inside. "Is he sure?" he hissed, moving boxes as quietly as he could to make room for himself. He stretched his senses, closing his eyes and reaching toward the burning inn. The corruption, the hollowness where humanity used to be, and the husks that were left behind stuck out like a fox among chickens now that he looked. "How did he know?" Leon should've sensed them long before they got close, but he hadn't used his god's gifts in ages. To think Kelan had figured it out before he did—

But that wasn't the issue now. He could panic over that later, after the husks were gone and he was safely away. Until then, he needed to hide and thank the gods the others didn't question why. His gray eyes were enough to get him hanged in some border towns, and those that killed him would call it a mercy. If the husks found him, they'd make the atrocities at the inn look like a summer picnic and then drag him before the Sister once they'd finished with the Band.

Shea shook his head and held a finger to his lips. "They've seen us." He jerked the curtains closed, and his shadow walked around the wagon, just visible on the other side of the canvas roof.

Leon made himself as small as he could, which still wasn't very small, and pulled bags of bandages and blankets over himself. It wasn't much, but it was better than nothing. The others would keep quiet about him, and they'd be on their way soon enough. They needed to be.

"That's far enough," Njeri's voice rang out sharply in the brisk late afternoon air. "We have no business with you."

"But we have business with you." The person that spoke had no inflection. Each word had the same weight and tone as the one before it, with no way to tell how the speaker felt. "The Protectors were searching for someone." The speaker paused, and the hollow nothingness around them writhed with unholy glee. "A mercenary. An oathbreaker. A knight."

Leon's heart seized. His breathing sounded deafening to his own ears, and his blood screamed.

Njeri's voice broke through his panicked haze like a rock through a window. "They're always looking for someone." The shadows on the outside of the canvas multiplied as dozens of footsteps marched between the husks and the wagons. Dark murmurs almost blocked out Njeri's next words. "What makes you think whoever they were searching for is with us?"

Leon knew without having to hear the speaker's answer. The seer must've died in agony before they strung her corpse alongside her guard and the family foolish enough to give them safe haven. The Brother might be gone and the Templesbane separated, but the Sister had talents enough that she could work through their tools. The husks' interrogations were legendary for their brutality and their indifference.

But the speaker didn't answer. The nothingness stretched, reaching toward the wagons like a maggot toward rotting flesh. Leon pulled his gift back, tucking it into a ball deep inside him, yet he could still feel that oily touch. "We seek those who walked the accursed temple ground before we freed the city of the gods." The speaker said those words with all the gravitas of an ancient prayer, the closest they had come to an emotion since they approached. "We seek those tainted by the foul, watchful god, to purify and make whole their wretched deeds so the Templesbane may continue freeing the world from the stain of divinity."

Njeri snorted, and the mutters took firmer form. Whispers became grumbles became an audible hatred. "As I said, you've no business with us, then. We are mercenaries—and proud of it—but none of us have ever broken our oaths or our contracts."

The nothingness lingered, caressing Njeri, but then pulled back. It wrapped around the speaker, whose voice became deader still. "And yet, the seer—and those who sheltered her—waited for you. Interesting, is it not? Perhaps there are those among you who haven't kept to their oaths."

Leon hadn't abandoned his oaths. They were to an order that no longer existed. A god that had been silent since he was a boy. They had no hold over him anymore.

"The treaty allows you to pursue Protectors, rogue gods, and Knights Vigilant," Njeri hissed. "It does not give you leave to harass innocent travelers this far from the border."

Innocent. Weren't the innkeeper and their family innocent? The poor souls seeking shelter in the inn? No. The Templesbane saw guilt in all who followed the gods they sought to destroy. There were no innocents in their eyes. The husks could not be bargained with. The nothingness within them wished only to consume.

But Leon couldn't tell Njeri that. To do so would mean revealing how he knew, and he wouldn't give up nearly two decades of hiding his true identity for that. He could make up a lie later and avoid any probing questions by hiding from them at the bottom of his mug. He could hope she was smart enough to realize fighting the husks would only end with the Band's corpses hanging from trees and gallows from here to the ruins of Dhuitholm. They needed to get out or—failing that—get him far away. The husks would leave the Band alone if they were chasing him instead.

He couldn't do anything more, no matter how much the unseen and unheard spirits around them cried out for justice, for someone to ensure what had happened to them was never allowed to happen again.

"And yet, we were allowed this. Curious, is it not? Justice was not denied." The nothingness curled tighter still, drowning out any fragment of the divine in the earth, plants, or insects crawling through the grass below them. "We will search the wagons." There was no room for disagreement in that voice. It was as certain as death and as inevitable as despair. "If our oathbreaker is not among you, we will release you with the apologies and blessings of our masters."

The protests were loud and immediate. But Njeri wasn't stupid, and the merchant, wherever she'd hidden herself away, trusted her enough to not interfere.

"I can't allow this," she hissed. "We were hired to protect these wagons, and that includes not allowing thugs to rummage through them. Unless you have cause to search the wagons and can prove it before a magistrate, we will be leaving, *now.*"

The husks had no response, and for a heartbeat, Leon allowed himself to believe that they wouldn't call Njeri's bluff. Their authority this far from the border was thin, and they'd pushed it far enough by slaughtering the Protectors and the innocents who'd sheltered them. Their only real defense was that the Band was escorting a merchant caravan, and the treaty gave them leeway with those if the Protectors were involved.

But without the seer or a witness to vouch for her words . . . perhaps they could get away with this.

Then, the nothingness surrounding the husks swelled and vibrated, silently humming a melody only they and Leon could hear. It relaxed and faded into obscurity, so small now Leon would've missed it if he weren't looking. He inhaled sharply and slid a hand down to loosen one axe from his belt. The Sister had spoken, and not even the gods knew what she commanded.

"Then we will take the gray-eyed one over there." The speaker—with his emotionless and unchanging voice—may as well have commented on the weather. "She is young, but oaths are sworn and broken as readily by children as adults. The Sister will make good use of her."

No. No, no, no, no. They couldn't take Jackie. Leon's fingers tightened around his axe, resolve growing as Jackie's stifled sob cracked the air. They would not take her. There weren't that many husks. If it came down to it, the Band wouldn't let that happen. Leon wouldn't let that happen.

"She's our quartermaster's daughter," Njeri said, lying without skipping a beat. "Her eyes are a trait from her father's side, not a god's gift. She's not a Knight Vigilant."

Bettany grunted, her voice coming from somewhere near Leon's head. She was too short for Leon to see her shadow, but her voice carried effortlessly. "Her father is a mercenary from Falte. Half his bloody country has eyes like ash, but I don't see your kind wiping out the Falten."

The Band protected its own. If asked, half of them would've claimed any of the others as their kin, even if blood made it clear the connection was impossible, and the other half would've backed up each word. And if the bond claim was not enough, they'd follow it through with their blades and their bows. Too many had lost family and village alike to the Templesbane to risk losing the bonds they'd forged in the Band, no matter how fresh.

Now that Njeri had spoken it, the entire Band would swear until their dying day—or until someone else claimed Jackie—that it was the truth. A good handful would follow it up with claims that they'd been present for both the courting that led to her, and her birth.

The speaker made a disbelieving sound. "How convenient."

"And yet true," Bettany drawled. "I've got the stretch marks to prove it."

The nothingness thrummed, but otherwise stayed quiet and still. "Very well," the speaker finally said. "We will follow you to the merchant den and the magistrate. A legion of the pure waits for us three days' ride away. It will be safer for you to travel under the banner of the Templesbane until the truth comes out."

Leon snorted, the sound hidden under dozens just like it. Safe, while traveling with husks, was a relative term. They couldn't refuse. Denying the husks the right to search the caravan was one thing; it was another entirely for a merchant in good standing to refuse their escort. If Njeri denied them, the husks would claim the Band had turned bandit and taken the caravan for themselves. They'd be worse off than when they started. Even if they escaped with their necks intact, they'd never find work again.

With the offer extended, they were trapped.

He was trapped.

The world pulled in on itself, narrowing down to Leon and the tiny scrap he could see through a hole in the blanket. Each breath became a battle made harder as he bit back any noise that could draw attention to him.

Breathe. He needed to breathe like Aoife had taught him. Deep breaths. Njeri's voice and another, only slightly familiar one, trickled in, but they might as well have been speaking one of the Sihianese or Alkan languages, for all he could understand it.

The world settled into its place again. It might not be safe here, but it was even less safe if he got caught because he was panicking. The way his heart leaped into his throat when three knocks came from the rear of the wagon was not a good sign.

Dodging around the now-scattered supplies he'd been hiding under, Leon crept to the curtain and cracked it open a hair. Kelan waited on the other side with two of the junior Band members beside him. To a casual observer, they looked bored out of their skulls from the ongoing but muffled negotiations. To Leon, they were clearly keeping watch.

"Njeri's bought you some time," Kelan said in a low voice without moving his lips. He turned his head a fraction, and the cat-like slits in his eyes widened to accommodate the light change. His nostrils flared, taking in a thousand odors Leon couldn't even begin to imagine. "But you can't stay with the Band. The husks have offered to 'escort us' to their legion, and Njeri wants you gone as soon as possible."

Leon nodded. That much was obvious. Even if they somehow managed to convince the magistrate that the husks didn't need to search the caravan, he was too large to hide for more than a few days. "I'll head out once it gets dark. Any chance I can get some food?"

If the gods were kind, he could've said where he planned to lay low, but as the last two decades had proved, they weren't. The less any of the Band knew, the less they could tell others. The only silver lining was that he'd travel faster by himself than the Band and the caravan would. He could get settled in whatever farm he chose to hide in and get a message to the mercenary guild who would get it into Njeri's hands.

Kelan nodded. "Bettany and Shea are putting a bag together. It won't be much, but it should get you to Mezeldwelf without any issue. Gods willing, we'll meet you there and pick up Jackie."

"Jackie?" Leon asked, louder than he meant to. Swearing silently, he shook his head. Starting again, in a much lower voice, he continued, "Why is Jackie coming with me? It's safer for her here." Not by much, granted, but the magistrate wouldn't let the husks take Jackie.

It'd be a dangerous trip to Mezeldwelf for one person, let alone someone traveling with a child. Between the husks, bandits, and peasants too scared of the other two to trust strangers, the main road would be too dangerous to use. He'd have to go on foot through the wilderness.

Kelan shook his head. "Njeri said the merchant we're escorting doesn't want to risk having her with us. The husks have been more aggressive lately, and she says that 'removing the obstacles' will get us back on the road faster." The corner of his lip quirked up. "At least you'll have a horse. The merchant offered up one of her packhorses to whoever can get Jackie away, and Njeri agreed."

Leon's jaw dropped. "She's offering a horse? That's almost half as much as we're getting paid!" Having a horse would cut their travel time in half, presuming it was healthy, and he could sell it when all was said and done.

"She says saving Jackie is more important than a horse." Shrugging, Kelan raised his hand and made a sign for the wagon drivers to launch. The two men he'd brought with him took their place on the driver's seat of the wagon behind Leon's. "And that any chance to screw over the husks is one she wants to take."

Leon let out a low whistle as the wagon started moving again. He could sympathize with that. After Dhuitholm fell, nobles and peasants across Hyderia had taken in refugees, like Leon, that escaped the city. They'd kept the survivors safe even though the Knights Vigilant were gone and doing so would make them a target of the Sister and her husks.

From that rabble of refugees and their caretakers, the Protectors were born while the merchant princes negotiated the Great Treaty.

"But Njeri wants me to take Jackie? Shouldn't Bettany do it?" As tempting as a horse was, it didn't make sense. The husks might want Jackie, but they'd kill for Leon. Better to be down two blades for a short while than lose one altogether.

"She said it'd be better if you did it. She's already told the lower ranks that you're Falten by birth and that you were scouting the road ahead before this. They've all agreed that's more or less exactly what happened." Kelan pulled himself onto the rear bench and settled down like he was keeping watch on the wagons behind him. "She also said that three people are more conspicuous than two." He paused, chewing over his words, and then smiled. "Besides, the less Bettany has to pretend to be a parent, the better. I actually think that horse you're getting would be better than she is."

Leon let out a hollow chuckle. The joke wasn't that funny, but it was either laugh or yell, and only one of those choices wouldn't get him caught.

"Does Jackie know?" he asked when the laughter went to its merciful rest.

"Yeah. She's not happy about missing dinner tonight, but she's lived on the border her whole life." Kelan's shoulders bowed, and he rubbed a hand over his face. "She doesn't want to go with the husks any more than you do."

Sighing, Leon shuffled until he could lie down. "Make sure Jackie and everything we need is ready to go when we stop. I don't want to stay longer than I have to."

Chapter 3
Legends of Old

The brisk wind cut into Leon as they rode down an old farmer's path. They'd been riding for two hours already and wouldn't stop until sunset. Jackie huddled in front of him, one of their blankets wrapped around her shivering shoulders like a second cloak. Their horse, a tall roan stallion, was older than Leon would've preferred, but he carried both of them without complaint.

"How much farther?" Jackie asked through chattering teeth. "We've been traveling for three days already, and my butt hurts."

Leon nudged the horse toward the middle of the path. "Three more weeks if the weather holds." And assuming they didn't run into any more husks. They'd spent most of the first night and day skirting the legion in the area and dodging patrols like the ones that attacked the crossroads inn. "If we're lucky, the main road will be clear, and we'll be able to cut about half a week off our trip."

Jackie grumbled and pulled the blanket tighter around her shoulders. "Can't we stop for breakfast? We haven't run into anyone since yesterday, and I want to get off the horse."

"No. We need to keep moving." Just because they hadn't run into any husk patrols since yesterday didn't mean he could drop his guard. Besides, there could be bandits. A man traveling with a child might make for a poor target, but a poor target was better than none to desperate folk. Still, the horse couldn't go forever. He'd need to rest and eat soon. "We'll stop for lunch," he allowed. "But we can have a snack before then. There's some dried meat in the saddlebag. Get me a slice and you can have two."

Jackie grumbled, but didn't turn down the offer of food. They ate in silence for a quarter of an hour before Jackie started fidgeting again.

"Tell me a story," she demanded. "I'm bored."

A part of Leon wanted to ask if she'd have preferred staying with the Band, but he bit that part back. Jackie was young, and she hadn't asked to live the life she had. Besides, he was bored too.

"What about?" he asked finally, stretching his senses out as far as he could. There weren't any husks nearby, just like the last six times he'd checked. The nothingness inside them stood out like a spot of color in a snowstorm, but he'd already been surprised by them once. He wasn't going to let that happen again.

With luck, they'd managed to escape the husks entirely. Once the husks had searched the caravan, it would've been clear that there weren't any contraband goods or people. They might kick up a fuss about Jackie being gone, but there wasn't anything they could do about it. The wilderness was a big place, after all, and without Jackie at hand—taken by her "father" before the husks could grab her—they had no reason to keep the caravan.

Jackie looked up at him through the mess of bangs and tangled braids she'd refused to let him help with. "Tell me about the Knights Vigilant." Her gray eyes met his, and he quickly looked away.

His heart ached. The wind rattled the tree branches and sent leaves flying in the air. It was as good an excuse as any to keep an eye on the surroundings and not on the little girl in front of him. "Why them?" he managed to ask, proud of how level his voice was.

Jackie, however, wasn't fooled. She slammed her head into his chest, then grunted from the impact. "Because the stupid husks made us leave the Band, and Kelan said—"

"Kelan says a lot of things." That was too sharp and too fast. He'd been on edge since the crossroads and now . . . he took a deep breath and let it out again. "He's a romantic. Very little of what he says matches up with reality."

Snorting, Jackie took another bite. Without bothering to swallow first, she continued like he hadn't spoken. "He said they were heroes. That they were giants with gray eyes and flying horses and that one day they'll destroy the Templesbane and bring back the gods."

He couldn't hold back a scoff. "I didn't think Kelan was a seer." A fog slid through the trees ahead of them, thick as soup. They must be near a lake or river. "The Knights are gone. They all died when the Templesbane attacked Dhuitholm."

Except him, but one man did not make an order.

Jackie shrugged. "Kelan doesn't think so. He says some of them must have survived, otherwise the Templesbane wouldn't still be looking for people with gray eyes."

He grunted. It was hard to argue with that logic. Especially since he was right here, even if no one else knew it. Maybe one of the others was hiding in plain sight the way he was.

They reached the mist, and he slowed the horse to a walk. Better to move slowly than risk an unseen root or ledge.

They traveled in silence for a time. The world narrowed to them and the tiny portion of the trees that were visible in the fog. Jackie huddled into him and pulled the blanket tight.

"People used to say gray-eyed folks were blessed by the Watchful Peace," he said in a low voice, staring into the fog. "That they were called to serve them in ways the Knights

Vigilant couldn't. Maybe the Templesbane thinks that, too, and that's why the Sister pursues them."

"Do you think that?" Jackie fiddled with the last of her meat, ripping it into two pieces and then three. "That the Watchful Peace wants us to serve them."

It wasn't true any more than the superstition about cats serving the Moon was true. There was a difference between a god's gift and something born of blood.

Kelan and his order were given the eyes and reflexes of a cat, but cats themselves were creatures of the Land and the Hunt. Likewise, Jackie's eyes might be gray, but they still held a tiny scrap of blue at the edges. Leon's eyes had been as brown as his hair before all the color had been stripped from them the day he swore his vows. Gods' gifts were a sign of devotion, given to followers to reward them for their faith and dedication, or so older godsworn liked to say.

But all the same, it comforted others to think that the Watchful Peace hadn't abandoned them when the Knights Vigilant fell. Perhaps Jackie would see it the same way.

He shrugged. "Maybe." It was true for him, at least. He'd sworn an oath, one that he couldn't fulfill any more than he could stave off death forever. Jackie didn't have that waiting over her head.

The mist swirled around them, distant trees taking forms that weren't theirs. The air itself felt thick and oppressive, like a storm was waiting for the first crack of thunder to fall. Wisps watched from beneath the distant branches. Figures wearing robes and armor from centuries ago and crests that hadn't seen the light of day in twenty years waited on the other side of the mist. Waiting for Leon to acknowledge them.

He resolutely didn't look at them. After twenty years, he knew the faces he would—and wouldn't—see among them. The

Knights Vigilant he had known were dead, and their souls belonged to the Templesbane.

Jackie pressed into him. Her hands toyed with the blanket hem. "Did . . ." She faltered, fading into silence before her question could escape. "Will I always have to run from them?"

"Probably," he said honestly. "Unless the Protectors actually manage to reclaim Dhuitholm and drive back the Templesbane without the Knights Vigilant, or the Sister stops chasing gray-eyed folk."

Neither option was likely. He'd been little more than a child when the Templesbane attacked Dhuitholm, and the Sister was still after him more than twenty years later. His knighting had been a matter more of desperation than anything he'd earned. There hadn't been time to teach him the rituals and spells the more experienced knights knew. He couldn't even purify husks.

The mist shifted and moved around them, passing through trees and spider webs and vegetation alike. A figure peered through the mist, no more corporeal than the air around her, and held a finger to her lips. Leon stopped the horse and stretched his senses farther still. Nothing stirred in any direction, but it was seldom a good idea to ignore advice offered by the dead.

At least not when he was traveling like this.

"It's not all bad though," he said finally, after he'd satisfied himself that whatever the Knights Beyond were worried about was gone. He nudged the horse's sides to get him going again. "The Band will defend you until you can fight for yourself, and if you stay far enough inland, you should be safe. The Sister doesn't normally send troops past the Lyrien River."

The Great Treaty forbade it without great cause. The Sister kept her troops on the other side of the river, and the folks stuck on the border kept their heads down and their gods close. Away from the border, the husks were only a problem if they suspected a treaty violation. He'd occasionally run into villages that attacked him for fear his eyes would bring the Sister down on them, but they were few and far between. The Band would keep Jackie safe the way they kept each other safe.

Jackie sniffled, and Leon gave her the dignity of pretending not to notice. Let her have her tears while it was safe to shed them. Life was hard. Protecting someone was one thing, but hiding those cruelties altogether did more harm than good.

Something barreled across the edge of his senses, and he reined the horse in. The figures in the mist swirled, some gesturing for him to wait where he was, some gripping weapons that couldn't defend him, and some staring into the distance.

"Leon?" Jackie whispered. "What're you doing? I thought you said we wouldn't—"

"Hush," he said in a low voice, "there's something ahead of us."

Now that he focused, he could sense it. It wasn't the nothingness of the husks, but it wasn't an animal either. Too big and too . . . intentional in the way it moved.

Swearing silently—less for the sake of silence and more because Shea made it clear he didn't want them swearing in front of Jackie—he examined the sensation closer. Some of the knights he'd known had been able to distinguish a cricket from a beetle and figure out what they were doing from two miles away, but that had never been where the direction his god's gifts lay. Still, he ought to have been able to tell the intent of whoever was approaching at least. By the gods, he should practice more.

The feeling moved and multiplied. Whoever was heading this way would find Leon and Jackie soon.

"We need to get off the path," he muttered under his breath. Dismounting, he took the reins in one hand and led the horse deeper into the trees. "Jackie, stay on the horse and if I tell you to run, kick him in the sides and hold on."

Hopefully, he was wrong, but better safe than sorry. With luck, whomever he sensed wouldn't be able to see them through the mist.

No sooner had they gotten out of sight than the first of the beings he'd sensed emerged from the mist. Seven people walked toward them, each armed but holding their weapons with a distinct lack of familiarity. Their clothes were ragged and dirty, coated in equal measures with dirt, grass stains, and dried blood.

A woman led them, a curved Alkan saber at her hip and a beat-up crossbow in her hands. Her blue dress had been fashionable once, and even the rags it was now would be worth a fair amount of coin in most markets.

A scrawny man, not much more than a boy, followed behind her. He carried a standard with an unfamiliar crest on it, one most of this bedraggled crowd wore in some fashion or other. The standard had been slashed in two, and black paint had been splattered across the crest.

A fallen noble, then. But how far had she fallen?

"Who are they, Leon?" Jackie whispered, leaning down over the horse's neck. "They don't look like mercenaries or merchants."

He shook his head and held a finger to his lips to indicate she should be silent. "I don't know, but I don't like the look of them." They were miles from the nearest village or trade road, and as Jackie said, these folk didn't have the look of someone with legitimate cause to be out this way. They moved with a stark desperation that painted the blood on their weapons and clothes in a darker light.

The leader's grumbling became audible as they drew closer, the sharp pitch of her voice cutting through the autumn air like an arrow. "We need to find somewhere wealthier. The food we got from that farmer's larder was hardly fit to feed swine, and the coin they had wouldn't even be enough for a decent bottle of wine."

The man carrying the standard stumbled over her skirts, and she yanked them out from under his feet, glaring at him like he'd spit in her face. "Be careful, you oaf! It's bad enough that this miserable fog is ruining my hair, but that fabric is worth more than your life."

He muttered an apology that went unheard underneath her continuing rant, but Leon had heard enough. Whoever this woman and her followers had been, they were little more than bandits now. Best to stay out of sight until they were long gone.

At least, that was his plan. The gods hated him, though, so that was the moment a bird erupted from a bush near his elbow. Even the thickest mist couldn't hide his frame or the horse when someone was looking right at them.

There was a moment where he fantasized the bandits would move on, letting them go after an awkward greeting that both parties would do their best to forget about. Alas, it wasn't meant to be.

"Get the horse!" screamed the woman in blue. She shot wildly toward Leon and almost struck Jackie. "Kill them—I want that horse!"

Cursing, Leon charged forward. "Jackie, go," he yelled, "I'll catch up to you."

Despite the risks, he couldn't help the feral grin that spread across his face. This was what he was good at. He might not be able to sense or heal or use most of the spells the knights of old could, but he could fight. With Jackie riding away, he didn't need to worry about hiding the full extent of his abilities.

Magic thrummed through his veins, quickening each step and strengthening his limbs for the coming fight. His axes were in his hands before the bandits finished drawing their weapons, and he leaped out to meet them.

The first met his end before he could untangle his sword from his belt. His head fell to the ground three feet from his body. The second dropped her spear and failed to reclaim it before Leon's axe cut through her stomach. She collapsed, scrambling to hold her innards in place while blood spurted through her fingers.

He spun from the downed woman, axes raised to meet the three people charging at him, and pulled at the magic, infusing it deeper into his bones and muscles. Two he could handle with ease, but three made things difficult. The world slowed around him. It was brighter like this, each root, rock, and leaf cast in perfect contrast with everything around it. His axes thrummed under his fingers, a promise of violence to come. He couldn't hold this state for long, but it would be more than enough.

The standard-bearer swung his burden like a club, and Leon chopped it in two, taking one hand with the same blow. Two women, identical in all but the bloodstains and muck covering their clothes, followed right behind him, their footfalls slowed to a snail's pace in Leon's eyes. The swords in their hands were chipped and battered, likely decorative items before they'd been put to their unsavory purpose.

As the standard-bearer fell to his knees, the women attacked. One came from the left, swinging high, and the other from the right, swinging low. There was a unity and grace to their movements, one that whispered that they'd sworn themselves to a god and been given their gifts. Dance, perhaps, or maybe some river god. It didn't really matter, since they were about to die.

The blade coming from the left cut into his palm as he dropped an axe to rip the sword from its wielder's hands. Momentum carried her forward, stumbling toward the ground, as his other axe caught the blade from the right before it could cut into his legs. Pivoting, he spun around the falling woman and allowed his hand to slip up the blade, grabbing hold of the blunted area before the hilt. He thrust the sword down and left it buried in the fallen woman's lung.

His axe slid free of the other woman's sword as she let out an anguished scream. She attacked him with renewed vigor, channeling some magic of her own to nearly match him for speed, but it wasn't enough. They traded blows twice before he got under her guard and sent her to join her twin.

He turned and bit back a wince. The magic he'd cast was already ebbing away inside him. Shooting pains darted up and down his limbs, sapping his remaining strength, and he regretfully let it go. He couldn't afford to exhaust himself yet.

One of the remaining bandits stared at him, horror in his eyes. The bodies of his comrades lay strewn around him, some dead, some dying, and one looking at the stump that was all that remained of his hand. All taken out in less than a minute.

Leon's grin grew wider still, and he hefted his axe. The magic might not be thrumming as deeply as it had at the beginning, but it still ran through him. This would end soon.

"Leon!" Jackie's terrified scream broke through his battle haze, and he whipped around, the remaining bandit forgotten.

Jackie had listened to him but hadn't gotten far. A crossbow bolt stuck out of the horse's neck, and he fought against Jackie's attempts to control him. The woman in blue had one hand wrapped in the reins while the other awkwardly tried to pull her sword out. Her mouth moved, but Leon couldn't hear what she was saying over the pounding blood in his ears.

He moved without thinking. His axe left his hands, spinning through the air, the handle coated in his blood. The magic flowed between them, and he willed it to go faster, to strike harder and true. That stupid woman would not hurt Jackie, not while he had any breath left in his lungs.

The axe struck her dead-on, burying itself deep into her chest. She dropped the reins and lurched back, her hands scrabbling at the axe. They gripped, tugged, and then she dropped like a stone.

Leon realized what was about to happen too late to stop it. As the woman in blue fell, her dress rapidly staining a deep and fresh red, the horse reared up and away from her body, his eyes wide and his nostrils flaring. Jackie scrambled for the reins, but her poor seat and small limbs failed to keep her on his back. She fell, screaming.

Leon charged forward, everything else forgotten. The horse jumped back and forth, bucking and rearing. One hoof came down with a sickening crunch onto the dead woman's head and then twice more. Jackie's screams grew louder still, and Leon ducked around the panicking horse, scooping Jackie up against his chest and sprinting away.

"Leon," Jackie cried, clinging to his shirt. "Leon, it really hurts."

He gently deposited her against a tree, whispering quiet platitudes, and spun around. The horse, now free of anyone on his back or fighting for his reins, crashed into the forest, screaming as only an injured horse could. The lone uninjured bandit had picked up the standard-bearer, and they were limping away. Leon let them go. They were no threat now, and he had larger concerns.

With the battle over, the magic that had been pumping through him fled. His limbs buzzed with exhaustion, but he couldn't stop yet. The horse was gone and with him, most of their supplies. The Knights Beyond, who'd vanished during the battle, reappeared, watching him silently from the shadows.

Swearing to himself, he spun back to Jackie. First things first, he needed to make sure she was all right. Once he knew that, he could make sure the bandits were dead and raid their corpses for whatever supplies they had.

"Where does it hurt?" he said in a low voice, kneeling beside her. "Did you land wrong?"

Jackie nodded, clutching her leg right below the knee. "It hurts," she said again, tears leaking out from under her closed eyelids. "When I fell, my leg got hurt. Make it stop, please make it stop."

Forcing back a curse, he gently pushed her hands away. "I need to touch it," he said as soothing as possible. "Let me know where it—"

She screamed as soon as his hands touched her leg, and he jerked back like he'd been bitten. "No," she yelled, "please don't, it hurts, it hurts—"

"Jackie, I need to touch it, I can't fix it without touching it." It was louder and harsher than he'd meant to be, but he couldn't find it in himself to be sorry. If the sinking feeling in his stomach was any indication, this wasn't going to be an easy fix.

She'd been thrown from the horse's back. He hadn't seen how she landed, but . . .

She sniffled, and when she looked up at him, her eyes were glassy with tears and pain. "I want Shea," she whispered. "I want Kelan and Njeri and—and I want to go back to the Band."

His throat tightened, and he set a hand on her shoulder. At the very least, she didn't flinch away from that. "I know," he whispered, "and we're going to meet up with them when we get to Mezeldwelf, but we can't do that unless you let me look at your leg, do you understand?"

Jackie shook her head. "No, I wanna go home now. This isn't—I don't want to go to Mezeldwelf anymore."

He rubbed her shoulder and nodded. "I know, I know, but we can't do anything unless you let me fix your leg."

Her jaw set tightly, but she nodded. She pulled her hands away only to dig her fingernails into her palms so hard she drew blood. "It really hurts."

Nodding, he moved as gently as he could. Jackie didn't scream again, but the quiet and hitching sobs weren't much better. As he inspected the injury, his heart sank from his chest, down through his stomach, and vanished into the ground below.

If the pain hadn't been enough of a clue, the swelling and twist that hadn't been there this morning made it plain to see.

"It's broken," he said in a low voice, forcing calmness he didn't feel. With the horse gone, they didn't have many resources. He couldn't even offer her ale to dull the pain, but he couldn't leave it either. The bone would need to be set soon, but for now, he needed to keep her calm. It wouldn't help anything if she saw him panicking. "I need to get supplies for a splint." He made to stand and Jackie's eyes widened.

"No," she yelled, latching on to his sleeve like she was afraid he'd disappear, her tears and pain forgotten for the moment. "Please don't leave me, I'll be fine. It's not that bad."

"Jackie—" he tried, but the words got all caught up in his mouth. Sighing, he knelt at her side, his knees digging into the soft dirt. "I'm not going far, and I'll be right back."

"No," she yelled again, holding tighter. "I'll be fine, I promise. I can still walk, I just need a minute."

"You absolutely cannot walk on it," he snapped, pushing down on Jackie when she moved like she intended to prove him wrong. He inhaled and counted to ten. He shouldn't have yelled. Jackie was young and in pain, and her childhood had been rougher than most. The gods alone only knew how long she'd been by herself.

There was a reason Njeri didn't let him talk to injured people. He didn't have the knack for it. Always too harsh, too rough. Shea, despite being a former Forge priest, was good at keeping the wounded calm while Kelan told stories and sang songs to distract them. They understood people in a way Leon didn't.

But he couldn't stay here, and he didn't dare bring Jackie with him. She shouldn't move until he'd immobilized her leg. He didn't know any healing spells, and the healing abilities the Watchful Peace granted him didn't transfer to others, so they'd have to do this the natural way.

Finally, he continued in a much softer voice, channeling his memories of how Shea and Kelan had acted when they'd rescued Jackie. "Stay here while I get wood and cloth for a splint. I'll be right back. I won't even go out of sight, I promise."

Jackie's eyes welled up, but she let him go, falling back against the tree like a puppet without strings.

His heart panged, and he moved as fast as he could.

The bandits, at least, were good for something now. The parts of the leader's blue dress that weren't coated in blood or muck made for excellent bandages, cut into strips with a dagger he pulled from one of the corpses. The pole they'd used to carry the standard was sturdy but couldn't stand up to his axe. Between them, there was a small satchel of coins, a handful of vegetables that were already starting to go bad, some moldy cheese, and three skins full of water. The only thing they couldn't provide was medicine.

Jackie stared at him the entire time he worked, her eyes digging into his back like a dagger. When he returned, arms full and heart heavy, she noticeably relaxed.

"What now?" she asked in a shaky voice, glancing back and forth between the splint materials and her broken leg.

"I have to set it," he said in a low voice. "It's going to hurt."

That would be an understatement. He'd broken his arm as a child and passed out in his master's arms when the healer set it. Shea or one of the others might have tried to soften that blow, but he didn't see the point. Not knowing how much it was going to hurt didn't make it hurt less.

Jackie's skin paled to a grayish white, but she still nodded. "It can't hurt any worse than this," she said, each word quivering. Her tears had slowed, and her smile, a poor attempt at bravado, was wide.

He grunted and pulled his belt off. "Here, bite into this." It wasn't much, but it should keep her from cracking a tooth or biting off her tongue. If the horse hadn't run off, they'd have some willow bark and a wineskin, but wishing never brought him the things he needed.

She didn't argue, just took the belt and bit down as hard as she could. The tension had faded when he returned to her side, but it was back now and worse than before.

"Hold on to my shoulders," he instructed, pushing back the panic swelling in his chest. "Hit or pinch if you need to. I only want to do this once, and you can't hurt me." May Death's sentinels drag those bandits to the lowest hell for landing them in this situation. If Jackie moved wrong, the bone would set poorly. He could cripple her or worse. Having wine or real bandages or even some food to comfort her would've helped.

But he didn't have any of that, and all the curses in the world wouldn't bring the horse back on its own.

He took a deep breath, placed the supplies in their proper places, and nodded encouragingly. "On the count of three."

She nodded, and her teeth dug farther into the leather.

"One."

Jackie's tiny hands gripped his sleeves so hard he thought they'd tear. Her eyes welled up, and he had to swallow around a ball in his throat.

"Two."

Her leg was so small under his hands. The lump where the bone was out of place pressed into his thumbs, as if declaring to the world that nothing could drive it away.

"Three."

The bones slid back into place with a sickening crunch. The leather could do little to hold back the way Jackie screamed or how her small fingers dug into him. There would be bruises when they were soon, but it was over. The bone was set.

Whispering soft encouragement, he moved as fast as he dared. Jackie swayed as he worked—slotting the wood into place, wrapping the bandages around wood and leg alike, not nearly fast enough to make up for how it had hurt—her eyes foggy and distant. She slumped over when he finished with the bandages, eyes closed and mind lost to the realm of dreams.

It was for the best. They couldn't stay here. Her leg might be set, but this was the middle of nowhere, and he needed to gather what supplies he could before they went. She couldn't worry about him leaving if she was unconscious.

He laid her down on his cloak, wrapping the ends around her and leaving an axe beside her. Her lessons hadn't progressed far enough that she was comfortable reading; otherwise he'd have written something in the dirt. Hopefully, it would be enough to convince her he was coming back if she woke up while he was gone.

Picking up a fallen sword, he turned to face the clearing. The mist had cleared and the Knights Beyond were gone. Both suited him just fine.

The bandits had already given up their worldly goods. It was time to see what the forest would provide while he chased down that bloody horse.

Chapter 4
An Unwilling Homecoming

Leon ached more than words could tell, and his stomach was on the verge of caving in on itself, but they were finally here. Mezeldwelf lay before them in all its glory. The setting sun shone on the red walls like fire that lit the Lyrien River and the sea itself ablaze. Riverboats, sailing ships, and merchant wagons alike pushed toward the city along with the occasional lone traveler, all eager to find shelter before the gates slammed shut for the day.

The world spun, and Leon swallowed back bile. He couldn't stop now. They were so close to the help Jackie needed. Once he got her into Mezeldwelf and safely handed off to Aoife—his aunt—he could rest, eat, and drink. Until then, he couldn't stop moving if he didn't want to stop permanently.

Magic could do much, but there were limits. He'd been running for the better part of three weeks with Jackie tied to his back on little rest and less food, sustained by the magic strengthening his legs. He hadn't had much choice in the matter. The bandit leader had seen to that.

He'd managed to track the horse's wild path through the trees—all the way to the ravine where the horse had met his end. The walls were too steep for Leon to climb, and their rope had been in the saddlebags. Leaving their supplies behind galled him, but he didn't have a choice. He couldn't risk leaving Jackie alone if he hurt himself trying to recover their things.

Fortunately, he'd managed to find a stream with which he'd rinsed out and refilled the skins, a willow that was willing to give up some of its bark, and a handful of bushes with berries still on them. It wasn't enough, but it would keep Jackie fed and soothe some of her aches for a bit, and that was the most important thing.

Then he'd tied her to his back with strips of cloth and their sole remaining blanket and run. The Knights Beyond whispered to him as he went, offering advice to strengthen his limbs and clear his mind of exhaustion's fog. Jackie woke periodically, her tears dampening his collar whenever she was conscious, but he didn't dare stop for long. Her skin had grown hot that first night, and the few herbs he'd been able to find did little to cool it.

Now, as if to remind Leon they'd dallied long enough, Jackie moaned and muttered something he couldn't understand. Swearing silently, for he'd long since lost his voice to thirst and overuse, he picked up his pace.

He'd tried to entertain her while they traveled, to keep her mind off how each step jarred her leg and the ties tugged against her bruises. He'd told stories his master, Delke, and his brother, Mael, told him when he was little, the ones he'd begged for on stormy nights and after nightmares, and a few that had become popular since.

Stories about the gods and the Knights Vigilant. How Magic had given the knights tremendous power, how the Sea and Sky together created winged horses to thank them for their vigil, and how Death held back on their due so those who completed their vigil could offer guidance even after their bodies passed. How the knights fought until the last and how the Templesbane was split—Brother from Sister, half from half, and entropy from destruction—and the knights' vigil ended.

She'd liked those stories, at least when she'd been awake to enjoy them, and despite how much it hurt to tell them, he didn't keep them from her. Not when they'd run out of willow bark on the first day. Not when her fevered skin burned against his back.

She slept now, or at least something like sleep. Her murmurs and tears kept him company over the last few miles, and he comforted himself with the knowledge that healers and gods still lived in Mezeldwelf. Aoife would bring Jackie to whichever was closer, and he'd escape outside the city before Padraeg found out he was there. Better to leave Jackie alone in the hands of someone he trusted than to stay and find himself inside a prison cell.

The walls drew near, and he slowed, trailing behind a small group of wagons. With luck, he'd be able to sneak inside with them. It wouldn't be the end of the world if he had to give a name to the guards, but he'd rather not. Between his height and his eyes—not to mention the child on his back—he stuck out in a crowd, and there was always a chance someone would recognize him. It hadn't been long enough for everyone he'd known on the guard to seek greener pastures.

The line slowed to a crawl. All the aches and pains he'd been trying to ignore flooded back, slamming into his consciousness like a battering ram at the gates. The magic he'd used to get here scraped over each nerve and burned where it touched. He'd held it for too long. The knights of old had been able to march for months and fight a battle at the end, but he didn't have their training or their strength.

Silently, he urged the line to move faster even as he took advantage of the wait to drain their last waterskin. His legs shook, his shoulders and back screamed, and Jackie burned against him.

The sun skirted low over the distant horizon, the waves that had been orange as an open flame now as red as a ruby, before the godsworn hunter in front of him, with towering antlers and cloven hooves instead of feet, led her wagon through the gates.

Taking a deep breath, Leon tugged his hood lower still and made to follow her in.

"Stop," called a bored-sounding guard. "We need your names before you can go through."

Leon let out an explosive sigh and turned to the guard. He kept his eyes low, focusing on the guard's neck—lily-white compared to the tanned skin on his face and hands—to avoid meeting his gaze. "Sorry," he mumbled, his voice harsh and cracked even after the water. "I need to get in. M' daughter needs a healer. I'll come back when she's settled, I promise."

The guard would have to be blind not to see Jackie was doing poorly, but it didn't seem to warm his heart any.

"Your daughter and half the folks we let in here," the guard snapped. "But that doesn't change that the princes need to know who is in their city. Name, please, and then we can get you on your way to the temple district." He paused and tilted his head, bringing his face into Leon's view. "And take off your hood. We need to get a good look at you."

Leon bit back a curse. "Is . . . is that necessary?" He didn't recognize this guard, but he didn't want to take the chance that he'd be recognized himself. "I don't . . . It wasn't like that last time I was here."

The guard shrugged. "Things have changed." He pulled a thick book from the table beside him and opened it to a half-filled page. "Now drop your hood and give us your name before we make you spend the night outside, praying the day guard is more willing to risk their jobs."

His counterpart, a dark-skinned woman with her hair done up in a bun made of a hundred braids, stepped between Leon and the city proper. Her lips dropped into a deep scowl. "You're holding up the line."

Sighing, Leon pushed back his hood with shaking hands and brought his eyes lower still, focusing on the first guard's knees. "There's no need," he muttered. "I wasn't expecting this, is all."

The first guard huffed. "That wasn't so hard now, was it? Name and purpose."

"Loran and Jackie Bladesworn," he lied smoothly, adjusting his grip on Jackie. "We're here to see a healer, as I said."

The others would know to look for him under that name. Or at least, Njeri and Bettany would. They used it often enough when they needed to keep a low profile. Having a shared pseudonym made it easier to get back together when all was said and done.

The pen scratched the paper like it had personally offended the man holding it. "Right. Do you know where the healers are, or do you need directions?"

Leon shook his head. "No, I've been here before. I know where to find them."

The first guard grunted, and his book closed with a thump. "Go on in. We'll find you if there are any issues."

Leon bit back a relieved sigh and tugged his hood back up. He stepped around the second guard, only to come to a stop when her spear blocked his path.

"Wait . . ." Her voice was harsh like steel. "I know your face."

Leon's heart sunk, but he made himself smile. Hopefully it didn't look too forced. "I get that a lot. One of those faces, I guess."

There'd been dozens of Alkan folks on the guard when he'd left Mezeldwelf, but she didn't look a day over thirty, so he couldn't have known her. The first guard barely looked old enough to wear that uniform.

She shook her head. "No, it's not that. It . . ." Her eyes widened. "Hob, run to the guardhouse and get the guard book. It should be near the end."

"This is unnecessary," Leon insisted. He stumbled back, his legs trembling under him. It was too late to get to one of the other gates before the end of the day, and he wasn't sure he could run there before she could tell the other gates to keep an eye out for him. "The other guard said I could go in."

"It's very necessary," she snapped, bringing her spear up to his face while her fellow guard ducked through a door on the far side of the gate. "I never forget a face."

Leon kept a smile plastered onto his face, but inside, he was panicking. There was only one reason someone's picture would be in a guard book, but he hadn't thought Padraeg would set the guard on him.

Before the bandits ruined everything, he'd intended on sending Jackie in by herself with a note for Padraeg and Aoife. Even if Padraeg was still angry at Leon, he wouldn't have turned Jackie away, and Aoife would've kicked his ass if he tried. Obviously, that wasn't an option anymore. Even if it weren't for the fever burning through Jackie, she couldn't walk, and he wouldn't force her to try for his comfort.

He could run—or try to, at least—but he wouldn't be able to go far. Even if he did, the closest village was miles away, and they wouldn't have a healer for Jackie, not when they were this close to Mezeldwelf. Even if he could get past the guards and into the city, it'd only be on borrowed time. Without food and rest, he wouldn't be able to avoid capture for long. With Jackie on his back, he couldn't exactly hope to fight and keep her safe. If he stayed here, they'd arrest him or worse.

His heart sank further down into his trembling legs. He stared at the spear in his face and swallowed around the lump in his throat. Only one of his options would see Jackie treated right away.

When the first guard burst from around the corner, clutching a battered book with a red cover to his chest, Leon had already made his choice. Five other guards, each armed and wearing armor stamped with the symbol of Mezeldwelf, spread themselves out in front of the gate.

"Catch him!" The first guard skidded to a stop, his chest heaving. He thrust the book toward the other guard and only then seemed to notice that Leon hadn't moved. "I mean—seize him," he ordered between heaving gasps of air. "Under the orders of Guard-Captain Quinn, this man is to be brought to the Citadel immediately."

Leon raised his hands over his head. "I'll go calmly," he said, forcing his voice to stay steady. "But please—"

"Your daughter will be tended at the Citadel," the first guard snapped as the new guards surrounded Leon. "We've already sent word to have someone meet us there." His face softened, and he patted Leon's shoulder awkwardly. "Don't worry. She'll be all right. The healers here are very good."

A part of Leon wanted to protest, to demand they stop right by the temples first if they were going to arrest him, but he bit his tongue. Padraeg had never been one to punish children because their caretakers broke the law. They would treat her—probably faster than he could get her treated by waiting in line at the temples—and Padraeg and Aoife would take care of Jackie until the Band got to Mezeldwelf. That was what mattered.

Besides, there was always the chance he could escape once he knew Jackie was safe. A miniscule chance, admittedly, but a chance nonetheless.

***

58

The Mezeldwelf Citadel was a sprawling fortress made of the same red stone of the city walls, located roughly equidistant from the gates and the wharf. Besides hosting the city guard and prison, it was where the business of running the city was done and where the merchant princes held their court. Leon was quite familiar with it. He'd spent countless hours there before he left Mezeldwelf, helping Padraeg in his office or training with the guards.

He'd never expected to see it again, and certainly not like this.

His escort led him down the road, past the merchant stalls and tradesfolk closing up for the day, past a handful of abandoned temples, and straight to the prison gate on the east side of the Citadel. The people they passed were more ragged than he remembered. Their eyes followed him, distrust and fear heavy in their faces and movements as they ushered their children away. Buildings that had been bright and well tended when he was a boy showed their age and wear in ways they never had before, thatch and shingles ill tended and in disrepair. There were stones missing from the road, and waste in each alley. Things had changed while he was gone, and not for the better.

Jackie never stirred, never even mumbled at the rapidly changing and deafening racket of the city. His back felt cold and his heart heavy when the healer came to take her away. Her eyes fluttered beneath her lashes, and she moaned when they transferred her to the healer's arms, but that was all. Leon's heart sank and he inhaled sharply. Letting her go hurt more than he'd anticipated.

They would treat her, he reminded himself when his escort pushed him toward the cells. That was why he'd let them take him. Jackie would be safe, and he'd figure out how to escape on his own. Somehow.

His escort didn't give him long to plan or to examine his surroundings. He was taken to the cells, his weapons and armor removed, and his name logged with the warden.

When the cell door slammed shut, he found himself in a small room four paces long and three wide. A mat and a blanket were rolled up in one corner next to a chamber pot. It was more than he'd expected, considering the situation.

Mezeldwelf prided itself on the quality of its jails, but unless they'd dramatically improved since Leon left, this was one of the private cells, meant for spoiled merchant children and those who needed protection from the other prisoners. Leon wasn't one of the former and definitely wasn't one of the latter, so by all rights he should be in the public cells.

But he wasn't going to question it too much. If he were in the public cells, he'd have to deal with the drunks, petty thieves, and thugs currently occupying them, and he was too tired for that. As it was, he wasn't sure he'd have the energy to eat the porridge and bread that a guard slid through the bars before he collapsed on the mat, let alone deal with a singing drunk.

He considered the food, and his stomach, gurgling audibly, made the decision for him. He pulled the tray toward him and slumped down on the mat. Magic took a lot out of its user, and this was better than nothing.

The porridge was tasteless but filling. When he wiped up the last of it with the bread, he wished for more. It would have been more than enough for a normal man but did little more than take the edge off the hunger that hollowed out his stomach.

The sun had finished its slow slide below the horizon before he was done eating. His cell would've gone dark if it weren't for the torchlight flickering in through the bars. The mat felt softer than a feather bed beneath him, calling him like a siren. He'd barely slept since Jackie was hurt. The thought of escape was briefly entertained and just as quickly dismissed. Even if an opportunity came up, he was too tired to move, and the cries coming from his stomach had been satisfied enough for other needs to make themselves known.

Bundling the blanket under his head, Leon stretched out and closed his eyes.

He was asleep within a breath.

***

The sun beat into Leon's face, and he groaned, flopping an arm over his eyes. Every part of him hurt. Moving took so much effort he debated whether filling the cavernous hole in his stomach was more important than going back to sleep. Or maybe he should find some water. His throat might as well have been sand.

"I know you're awake."

Leon's breath caught in his chest. He knew that voice. The last time he'd heard it had been right before he left Mezeldwelf. Its owner hadn't been this calm though.

"I didn't think you'd come down here yourself," Leon rasped, willing his heart to slow. He pulled his arm back and then pushed up into a seated position.

Padraeg Quinn—called the Red by enterprising guards and admiring citizens—guard-captain of Mezeldwelf, and Leon's adoptive father, stood outside the bars. The years had stripped the color from his braided hair and most of his goatee, but the eponymous red hadn't lost the battle altogether. The polished steel of his armor shone in the sunlight like a star had come down from the heavens, which only made Leon's head hurt more.

Fuck, he'd hoped he wouldn't have to see Padraeg again. They hadn't spoken in over a decade, and Leon had been hoping to extend that record.

61

Padraeg let out a harsh laugh. "Who else would come collect the errant son of the guard-captain?"

Leon let out a laugh of his own and didn't bother to hide the frustration and anger behind it. "You're collecting me? What am I, a child? Are you going to send me to my room next, or are you going to finish twisting the knife in my back and turn me over to the council?"

It was a low blow and Leon knew it, but he was hungry, tired, and Padraeg hadn't even given him the decency of an update on Jackie. He'd have thought that if anyone understood how it felt to have a child in your care injured, it would've been him.

"Perhaps," Padraeg said in a low voice. He moved to the right, out of the sun but still visible to Leon. His voice dropped into a register Leon definitely hadn't missed, the same one he'd used whenever he caught Leon in the wine cellars or picking fights down on the docks. "That depends on what you were planning to do in my city."

Shrugging, Leon stood and stumbled over to the water pitcher. A bowl of no doubt cold porridge and more bread waited by the door, but that would require getting close to Padraeg. He'd stay here for now. "I wanted to get a healer for Jackie."

The water was warm and stagnant, but Leon didn't care. He drank half the pitcher before he stopped for breath.

"I know," Padraeg said once Leon set the pitcher down. "The gate guards told me you insisted on it." He tilted his head again, and his voice took on a strange pitch. Somehow hopeful and despairing all at once. "Aoife took the liberty of bringing her to the house. She said it was the least we could do for her, considering who she is."

Leon let out a relieved sigh and slid back down the wall onto the mat. It wasn't much of a surprise. He might have been too exhausted to ask the guards to contact Aoife, but that had been his plan all along. "That's good." He turned and pointedly stared at the opposite wall. "I was going to send her to Aoife anyway once the healers got done with her."

Padraeg sputtered, and Leon bit back a smile. It felt better than he'd expected to get that reaction out of him.

"You just wanted to take her to the healers, then?" he asked in a strained voice. "You didn't even—"

"I'd hoped to be out of the city before you found I was here," Leon cut in. "If I'd had my way, you'd have never known. I didn't anticipate you'd throw me to the wolves like this."

"To the—no, I'd never do that," Padraeg hissed. "Your warrant didn't say why you were to be brought in, just that you were supposed to be if you ever came back. I'd never do that to you." The disgust in his voice could've curdled milk, but it still made for a poor sort of comfort.

"Abusing your rank for personal advantage?" Leon said sharply. "For shame, Padraeg, I didn't think you had it in you. What would the council think?"

Likely nothing. As guard-captain, Padraeg had almost as much power as one of the merchant princes and almost as much responsibility. To have lasted over two decades in that role meant that the council and the people of Mezeldwelf thought his work more than adequate. They wouldn't remove him for the simple charge of arresting someone who lied to the gate guards.

"I didn't—" He took a deep breath. "Since you lied to the gate guards, one of the princes will need to review your case." His face softened. "I imagine you're eager to see your daughter again, but you'll need to wait until I've filled out the paperwork to release you into my custody."

Leon eyes widened. "You trust me on parole? That's hard to believe." There were other things he should address in that comment, mostly that Padraeg actually believed Jackie was his daughter, but frankly the idea that he'd be trusted with even a scrap of freedom was almost too much to believe.

Padraeg let out a sound that could've been a growl. "A monitored parole. We can't have you leaving before your case has been reviewed, or even I won't be able to get you out next time."

"Next time," Leon muttered under his breath. Pointedly ignoring Padraeg, he pushed up to his feet and retrieved his food. "There won't be a next time," he said, sliding down the wall by the door and setting the small tray between his legs. It soothed a petty part of himself that Padraeg would have to crane his neck to look at Leon at this angle. "I'm leaving as soon as I can."

The porridge had solidified into an unappealing gray mass, but it was food, and his stomach felt like a bottomless pit. Besides, it softened up the bread.

Padraeg, unused to being ignored, spoke. "Was that your plan, then? Leave her with Aoife and me so you can go back to gallivanting around the countryside with whichever mercenary band you've tied yourself to?"

Leon shrugged. "Only for a while," he said through a mouthful of porridge and bread. "The Band has a job here, but we ran into a legion of husks on the way from Amberbrook. The others should be here in a few days, and they'll pick her up then."

"Is that it?" Padraeg stepped close, his thick eyebrows furrowing. His eyes sharpened to a deep glare, one that would've sent Leon running away with his tail between his legs a decade ago. Now it irritated him.

Leon shrugged. "There's not much more to tell. If Jackie hadn't been hurt, I wouldn't have come here at all, but I couldn't exactly leave her at the gates with a broken leg."

"You would've left her alone?" Padraeg's expression had shifted from a disappointed glare to a storm front of rage. His chest heaved, and he looked one second from reaching through the bars to strangle Leon himself. "I thought you were better than that. You were raised better—"

"What would you know about how I was raised?" he shot back, returning Padraeg's dark look with one of his own. "I was almost full grown when the Te—" His mouth snapped shut and he took a deep breath. He had no idea who was listening besides Padraeg. This city wasn't safe for him to talk openly. Anyone associated with the Knights Vigilant had been exiled when the Great Treaty was signed. "I don't understand why you care so much. This is the first we've spoken since I left."

"It's not . . ." Padraeg took a deep breath, and his face smoothed. He pulled his hands off the bars and held them behind his back. "You have responsibilities now," he said firmly. "She's your daughter. It's safer here than it is on the road. Why would you want to go back to that? To throwing away your life and loyalty on anyone with gold?"

Leon stared at the window. The sun was high in the sky by this point, and there wasn't much to see, but that endless blue was better than looking at Padraeg right now. "She's not my daughter." He should've brought that up when Padraeg first mentioned it, but he'd hoped Padraeg would figure it out on his own. "She's . . . The Band picked her up near the border of the Fallow Lands two months ago, and she's been following us around ever since. We've all kind of adopted her."

There was more he could've said, but none of it fit. This was part of a conversation they'd failed to have before he left Mezeldwelf. The care had been lost beneath the harsh words and raised voices. Leon hadn't seen how much Padraeg wanted the best for him, and Padraeg hadn't realized that following that path would've killed Leon ages ago. The Knights Vigilant were gone, and Leon hadn't the heart to keep chasing their ghosts.

"I can't stay," he continued, twiddling his thumbs, grateful beyond words that Padraeg hadn't interrupted. He'd thought about what he should've said to Padraeg a hundred thousand times over the years. He'd never quite found the right way to phrase it. "It's not safe here for anyone that could be linked to the Knights Vigilant, and Jackie's eyes are almost as gray as mine. Once I know Jackie will be all right, I'm leaving." It wasn't just Leon that would be in danger if he stayed. The whole city was at risk as long as he was inside its walls. "The others should be here in a few days, and they'll take her off your hands. I don't expect to come back."

The silence stretched on between them. Through the window, Leon could hear the sounds of a city going about its day. The smiths working at their trade, the fishmongers and artisans hawking their wares in regional variants of the trade language that was Mezeldwelf's native tongue, and the repetitive thuds of the guards training.

"I . . . see," Padraeg finally said in a muted tone. Disappointment leached into the air around him so loudly Leon didn't have to look at him to know his face had fallen. "I'll finish the paperwork, then, and collect you in a few hours."

Leon didn't answer. The echo of Padraeg's heavy footsteps faded away, leaving him to stare out the window, listening to a world he'd never get to participate in.

***

Padraeg returned right before sunset, when the golden rays of the sun turned to fire. He returned Leon's gear and waited silently for him to dress. A clerk waited outside Leon's cell, a tracking sigil in hand to ensure Leon couldn't leave until his case had been heard.

The clerk wasted no words explaining any of this to Leon. Their voice was clipped and sharp as the sigil burned into the flesh of Leon's arm and softer as its match practically melted into Padraeg's arm.

They were linked now. Leon wouldn't be able to go anywhere without Padraeg knowing until the sigil was removed or either of them died. If necessary, it could stop Leon in his tracks, making him writhe in pain as it cut deeper and deeper into his arm. If he resisted enough, the mark of the sigil would scar and never fade.

There was a reason this sort of magic was illegal outside of the Citadel. Only sworn followers of Justice could cast it, and only elite members of the guard could bear the corresponding mark.

Leon and Padraeg exchanged no words as they walked down the familiar streets to Quinn Manor near the docks. The streets came alive as they went. Temples, taverns, and shelters rang with cheer as their patrons spilled onto the streets to enjoy each other's company in the sun before winter's chill drove them all inside. The darkness hid the wear on old buildings, the garbage in the streets and alleys, and the exhaustion of each resident. The screaming of the gulls melded with laughter and drunken singing, a familiar cacophony Leon had never thought he'd hear again.

It was almost peaceful. Idyllic even, if it weren't for Padraeg striding beside him like a storm front given human form.

Quinn Manor loomed out of the encroaching darkness. Even now, despite all the years that had passed, the sight of it brought ease to Leon's heart. He'd been happy here, for a time, in a way he'd never thought he'd be again after Dhuitholm fell.

"Aoife is out on business," Padraeg mumbled as he unlocked the front door, the first words he'd spoken to Leon since that morning. "Some ship came late into the port. The girl is in your old room. Aoife brought a healer in to see her last night. I trust you remember the way."

Not trusting himself to speak around the lump in his throat, Leon nodded. He followed Padraeg in and then pushed past him and sprinted up the stairs. His feet remembered the path as if he'd walked it yesterday.

Down the hall he ran, ignoring the pangs in his heart as a thousand memories came flooding back. It had been easy to put his concerns aside while he was in that cell, but now that he was here, he found he couldn't bear waiting a moment longer to see Jackie.

He skidded to a halt, a rug that was older than him bunching up under his feet, in front of a familiar wooden door with an owl carved into the doorframe. It had been made by a much younger, more foolish boy. One who'd still believed the Templesbane hadn't destroyed the entire order and could be driven back by blood and blade and with the might of kingdoms behind him.

Leon hadn't been that boy in a very long time.

Swallowing, he pushed the door open and entered.

It was more bare than he remembered. A desk and chair, a bed, and a chest he'd once stored his entire worldly belongings inside.

A servant woman he didn't know rose from the desk when he came in. He wasn't sure whether she recognized him or simply had been told to expect him, but she gave him an update and then left him to tend to Jackie.

Leon pulled her abandoned chair to Jackie's bedside. Jackie lay flat on her back in the bed, each breath deep and even, and made no reaction to any movement or noise. The fever no longer burned his skin when he touched her, and her color was better, even in this dim light. The white cloth wrapped around her broken leg gave off a faint light, confirming for Leon that the healers weren't done yet. They'd left their magic to do its work and put Jackie into a deep healing sleep in the meantime.

He let out a sigh that had been trapped in his chest since yesterday. Jackie would be fine. She would recover, and he could leave Mezeldwelf as soon as the sigil was removed.

It would be all right.

Chapter 5
Reunion at the Tavern

Jackie slept for the better part of three days. The healers came by twice a day to wake her long enough to eat and wash and then sent her back to sleep. Leon stayed at her side the whole time.

At least, he stayed at her side until she woke up for good and prevailed on Aoife to kick him out so she could have some privacy.

"For not being your child, you certainly dote on her," Aoife said, gathering up the soaps and hair oils she'd sent a servant out for that morning and shoving them in a cabinet. "I don't think I've seen you so focused on someone's recovery since Padraeg caught pneumonia when you were fifteen. Do you remember that?"

Leon shrugged and squeezed the water from his hair. Aoife had taken one look at him when he'd emerged from Jackie's room and dragged him by the ear to the washroom, calling over her shoulder for the servants to meet her there as they went. He considered himself lucky that Aoife had only insisted she help tame his hair after he washed. Padraeg had a list of stories a mile long about Aoife aggressively managing his wardrobe and hairstyle choices when they were young.

"She's part of the Band. The others would kill me if they thought I'd abandoned her while she was injured."

Laughing, Aoife threw a towel at him. "If you say so. Here, dry your hair."

Leon caught it and did as he was told. The towel, which was as fluffy as a frightened cat and more expensive than most of

Leon's clothes, was big enough for Jackie to use as a blanket. Draping it over his shoulders, he stood, only to be pushed back onto his stool while Aoife attacked his hair with a comb and a pair of scissors.

Aoife Quinn was a stout, middle-aged woman with dark red hair and a pleasant countenance. She managed the Quinn household and affairs while her brother, Padraeg, occupied himself with the minor concerns of the guard, or so she liked to say.

Padraeg had teased—repeatedly while Leon was living there—that running their small fishing fleet and their wharfside shop couldn't begin to compare to how much work he had to do to keep the guard running since he'd left the family business. Aoife, master of pettiness that she was, had taken that to heart and turned the Quinn fleet into a force to be reckoned with. Truthfully, Leon hadn't been surprised when she told him she'd expanded the business enough to earn a place as a merchant prince a few years after he left. She'd more than earned it. Apparently, she'd taken great pleasure in making Padraeg eat his words at her investiture ceremony.

"There you go, love, that should keep the tangles out," Aoife said, smiling as she set her tools down. The freshly clipped ends of his hair reached just past his shoulders now. "Now, I've got to go, I'm running late for a meeting. I've had your old things moved into the room next to Jackie, and the staff will get you anything you need."

Leon nodded and stood, hanging the towel over a rack left by the tub for that purpose. Aoife had pulled some of his old clothes out of storage when she heard he was coming. They were a bit tight around the shoulders and gut, but they fit well enough. At least the pants weren't short. At his height, he'd had more pants that didn't even reach his boots than actually fit. "What kind of meeting?" he asked, pulling a red shirt over his head. The fabric was finer than anything he'd worn in years. Even the embroidered Quinn crest was made of golden thread. "Do you need someone to come along?"

"I'm meeting someone at one of the guild taverns," Aoife called, her voice resounding off the worn tile. She'd already left the hall, and Leon took long steps to catch up to her. "A mercenary group one of my caravan masters recommended. She said they work near the border most of the time, which makes them perfect for this."

He slowed his pace when he reached her side, and frowned. "Why do you need to hire mercenaries? Is there an issue with the local groups?" The Mezeldwelf mercenary guild was one of the largest in Hyderia and was very well regarded. The Band was just one small part of it, which was the only reason they could even take contracts in this area.

Aoife's face soured. "Smugglers," she snarled. "I've got a bunch of records that don't match up and a bad feeling about it. I'd rather bring in an outside group than someone too close to one of the other princes."

Leon whistled. Smugglers were the bane of all the merchant princes' existence, but nothing could be done without definitive proof. Finding proof of smuggling was a job that could fill a mercenary's pockets for years on end. If it was a big enough ring to earn the ire of a merchant prince, like the contract that the Band had accepted, then it would fill the pockets of an entire mercenary troop. "The guard can't find anything?" he asked when they reached the door.

Shrugging, Aoife took a shawl from one of the hooks by the door. "Not as such." She paused, the shawl already over her shoulders. Turning back to him, she smiled. "You're welcome to come if you like. You can check for any message from your friends while we're there. Perhaps you'll be able to find out more information about the contract they were supposed to take."

A small part of Leon wondered if Aoife's contract and the job the Band had been hired for were one and the same, but he dismissed it without giving it much thought. There were thousands of mercenaries in Mezeldwelf and forty merchant princes. The odds of her choosing the Band, of all groups, were astronomically small.

That being said, it would be good to get out of the house. Njeri and the rest of the Band would be getting here any day now, and he hadn't heard anything from them. He hadn't even been able to scout out lodging for them, like he ought to have done. "I'd like to, but . . ." He glanced upstairs, toward Jackie's room, and Aoife patted his arm.

"She'll be fine. I arranged for a healer to visit her for a few hours, and we'll be back before they're done." Her face softened into a smile. "Why don't you leave a message with the cook? He'll deliver it when he brings lunch up."

It'd be better if he went himself, but Jackie had been very clear she wanted some time to herself today. Besides, she generally trusted people the Band let make food for them. She wouldn't worry if the cook was the one who gave her his message. "I'll be right back," he finally said.

A quick conversation with the cook later—with deliberate focus on the wording to hide one of the Band's code words inside Leon's message, due to Jackie's reading difficulties—and Leon and Aoife were off.

Aoife took Leon's arm as soon as they were outside; it was a bit of a stretch for her, since her shoulders were even with Leon's elbows, but she managed. The sun was making a valiant effort to dry up the mud and puddles from the rain that morning but hadn't quite managed it yet. It didn't stop the town though. The roads were packed with sailors, craftsmen, pilgrims, and more children running around underfoot than Leon had seen in years. Songs and chatter in over a dozen languages filled the air like water filled the sea.

"It's busy today, isn't it?" Aoife asked, waving to a blacksmith in front of a shuttered Forge temple. "Everyone's rushing to finish the preparations for the harvest festival. Padraeg's been tearing his hair out trying to ensure everyone that needs shelter gets it."

Leon shrugged. "The harvest is the same everywhere." Although this festival was particularly popular. Ever since Dhuitholm fell, all the religious rituals that had been held there had been moved to Mezeldwelf instead, and the city had never quite adapted to the seasonal rush that came with becoming the de facto religious center for Hyderia.

"Has he told you anything about it? I remember you used to love going to the guard initiations with him."

He shrugged again. "I haven't seen Padraeg since I got to the manor." He lifted Aoife over a puddle that covered most of the street to spare her from the mud. His boots could take the mud better than her silks. "I think he had grand dreams of me finally settling down and joining the guard that I kind of . . . shattered."

Aoife let out a sharp laugh as he set her back on the ground. "I don't doubt that. He was thrilled when he heard you were back—and with a child no less!"

"She's not mine," Leon said automatically. It was one thing to tell that lie to strangers and another entirely to tell it to Aoife. She loved children, even if she'd never desired any of her own.

"And we know that now, but then . . . I don't think I've ever seen him so happy. He thought you'd finally come home." She paused and her steps slowed. "When you said you hadn't planned to even visit, it broke his heart. He might be trying to honor your wishes until this whole affair is sorted out."

Leon grunted. He didn't know how to respond to that, so he didn't. Luckily, Aoife didn't need his answer to keep the conversation going.

"You know, he did miss you. He always regretted his actions during your last fight."

"He had a funny way of showing it," Leon muttered under his breath. The only reason he hadn't been thrown straight into a cell was because he'd charged out of Mezeldwelf right after their argument. He'd been fortunate that the Band spent most of the next few years near Beldown, in the south, because the rumors said Padraeg had torn Mezeldwelf and the surrounding countryside apart looking for him. He'd had to talk Njeri out of accepting one of the numerous bounties Padraeg had put out for information on his whereabouts without cluing her in to his past.

This time, Aoife was the one who didn't answer. She patted his arm, and they walked in silence until they reached their destination.

The mercenary guild tavern was a large and ramshackle three-story building that doubled as a meeting place and information den. Each guild master for the last three hundred years had added their own twist on it, and there wasn't a single building like it in all of Mezeldwelf.

Leon liked it. The eclectic mix of Alkan latticed windows, Hyderian stonework, and Falten murals made it stand out from the buildings around it. There were even two Sihianese lions that were allegedly a gift from the first delegation to Hyderia by the front door. The mercenary guild had arranged and facilitated the trade agreement between Sihia and Hyderia centuries ago, according to local legend. They'd provided protection for the visiting merchants in honor of that agreement until the war with the Templesbane cut off communication and trade between the two countries.

The decorations inside were even more varied than the ones outside. Weapons from all nations, creeds, and gods covered the walls. No two sconces matched. Some were iron, some steel, some bronze. A handful held four or five candles, but most only held two or a single large torch. The tables and chairs were mismatched in all ways, some ornately carved from exotic woods, and others little more than a stump pulled straight out of the ground. More than half were filled with mercenaries as varied as the furniture. Dozens of languages Leon only vaguely recognized mixed together in a low roar of sound. From the kitchen, there came a thousand beguiling scents that fought the smoke and burning wax for Leon's attention.

"It looks like we beat them here," Aoife said, squinting into the crowd of mercenaries. She dropped Leon's arm and stepped away. "Why don't you go ask the bartender if there's been any news from your friends? You can get us something to drink while you're up there."

Nodding, Leon waved Aoife away and headed to the bar. He wasn't too concerned about leaving her alone like that. There wasn't a mercenary in Mezeldwelf that didn't recognize the merchant princes on sight, and none would risk their membership in the guild by letting someone attack her on guild property. If anything, the most she'd have to worry about was overzealous leaders offering their services.

To Leon's dismay, he didn't have any messages at the bar. He tried not to worry as he quickly wrote one out for Njeri. The bartender would get it to her as soon as they checked in. It was a long journey to Mezeldwelf on foot, and the earliest he could've expected to hear anything was yesterday. Besides, Njeri still had to meet the merchant prince's representative before she could try to find Leon and Jackie.

He settled down beside Aoife, nudging a large Falten man with glowing and shifting tattoos out of the way to do so, and set both mugs on the table. "Who are we looking for?" Over the years, he'd become familiar with many of the mercenary bands based out of Mezeldwelf by reputation if not by the periodic joint jobs they worked on. At the very least, he might be able to give Aoife some advice for dealing with them.

"I actually think that's them." Aoife pointed to the door, where two figures had just come in out of the sunshine.

Two very familiar figures.

"Njeri? Kelan?" Leon's lips pulled back in a wide smile, and the knot in his stomach unwound. They'd made it. They were safe. "What're you doing here?"

The dots that had been laid out plainly in front of him connected, and he wanted to kick himself. Small odds did not mean impossible, and one too many coincidences should've clued him in to the identity of the Band's prospective employer.

"Same to you," Njeri shot back, settling into the seat opposite Aoife. They must've just gotten to town because their clothes were still stained with the dust from the road. "I thought you were going to wait outside Mezeldwelf for us."

"I was, but—" His jaw worked up and down, and he waved vaguely. No need to mention that he couldn't leave the city until that blasted sigil was removed. This job would keep them in Mezeldwelf for a few weeks, and the courts moved quickly in cases like this, so it'd be resolved before it became a problem. "There were complications with some bandits, and Jackie needed help. I couldn't just leave her alone."

"Is she all right?" Kelan asked, pulling out the stool next to Njeri and plopping into it. It groaned under his weight. He flashed a brilliant smile toward Aoife and then turned back to Leon. "And what the hell are you wearing? That's the Quinn crest. Have you gone noble on us? Sworn on as a house guard?"

Aoife answered before Leon could. "She's fine and staying at the family manor. Leon is my nephew, and those are some of his old clothes." She gave Leon a stern look he wasn't certain he deserved. "I had no idea he belonged to your group."

"I had no idea you were hiring them," he shot back. "All the merchant princes deal with smugglers." If he were in a less charitable mood, he'd have suspected she'd hired the Band intentionally to get him back to Mezeldwelf, but he'd covered his tracks well. He was far from the only person in the Band to use a different name than the one he'd signed the charter with.

"Why are you a mercenary, then?" Kelan asked, flagging down a server. "Were you the spare or something?" He paused to order two ales and two meat pies before continuing. "I know you don't like to talk about your past, but it had to be something like that to make you leave the family business."

Leon snorted. Kelan was many things, but he had no subtlety where his friends were concerned. "I'm not in line to be head of the house." That dubious honor belonged to a distant cousin in Falte, since Aoife didn't want children. He'd never even met the man. "My adopted father is the guard-captain, so he renounced his rights to the title. By law, that means it skips me too."

"Did you want to travel, then, or—"

"Enough," Njeri cut in. "You can badger Leon about his choices later. We're here for a job." She looked meaningfully at Aoife. "Unless you'd rather not hire your delinquent nephew's mercenary band?"

Shrugging, Aoife took a delicate sip of her ale. "I wasn't the one who drove him to delinquency. In fact, his membership in your band speaks well of you." Then she took a larger gulp, finishing her ale. When she finished, she belched and wiped her mouth on her handkerchief. "He's told me a bit about you since he arrived, and it only confirms my decision to hire you."

The server arrived and deposited Kelan's order onto the table. Aoife handed her enough to cover the bill before Kelan could finish getting his coin purse out.

Laughing under her breath, Njeri pulled a pie and an ale toward her. "That's a relief. I'd hate to lose out on a job that pays this well because one of my blades didn't realize he was feuding with our employer." This was delivered with a sharp note of rebuke that Leon *did* deserve. He really should've read the message that outlined what this job was when he had the chance. He wouldn't have gone into this blind if he had.

"Once more," he grumbled into his mug, "I had no way of knowing which merchant prince it was. I never even read the contract."

"A poor show of judgment on your part," Aoife said dryly, "but then, based on your actions since arriving, I'll assume you never intended to participate."

Kelan snorted into his pie, and Leon made a rude gesture in his direction when Aoife looked away.

Njeri wasn't looking away, though, and she rolled her eyes. "If the boys are done misbehaving, I have a few questions about the job."

"Of course." Aoife set down her mug and smiled. "Let's begin the negotiations."

***

Leon had been to a few contract negotiations in his time with the Band. He'd even led a few when Njeri and Bettany were out of commission. This was another thing entirely.

Aoife had earned her merchant prince title. Each line of the contract was gone over with a fine-tooth comb. Each duty was clarified, expounded upon, and broken down into its base parts. It was more than fair, but by the gods, it was terrifying to witness. And since Leon was right there, he got a much more in-depth explanation about what the contract entailed than he'd normally get.

Which was good, because he hadn't paid any attention at all when he thought he'd spend this mission getting drunk in a village outside of Mezeldwelf.

The job itself didn't seem too hard. Aoife was concerned that a number of ships came in low in the water, but their manifests didn't have enough goods on them to weigh them down like that. The guards hadn't found anything, but Aoife had a bad feeling of the kind only a devout follower of Commerce could have. She wanted them to keep a watch on the warehouses and tail the sailors and merchants to confirm they weren't off-loading their goods somehow.

It wasn't the most exciting job, but it needed to be done, and the guards had already done everything they could. It was on Aoife to prove that the wharf was being used for smuggling, and it was her reputation—and pockets—that would take the hit if she set the Band on innocent folk.

"Excellent, I think that's everything." Aoife lifted her mug— her third since they sat down—and saluted Njeri and Kelan. "I'll send Leon over with the final contract in the morning, and the next suspect ship arrives tomorrow afternoon. I look forward to working with you."

Njeri returned the gesture and drained her mug. "Likewise."

Kelan, who'd migrated over to Leon's side while Njeri and Aoife were elbow deep in negotiation, slapped Leon's shoulder. "Come on, don't look so glum. This'll be fun!"

Leon grunted. The longer they'd talked, the more an uneasy feeling had settled in his chest. Something wasn't right about this whole thing, but he couldn't figure out what it was.

Aoife tossed down a few more coins for the servers, and they went their separate ways. Njeri and Kelan—who'd made it clear he intended to tell the entire Band that Leon's aunt was a merchant prince—went to find lodging for the Band, and Leon and Aoife went back to Quinn Manor.

Njeri hadn't questioned why Leon would be staying at Quinn Manor instead of with the rest of the Band. Between Aoife insisting on caring for Jackie until she finished healing and the fact Leon hadn't seen his family in ten years, she'd made it plain that she expected nothing less.

"Your friends seem nice," Aoife said, once more grabbing Leon's arm as they left the tavern. "Especially that Njeri. Strong too. An old friend?"

He shrugged. "She's led the Band since before I joined. It's an honor to serve under her." It was, perhaps, unnecessarily diplomatic, but he knew without having to be told what Aoife was fishing for. She, even more than Padraeg, had always wanted Leon to settle down. She didn't much care about who or what he was with, but she hadn't liked the fact that he'd wanted to leave Mezeldwelf, even before he and Padraeg had fallen out. She'd wanted him to build roots here too. She'd just been quieter about it.

But he and Njeri had been friends for years, and there wasn't any chance of anything more. The fact that they'd already tried it was proof enough of that. Things would never work out that way between them. Not while he had the Templesbane and the Protectors after him and the weight of his own secrets holding him down. Not while she still looked at every member of the

Band like she'd die to protect them, hang anyone or anything else she left behind.

They'd fought side by side and saved each other's lives more often than he could count, and she knew all his secrets except one. He trusted her and she trusted him. They'd ended things before it destroyed them.

Aoife nudged him, a twinkle in her eye, to break him out of his distraction. "What about the man who was with her? He's handsome."

That was more for her own pleasure. She knew how Leon's preferences ran, and Kelan didn't fit them for many reasons.

"He, ah, isn't fond of that sort of thing," Leon said, rubbing the back of his neck.

Aoife arched an eyebrow and skipped over a muddy puddle without breaking eye contact. "Women or in general?"

"In general." Leon shrugged. "He says he doesn't see the appeal even after trying with . . . a variety of folks."

What Kelan actually said was that he'd rather spend a night trading stories at a fireside than in someone else's bed, and he'd never met anyone who changed that, but Aoife didn't need that level of detail. And more importantly, Leon didn't want to give it. The less he thought about her bedroom inclinations, the better. Especially with people his age.

***

Aoife left for her office in the Citadel once they returned to Quinn Manor, and Leon went to check on Jackie. He heard three voices through the door when he approached. Two were familiar, but the third was unknown to him. The healer must still be here.

When he pushed the door open, Jackie was the first to greet him.

"Leon!" she said, bouncing on the bed. "You're back. Did you find the others? Are they coming to visit? Kelan owes me dinner—he was supposed to cook when we left."

She looked healthy. The bandages had been removed, and the wan tint had left her rosy cheeks.

Leon smiled back at her and nodded at Padraeg, who'd taken the chair at her bedside. Padraeg nodded back. "Yes, Njeri accepted a job from Aoife, so we're staying here for a bit. They were very concerned about . . ." He trailed off, eyes transfixed on the third speaker, who sat on Jackie's bed.

They were little more than a child and eternally more than that. Their clothes were simultaneously a white robe and rags, their hair long and tangled and elegantly braided, and their cheeks hollow and plump as a fattened calf. Leon's senses rattled against the corners of his mind, struggling to comprehend what was before him when he knew that sight was a lie.

"Hello, Leon Quinn," they said, their voice rattling the rafters. Their clothes shifted in a wind that didn't exist, and each shifting fiber was a child in need, a widow struggling to survive, a beggar looking for a scrap of bread. "Once knight, lost knight, fallen knight. I've been waiting for you."

He dropped to one knee out of reverence and fear. Blood pounded through his ears, and his heart threatened to leap from his chest. There were gods still in Mezeldwelf, those few who'd taken physical form. They recognized when humans bore their siblings' touch. "Your Grace," he said in a hushed voice. "To what do I owe this honor?"

The figure laughed and crossed their legs. "So you can still recognize us, even when we've hidden ourselves from others. I was concerned." They turned back to Jackie, who frowned at the sight of Leon kneeling. "But Subtlety said I should try to keep the specifics of your situation quiet."

They raised a hand, tapped twice on Jackie's forehead, and Jackie slumped over. Leon leaped up before he knew what he was doing, and the god helped him lay her down.

"Here we go," they said pleasantly. "She'll sleep for twenty minutes, which is more than enough time to discuss the matter at hand."

Padraeg grunted. "That was unnecessary, Your Grace. We could've gone to my office."

They shrugged. "It was kinder though. She wouldn't have been able to rest until she knew the others were here. She'll recover faster now. When she wakes up, she should even be healed enough to visit her friends."

Leon opened his mouth and shut it again before stepping away. The doorknob dug into his back, and he forced himself to take a deep breath. "May I inquire after your nature, Your Grace?"

Padraeg trusted them around Jackie—and none of the crueler gods had aspects in Mezeldwelf—but most of the gods that lived here when Leon left had given themselves over to the Templesbane. He didn't think he'd ever seen one with an aspect this young either.

Laughing, they stood on the bed, and the top of their head didn't even reach Leon's chest. "I'm surprised you don't recognize me. The Knights Vigilant often did my work in their orphanages and schools." They smiled, and their eyes glittered like stars. "They cared for those wearing my mark until the Templesbane brought them low." This time, they scowled, and it chilled Leon to the bone. "The Sister has added greatly to my flock since the Brother was imprisoned."

The orphanages and schools . . . Leon had lived under the care of the orphanages at Dhuitholm until Delke had taken him and Mael under her tutelage. They kept the poor and destitute fed, clothed, and healthy. The Watchful Peace ordained those who kept the peace, and the peace was kept by ensuring that the needs of the populace were met. It was kept by attending to—

"Charity," Leon said in a low voice. "You're Charity, aren't you?"

Charity smiled and their appearance swirled. The confusing mishmash of images settled into that of a young, dark-haired child wearing worn clothing. They laughed, a sound like a temple bell. "I knew it. My siblings were worried you might have forgotten how to see us, but I knew you'd recognize me."

Padraeg also let out a chuckle. "You got it faster than Delke did," he said in a low voice. "When we first met this Charity, she spent ten minutes trying to piece it together."

Leon shrugged, ignoring the sharp jab of pain hearing that name sent through his heart. "She tended the winged horses, not the people. She wasn't—" He cut himself off before he could say something he'd regret. Now wasn't the time. Padraeg had known Delke as well as anyone. Better, even. There was a reason Leon had come to him after Dhuitholm fell. "Are you here for a reason, Your Grace?"

Charity had worked closely with the Knights Vigilant, pointing them toward folks who needed help, to the point some questioned who the true patron of the order was. Leon had known an aspect of them then, but in Dhuitholm, they had preferred the form of an elderly man with one leg.

Charity sat down again and arranged their robe so they could sit cross-legged. "To the point, as usual for one of the Vigilant." They huffed and reached out to stroke Jackie's hair. "It's a message. Or rather, a nudge. The others weren't sure we should say anything yet, but—"

They sighed. "A lot more people are going to enter my flock soon," they whispered. "I can feel it. Compassion went early, and

85

without them, even the other gods struggled to remember why we fight the way we do. It grows more and more difficult to find major aspects willing to surrender themselves ever since the Forge went."

Leon nodded but didn't speak. It was a strange sacrifice humanity asked the gods to make, and no one knew why they'd agreed to do it.

Charity leaped from the bed and took his hand. Their skin, a dusky tone like the sun reflected off the water, glowed in the dim light. "I know where your mind wanders," they whispered. "Mine goes there as well. It'll be my turn soon enough."

Padraeg stiffened and exhaled shakily. "Your Grace, you can't mean—"

"I couldn't put it off forever, Padraeg Quinn," they said in a low voice. "And when I go, many of the things that keep the city strong will begin to suffer."

"But—you don't even have priests or godsworn," Leon snapped, his heart hammering in his chest. He dropped to his knees beside the bed, squeezing Charity's hand. "How can they take you without them?"

Commerce might be at home in Mezeldwelf, but they allowed themself to be tempered by Charity and Compassion. Without them, the baser urges of humanity would be overcome by greed and the desire for power. Now that Compassion was gone, Charity was the only thing holding their sibling back.

Charity shrugged. "It's not my place to question it. The Templesbane made their demands clear." They smiled up at Leon, and the stars in their eyes twinkled. Their voice dropped lower still, until Leon struggled to hear them. "But I am glad to see you one more time before the autumn festival. There have been stirrings in the ruins of Dhuitholm. Walls are starting to crumble, and familiar whispers linger on the wind, and . . . I believe there might be hope again."

Hope? What kind of hope could there be? The other knights were gone. If the Brother truly was stirring from his imprisonment in Dhuitholm, then Leon couldn't hope to stand against the combined forces of the Templesbane, even if he had all the armies of all the countries in the world at his side. The Watchful Peace had been silent since Dhuitholm fell, not consumed but not guiding either. Without them, he couldn't save anyone. With them, there was no hope.

They dropped Leon's hand and turned to Padraeg. "Please keep this between us for now. It won't do to let everyone know I'm this year's sacrifice before the harvest festival and—I'd ask for a personal favor, if you don't mind."

They pulled Padraeg down and whispered in his ear. Padraeg started and then nodded.

Charity smiled, bowing their head. "I'll take my leave."

Then they were gone, like they'd never been there in the first place.

Padraeg huffed and rubbed his face. "I'd wondered why they came here, and to think . . ."

"What did they want?" Leon asked, clenching his hand into a fist.

They couldn't expect him to save them, could they? They were a god and he was a drunk, a mercenary that had been a knight for all of an afternoon before his world ended. He couldn't do anything.

Sighing, Padraeg ran a hand through his hair. "We should talk."

Chapter 6
Conversation Delayed

Dinner was possibly the most awkward thing Leon had participated in since those first few days after he and Njeri ended their relationship. The more romantically inclined members of the Band had tried to get them back together by tricking them into a stakeout in a tavern room with one bed. It hadn't worked, but Leon and Njeri had devised some truly terrible punishments for the ones responsible, which helped break the ice between them, so it all evened out in the end.

This time, though, it didn't look like there was anything coming that could spare Leon the sheer tension of sitting across from Padraeg at dinner for the first time in a decade. He'd hoped he could slip away, but Jackie woke up after Charity left and started begging him to invite the others to visit now that she was awake. Then, Padraeg had started asking her questions about her life with the Band, and Leon hadn't been able to figure out how to sneak out without Jackie realizing he was gone.

Which led them to dinner. While Leon and Aoife were out, Padraeg talked up the abilities of the Quinn cook and promised Jackie all kinds of new food. Jackie, in turn, had made it clear she expected Leon to come so someone else would be able to help her keep track of the ones she wanted Kelan to recreate later.

Padraeg hadn't pulled Leon aside at any point in that conversation. He'd led Jackie to the dining room and sat at her side, never once looking at Leon, even as the food started rolling out of the kitchen.

For Jackie's first dinner out of the sickbed, Aoife had gone all out. She'd sent servants to get candied fruits and nuts, arranged for fish fresh from the harbor to be fried with all manner of spices and herbs, and allowed Jackie one glass of wine with dinner. There was honeyed boar, fruit tarts, savory stews, and fried vegetables. They finished up with cinnamon apples roasted in the fire. Even Jackie found her limit after her fourth full plate and three servings of dessert, although she'd probably have gone back for more if Aoife hadn't promised her all the extra candied nuts.

Leon did feel a little guilty he hadn't thought to do that. Jackie normally kept a bag of nuts or dried fruit on her at all times for emergency snacking purposes, but they'd lost it when the bandits attacked.

What little conversation took place was between Aoife and Jackie. Leon and Padraeg ignored each other, speaking only to ask Jackie how she liked the food and to inquire—repeatedly—how Aoife's day had gone.

It was after dinner that things changed from awkward to downright miserable. That was when Aoife took Jackie aside to treat her to an extended bath and skin treatment, and Padraeg took Leon to his study.

The study was in the back of the manor on the second floor. It had seemed a lot bigger when Leon was thirteen. Back then, he'd never seen this many books outside of the great library at Dhuitholm. The bookshelves drowned out all the outside noise, and the window—which looked north, over the harbor—was the only evidence the world still existed once that door closed.

It had been a safe place for him then. Padraeg let him borrow as many books as he wanted and kept a small bowl of walnuts on his desk for Leon to snack on. He'd been able to hide away in there when the streets felt too crowded and the children playing sounded like screams and the smoke from the Forge temples overwhelmed him. When Leon was ready to emerge, Padraeg had waited with tea and stories about Delke from when she and Padraeg were young and in love.

It was the first place Leon had felt at home after escaping Dhuitholm.

Now it felt disturbingly like he was being taken into the caretaker's office at the orphanage or dragged in front of Delke to be told off for whatever prank he and Mael had pulled off.

Padraeg settled into one of the plush armchairs in front of the fireplace and indicated Leon should sit in the other. Leon's heart sank, and he bit back the urge to run out. Padraeg had been kind enough to leave him be once upon a time. He wouldn't pursue Leon if he left now.

Or at least, he might not.

But the uncertainty drove Leon to sit opposite Padraeg, in the armchair he'd always preferred as a boy. It still sat in the spot he'd dragged it into on the first day he'd been allowed into the study, in the only place he could see both the window and the door.

"I never thought I'd see you here again," Padraeg said in a low voice. He grabbed the poker and stirred up the coals. A rush of heat came out, driving away a chill Leon hadn't even realized had sunk into his bones. "The last time we were here, we both said harsh things, and I—"

"It was a long time ago," Leon interrupted, keeping his eyes fixed on the fire. "I tried to stay away."

Settling back into his chair, Padraeg sighed. "And I regret that. I never meant to make you feel like this wasn't your home—that you wouldn't be welcome here."

Unbidden, a harsh laugh burst out of Leon's mouth. "You had an odd way of showing it," he ground out. "You threatened to arrest me if I didn't join up with the Protectors or the guard after the Great Treaty was signed. You—" He clamped his jaw shut and took deep breaths. "I've spent most of my life running from the Sister. The Knights Vigilant are gone, and I don't want to spend the rest of my life trying to live up to their legend."

He'd fled Mezeldwelf in the initial wave of Dhuitholm refugees who refused to renounce their ties to the city in accordance with the Great Treaty. The Protectors had snatched up everyone they could, recruiting them into their hopeless fight against beings that could devour gods. Beings that stripped captives of everything that made them individuals, leaving them nothing but husks of their former selves.

He'd seen what happened to people the Templesbane captured. He'd known too many innocents trapped in Dhuitholm when the city fell, and it would destroy him to see their faces on the wrong side of his axes, to see the brief flash of recognition when he cut them down and the Sister abandoned the husk they had become.

Padraeg sighed. He slumped into his chair and, for once, looked each one of his sixty-three years. "I know," he whispered. "I shouldn't have pushed you like that. You weren't ready, and it drove you away."

A shadow shifted behind Padraeg, and Leon refused to meet the gaze of the figure that emerged. A ghostly hand rested on Padraeg's shoulder.

"Why did you call me here?" he asked, returning his eyes to the flames. "I can't stop Charity from giving themself up. No one can." The flames in Dhuitholm had turned green as he fled, some remnant of whatever magic the senior knights and the Vigilant General had used to trap the Brother there. If they'd thought it would be enough to stop the Sister, too, they were sadly wrong. They'd paid for it with their lives and the lives of countless innocents that couldn't escape in time.

"It's . . ." Padraeg sighed and rubbed his eyes. "I wanted to ask if you'd reconsidered. The Protectors are planning another campaign in the spring. They want to try reclaiming Dhuitholm and Charity—"

"No." He took a deep breath and let it out. His voice didn't shake even though his hands did. "It's a lost cause. Dhuitholm is too deep in the Fallow Lands." Even the thought of returning to Dhuitholm, of seeing the ruin and graveyard the city had become, took the strength from his limbs and the air from his lungs. What good would it do to reclaim a city they couldn't purify? Without the Vigilant General and the Watchful Peace, all they would do was waste lives for something they'd never be able to hold.

"If you joined them—"

"I'm not a knight," Leon exploded, jumping to his feet. He ached to pace, to soothe the wild energy swirling through his limbs, and the three paces from one side of the study to the other did little to help. His lungs ached, and his hands wouldn't stop moving. "It was a formality. I can't purify anything the Templesbane have corrupted, I was never taught how, I can't—"

He stopped, dead in his tracks. A man wearing the ceremonial armor of the Vigilant General stood between him and Padraeg. The heavy silver plate, which in life had been painted with gold and studded with emeralds, glowed dully in death. The owl inlaid on the breastplate stared at him through amber eyes. He recoiled and snapped his eyes shut, sinking back into his armchair. He couldn't deal with them now. The Vigilant Generals were always the most insistent that he take up arms against the Templesbane, but he couldn't. He wasn't a knight.

He'd proved that when he'd fled the city instead of fighting alongside everyone else.

"Do you still see them?" Padraeg's voice rumbled through the room like thunder. He glanced around, like this time he'd finally be able to see the ghosts that haunted Leon. "The Knights Beyond, I mean."

Jaw clenched, Leon nodded. "More than I'd like." The first time they'd come to him was in Mezeldwelf, when he'd started talking again. He'd been so grateful that he wasn't the only one left, that there were others and they'd have a chance to get revenge for everyone he'd lost. For Delke. For Mael.

Padraeg had thought him lost to battle sickness when he started talking about the knights teaching him to fight and telling him the history of the Knights Vigilant.

When Leon had realized the truth—when the Knights Beyond revealed he was the only one left—something had broken deep inside him. He'd stopped listening to them, and they'd stopped teaching him when they realized there were things the dead would never be able to pass on to the living. Powers he'd never be able to touch with an absent god.

One man did not make an order, despite what the Knights Beyond believed.

Padraeg faltered, and his fingers dug into the armrests. "Have you seen her yet? Or your—"

"No," Leon said harshly. "No," he said again, softer this time. "I still haven't seen anyone who was in Dhuitholm that day." He'd looked a thousand times that first year, a million times the second, in the vain hope that there were knights who had held out against the siege, that had only recently died. Each time the Knights Beyond had come to speak with him, he'd searched through their ranks and seen nothing. None of the knights he'd left behind were there. Not the Vigilant General, not the senior knights or the other squires or Delke or—

Some cruel magic of the Brother or revenge of the Sister had kept their souls from Death's sentinels. The magic that was supposed to sustain them in death wasn't enough to stand up to that cruel appetite. The knights were gone, and Leon would never see them again.

They will return, a voice said, familiar and foreign. Dozens more joined, far more than should fit in a room this size. **Death cannot be held off forever.**

Padraeg's hands settled on Leon's shoulders, and he let it happen. His breath quickened, and he collapsed in on himself, hands over his ears. They would leave eventually, but not until they had their say, and there wasn't anything he could do to make that happen faster.

He was too sober for this. He should've had more than a glass of wine with dinner. It was louder when he was sober and much harder to ignore.

By the gods, they'd left him alone since the bandits attacked. Why did they have to come now?

The Watchful Peace stirs. Ghostly hands pressed on Leon, touching, pushing, reminding him of everything he'd tried to forget. **The time has come to take up the duties you left behind. To avenge the fallen and save the captive.**

No, no, no . . . It wasn't time. The Watchful Peace hadn't answered his prayers since Dhuitholm fell. They'd abandoned him. They'd left him with their mark and their gifts and had forgotten about him when the older knights died. There wasn't an order, so they left him alone.

The Sister will come, the voices whispered, their words thrumming through Leon's chest. **The city will fall.**

Padraeg's hands came to cover Leon's, but it didn't quiet the Knights Beyond at all. Leon's breath came fast and hard and didn't do anything to soothe the ache in his chest. He might as well not have been breathing at all.

You must fight, Leon Quinn. The time has come to stop running. The city will fall if you fail to answer the call.

He lost track of how long they sat like that. The voices came for ages, pushing into Leon like a tidal wave, and he couldn't escape them. Padraeg's voice rumbled underneath them, and he tried to focus on it, to block out the endless barrage around him.

Breathe. Breathe. It would be over soon.

***

"Gods, do they not believe in sleeping draughts here, or are you hungover?" Kelan's stage whisper grated on Leon's ears like an infant's wail.

"Shut up," he snapped, regretting it when a burst of pain ripped through his skull. "Pay attention." They'd been patrolling for a week already, and he was ready to drop from exhaustion.

The Knights Beyond were more active than they'd been in years. After that first night, where Padraeg hadn't left his side, they were always there. They never spoke, but they lingered over each meal and conversation. Dead knights watched his every move and listened to every word. A crowd of them followed him now, staring silently as he went about his day. He did his best to ignore them.

Once the contract was signed, the Band's work began in earnest. Aoife and Njeri decided where the Band would devote their effort, and Padraeg had provided all the research he'd gathered when the guard was looking into the matter.

Most of the Band were either cozying up to the sailors or tailing the merchants involved in the alleged smuggling. Whoever was left got sent on errands to investigate tips and rule out false leads. It would've been easier if there was some sort of link between the merchants, but as far as Aoife could tell, the only thing they had in common was that they'd used small ships, typically docked late, and came in with their holds less than half-full, according to their manifests.

Leon had drawn patrol duty with Kelan and Shea. They were investigating an area near the old Forge temples, and he regretted not trading with Bettany with each hammer swing and drunken shanty. At least she got to drink in the taverns while swindling sailors out of their pay. If his head was going to hurt, he'd rather it be for a pleasant reason.

"Nothing here." Shea's voice beat him from the old Forge temple by bare seconds. Ash lingered on his clothing and his forehead. His hand tightened around the haft of his war hammer, and he scowled. "The forgemaster says there've been no unusual orders from any of the merchants. They haven't even asked for extra nails. Let's move on."

Kelan and Leon exchanged looks and hurried after him without another word.

Leon had wanted to be surprised when Shea volunteered to cover this patrol, but he couldn't be. Even with their god consumed, many Forge priests hadn't left their temples. Shea had friends left here, and they heard more gossip in a week than most people heard in a year. And without worship to keep them busy, many found alternative ways to stay occupied. Alternative ways that saw them in and out of the seedier parts of town.

Leon didn't doubt that it hurt Shea to see the people he'd admired sink into drink and depravity now that their god was gone. The Forge had been a kind god, and their worshippers came from all walks of life. Many of them simply didn't have another place to go after the temples closed, and had fallen back into old vices.

"Can I talk to the next one?" Kelan asked, taking quick steps to catch up to Shea. While not a short man, he was still head and shoulders smaller than both Leon and Shea, and he needed to take three steps for every two they took. "You look tense."

"I'm fine," Shea said through gritted teeth. "We're almost done."

Leon snorted. "Are you sure? I've seen wildfires putting off fewer sparks." He tugged his hood forward to make sure it covered his eyes. It probably wasn't necessary, but gossip traveled fast, and it was likely that more than a few of the guards involved in his arrest had told their friends and family about their part in that affair. Not for the first time, Leon cursed his height. Between that, his eyes, and his notoriety as Padraeg's estranged son, he was too recognizable to participate in undercover work in Mezeldwelf. That was one of many reasons he hadn't been sent to tail anyone. There weren't many gray-eyed men whose heads brushed the ceiling beams.

"Yes," Shea bit out. He looked ready to strangle the next person who questioned his suitability for this task. "I'm fine."

Kelan and Leon exchanged a look as Shea charged ahead.

Kelan wiggled his eyebrows and scowled. "I'm fine," he whispered in a passable imitation of Shea's voice. "I'm Shea, and I always look ready to bite people's heads off. Let me ask people questions, I'm sure it'll go well."

Biting back a laugh, Leon shoved Kelan's shoulder. "Shut it before he hears you." He needn't have bothered being cautious. Shea's steps quickened, and soon he was ten feet away. His height was the only reason Leon could track him in the crowd.

Kelan rolled with the punch and laughed. "I don't know why he's bothering. Half of the former priests are drunks, addicts, or worse, and the ones that aren't hardly lift their attention from their anvils. Anyone could talk to them." His voice dropped lower and his brow furrowed. He continued, a deep frown painting his face with worry, "He doesn't need to do this to himself."

Shrugging, Leon tugged his cloak closed as a brisk wind blasted down the street. Kelan, the bastard, hardly seemed to notice the cold, even though he was wearing a linen shirt and loose breeches. "Wouldn't you? I know you left the Order of the Risen Moon, but you were raised in their monastery. These priests were his family like the monks were yours."

Kelan huffed. His yellow eyes never left Shea's back. "Not the way he does. The order believes that relationships come and go and should be released when the time comes. Forge priests may have shared the fire, but he acts like each one's struggles are on his shoulders."

The fires of the Forge seared their followers the same way the Hearth called everyone home at the end of the day. The flames burned brightly, churning out ideas and inventions and creations never seen before and brought to life in the forges of each temple. With that wellspring gone, the Forge priests' fire had gone out. It was no wonder that most had succumbed to the evils they'd left behind when they joined the priesthood.

If any of the senior knights had survived and the Watchful Peace had been consumed, Leon didn't doubt he'd act just like Shea. To see brilliance like that disappear into despair and self-destruction . . . well, it wasn't a surprise that Shea wanted to prop them up where he could.

Or that he'd left the Forge priests in the first place.

But before Leon could share any of this with Kelan, he realized that Shea's familiar shape was gone. He'd disappeared between one blink and the next.

"Gods damn it," he snapped. "Did you see where he went?" There weren't any Forge temples in sight. There weren't even any unaffiliated smiths Shea could've known as a child.

Kelan stood on his tiptoes and shaded his eyes. He scanned the crowd and let out a frustrated growl. "Fuck, he's almost as tall as you and built like an ox, how did he disappear?"

Leon scanned the road ahead of them, even standing on his tiptoes, and let out a victorious shout that made his head pound like one of the Forge priests was using it as an anvil. "There! There's an alley just past the baker. I'd bet he went that way."

"So there is," Kelan said, dropping his hands. He darted forward, gesturing for Leon to follow. "Hurry up, he'll be insufferable if he thinks we got lost."

But there was no sign of Shea. There wasn't even a business or open door he could've ducked into, and the alley was too long for him to have gotten all the way through unless he sprinted. It also was empty apart from piles of rubbish, a cart with eight large barrels on it, and a small pack of children dressed in simple temple clothes, who all looked up nervously when Leon and Kelan ran in.

"Damn it," Kelan swore, rubbing his forehead. "I thought we'd catch him here." He glanced back into the busy street they'd just left, and then turned to squint down the alley, to the busy street on the other side. "Well, which way do you think he went?"

"We could split up? Flip a coin?" They might find him eventually, but it was more likely that Shea would find them. Unlike Leon, who'd spent less than ten years there, Shea had been born in Mezeldwelf and likely would've died without ever leaving if the Forge hadn't been consumed. Most of those years had been spent running in alleys and back ways as only someone with the city in their blood could. He knew more shortcuts and back roads than Leon had known knights or city guards.

Kelan considered the alley and shook his head. "I don't think so. He should be close by." His eyes lingered on the children, who were still looking warily at them, and he smiled. "I've got an idea."

Before Leon could stop him or ask what he intended, Kelan stepped forward with his coin purse in hand.

"Hey, I'll give a silver piece to anyone who can tell me if they saw my friend." He waved his coin purse above their heads, and the clank of the metal inside was audible. "And two if they can describe him well enough for me to confirm it's him."

The oldest of the children, a scrawny Sihianese girl who couldn't have been older than Jackie, squinted at him. A toddler, who shared her straight, black hair and almond-shaped eyes, clung to her hand, and she pulled him close. "What's your friend look like?" she demanded. "There are a lot of people on these streets."

Kelan raised his hands placatingly. "Fair enough." He pointed to Leon, who hadn't moved from his spot at the alley's entrance. "He's almost as tall as my friend back there, and he's Sihianese like you, except he's got a huge nose, and his hair isn't as dark as yours."

Leon snorted under his breath. That was one way to describe Shea and likely not one he'd have appreciated if he were here. His nose and his height were the only thing he got from his Hyderian mother. Apparently, they hadn't been on good terms when he joined the Forge priests, and he disliked being reminded of her.

The little girl frowned. She exchanged a look with a redheaded Hyderian girl, who shook her head. "No, we didn't see anyone like that. Or at least, they didn't come through here."

"They didn't come through here?" Kelan asked, perking up.

She shook her head. "No. There've been a bunch of people walking by, but ever since those merchant guards cleared out the beggars and drunks, this alley's been empty. It's why we can play here."

Leon came closer, his head cocked. "A merchant cleared out the alley? Did you see their crest?"

There wasn't much in this alley. A handful of warehouses and the back doors to some of the shops, but nowhere to hide and nothing that looked fragile or important enough to keep drunks away from.

The children nodded nearly as one. "Their clothes had golden roosters on them," a little boy volunteered. Frowning, he rubbed his arm like he was hurt. "One of them threw a bottle at us last week. I had to go to the healer because I got cut on a shard."

It was Leon and Kelan's turn to exchange a look. That wasn't normal behavior. At the very least, it warranted reporting to Padraeg before someone got seriously hurt. Sometimes a little power turned decent folks into horrible ones, and it had only gotten worse since Compassion was consumed. Best to curtail that early, before someone decided to take their anger out on someone who didn't deserve it.

"Did you see anyone else?" Leon asked in a low voice. He dropped into a squat to get closer to their level. Jackie had told him once, in no uncertain terms, that it was scary when he loomed over people. Squatting may have been uncomfortable, but it should help make the children feel safer. "If you tell us, we can stop them from hurting you again."

The redheaded girl spoke up. "We saw a Sihianese man with dark skin and curly hair, but he was short. He brings the barrels, and then the rooster people switch them."

"Oh yeah, I forgot about him," the first girl said, picking up the toddler and settling him on her hip. "We haven't seen him since he dropped the cart off yesterday though." Her voice dropped into a whisper, and she leaned close to Kelan like she was sharing a secret. "I think he's blind. His eyes looked like my grandmother's hair."

"He can't be blind," the little boy interjected. "I saw him reading a message."

Leon's breath caught in his chest. "White eyes?" he asked in a low voice. "And he could read? Are you certain?" It could've been a blessing from a god, but he hadn't lived this long by not being paranoid. Children saw things adults often missed.

The little girl nodded. "Yes. He's creepy, even if he doesn't chase us off like the others. He keeps asking questions about where we live and what our parents do." She shivered and clutched the toddler close. "I didn't like the way he looked at us. It felt weird."

Leon jerked to his feet and stretched his senses out as far as he could. A thousand minds lingered against his, but none of them had the emptiness of a husk. They were full of worries and fears and gods and life. They weren't hollow and blank, a template for the Sister to force herself upon the world.

The children must be mistaken. The husks weren't allowed in Mezeldwelf. To come into the city outside of the harvest festival, when they came to take the god that was giving themself over that year, would break the treaty. No matter the Sister's greed, she wouldn't risk losing the gods of Mezeldwelf and driving the city to partner with the Protectors just to have a few more eyes around.

Kelan thanked the children, slipping each of them a silver piece, and then pulled Leon aside. The children ran toward the far side of the alley, talking excitedly about what they were going to buy before the stores closed for the day.

"You look like you've seen a ghost," he said in a low voice. "Care to fill me in?"

"It's . . ." No, it was just a suspicion. He was being needlessly paranoid. Searching the whole city based on hearsay like that was unrealistic. "It's nothing. The husks from the crossroads are still on my mind, is all."

Snorting, Kelan leaned against the wall. His pupils flexed in the changing light of the alley, narrowing into slits and then widening back to circles. "You, too, huh? Someone in a merchant's colors is switching out barrels, driving drunks and children away, and being mighty sneaky about it. It's also not too far from the inns where the visiting merchants stay. You think it's connected?"

"At the very least we ought to let the guard know about it. Even if they're not our smugglers, they're not good people." He paused and considered the cart. The barrels inside weren't anything fancy, but all the same, they weren't something to leave outside and unguarded at all hours. "Something's not right here. I think we should look deeper into this."

"I agree." Kelan stroked his chin. His eyes raked up and down the walls as he considered which windows, balconies, and overhangs were sturdy enough to support his weight. "Someone will need to stay here to keep an eye out for our friend who takes the cart away. Do you want to do it, or should I?"

"You see better in the dark," Leon answered. "With the sun going down, I imagine our friend will try to hide in the evening crowd. I'll keep looking for Shea, and we'll let the others know to keep an eye out for you."

But Kelan was already gone, halfway up one of the buildings and bouncing back and forth off anything sticking out more than an inch or two to get higher. That was another reason Leon wanted him to follow the man with the cart. Few thought to look up when trying to stay inconspicuous, and Kelan was as comfortable scrambling across a roof as he was at a fireside telling stories, especially after dark.

Leon slid out of the alley and set about looking for their missing friend.

Fortunately, he didn't have to look hard. No sooner had he poked his head out from the alley than he heard Shea calling him over the crowd. A few minutes more—and some silver paid out to buy some different and more nondescript clothes from a forgemaster—and Kelan had a second pair of eyes looking after things from the ground while Leon reported to Njeri.

Chapter 7
Unexpected Help

"I still can't believe Shea left you like that," Njeri muttered, lengthening her stride to stay close to Leon. "Even if he saw his old forgemaster. That's irresponsible."

Leon shook his head. The Knights Beyond had been quiet last night, and he'd gotten more sleep than he had since arriving in Mezeldwelf. "He thought we'd seen him follow her into her house. It was an honest mistake."

A profitable one, since it led them to their current lead, which even Aoife admitted looked like it was paying off. The mysterious blind Sihianese man had come for his cart an hour after sunset and left another behind him. Kelan had followed him from the rooftops, and Shea had taken his place to watch over the remaining cart.

Shea had returned at dawn—smelling like a brewery from his nightlong stint outside of one but as sober as the day he was born—with more news about the rooster men the children had seen. They'd emerged from the storeroom behind the cart after moonset, removed jars light enough to be carried by one person, and replaced them with ones that were so heavy two people struggled to carry them.

For people trying to avoid attention from the guard and the tax houses, they made almost no effort to hide their identities. The "golden rooster" the children had seen was a cockatrice, the crest of the Mesley family, a wealthy merchant family who sponsored a third of the minor merchants in Mezeldwelf. Only one of the men swapping the barrels had even bothered to wear a cloak to cover it up.

Unfortunately, it wasn't quite enough to get to the root of the smuggling. A drop-off point was easily changed, and the actions of a handful of men could be brushed off as acting independently. The current head of the family, Prince Artur Mesley, had been leading his house for longer than Leon had been alive. Leon had known his youngest child—a reprobate, bully, and scoundrel by all accounts, including Leon's—but even Myrrdin's poor reputation hadn't tarnished the shine of their father's decades of service on the merchant council. They'd need more proof if they wanted to accuse Mesley or to prove he needed to investigate his servants.

Kelan, on the other hand, had followed the blind Sihianese man all the way back to the docks, to a warehouse near the port. The heavy barrels had been dropped off inside, and the blind man had disappeared into the living quarters there. There was no mark of ownership on the warehouse, but the city clerks had traced its history back to House Carrick, a merchant clan that had fallen apart a few years ago. Most of their property had been seized to pay debts, and the ones they retained barely made enough in rent to pay off the fees to run them.

Neither lead was enough to bring the guard in, but the warehouse was solid enough. Njeri had seized the chance to free herself from the mire of planning and paperwork and stretch her legs on a simple scouting job. That was how she and Leon found themselves outside the warehouse on the docks. Allegedly, they were exploring the small shops and stalls in the area, but it was simple enough to do that and to keep a careful watch for potential entrances and guard rotations at the same time.

Or at least as careful a watch as someone could manage while cold, hungry, and distracted by spectral figures that had taken up position in the corner of his eye.

Njeri huffed once more. "I swear, I'm going to put him on first watch for a month if he pulls something like that again."

"So you've said," Leon shot back, scanning the next stall's offerings. The fish was starting to reek in the way that only something left in the sun near a tannery could. Gagging, he pushed Njeri forward. It smelled worse each time they came this way, and the less time he spent enmeshed in that smell, the better. "And I've agreed each time."

They'd been here for two hours already, and they'd gone through most of the stalls, haggling over goods they ended up not buying and loitering as inconspicuously as possible. It was all to no avail, though, because the single entrance to the warehouse was constantly guarded by at least one person, often two. The only other way in was a handful of windows on the second floor. Even Leon on Shea's shoulders wasn't tall enough to climb through those.

The sound of arguing drew Leon's attention before he could suggest they move on. A squat Hyderian man, one of the two guards on duty right now, stood near the warehouse door, yelling at a child in an oversized red tunic and brown leggings. As they walked closer, the child's voice became clearer, and the insults they were hurling at the squat man could've curdled milk.

"For gods' sake," Njeri muttered under her breath, catching Leon's arm and pointing toward the warehouse. "What's Jackie doing here?"

Leon's head spun so fast his neck cracked. Now that he was looking closer, his heart sank and he swore. Jackie was currently telling the squat man the things he could shove where the sun didn't shine in florid terms. "I have no idea," he hissed under his breath. "She's supposed to be staying at Quinn Manor unless someone escorts her out."

Padraeg and Aoife had insisted on it, and none of the captains had protested. Mezeldwelf was a safe city most of the time, but the neighborhoods the mercenary guilds favored were rough and ill-suited for one recovering from a broken leg. Not to mention the decay the city was undergoing as its gods were consumed. It hadn't been this rough when Leon was a boy.

Njeri looked back and forth between Leon and Jackie, and her brows furrowed. "One of us needs to get her out of there."

"No, really? I thought we'd leave her there," Leon snapped back, shuffling so he could pretend he was talking to Njeri while still keeping an eye on Jackie, who'd moved on to describing, in detail, what she thought the squat man's parents looked like to produce a child such as him. She was drawing too much attention to herself, and the wrong sort of people paid attention to random children that appeared in the homes of merchant princes. He ought to know.

"Do you think you could pull off a concerned father right now?" Njeri asked. "Except make it big?"

Leon's eyes narrowed. "Like that time at the Bandarin fishery?"

"Exactly." Njeri's eye gleamed with a feral light. "Except much bigger. They'll all be looking at you, and I might be able to sneak in."

Leon swore once more but tugged back his hood and grimaced. It would be easier to sell father and child if people could see his eyes, but that didn't mean he had to like it. "Fine. Just hurry."

He didn't want to do this. The only reason it had worked in Bandarin was that he hadn't grown out of the gangliness of youth yet, and the quartermaster at the time was almost sixty. They'd managed to distract the guards there with an argument that scared off most birds in the area. Jackie couldn't yell loud enough for that, and doing so would get the guards called on them.

He jogged toward Jackie and the squat man, who had barely stopped insulting each other long enough to breathe. "Jackie Bladesworn," he roared at the top of his lungs. "What do you think you're doing?"

Jackie spun to face him, a curse already halfway out of her mouth, and froze. "I—I—"

But Leon plowed on, not even giving her time to come up with a lie. "Your aunt and I have been worried sick," he yelled again, yanking her away from the squat man. "We've been looking for you for ages, and now I find you here, insulting this poor man."

It was working. Leon's voice was enough to draw attention in a way that a single child yelling at an adult couldn't, if only for the lure of a fight. More importantly though, the other guard, a tall Hyderian woman, was paying attention. She'd even gotten to her feet to get a better look at Leon and her partner. Leon glared at Jackie and subtly tapped his left leg three times. Jackie's eyes widened and then narrowed. Njeri had insisted she learn their signs, even if she wasn't allowed to help on jobs yet.

"You're the one who got lost," she yelled back, setting one hand on her hip. She pointed to the squat man, then stuck her tongue out at him. "This bag of rotten fish entrails and dung wouldn't let me stay here until you could find me again."

It was a thin excuse, but thin was better than none. Leon scooped Jackie up and shifted her onto his hip while she wrapped her skinny arms around his neck. "If I've told you once, I've told you a hundred times, you're not to wander the markets on your own." His head snapped up, and he gave a fake—and hopefully frazzled—smile. "I'm so sorry, sir, I don't know where she gets this language from."

The squat man spat, and his saliva glimmered in the dirt. "She tried to get in the warehouse," he growled. "No one's allowed in the warehouses without permission. Not even skinny little rats."

Leon sputtered and tightened his grip on Jackie before she could lunge at the squat man. She did her best anyway, and he almost dropped her. "Jackie, behave," he growled. He looked up again and shook his head at the squat man. "And that, sir, was uncalled for. She's a child. All businesses in Mezeldwelf are supposed to report lost children to the city guard; you'll be lucky if I don't let them know that you threatened a child."

The other guard took a step closer, but no more. Njeri had snuck close to the warehouse, far enough that Leon could see her, but she couldn't get closer as things stood. He'd need to go bigger.

But the squat man did it for him. "This ain't city property," he snapped, stepping within arm's reach of Leon and glaring up at him in a way that might've been intimidating if he weren't more than a foot shorter than Leon. "Your brat was trying to steal something, mark my words."

"Liar," Jackie shouted, lunging forward and knocking the squat man's straw hat over his eyes. "I was nice at first! I asked you if you'd seen Da, but you didn't listen! You started shouting at me." She turned back to Leon, tears shimmering in her eyes. "He called me names! He said he would—" She stopped, and the fake tears couldn't disguise the genuine fear in her eyes. She leaned in and whispered in Leon's ear. "I know you're just pretending to be my Da, but he really did say something nasty."

He grabbed the back of her head and pressed it close to his chest. "How hard do I have to hit him?" he whispered into her hair. A proper fight would pull more attention still, especially since the second guard looked increasingly bored with how things were turning out.

"Pretty hard," Jackie mumbled. "He said gray-eyed bastards like me deserved what the Templesbane did to them, and he'd make sure they found me."

Leon's heart stopped and rage flooded his veins. He set Jackie down and nudged her behind him. "Go wait by the jewelry stall," he said in a dark voice. "Da's got to teach a man to mind his manners."

They may have been pretending, but there were times when the games became reality. This was one of them.

The squat man grinned like a rabid wolf and cracked his knuckles. "Teach me manners? What are you, my mum?"

"You threatened her," Leon said again, stalking forward. "You said you'd give her to the Templesbane."

The crowd gasped and muttered, just like Leon intended. To call upon the Templesbane was a blasphemy and a curse. The folk here might not face the terrors of the borderlands, but they suffered from the Templesbane's cruel appetite all the same. They'd seen the city decay as gods died and their godsworn lost the abilities they'd been given, lost the ability to heal or create. To call the Templesbane down for something as simple as a lost, or even a thieving, child was worse than taboo. Leon had no idea what the squat man had been thinking, and he didn't care.

He'd threatened Jackie with a fate worse than death. For that, Leon would hit him as hard as he deserved.

The squat man didn't deny it. "She's got gray eyes," he spat out. He grinned, and the sight of his silver teeth, each as sharp as a dagger, turned Leon's stomach. How could a godsworn invoke the Templesbane against someone? What kind of god must he serve that he retained his gifts after doing something like that? "Do you have any idea what the bounty is on those in the right market?" His grin turned into a leer. "You've got them too. I should turn you both in and save this city a god or two—"

Leon's fist hit him before he could finish his sentence, and his nose collapsed with a satisfying crunch.

Screaming, he reeled back into the encircled crowd, who shoved him back toward Leon. Blood poured down his face, and he swore violently. "You fucker, you'll pay for that. You and your brat." He swung at Leon, who easily dodged. "I'll turn you both in, I'll—"

This time Leon hit him in the stomach, and he doubled over to the cheers of the crowd. Through the red mist, Leon struggled to remember that he couldn't finish this too early. Njeri needed time to get in and out before he stopped, but he couldn't let this stand.

He pulled back, his fists raised. "Apologize," he hissed, guttural and deep. His arm burned, and he swallowed back the pain. He hadn't hit the squat man hard enough to injure himself, had he? "Apologize for invoking the Templesbane against my daughter, and maybe I'll leave you with a tooth or two in your mouth."

The squat man spat out a bloody gob. "Fuck off, your brat deserved it." He lunged at Leon and this time managed to grab onto his cloak. His lips spread in a bloody smile. "And maybe, she deserves a bit more than that." His forehead slammed into Leon's chin, and stars erupted behind Leon's eyes.

Leon stumbled back into the crowd, the coppery taste of blood flooding over his tongue. He struck without thinking, without seeing. His first blow struck air, but the second hit home.

Distantly, he heard Jackie calling for him, but he couldn't understand it. His head settled in time for a blow to connect across his temple and send it spinning again. Unbidden, the world expanded. His senses lashed out, and things came into a terrible sightless focus before the stars faded. He could smell the sweat soaking through the squat man's tunic, heard each gasping breath and quiet whimper, felt each step on the muddy cobblestone.

Jackie's voice rang out above it all, warning him to turn around.

His hands shot out, and he caught the next punch before it could make contact. His vision sharpened, and he moved without thinking. Each strike hit harder and faster than a normal man could ever hope for.

He should stop. Someone would notice; they'd make connections. He knew that, but his fists wouldn't stop moving. If he'd taken his axes today, he'd have pulled them out without question. There was something here, something that was pushing him, stoking the worst parts of himself. Something was wrong.

"Stop," a new voice ordered.

At the same time, Jackie screamed in terror. "Da, help me!"

He spun toward Jackie's voice, fists raised high. The crowd parted to reveal the other warehouse guard with Jackie in her arms.

"Stand down," the guard said, snarling. Jackie wriggled in her grip, but her struggles didn't help her any. "You've more than made him pay for what he did."

Not nearly enough, in Leon's opinion. He was still breathing. "He hasn't apologized," Leon slurred. "Do you know how much bad luck he's brought on my daughter? On me? We deserve more than a little blood."

The Sister wasn't omnipotent. She wasn't a god and couldn't be summoned by the simple act of saying her name, but Luck and Fortune were fickle gods. Being marked with her name or sign was more than enough to persuade them to turn their backs on someone.

The squat man was on the ground, stunned by Leon's last blow. Blood stung Leon's eye, and he blinked furiously, but the stinging only stoked his rage higher. Even dismissing the magic fueling his movements was agony. What normally needed to be pulled from the depths of his soul fought against the limits he tried to enforce, desperate to lay waste to his enemies.

The guard shook her head. "We'll report him for blasphemy, but whoever your god is won't want to see him killed. If you're arrested, who will look out for your little girl?"

"Da," Jackie cried, "please, let's go." Her eyes welled up again, and she sobbed. "Please, I wanna go home."

Jackie was an excellent actor, Leon noted absentmindedly. He stepped away from the squat man, who groaned and whimpered, and went toward the second guard. It was easier to go that way, toward the greater threat, but something tugged him back to the squat man. "Let her go," he slurred. His tongue felt thick and swollen. He must've bitten it when the squat man headbutted him. "Now."

The guard shook her head. "No." She pulled away, matching each of Leon's steps with her own and dragging a struggling Jackie with her. "Let me get my partner, and I'll let her go."

Leon took a step closer out of the shadow of the warehouse, and Jackie gasped when the guard's grip tightened. Leon stopped just out of arm's reach. The magic, the rage drained away, like someone had pulled a plug. His forearm burned, his knuckles bled, and he became aware of a hundred aches all across his body. How long had it been? How had causing a scene and protecting Jackie turned into this?

The squat man moaned, drawing Leon's attention back to him. Blood bubbled out of his mouth as he rolled onto his front, struggling to push up off the ground. What manner of god had the squat man sworn himself to that gave him such single-minded focus? That brought out a reaction like that in Leon?

"Now," the guard hissed. "Before he gets angry and tries to hit you again."

"All right," Leon said, lifting his hands higher still. "I'll go. I'll come back for my apology later."

The guard frowned but didn't argue. When she decided Leon had moved far enough away, she dropped Jackie and ran to her injured partner.

"Jackie," Leon gasped, relief washing over him and wiping away any anger he had left. Even the pain radiating from his knuckles stopped bothering him. He dropped to one knee and opened his arms. Jackie, obligingly, ran right in. "Are you all right? Were you hurt?" It probably wasn't necessary to keep the charade up now, but it didn't hurt either.

She shook her head, buried as it was in Leon's shoulder. "No, I'm fine, she just scared me."

"What were you doing out here?" he grumbled, pulling back. "You weren't—"

"I followed you." She beamed like the sun had come down to play, even through her tears. "I saw you were scouting the warehouse, and I decided to sneak inside. That dung sack caught me before I could get in though."

"You—" Leon took a deep breath and stood up, wiping the dirt and mud from his knees. "That was dangerous. You're not allowed to help during jobs, you know that."

It was then that he noticed that the square was distinctly lacking ghostly figures. They'd disappeared during the fight, and he couldn't help but be grateful for it. The last thing he wanted to deal with was their judgmental glares when he felt this bad.

"You got her!" Njeri's relieved voice cut through the growing buzzing in Leon's ears. "Thank the gods, I thought we'd have to go to the guards the way you were hitting him."

"Auntie," Jackie yelled, glancing around to see if anyone was listening. "Da saved me."

"I saw." Njeri glanced up at Leon, disapproval warring with amusement in her lovely brown eyes. "A little extreme, don't you think?"

He shrugged and regretted it when the action sent a searing bolt of pain through one shoulder. "He deserved it," he muttered, massaging the aching muscle. His forearm hadn't stopped burning yet either, and he was tempted to pull his sleeve back to see if he'd gotten cut and somehow missed it. "And . . . well, I'll tell you when we get back."

That rage hadn't been his. Now that his mind was clearer, it was easier to piece together what happened.

He hadn't lost control like that since he was a teenager, when the Sister had first sent her husk to negotiate with the merchant princes. War and Vengeance had grown powerful during the negotiations, and they reveled in the chaos their followers could cause. It made sense that not all of the troublemakers had left to join the Protectors. With the squat man out the way, things should settle down, but they needed to go home before Leon did something else he'd regret and end up arrested, killed, or worse.

Snorting, Njeri helped him to his feet. "Come on. You're lucky that worked and no one called the city guard. The last thing I want to deal with is explaining to your aunt—our employer, in case you've forgotten—and your father that you blew the whole job because you lost your temper."

She took Jackie's hand and squeezed it. Her smile was not pleasant. "And you—you're going to explain to me exactly why you decided to follow Leon." Her smile grew wider still, and Jackie shrunk away. "Then you're going to work very hard to convince me that you deserve to keep staying at Quinn Manor to finish recovering instead of the mercenary quarter, where I can keep an eye on you."

***

"This is all you found?" Aoife asked, paging through Njeri's report, which included a logbook she'd stolen from the warehouse. "We've already searched the merchant logbooks."

They'd reconvened at Quinn Manor to drop off Jackie and discuss the latest developments with Aoife. Padraeg had offered his study for the discussion, and as it turned out, four adults were a bit much to cram around his desk. Padraeg and Aoife sat on one side, and Leon and Njeri on the other, the open logbook between them.

Leon had convinced Njeri to stop at a healer so he could wash up and mend the cuts across his eyebrow and knuckles. Padraeg already didn't like that Leon was a mercenary. If he thought Leon was using it as an excuse to get into fights in Mezeldwelf, that blasted sigil—which Leon only realized at the healer's had been the cause of the burning he'd felt after the fight—might never come off. Thank the gods that particular effect only went one way; otherwise Leon might have found himself confined to the manor the way Jackie was now.

They hadn't had an opportunity to change, though, which meant Njeri was still in the leathers she'd worn to the market and Leon was in his old clothes, which were stained with mud and blood.

"Yes, but the warehouses in here aren't affiliated with any of the merchants that are on your list." Njeri smiled wolfishly, leaning back in her chair. "There's a new player in the game."

Humming, Aoife gestured for Padraeg to come closer. "Come look at this. That seal, doesn't it look—"

"Forged," Padraeg confirmed. "But a high-quality forgery based on the ink. If I didn't know to look for the right signs, I'd assume it was legitimate. Whoever they bribed to sign off on this must have access to the tax houses."

Leon almost had a conniption when Njeri pulled the logbooks out while the healer was attending to his wounds, but he had to admit it was a good find. At the very least, it proved they weren't wasting Aoife's money. They'd found evidence of illegal behavior, and—since the guard had already passed on this particular job—that meant they had authority to do things like this.

"I agree." Njeri leaned forward, tugging the logbook toward her so she could point to a particular page. "Here especially. The goods they're supposed to store here match the ones that the suspected smugglers are reporting to the tax houses. Even if they're only filling a third of the barrels with contraband, that's still an awful lot of goods flowing into the city without the proper duties being paid, to say nothing of whatever those goods are."

"The carts were weighed down by the barrels," Leon pointed out, "which means that whatever they're carrying is heavy. Money laundering perhaps? Or maybe ore."

"They were wearing uniforms with a golden cockatrice on them?" Aoife tsked and leaned back in her chair. Steepling her fingers under her chin, she hummed. "Artur Mesley has been awfully quiet at council meetings, but I never thought he'd get involved in smuggling. He's been a prince almost as long as I've been alive."

"It could be his youngest child," Leon reminded her. "Myrrdin? You remember them, they were about my age. They were trying to start their own shop when I left, trading in wools. They always liked hanging out in the rougher taverns." They'd looked down on Leon for being a Dhuitholm refugee, as if their father hadn't grown up in the gutters of Mezeldwelf before his predecessor, Natalia Mesley, took him into her house.

Padraeg shook his head. "No, Myrrdin left on the last voyage to find a new sea route to Sihia. No one's seen anyone from that ship in three years, and their sister hasn't spoken to their father since she joined the Protectors, so Mesley himself has to be involved." His fingers thrummed on the hilt of his sword as he considered the logbook. "He's in charge of the tax houses this year, isn't he?"

Leon let out a sharp whistle. If that was the case, Artur Mesley had changed a lot. Myrrdin had been a little shit and a pain in the ass, but their father was a good man. He'd run the city treasury when Leon was young, which was as close to a king among the merchant princes as there could be, and the tax houses weren't far off from that in terms of responsibility.

There wasn't a city in the world like Mezeldwelf. The merchant princes ran it entirely, devoting their time and fortune to improving the city that brought them wealth in the first place. Each controlled a section of the city—like Aoife controlled the wharf, and Artur Mesley controlled the tax houses—in exchange for using their purses to fund development in that area.

Everything, from the orphanages and shelters to the schools and public parks, was funded by a merchant jockeying for power, position, and trade concessions. A merchant that failed to keep the peace and health of their district would lose their position and as much of their wealth as it would take to restore what their negligence had caused.

Losing the title of merchant prince to anything but retirement—in which case the title passed on to the house or company heir—was worse than death. Houses had been ruined by Greed convincing an unscrupulous prince to cheat on their public duties. Those houses rarely recovered.

Aoife nodded. "Yes. He mentioned a handful of seals had been stolen, but swore he had recovered them all. We didn't think to question it once the clerk involved had been punished, but now . . ." She paused and pursed her lips. "Perhaps the time has come for the merchant princes to account for our management." She raised her head and turned to Padraeg. "What do you think, is the harvest festival too close? I'd love to announce it to the public then—they always love when the princes are taken to account. It cheers people up after losing a god."

"That's a matter best discussed with the other princes," Padraeg said. "As it is, I suggest we wait to begin the motions for that until Mesley has enough rope to hang himself."

"I agree with Padraeg," Njeri said, nodding. "If you move too fast, you'll scare him away. Right now, all we can do is link his servants to the smuggling, not the man himself."

"And he's too clever to not have a backup plan if this operation goes wrong," Aoife muttered. She sighed and ran a hand through her rapidly disintegrating braid, a red twin to Padraeg's silver one. "Very well. Keep investigating and let me know if you need any research done. I have my own contacts in the tax houses, and I don't mind using them to get inside information."

The conversation turned to patrol rotations and where the Band could look for further merchant activity, as well as the possible identity of the blind Sihianese man and what to do with the logbooks now that they had them.

The candles had burned low before they finally made the last decision.

The logbooks would be copied that night and then returned by the sneakiest cutpurse currently working off their sentence by helping the guard. A constant watch would be kept on the warehouse, and Mesley's dealings would be closely scrutinized. In many ways, the Band's work had become easier. They had a target and could narrow their scope down to the essentials instead of having each member scattered throughout the city, chasing down leads that might never materialize.

However, now that they had leads, things would also become harder. Mesley was an intelligent man who hired intelligent servants. Someone would notice they were being followed if the Band wasn't careful, which meant the stealthier of their members would need to work harder while the rest twiddled their thumbs.

The meeting came to an end an hour after dark. Njeri had her orders for the next few days, and Aoife had the report and the logbook to pass on to her scribes.

Leon stood to follow them out. Njeri had sent Jackie to the kitchen with firm orders to help with the cleaning as punishment for sneaking out, and he wanted to check on her before he washed up. Padraeg put a stop to that, grabbing Leon's arm as soon as he straightened.

"Stay behind. We need to talk."

Leon's stomach sank. He hadn't done anything that could make it back to Padraeg—even the fight had been resolved without calling the city guard—but it was hard to push aside the inherent guilt caused by a parental figure saying those words. He'd tried to limit his involvement in the discussion, hoping and praying that Aoife's vague mentions of his having caused a distraction would be enough to keep Padraeg from asking questions.

Njeri and Aoife both looked sympathetically at him but left anyway. The fading echoes of their voices were his only company when Padraeg closed the study door.

"Take a seat," Padraeg said in a dark voice, taking his place in the chair Aoife had abandoned.

Leon's heart clenched and he sank into his chair. He hadn't done anything Padraeg could yell at him about.

Padraeg crossed his hands on top of his desk and scowled. "Care to explain why my sigil lit up like the harvest festival during my meeting with Prince Toren?" he asked, pulling back his sleeve to reveal the sigil on his forearm.

A sigil that was still faintly glowing.

Fuck. Sigils weren't supposed to work like that.

"We needed a distraction," Leon said honestly, biting back the residual anger pounding in his chest. He placed his hands across his knees and forced them still. "We needed to get into that warehouse, and hitting the guard seemed like a good idea at the time."

He hadn't known that the sigil wasn't just a tracking sigil. The ones used for suspected smugglers—which he was, since he'd lied to the gate guard—weren't supposed to be anything more than that. Even if he had known . . . well, he wasn't certain he'd have reacted another way. It might have been over the top, but the squat man had threatened Jackie.

"There weren't any other options?" Scoffing, Padraeg pinched the bridge of his nose. He looked like he couldn't decide whether strangling Leon would be worth the paperwork it would take to cover it up. "You were supposed to keep a low profile. Gods, if your sigil were on anyone else, they'd have hauled you into the Citadel already."

"We didn't have a choice," Leon shot back. "Jackie—"

"And you got Jackie mixed up in this." Padraeg inhaled through his nose and out again before he continued. "She's a child, and you got in a fight with her there? You're supposed to be taking care of her."

"Hey, she mixed herself up in this," Leon snapped back. He dug his nails into his palms and took a deep breath. "Njeri and I have dealt with her. She knows not to do it again." Which Padraeg knew. Njeri had explained what happened, even if she'd downplayed Leon's role in the matter a little.

Aoife and Padraeg might have grabbed them as soon as they got back, but Jackie had scurried straight for the kitchen like a dog with its tail between its legs. She knew better than to not be where Njeri expected her to be when she was in trouble. They'd taken turns lecturing her on the way back. The gods alone knew if any of it had taken, but at the very least she understood what she'd done wrong this time.

Besides, Jackie wasn't like the children in Mezeldwelf. She'd grown up on the border of the Fallow Lands. She could handle herself in a fight if it came down to it. That was why the Band worked so hard to make sure she never had to.

"You should've sent her home immediately." Padraeg pushed back in his seat, glowering at Leon like he'd caught him with his hand in the family vault. "She's a child, not a mercenary, and you shouldn't have put her in that situation. Njeri could've brought someone else back later to cause a distraction *after* you brought Jackie back here."

Leon ground his teeth and bit back an oath that would've seen Padraeg washing his mouth out with soap when he was a teenager.

Padraeg paused a moment and continued when Leon didn't say anything. "The facts are that you can't do that again. Our family is important, and people pay attention to what we do. Rumors have already begun spreading that you're staying with Aoife and me as a condition of your parole. Aoife's got enough to deal with right now without you causing more problems."

A stab of guilt shot through Leon's heart, and he forced it back down. He didn't want to be sorry. Yes, he could've explained everything more thoroughly, but it wouldn't have changed anything. A fight on parole was a fight on parole, even if he hadn't known that was a part of the deal. Although perhaps he should have expected it. Padraeg had always been overprotective.

"I . . . apologize. If I caused any issues for you," he muttered, sinking into his chair. Facing Padraeg's disappointment hurt. Still, he couldn't resist one more shot. "Although I don't recall staying out of unnecessary fights being a parole condition for suspected smugglers."

Padraeg met Leon's sharp look head-on. "Things have changed since you left," he said, tapping his fingers on the desk. "With each god we lose, the guard has a harder time keeping the peace. The smuggler sigils were changed years ago. I'd assumed you knew."

Rage and shame mingled in Leon's stomach, and he sat up straight. "You—" His jaw worked open and closed, and he swore. "You don't trust me."

The sigils were standard, yes, but they could be changed if the situation called for it. A smuggler could be allowed to leave and return, a spy could be trusted to carry messages, or a murderer could have a weapon. Padraeg had chosen not to change the conditions for Leon's sigil.

"No—it's not that. I do trust you." He rubbed his forehead and let out an explosive sigh. "Things have changed, this isn't the city you knew and—"

"And I've been fighting in the fucking borderlands for a decade," Leon snapped. He shot to his feet, knocking his chair over, and began to pace, three steps from one side of the study to the other. It wasn't much, barely soothed the itch underneath his skin, but it was something. "I know how to take care of myself. Njeri needed a distraction, and Jackie gave us an opening. Would I have preferred not to fight? Yes, but I didn't have a choice, and we were running out of time to get her out of there."

"There's always a choice," Padraeg said, standing to match Leon. Even though he was a good six inches shorter, he still managed to look down his nose. "Especially when you have someone depending on you. Fighting should always be your last option and—"

"The last option?" Leon let out a hollow laugh. "I should have known. The great Padraeg Quinn, guard-captain of Mezeldwelf, was never one to fight unless it was the last possible option."

Padraeg's eyes narrowed, and his voice dropped to a dangerously low pitch. "Care to elaborate on that?"

"You know very well what I mean," Leon said. His lips pulled back in something that could've been a smile if it weren't so cruel. "You've always preferred the peaceful route, and that's why your city sacrifices their gods."

Leon spun around and stormed out before Padraeg could formulate an answer. Fire burned in his blood, hot enough to drown out the shame of what he'd said. The dark cloud following him scared off everyone on his way to his room.

Chapter 8
Secrets Revealed

Padraeg found Leon the next morning. If Leon had been concerned their argument from the night before would pick up again, he needn't have worried. That didn't mean the news Padraeg had come to deliver was any easier to swallow.

Leon was still struggling to digest it when he joined Kelan on patrol.

"So, now you can't fight—at all—unless your life is in danger, or you'll be put under house arrest?" Kelan asked, incredulity straining at each word. "He does know you're a mercenary, right? That kind of comes with our job description."

Unfortunately, Leon's parole conditions had tightened, and there wasn't anything Padraeg could do to loosen them again. The sigil was already triggered, and the next phase had gone into effect before anyone could stop it. Padraeg had tried to reverse it, but the damage had already been done. The only concession he'd been able to get was that Leon was still able to join patrols.

"It's . . . complicated." It really wasn't, but he didn't want to discuss it with Kelan. It was bad enough that Njeri had learned about the sigil from Aoife. Apparently, Aoife hadn't realized Leon hadn't told any of the others about it yet.

When Leon had come to get his assignment for the day, Njeri had yelled at him. Loudly.

Much to his displeasure, the other captains had been waiting outside Njeri's room when she let him go. Shea and Bettany had been kind enough to not comment, but Kelan had no such qualms.

Between him and Njeri, Leon had no choice but to explain everything that had happened after he arrived at Mezeldwelf and before he found Njeri and Kelan in the mercenary guild tavern. If it hadn't been for Bettany pointing out that making Leon stay out of it would leave someone without a partner, Njeri would've dumped him at Quinn Manor and left him there.

One of the merchants Njeri suspected of helping Prince Mesley with the smuggling was supposed to be coming into port tonight, right before the sea gates closed. Most of the Band had been dispersed throughout the wharf, keeping a close eye on the cargo as subtly as a bunch of mercenaries could. Njeri had ordered them to linger near the dock where their suspect merchant would be unloading. Leon's absence would create holes in their net that they'd struggle to fill, which was the only reason Njeri had allowed him to stay until the sigil was gone.

He wasn't certain if he was angry about it or not. If one of the junior Band members had pulled something like this, he'd have left them at camp to watch Jackie and prepare dinner. Since it was him, though, Njeri's anger felt out of place. He wouldn't even be in Mezeldwelf if the gate guards hadn't recognized him.

"I dunno, seems pretty simple to me," Kelan said, crossing his arms behind his head. His eyes gleamed as they turned a corner and entered a shadowy alley near the dock where their merchant was supposed to land. "Your father is angry at you, and it sounds like you're one punch away from house arrest."

"It's not—" He inhaled through his nose and counted to ten before he spoke again. Gods, he couldn't believe he was even defending this. "It's a standard intensification of my parole stipulations. Padraeg apologized that he couldn't lower them again."

"Right . . ." Kelan dragged that single word out far longer than necessary. "And it has nothing to do with the fact that he hates that you're a mercenary."

"Nothing at all."

Gods, if only he'd been able to convince Shea or Bettany to switch with him tonight. They'd been assigned a position on the other end of the wharf as a servant of Beauty and his client, which wouldn't draw any attention at this hour. Half the balconies, gardens, and appropriate viewpoints had aspiring artists using the golden hour before sunset to practice their crafts, so Shea—with his sculpted body and actual knowledge of art—and Bettany fit right in.

Thank the gods that Beauty didn't require their priests to swear to them. They accepted anyone into their service, provided they sought to bring Beauty into the world, whatever that meant to each individual, and abstained from unnecessary violence.

It did mean that neither of them could wear armor—not even the chain mail Leon and Kelan hid under their loose linen shirts—or any weapon larger than their daggers. Shea couldn't even wear a shirt that closed all the way. They might be lookouts tonight, but if things went wrong, they'd be sitting ducks.

That, and Bettany had promised to give any sketches she produced to Kelan when all this was over. Shea had allowed it without too much grumbling, which made Leon glad Bettany was with Shea and not him. She was a much better artist than him, and whatever relationship Shea and Kelan were building was nothing he wanted to get in the way of.

Thankfully, Kelan lapsed into silence after a few more pointed comments Leon did his best to ignore. They found a pile of boxes near the dock, and Kelan pulled wine bottles filled with red juice from his bag, set them down, and then pulled out a bottle of cheap rum he splashed over their clothes to sell the look and smell of two drunks. They settled in to watch, chatting about the weather or the docks and generally doing their best to look like sailors instead of mercenaries.

The ship they were waiting for was certainly taking its time. It came in as the sun crept below the horizon, and still hadn't finished docking now that the sun was long gone. By now, even the dregs of Leon's patience were drained, and Kelan had taken over the bulk of pretending they were passing the time until they needed to report to their ship for night watch.

Leon let his mind wander while Kelan spun a story about a drunken blacksmith he'd met in Beldown who'd inadvertently introduced him to Njeri.

Leon had been there for that series of events—and Shea's pride had never recovered from them—so he felt no shame in only paying the barest attention.

The Knights Beyond had been quiet today. He'd only caught glimpses of folk no one else noticed in crowds and in the corner of his eye. It was almost peaceful. They hadn't left him alone this long since Amberbrook. He'd even managed to get some sleep last night after liberating a bottle of cooking wine from the kitchen.

Absentmindedly, he let his senses stretch out. It felt good to do so. He'd ignored them for years, terrified that the wrong person would figure out what he was doing and drag him in front of the Protectors or right to the Templesbane. He'd used them more since Amberbrook than he had since fleeing Mezeldwelf, and it was so freeing, like he'd finally been released from a cage.

He was safe here. The husks weren't allowed inside the city, and anyone who looked at him would only see a drunk closer to passing out than his friend was. With Kelan at his side, he didn't have to worry. He could let his guard down and keep a better watch while he was at it.

It was quiet on the docks. If he looked, he could see other Band members standing and sitting in groups like theirs farther down the pier but much louder. Thousands lived in the wharf district, and the quiet hum of their lives soothed his soul.

Delke used to do this with him and Mael. She'd take them to the busy parts of Dhuitholm and make them sit at her side while she prayed. He hadn't understood it at the time—without the gifts of the Watchful Peace, he couldn't even hope to—but he'd always enjoyed those quiet hours spent watching the people of the city go by.

By the time he'd gotten his gifts, there'd been no time to sit for hours, and the people they'd watched had either fled, died, or become trapped.

"Wake up," Kelan whispered, hitting Leon's leg. "Shea sent the signal. Our friend with the cart is on his way."

Leon opened his eyes, only half-aware he'd even closed them in the first place. "Give me a bottle." It was easier to excuse odd behavior from drunks, and even if whatever was in these bottles wasn't alcohol, it certainly looked that way.

By now, everyone should be in place. Aoife had pulled some strings and gotten a handful of Band members onto the ship docked opposite their target. Once the crew went ashore for the night, they'd sneak aboard and find any paperwork or proof the tax house seals were being forged, while the others convinced the sailors that weren't stuck on watch duty to come to the taverns with them. Leon and Kelan were supposed to keep watch and, if necessary, provide a distraction so the ones on the ship could get off again.

The sailors moved fast once the ship was docked. The barrels were unloaded onto the dock, and when the first one hit the deck, Leon's heart stopped, and he almost dropped his bottle. That was—no, it couldn't be—but it was.

There was an absence inside those barrels. A void that wanted to consume every good and bright thing around it.

He leaped to his feet. All color drained from his face as he stretched his senses as far as he could toward the ship. It had to be a coincidence. He'd lost his touch, there was no way—

He swore brokenly.

The absence was real. It was all over the ship, touching and consuming it. There were good souls on board, but the absence threatened to drown them. It swirled, writhing and dancing like a flame, around the crew as it sucked tiny portions of their light and life away to satisfy its unholy hunger. The nothingness was a physical thing that tugged on Leon, a hound on the scent, that wanted to follow his touch until it caught him between its jaws. The things on that ship were empty and hollow inside, like a corpse that somehow kept walking after Death's sentinels took the soul away.

"We have to get out of here," he hissed, throwing his bottle back to Kelan. "Now." Leon wanted to vomit. If they hurried, maybe he could get away, but that would mean leaving the others behind. By the gods, they were going to sneak on board. They'd be seen and captured.

"Why?" Kelan asked, already swinging his bag over his shoulder. "Did you see something?"

Leon didn't answer. "Send the signal for everyone to come back," he rasped, tugging Kelan into an alley. His heart pounded in his chest, and he sank to the ground, his breath coming in quick, sharp bursts. Husks couldn't be here. It wasn't allowed. The merchant princes were supposed to stop that from happening, no matter what it took. "Now."

"Why?" Kelan demanded again. "Leon, if this is some stupid thing with your father—"

"It's husks," he hissed, trying and failing to keep the shaking from his voice. "They're what the merchant is smuggling into the city."

"What do you mean?" Kelan asked, crouching to look Leon in the eye. "Leon, that's impossible—"

"He's not blind, the kids were wrong, he's got white eyes. I can—" He couldn't tell the truth, and Kelan would know he was lying, but— "I just figured it out. Please, we have to—" They needed to go. Now. If the husks realized they'd been found out, they'd take half the Band with them, and the Templesbane would know that Leon was still alive. The Sister would take Mezeldwelf as revenge for the Brother, and he'd be lost, the way the other knights were.

Kelan stood, and Leon watched him creep back to the entry to the alley. His lips moved in a silent prayer, and his eyes glowed as he sniffed the breeze coming off the ocean. "Shit," he whispered under his breath. "I think you're right. That smell, it's—"

Worse than death or rot or disease. A complete emptiness that nothing would fill. Leon didn't smell them, but their touch against his senses made him want to rip his skin off.

"It's stronger than anything I've ever smelled," Kelan finally finished. His voice shook but still didn't contain even a fraction of the horror racing through Leon. "I thought it smelled bad at the crossroads inn, but the smoke and burning bodies must have covered it, gods."

"They're in the barrels," Leon rasped out, his breathing getting harder and faster. Aoife had been tracking these shipments for months. Even if it hadn't all been husks, they'd smuggled enough of them into the city to make the ships sit low in the water. "Mesley's men must be hiding them in the storehouses. Gods, how many of them must be here already?"

Now was not the time to be making those connections, but Leon's brain wouldn't stop. It wasn't proof, but if he could get Aoife and Padraeg to believe him, then they'd have to investigate Mesley. The city charter forbade any prince from harming the city, and Mesley had helped bring—

"We need to follow them," Kelan said suddenly, kneeling in front of Leon. He looked up and waved at the woman they'd stationed on the roof. She'd let the others know to retreat. Someone would find Leon and Kelan later, but they'd be away by then, gone and out of danger.

If Leon had been able to breathe, he would've waved, too, to make her hurry, but he couldn't. The beat of his heart pounded like a thunderstorm. His clothes, his armor, the alley—everything seemed too small. The world shrunk down to the ache in his chest and the tension thrumming up and down his legs. He needed to get away; he needed to run. They couldn't be here. It was impossible. There was no way a prince would betray the city like that.

"Are you insane?" he hissed, unable to get any louder than that. "We can't follow them. We need to tell Padraeg and Aoife." They would report it. Padraeg had fought the husks before the Great Treaty had been signed. He'd know what to do. He'd help make it right again.

"You realized it first," Kelan shot back. "I don't know how, but you knew, and don't give me that nonsense about you figuring it out. I don't know what god you follow, but I can't imagine they'd like it much if you let the husks escape because you were a little scared."

Scared? No. Leon was far past scared. His whole body was shaking, and his lungs refused to expand, and the husks couldn't be here, but they were, and—

Kelan came close and cupped Leon's face in his hands. They were cool and calming. Something for Leon to focus on even as the walls closed in around him.

"The sentry has already sent the signal. The others should be falling back. I need you to breathe, Leon. It's up to us."

He couldn't breathe. Couldn't Kelan understand that? Mezeldwelf was supposed to be safe. Even if the Knights Vigilant—even if *he*—couldn't be here because of the Great Treaty, the husks couldn't be here either. He'd already survived one of Hyderia's great cities falling—he wouldn't survive another.

"Look at me, Leon. I'm going to be here with you the whole time. We're just going to follow them. They didn't know you were there at the crossroads inn; they won't know you're here now. Focus on my face and breathe."

Kelan was right; they couldn't sense him. They could track him, though, and if they followed him back to Quinn Manor, everyone there would pay the price. The Knights Beyond had known; they'd been trying to warn him, but he hadn't listened. He should leave now. He'd send Padraeg a letter and hide somewhere as far from the city as he could, he—

Pain exploded across his cheek as his head snapped right. He turned back, eyes wide, and *breathed*. His lungs filled, and the dizzying panic faded into the background. Still there, still just as loud, but now he wasn't drowning in it.

"You back with me? Good." Kelan shook his hand out and then set it back on Leon's shoulder. "I can do it again if you need, but we have to go. They've loaded up the carts."

Leon nodded, still rubbing his cheek. "Carts?" he asked hollowly.

"Yes, carts." Grimacing, Kelan crept to the end of the alley and peeked out over the boxes. "I can see six of them. It looks like they're unloading the entire ship."

Normally, merchants bringing goods in would bring them in for inspection, but in rare cases, the inspectors would come to them. Like, say, when the goods being brought in were too large to move through the streets. Or if they had bribed an inspector.

Swearing again, Leon pushed to his feet.

The absence, the nothingness, called to him. It tainted everything around it. He wanted to shrink back again, to run and hide, but he couldn't. He couldn't. Kelan was right. Someone needed to find where the husks were hiding. The ship might be empty now—with the whole crew gone ashore except for a single watchman left behind to mind things—but the nothingness lingered, soaking into each rope, board, and sail. In a few hours, even that would be gone.

"Who are we following, then?" His throat hurt like he'd been screaming, and he swallowed painfully. Right now, he'd give anything for a mug of ale. "And how long can you track them?"

If Leon had the power to reach out to the others, he'd have sent people to follow all the carts. Tracking down where they went and where the husks were hiding was more important than anything they were doing.

Kelan shrugged, then pulled a rope from his bag. "Over the roofs and at night?" He grinned wolfishly. "Long enough. What about you?"

Leon could've followed them from one end of Mezeldwelf to the other as long as he was close enough, but he couldn't tell Kelan that. There were only a few gods that offered their followers mental abilities like the ones the Knights Vigilant had, and the people who worshiped them were not the type who came to populated places very often. Kelan would never believe it.

"As long as I can see them," he said finally. "But I don't want to get close."

Kelan smiled, a feral grin that wouldn't have looked out of place on a stray cat. "To the roof is it, then."

***

Kelan climbed up to the roof like a squirrel and dropped the rope down for Leon. Once they'd sent the sentry off to alert the others—and Njeri—to the new plan, they went off with varying levels of grace.

The roofs in Mezeldwelf were all made of the same red tile, which was slippery at the best of times and deadly at the worst, especially after dark. Kelan, of course, pranced over them like a cat. His eyes gleamed in the darkness, cataloging each slope and crack in the tile as he sprinted over them.

Leon followed him with much less grace. Magic thrummed through his limbs, heightening his reactions and his speed, but he still struggled to keep up without slipping. If it had been raining, as was so common in the fall, this journey would've been impossible. Even now, Leon wouldn't have attempted it without the rope still connecting him to Kelan. Especially not since the shadows had been getting thicker and more humanoid ever since they started their pursuit.

The carts carrying the husks split up once they reached the main road out of the port. Some went northeast, toward the dock warehouses; others west, toward the market district; and still others south, toward the temple district and the estates of the nobility. Kelan, for reasons of his own, picked one that was heading toward the temples. Leon followed without question.

The Moon was a lord of the sky and one who offered many different kinds of gifts to their followers. If Kelan said that cart was the one to follow, then Leon would believe him.

Prophecy called the Moon mother, after all.

The cart traveled noiselessly through Mezeldwelf. Past the craft district, past the Citadel, and through the poorer part of town. It finally came to a halt right outside the temple district, next to a ruined manor covered in vines and damaged by flames. The city had marked it for conversion into a shelter, but there were no signs anyone—not even one of the city guards—had been near here in ages. The sailors rolled the cart through the gates and left it there, out of sight of the road.

Kelan and Leon managed to stay on the roofs the whole time, if only barely. Kelan leaped without looking, trusting that his feet would find solid ground, and Leon followed as closely as he could, doing his best not to flinch whenever he passed through a shadow rapidly gaining human form. The nobles' houses were grand, but still tightly packed together. The distance might be too far for the average footpad, but for one blessed by the gods, it was well within reach.

Whatever calamity had struck the mansion had been intense. The heat had cracked and broken the cobblestones outside in the same way it had scorched the walls and twisted the metal of the gates. Even the autumn rains hadn't been enough to wash the ash away.

They found good perches on top of a pair of matching bell towers on the building opposite the ruined mansion, and Kelan settled into a crouch atop his tower. The moon had retreated behind a passing cloud, and even the brightest torches couldn't hope to reveal them up here. It was safe. Or, at least as safe as it could be this close to the husks.

Leon glanced over at Kelan, over ten yards away, and crept to the far side of his tower. Rage twisted his stomach in knots, and he breathed deeply as he glared into the night. He had business to take care of, and he couldn't let Kelan hear. If Leon kept quiet, this should be more than enough distance to stay hidden.

Shadows had been following them since they left the docks. By the time they passed the Citadel, they numbered in the thousands. Leon had ignored them. One, to lessen the risk of a fall, and two, because he didn't think he'd be able to hold his temper with the knights who could have warned him and yet chose not to. "Why didn't you tell me?" Leon hissed at them under his breath. "You kept me from my sleep for over a week, so you certainly had time."

They're all around, the knights whispered, their voices layering on top of one another like temple bells. **The echoes are deafening. Can't you feel them?**

Of course he couldn't. The only thing he could feel was the vast nothingness from the ones in the cart. He'd counted them over and over again on the way here, and each time, his stomach had sunk lower. There were sixteen husks down there, and it chilled his heart to think that he could've missed them entirely if he'd been a bit farther away when the ship was unloaded. "All I can feel are the ones down there," he whispered. "I lost the others ages ago."

He should've practiced more. If he had—if he'd been anything like the old knights, who could sense things from miles away and had always known where their enemy lay—things might have been different. But he only had himself to blame. He'd grown lax over the years, too scared of what he'd find or what could find him to risk using all his abilities.

The husks had never been this much of a concern before. They stayed in the Fallow Lands if they weren't hunting for Protectors or any lingering remnants of the Knights Vigilant and the Watchful Peace. As long as he stayed out of their way, he could drink and fight and protect himself, and now he was paying the price for refusing to honor his vows.

It is deafening, they repeated. **You do not listen.** They spread out around him, circling the tower like wolves circled a wounded lamb. **We warned you. The walls cannot hold. The Templesbane wishes to see the light in this world snuffed out, and you must stop them.**

"I can't," he snapped, louder than he meant. A thousand and one heads snapped toward Kelan, who hadn't moved from his position on the other tower. Leon let out a heavy sigh and rubbed his face. "I can't," he repeated, quietly this time. "The whole bloody order couldn't stop them. I was never even properly trained. What am I supposed to do?"

The knights of old had powers he couldn't even imagine, powers most godsworn couldn't even conceive of. Gifts from Purity, from Healing, from Salvation, for those who protected the world at their sibling's side. They could wipe all traces of the Templesbane from the land and its people, release gods consumed whole, and channel magics that would burn a lesser warrior to ash.

He was not—he wasn't any of that. He was a blade, and a broken one at that. He couldn't be what the Knights Beyond wanted him to be.

You are a knight. Your oaths demand this of you.

"It'll kill me." One man against an army. Against beings so powerful that generations of knights fighting with the support of countless gods hadn't been able to do more than temporarily drive them back. Against the horrors that still haunted him when he closed his eyes.

Then you will give your life if asked of you. Your children and your children's children will rejoice in the world you have given them.

He slumped against a pillar and bit back a sharp cry. "And is that how you want the Knights Vigilant to end? If I die fighting the Templesbane, that's it. There aren't any squires, and there's no one who can give the oaths. The Vigilant General is gone, and that magic went with him."

It was a weak argument and a hollow one, but Leon had used it for years. Normally, it split the Knights Beyond, and they left him alone while they argued, but now . . . now all those faces stared at him, set into the same harsh expression.

The Watchful Peace stirs. There will be others, even when you are gone.

"Weren't you listening?" Leon spat out. "There can't be. I'm the last. I'm—"

"Can you see anything on your side?" Kelan called before Leon could say anything more, his voice barely audible over Leon's breathing. The Knights Beyond disappeared, a lingering mist the only sign they'd been there at all. "The sailors are leaving and they're empty-handed."

Leon let out a shaky breath and closed his eyes. The Knights Beyond would be back, and perhaps he'd have an answer for them that wouldn't end with his death. He stretched his senses as far as he could. Down to the ruined mansion, weaving through the shattered walls and burned furnishing. It was empty and cold. "No," he called finally. "They're gone."

Would the sailors return tomorrow to pick up the goods for the tax houses to inspect, or would another husk come to collect their brethren? The Band would need to keep an eye on it. He levered himself off the stone and forced his shaking legs to stand firm.

"Do you want to stay here for a bit and see if anything changes, or should we head back?" Kelan asked, squinting down at the street below.

Leon scrambled down his tower and up Kelan's in lieu of answering. The mansion, cloaked in shadow, loomed across from them.

They'd need to talk to Njeri as soon as they got back, and it'd be easier to discuss this if they weren't yelling across the abyss. The sentry would've told her why they pulled the others back, but she always preferred to hear their side of things. When they told her, both Kelan and Leon could confirm exactly what they were facing, and things would change.

On the other hand, it would be best if they could keep eyes on the mansion. Ideally, a godsworn with gifts similar to his or Kelan's would take their place, but there weren't any like that in the Band. He didn't feel comfortable staying here by himself or leaving Kelan alone either. The husks were not to be trifled with. Standard orders when working around them were to never approach alone.

"Want to stay for a bit longer before we go back?" Kelan suggested, shifting to sit cross-legged on the roof. "Njeri won't send a search party out for another hour or so."

Nodding, Leon joined him, rubbing his shaking legs to ease the pain. "That's a good idea." And that way Njeri couldn't say they hadn't done their due diligence. "At least until we can know for certain if they're coming back or not."

It would hurt to keep his senses stretched out that long, but it was also the only way to make sure the husks didn't come back, short of exploring the mansion himself, which he'd rather die than do.

The silence settled around them like a blanket, and Leon was content to let it. He needed to organize his thoughts before he presented them to Njeri.

"You're one of them, aren't you?" Kelan asked casually. He leaned back against a pillar and brushed ash and dirt from his clothes, the products of using chimneys and gutters to support himself when loose tiles threatened to put an end to his adventures. "The Knights Vigilant, I mean. You're obviously not a husk, and I don't know who you were talking to, but you weren't exactly being subtle."

Leon's breath caught, and his right hand, hidden from Kelan, curled around the dagger at his belt. He should've been more careful. Whatever panic he'd felt was no excuse. A darkness inside him raged. He'd defended his identity for two decades. Never putting down roots, never truly moving on. Kelan was a good man, but good men had given secrets to bad ones countless times over the centuries, and Leon wasn't sure if he was prepared to risk that.

"I won't tell anyone," Kelan continued. His eyes were focused on the mansion, and his hands, the same hands that Leon had seen shatter bone and rend flesh, rested on his knees, palm up. "My order knows the value of secrets, and revealing yours would do more harm to the world than good."

Leon bit back a hysterical laugh. His hand tightened around his dagger. The hilt dug into his fingers, and he wished desperately he could take back the last hour. The Order of the Risen Moon gathered stories and any secrets revealed under the light of their patron, hoarding each scrap of knowledge like a squirrel hoarded nuts. Kelan had left years ago to gather the secrets that the Sun claimed dominion over.

"I'm not a monk anymore," Kelan said finally. He was calm and his voice was even. If Leon were judging by tone alone, he'd have thought Kelan was discussing what to make for dinner and not a secret that could ruin Leon's life if it came out. "But like you, I keep my oaths." The clouds shifted, and the patron in question revealed their luminous face. "I swear, by the Moon and the Night, I swear by the bonds we share and the ones we don't. I ask only to give you another shoulder to lean on. I won't tell anyone without your permission. Your secret is safe with me."

Leon's heart hammered, and blood pounded through his ears. Kelan's eyes were glowing, pulling in the moonlight and adding weight to his words.

The oath was sworn, and Leon . . . dropped his hand from his dagger and sighed. "Come on. We're not going to find anything else out by sitting here."

Perhaps it was his imagination, but he did feel lighter now.

Chapter 9
A Step Forward

"What do you mean the guards didn't find anything?" Leon asked, spraying crumbs over the table. He swallowed with some difficulty and kept going. "We tracked the husks to at least twenty different places in the city, all across the districts."

He and Kelan had returned to the Band's lodgings an hour after sunset. Njeri had been waiting for them with fire in her eyes and a frown fit to curdle milk. The sentry had told her why everyone had been pulled back and that it was only through Bettany's quick thinking that the others had been redirected into following the carts from a safe distance.

When they'd broken down what they'd found—and Kelan confirmed he'd smelled the husks the entire time—her frown had eased somewhat, but she'd still been upset. They hadn't consulted her or Bettany, her appointed second-in-command, before pulling everyone back, and then they'd disappeared. An entire night of work that was only salvaged because Bettany thought quickly on her feet.

Njeri dragged Leon and Kelan to Quinn Manor to tell Aoife and Padraeg exactly what they'd told her and what she'd gathered from the other teams. They'd marked each location on the map, and Padraeg had absconded with it. Leon lay in bed for hours after they got back, the events of the evening too fresh in his mind to encourage sleep. When he'd finally given up on getting any more rest, he'd dragged himself to the dining hall and found Aoife eating breakfast. Her news destroyed any hope he could've had of having a pleasant morning.

"Exactly that," Aoife said, frowning. "Swallow before you speak. Jackie may not be here, but I know you were raised better than that."

He took another bite of his toasted cheese and bread and swallowed before he spoke again. "That list was over a page long. Didn't they bring trackers or anything with them?"

He'd assumed the husks he and Kelan followed had gone into a basement of some sort, out of reach the way they'd gone out of sight. But there were only so many places one could hide. This wasn't a bard's tale or moral play where hidden tunnels and caverns were under every other building; it was a city with very strict building codes that even smugglers were careful not to violate.

Aoife shot him a dirty look, and he dropped his eyes back to his food. "A few pots without maker's marks, muddy footprints, and an empty Falten rum bottle." She grunted and viciously cut into the salted pork she'd chosen for her breakfast. "The issue is we've shown our hand now. Padraeg sent teams to raid unrelated locations at the same time, but if Mesley's behind this, he knows we're onto him. He's too smart to be tricked like that."

"Fuck," Leon whispered meaningfully. His stomach churned, and his food looked far less appetizing now. "What's your plan?"

A grape hit him on the side of his head, swiftly followed by another. He caught the third before it made impact.

"Mind your language," Aoife chided. "You might only be visiting, but the rules haven't changed. Even Padraeg isn't allowed to curse at the table."

Leon rolled his eyes and popped the grapes into his mouth. Some things would never change. The sweet juice burst across his tongue, a nice counterpart to his next bite of cheese and toast. "Do you want me to take any messages to Njeri when I see her?"

What went unspoken was the question of whether Aoife still needed their services. They'd proved that something was going on in the city, and it would be enough for Padraeg to open a formal investigation.

It was a long shot, but Njeri wouldn't want to stay in the city if there was going to be a showdown between the merchant princes and the husks, not if there wasn't a contract that required her presence.

Shaking her head, Aoife stood. Her meal was only half-eaten, and she showed no shame about scraping what was left onto Leon's plate. For his part, he certainly didn't mind, even if his stomach was still churning. He'd had worse breakfasts over the years, and since Jackie hadn't gotten out of bed yet, he might actually get a chance to finish it.

"If you and that monk friend of yours, Kelan, could take a look through the city, I'd appreciate it, but I don't have any news beyond what I already told you." Her lips cut down in a steep frown as she set her plate on the table. "The council is meeting this evening. If you could find some solid evidence before then, I'd appreciate it. I figure you two have a better chance than most, what with the—" She waved a hand around her head as if shooing away a persistent fly— "your gifts."

"Of course." He swallowed his disappointment with his next bite. He'd hoped that they were done now. The guard knew the husks were in the city, and they'd have to investigate, but until the Band was freed from their contract, they were stuck here. "Are there any places in particular you'd like us to look at? Any place the guards did find something?"

"No." Her voice dropped into a hushed whisper. "And that concerns me. The Sister's representatives will be here in less than a week to take Charity. If we can't find proof they're smuggling soldiers in before then, we may not have any chance to prepare our defenses."

He hummed and pushed the remaining ham around his plate. "You think the husks are planning to attack during the festival, then?"

"It's the only logical choice." She glanced around as if checking whether any of the servants were close enough to hear. An odd look settled on her face, one that was relieved and disappointed at the same time. She laid a hand on his shoulder, and the look on her face got even darker. "Even if they've only been sneaking a few dozen husks into Mezeldwelf with each shipment, that means they've got an army inside our gates, and we have too many temples with too few priests to guard them for that not to be a concern."

And too many people. There were fewer than two thousand godsworn in the city and surrounding area and more than a hundred temples and holy places. Even if the common folk took up arms alongside the godsworn, it would be a bloodbath. The city would fall, and with it, all the gods that called it home.

If the Sister took Mezeldwelf, Hyderia's lifeline would fall, and her army of husks would swell. Without trade, without the merchants and the news and knowledge they passed, Hyderia's people would crumble in front of the advancing husks.

"We'll start at the docks, then," Leon said. He reached up and squeezed Aoife's hand, which still covered his shoulder. "We'll see if we can't find anything in one of the warehouses." Aoife controlled the wharf district, so they could do more if they managed to find something there. In other parts of Mezeldwelf, they'd need permission from the controlling prince or a warrant and a guard tagalong to do anything more than ask questions. He was already in enough trouble with Padraeg. If there were any more problems, he'd be locked in his room until his case was cleared.

If the gods were kind, they'd actually find something big enough to justify a full-scale raising of the guard. Without a miracle or two, that was the only way they'd figure out where Mesley had hidden the husks before the harvest festival.

***

"Nothing?" Kelan asked quietly.

"Nothing," Leon confirmed, sighing.

They'd been searching for six hours, and the only traces they'd found of the husks were a handful of long-faded scents—and a few foolish cultists heralding the rise of the Sister and the defeat of the Knights Vigilant as proof that the end of all gods and the darkening of the world was nigh. A rather dramatic way to give up hope, but even the cultists had nothing more to offer right now.

Kelan swore, and Leon considered joining him.

"Should we move on to the craft district?" he asked, rubbing the bridge of his nose.

To say his head ached would've been an understatement of colossal proportions. Leon's skull felt like it had been used as the center anvil in a Forge temple and some apprentice blacksmith was hammering away even now. Each rumble of wagon wheels over the cobblestone, each vendor hawking their wares felt like a personal attack on his eardrums. He'd never used his senses this much before, and he was paying the price for it.

He wanted to be done. He wanted to retreat to his room, block out all the light, and get roaring drunk. But no, here he was in the market. In the middle of the day. With nary a bottle of rum, ale, or wine in sight. Gods, he'd even take some of the Falten herbs that Bettany liked to smoke. At least that was supposed to be good for a headache.

And the haze the herbs caused might convince the Knights Beyond to come out of whatever hole they'd disappeared into. They were never very active when the sun was out, but he hadn't seen any since the husks disappeared. The Knights Beyond always liked lecturing him when they thought he was neglecting his oaths, so maybe that would actually convince them to tell him where the husks were if they had any idea.

"We've been all over the market, so we may as well." Kelan's exhaustion faded for a moment, and he smiled like he'd been given the key to the city. "Besides, we're close to the old Forge temples, and Shea said he'd be helping some of the smiths today. I'd bet we can persuade him to eat lunch with us."

Rolling his eyes, Leon punched Kelan's shoulder. "If you wanted to eat, you could've just said so. No need to drag Shea into it."

Shea got mad when his work was interrupted. Whenever the Band had the opportunity to set up their traveling forge, he spent the whole night there. If the Forge hadn't been consumed, Leon had no doubt that Shea would've stayed in Mezeldwelf for the rest of his life.

"Nah, he'll be looking for a break." Kelan shoved his hands into his pockets and strode off into the market, leaving Leon to catch up. "Smiths don't like working in the early afternoon. Shea says it's bad for the metal."

Leon shrugged. "If you say so." But he didn't offer any more arguments. Despite the nagging feeling in the pit of his stomach, getting something to eat was the best option. The husks would still be there in an hour, but he'd be better suited to catch them with a full stomach and a bit of time out of the sun.

Still, there were a lot of Forge temples in this part of Mezeldwelf, and they wandered for an hour before Kelan caught sight of Shea.

By now, Leon's headache had grown from a single apprentice hammering on the anvil in his skull to a full parade of armed and armored knights yelling at the top of their lungs while running around. Even thinking of using his abilities anymore brought tears to his eyes and threatened to upend his stomach. Far faster than he'd like, his mind became fixed on the elusive goal of getting out of the sun and finding something to dull the agony ripping his skull in two.

"Shea," Kelan yelled, his normally gentle voice driving a dagger into Leon's temples. "Over here!"

Leon dragged his gaze from the back of Kelan's orange tunic and was hit with a wave of sensory hell. Dozens of voices, colors, and shapes all melded into one giant puddle of life, so it took Leon a moment to distinguish Shea's familiar towering, albeit blurry, shape from everything around him.

"I thought you two were on patrol today?" Shea wiped his ash-stained hands on his apron. His voice, softer than Kelan's, still beat against Leon like a fist when added to everything else screaming for his attention. "What're you doing here?"

Kelan shrugged. "We decided to take a break." He jerked a thumb back over his shoulder at Leon. "And this one, despite his vicious claims about my stamina being poor, needs to get out of the sun for a bit."

If Leon had the energy, he'd have sniped back, but he was struggling to think clearly right now, so he settled for glaring.

"See?" Kelan spun so he could look at both Leon and Shea at the same time. "He's been in a snit all morning, so I thought we'd try to find you and grab some food together."

Shea snorted. "And he could have a drink to soothe that hangover."

"More an unfortunate encounter with a doorframe on patrol last night," Kelan said, his smile taking on a harried edge. He shot a worried look at Leon and seemed to notice for the first time how fast Leon had deteriorated since they decided to find Shea. "But regardless, I'm hungry, and food tastes best with company."

Laughing, Shea said, "True. Give me a moment, then. I'll let the forgemaster know I'm leaving and grab Bettany."

Kelan waited for Shea to disappear into the crowd, then turned to face Leon. "What's going on? Are you sensing anything?"

Leon shook his head and breathed through the crashing waves of agony it caused. "Not since last night," he hissed. "I think I've overdone it though. My head is killing me."

Kelan swore quietly and then set a hand on Leon's forehead. "Gods' sake, I should've thought of that. You don't use this part of your gifts much, do you?"

Shaking his head once more, Leon bit back a whimper. When he'd first been learning to strengthen his body with his gifts, as well as when he'd run to Mezeldwelf with Jackie on his back, he'd gotten sick from the strain repeatedly. He hadn't had to worry about that since he was fifteen, and it had never been this bad before, and he'd never had to worry about it when using his senses.

"Well, you don't have a fever," Kelan said, dropping his hand, "but that'll be coming soon. I've never seen someone sworn as long as you get gift sickness, but I'll order some ginger tea in the tavern. It won't solve all of it, but it'll hold you over until you can get into a dark place to sleep the headache away."

"And ale?" Leon asked. Tea was good and all, but he'd kill for some ale right now. Even if it didn't help his headache, it would help him sleep later.

"And ale."

It was strange to have someone know Leon's identity. He still wasn't sure how he felt about it. On one hand, he'd been hiding for twenty years. No one but Padraeg and Aoife knew the truth, but even with them, he couldn't discuss it openly anywhere that wasn't Padraeg's study for fear of an eavesdropper revealing the truth to the wrong people.

On the other hand . . . it was nice to have another godsworn around who knew what and who he was. There was only so much Padraeg and Aoife could teach him when the power of the Knights Beyond failed, and they couldn't demonstrate what it meant to use his gifts. Try to understand as they might, neither had given themselves to a god the way Leon had. They were passingly familiar with the benefits of such an arrangement and completely unfamiliar with the consequences.

True to his word, Shea returned before they could discuss anything further, with Bettany in tow. He'd taken the time to rinse off and was marginally cleaner and slightly damp. He took the lead and directed them to a nearby tavern, which he swore had the best ale in the district.

Once they were inside, Leon collapsed onto the bench and rested his head in his hands. It was darker in here, and the thick tapestries on the walls absorbed much of the noise.

"Gods, how much did you drink last night?" Shea asked, settling onto the bench next to Leon, "and why didn't you share any with the rest of us?"

Leon shot him a withering glare and grunted.

Kelan saved Shea from the ravages of Leon's harsh look by returning with Bettany and four mugs of ale. "I took the liberty of ordering you some tea as well," he said, pulling out the stool opposite Shea. "I figure that might settle your stomach."

Bettany grunted and kicked a stool out so she could sit across from Leon. "If your head hurts that much, you should stop by one of the temples." Her eyes slid shut, and she moved her lips silently as if counting to herself. "Yes, we should still have enough supplies to make the necessary donations. Even considering . . ."

The mood at their table, already low, sank to the ground.

"If you ask Aoife, she'll help you restock," Leon rasped, then took a large swig of his ale. It was sweet across his tongue, like it had been mixed with berries at some point in the brewing process. It was very good but risky on an empty stomach. "She knows about our friends, so she'll be quick about it."

Njeri wanted to be gone as soon as they had their money in hand and could pass this whole matter on to the guard and the merchant princes, which meant they had to restock all their supplies as soon as possible. That was difficult, since most of their money had been put toward housing and food in hopes that their pay would come fast enough that they wouldn't be tossed into the streets beforehand. Since merchants in Mezeldwelf weren't the type to offer credit to visiting mercenaries, they couldn't even place orders without the funds to back them up.

It was a tricky situation, made worse by the fact that they couldn't tell anyone what was coming and what was in the city. Only the captains, Njeri, Padraeg, and Aoife knew what they were really facing. Even the rest of the Band was in the dark about it.

As guard-captain, Padraeg was supposed to keep the peace and to minimize the danger that not keeping the peace created. He'd forbidden anyone who knew what Kelan and Leon had discovered from telling anyone else on pain of death. If folks found out that husks were being smuggled in this close to the harvest festival, things would get bloody and gods might go missing.

They still had to take precautions, though, which was one of the reasons that Njeri made everyone, regardless of whether they knew the truth or not, travel in groups of two or more. Encountering husks alone was often the last thing one ever did of their own free will.

Shea arched an eyebrow. "You think Njeri would approve of asking for an advance on our pay? I mean—"

Kelan's foot hit Leon's under the table and then hit Shea and Bettany in quick succession. "Don't react," he whispered as his eyes flashed golden for a second. "But I think we've found our friend with the cart, and he reeks."

Bettany brought her mug up and whispered behind it. "Should we take him?"

Leon drained his mug in one go. The alcohol took the edge off his headache enough for him to focus. "Not here," he said in a low voice. "If we can get him into the alley . . ."

"We'd still need to get him to the Citadel," Bettany pointed out. "Maybe we should follow him instead. At least until he gets to the wharf, where we have permission to arrest people."

Shea took a large drink from his mug and then shook his head. "No. We'll lose him if we do that. He's already ditched every person we've had tracking him. Best to snag him while we have eyes on him."

Leon had to admit he agreed with Shea, even if it made his stomach sit heavy. Padraeg wouldn't be happy about this. If they could keep it quiet—and if Leon found him as soon as they got back to the Citadel to explain—he might be able to avoid house arrest.

Kelan slid his mug to Leon. "I'll wait outside, then. Shea, join me in a minute. Leon, Bettany, keep an eye out for him in here. Follow him if he tries to go out the back."

With the plan made, they went into action.

Making a show of his goodbyes, Kelan strode out of the tavern, singing a Falten drinking song as he went. Shea barely waited the full minute before he pushed his mug to Bettany and followed, grumbling about chasing Kelan down before he threw up somewhere.

Leon shifted so he was sitting next to Bettany and kept his eyes fixed on the bar.

"He's sitting at the table by the door," Bettany said in a low voice. "At the table with the man in the yellow hood."

Leon sipped Kelan's abandoned ale and chanced a slow look across that side of the tavern. Since there was only one person in a yellow hood, it was easy to find the right table.

The man with the cart, the person Kelan had tracked to the warehouse in the docks, was a slightly built man with Sihianese features, thick Alkan braids, and skin too dark to be entirely due to the sun. His partner was a muscular Hyderian man with a bright red beard and lily-white skin. Whatever they were discussing was unintelligible from across the tavern, but that didn't matter. Especially when the man in the yellow hood drew back his coat to pull out a small coin purse, and Leon caught a snatch of a cockatrice on his breast.

One of Mesley's men, then, likely here to pass payment and orders. If that was the case, they didn't have much time. He doubted their Sihianese friend would stay for lunch.

He swallowed another large gulp of ale and considered the tavern. It was a good size and over half full. The only way out other than the front door was through the kitchen, and the bartender seemed unlikely to let someone pass by him to go that way. A handful of the other customers were already making noises about going back to work. If they timed it right, they'd be able to leave alongside them.

"Ready to go?" Bettany asked. Her drink was hardly touched, and Leon mourned leaving it behind, but no doubt she'd made the same calculations he had. They needed to be outside as soon as possible.

"Aye." He finished his ale and shoved the bench back as he stood. As if cued, four other tables emptied, and their former occupants made their way to the door. "Let's go see where those two idiots ended up," he groused for the sake of anyone listening. It didn't look like anyone was, but it was better to be safe than sorry.

His head ached less now than it had a bit ago, but they still needed to hurry, or the ale would wear off. He pulled his hood up and tugged it as far down over his eyes as it would go.

Bettany followed at his heels, chattering about a made-up acquaintance as they went. Leon turned right and ducked down the alley next to the tavern. Bettany casually leaned against the door and pulled a dagger out to clean her nails.

Kelan and Shea had propped themselves up on two barrels outside the cooper opposite the tavern. Kelan winked, then nodded toward the alley behind Leon, all without losing track of his conversation with Shea.

Leon nodded back and turned, scanning the alley for whatever Kelan had left there. His eyes drifted over the refuse pile, the stacks of firewood, and settled on the medium-sized cart with six large barrels inside it. A very familiar cart with very familiar barrels that were large enough for a grown man.

A feral grin stretched over Leon's face. He darted over to the barrels. Carefully, he stretched his senses out enough to confirm that there wasn't anyone inside them—and regretted it when a blinding flash of pain almost made him vomit. Breathing deeply to stave off the nausea, he removed the lid from one and smiled again, albeit pained this time. Empty.

He knew just what to put inside it.

Kelan's sharp whistle brought Leon's attention back to earth, and he lifted the empty barrel out of the cart with ease. Once it was on the ground, he pulled his cloak off and hung it on the edge of the wagon. It wasn't much, but unless Shea or Bettany had some rope, it was all they had to keep the lid on.

"What are you doing?"

Leon's head jerked up. The Sihianese man stood at the alley entrance, his otherwise pleasant features twisted in rage. His eyes, which the children had called white but were actually a light silver, narrowed. He opened his mouth, presumably to yell for help, but never got that far.

Unfortunately for the Sihianese man, he didn't see the three shadows behind him or the bag that closed down around his head. He also missed the fist that hit his gut, the foot that sent him stumbling to the ground, and the rope that bound his hands behind him.

"Get him into the barrel," Leon hissed as loud as he dared. The Sihianese man was already struggling against his bindings and the hands that held him down. It took Shea and Bettany both holding various limbs to wrestle him into the barrel.

"You're a man after my own heart," Kelan praised, slamming the lid down and pressing his full weight against it. It muffled the yells of the Sihianese man dramatically. "I knew you'd follow my line of thought."

Bettany rolled her eyes and flicked her braids over her shoulder. "Let's get him to the Citadel. Shea, can you lift him?"

"Why bother?" Shea asked, considering the barrel. "The cart's still here and his contact is still inside. If we leave the cart here, he'll know something's gone wrong. If we take the cart with us, we'll save my shoulders and stop him from figuring it out for a while."

157

"An excellent plan," Kelan crooned, "but we still need to seal this. Bettany, do you have any more rope?"

Rolling her eyes once more, Bettany indicated Shea should lift the barrel a few inches and asked Leon to help her fasten it. Kelan checked the other barrels, knife in hand, to confirm they were empty. Once the barrel was tied shut and Leon's cloak wrapped around it to further muffle any sound, Shea moved it back into the cart, picked up the cart handles, and led the way to the Citadel. Mixed in with the chaos of a market town, the muffled yells coming from their cart went unnoticed. Or if they did, the four well-muscled folks accompanying the cart persuaded them it was better to ignore it.

Still, a knot in Leon's chest unraveled when they got through the Citadel gates. Even his headache felt less horrible now. "Let's take our friend to the cells. The jailer should've been told we were authorized to make arrests."

The others had agreed not to mention Leon's presence during the arrest, which was a load off his shoulders.

Shea nodded and dropped the cart handles. They hit the ground with a thud that made the occupied barrel squeal. "Got it. Why don't you and Kelan put the cart somewhere? I can't imagine your father would appreciate it if we left it there."

Bettany nodded and gently shoved Leon's shoulder. "You can head home once we're done. Get some rest and stop at a temple if you need to. We'll let Njeri know what happened."

The duties thus split, they separated. Bettany and Shea to the cells, and Leon and Kelan to move the cart to the side of the yard.

Kelan glanced at Leon as they both leaned against the cart when all was said and done. "Are you all right?" he asked in a low voice. "You didn't have the tea."

"I'm fine," Leon insisted. His head did still hurt a lot, but it wasn't as agonizing as it was before. Since they were in the shade, it was nearly bearable. The ale had helped, but it wouldn't last forever. "I just want to get my cloak back before I head home."

Kelan let out a sharp laugh that did nothing to soothe the pain in Leon's head. "Sure. A migraine like that just goes away with a drink or two? Leon, you need to sleep. And eat. And have a hot bath, if you can get it."

What Leon ought to do was check in on Padraeg before he left. No doubt he'd hear about what they'd done, and it was better he heard it directly from Leon or Njeri. Without his permission, they couldn't interrogate their prisoner anyway, and once he did, it would become clear that they hadn't been by the docks when they took the Sihianese man down.

"In a bit," he mumbled, resting his head in his hands. "I'm tired."

In a few minutes, he'd get up and go find Padraeg, who always spent the afternoons in his office, listening to reports and answering any mail he'd accumulated since the day before. All the senior officers knew Leon was back in Mezeldwelf now, so it wasn't like he'd be stopped. It'd be easy. He just needed a break first.

"Get up," a very familiar voice rumbled.

Leon chanced a glance up and silently swore. It looked like he was talking to Padraeg now.

Chapter 10
The Man with Silver Eyes

"My office," Padraeg rumbled. "Now." His voice brooked no disobedience, and his face was somewhere between a storm cloud and a volcano. Leon leaped to his feet and fell into step beside him.

Kelan shot Leon a pitying look and stayed right where he was.

Padraeg led Leon into the Citadel like a jailer leading his ward to the executioner's block. They entered the great hall, skipped past the court rooms, and went into the private areas in the back. In all that time, Padraeg never made a word nor sound.

"I was coming to find you," Leon said after a long while. "We managed to—"

"I said my office," Padraeg interrupted without skipping a beat. "This is not my office."

Right. Privacy. Leon glanced around the hall and only winced a bit when the sun sent a ray right through a window and into his eye. He wasn't sure they could get more alone than this. He hadn't seen anyone except the occasional passing squire since they left the public areas. There weren't even flies this far back from the streets.

When they finally reached Padraeg's office, Leon had to do a double take. It was like he'd stepped a decade back in time. Everything—from the thick books lining the shelves on the rear wall to the stained-glass window with the crest of Mezeldwelf on it to the battered chest under the cloak hooks—was exactly the same as it was when he'd last been here.

"Close the door behind you." Padraeg sat on one side of his great oak desk, and the wings of his armchair peeked over the edges of his armored shoulders. Once Leon had done as he asked, he leaned forward and folded his hands. "Now, explain to me why I have a smuggler in my cells that came to me inside a barrel."

Leon's eyes widened. Somehow, this wasn't quite how he pictured this going. At the very least, Padraeg could've given him a seat. His body ached far more than it should from the work he'd done today, and his headache was starting to make itself known again. Not that Padraeg knew any of that.

"What about it?" he asked, putting his hands behind his back. "We did our job. We were about to come find you so we could interrogate him."

"Your job?" Padraeg scoffed. "Is that what you call what you've done?"

"Yes." The sun coming in through the window behind Padraeg had gone from an annoyance to a threat faster than Leon could've ever believed. Had he only been outside a few minutes ago? It felt like hours now.

Leon's hands trembled from the effort it took to keep them at his sides instead of clutched around his head, and his legs shook from the strain of keeping him up. The ale had long since worn off. He blinked back tears and tried to focus long enough to string words together.

"We arrested someone we know was ferrying husks around," he said as evenly as he could. Every word felt like daggers digging into his ears. "He was meeting with one of Mesley's men, and we—"

"If we wanted to get someone involved, we'd have grabbed one of the sailors or taken one of the merchants in for questioning." Padraeg ran a hand through his hair and sighed.

"You can't take people off the street, especially when you only had authority to make arrests in the wharf."

"It wasn't—" His head screamed for attention. He wasn't sure if Kelan's tea would've helped, but he felt like he might throw up, and he desperately wished he'd had time to drink it. This needed to end. Soon. Padraeg was already upset with Leon. If he found out Leon had worked himself sick, Leon would never hear the end of it. "He's the one the kids were talking about. The ones in the alley where we first found Mesley's men," he ground out. "He's not—his eyes aren't white, but Kelan says he smells like a husk too strongly to not either be one or be close to them."

"You couldn't confirm it?" Padraeg's lips curled down into a sharp frown, and he rubbed the bridge of his nose. "I know you can sense them. We already showed our hand with the raids. If he doesn't know anything, then everyone who wasn't scared off will go into hiding, and we'll have to start all over again from the beginning."

"Does it matter?" Leon shot back. "We have proof he's assisting in smuggling. We saw him accepting the bribe. All you need to do is question him—"

"Question him?" Padraeg said, his voice sharper than a knife's edge. "Of course we're going to question him. I've already got my second-in-command reaching out to the temple of Truth to hire some of their priests, but that doesn't change the fact that your Band acted against orders. My jailer says you took him from a tavern near the Forge temples. You were not authorized to work there. You and your friends are close to overstepping the line of your contracts, and you're going to get someone killed."

"I know, but if we'd waited for him to go to the wharf or gotten a guard, we'd have lost him." Just like the guards had, but

162

Leon didn't say that. Aoife had shown him the reports. They'd raided the warehouse where their prisoner spent his time. He hadn't been there, even though they'd watched him go inside. "We saw an opportunity to grab him quickly and quietly. Once we had him restrained, we brought him here."

Padraeg let out a harsh laugh. "I should've known better than to let Aoife hire mercenaries," he said with a growl, pinching the bridge of his nose. "They always think they're above the law, above the rules." He raised his head, and his glare could've frozen the heart of a lesser man. "I've given your group a lot of leeway, because Aoife trusts your leader, and I trusted your judgment in companions, but if you can't follow the rules, then I'll shut you out of the investigation."

"That's not fair," Leon snapped, surging forward. He slammed his hands down on the desk, heedless of how the movement sent his world spinning. "We've done our job and stayed well out of the way of the guard. We've followed the rest of the rules and—"

Padraeg leaned back and sighed, rubbing his temples like he had a headache to match Leon's. "You're mercenaries," he said finally. They stared at each other from opposite sides of the desk, so close Leon could count the red hairs remaining in Padraeg's goatee. "Mercenaries don't care about the people who hire them or the damage they leave behind as long as they get paid. They have no loyalty to anyone but their bands and their guild. They are allowed to operate in the city because the guild agreed to abide by our laws, and you—"

A knock interrupted Padraeg midsentence. "Come back later," he snapped, irritation giving each letter a sharp edge.

The door burst open like he hadn't spoken. Bettany marched through it, her mouth set in a firm line. "I'd say sorry, but I'm not. We have an issue with our friend in the barrel."

Padraeg swore in a manner unbefitting his station. "What is it now? He didn't die in that barrel, did he?"

Bettany shook her head and gestured for them to follow her. She turned and marched down the hallway, each step pounding on the stonework. Leon and Padraeg exchanged glances—Padraeg had the grace to look ashamed that he'd been overheard—and followed her.

"The good news," Bettany said without turning around, "is that he's not hurt." Her steps picked up so she could stay ahead of Leon's and Padraeg's much longer strides. "The bad news is that he's asking for Leon by name."

"Me?" Leon asked, dread swelling to fill his stomach. "Did he say why?"

Bettany shrugged. "He did not. I figured you can ask him yourself, since he refused to say anything else until you were there."

All too soon, they came to the cells, and Bettany ushered them in. Kelan, who was leaning against a wall outside the cells, caught Leon's eye as they passed, and tapped his nose. Whoever was in the barrel, he still stank like a husk.

Leon nodded and entered the cells. It was darker here than the halls or Padraeg's office, but still too bright for Leon's taste. Bettany led them to one near the back, far away from the drunks and the petty thieves, and then left once more.

The Sihianese man sat inside, sitting cross-legged on the ground with his eyes closed. His black braids were frazzled and falling apart, and a nasty-looking bruise was forming over his right eye, but he looked nonplussed about the situation.

It was the first time Leon actually got a good look at him. His nose had been broken at least once, as evidenced by the thick scar across the bridge and the crooked angle it sat at. His clothes had the look of something that had been fine once, but age and poverty had worn them far past when they ought to have been replaced. He was, by all accounts, a normal person. Nothing about him screamed that he'd allied himself with an ancient evil, but nonetheless something about him bothered Leon, like an itch he couldn't quite scratch. Something beneath the surface, beyond his silvery eyes or his ragged clothes or the scar across his nose.

The Sihianese man looked up, and recognition filled his face. His smile stretched too wide to be real. "So my eyes didn't deceive me," he said, practically purring. His words were sharp and pointed, the way Aoife's and Padraeg's were. A Mezeldwelf native perhaps? "Leon Quinn, has it really been ten years?"

Ice filled Leon's heart, and it was nearly enough to make him forget about his headache. "How do you know that name?" he asked. This man had helped smuggle husks into the city. If he knew Leon's name, then his masters could too. If his masters knew about Leon, they might know what he was. Leon stepped closer to the bars and squinted, pushing aside the agonizing thump of his headache to focus. It only sort of worked.

The Sihianese man let out a sharp bite of laughter. "I know it's been a while, but surely I don't look that different." His grin turned feral as he pointed to his face, to his broken nose. "You left your mark on me all those years ago. I'd think you would've remembered that at least."

"It can't be . . ." Padraeg whispered. He came closer, within arm's reach of the bars. His face paled to match his hair. "Your ship never came back. We'd given it up for lost. We thought you were dead."

"Dead?" He shifted, leaning forward to rest his chin on his upturned hands. "No, not dead. Not all of us at least." Something—the way he moved, the little upturn in tone when he reached the end of his sentences, or even that bloody scar—scratched that itch Leon couldn't reach.

"Ranon?" he whispered. "Ranon Carrick?"

"I don't go by that name anymore," Ranon said, his smile fading away into something like sorrow. It felt hollow like a bell was hollow. A veneer of realness flickered inside and around the edges, but closer examination would reveal the emptiness inside. "I was quite surprised to see you again. Myrrdin and I were sure the husks swept you up when you disappeared. Myrrdin even fancied we might run into you on our adventure." He paused and bit his lip. "Of course, they always believed it would be at the other end of a blade, but we can't have everything."

"Shut it," Leon snapped. His knees shook, and it took a tremendous amount of will to keep from sinking to the floor. Between the pounding agony of his skull and the shock twisting his innards into knots, it was a miracle he stayed on his feet.

Ranon Carrick and Myrrdin Mesley had been best friends who delighted in lording their relatively high status as second children to merchant princes over others. Leon, as the adopted son of the guard-captain, had been one of their favorite targets. When he was sixteen, he'd broken Ranon's nose and knocked out two of Myrrdin's teeth after one too many *theories* about his past and taunts about his eyes.

His eyes.

"What happened to your eyes?" Leon asked, heart sinking.

Ranon's eyes had been brown. They were silver now and shone like a star had been taken from the heavens. Not white, never white, but a far cry from brown and too close to Leon's gray for comfort.

Ranon snorted and leaned back again, crossing his hands behind his head. His eyes slid shut. "We all have our gods. Our oaths too," he answered as casually as if Leon had asked how he preferred his tea. "I've come to appreciate that in the years since I left."

"What happened to you? To the ship and Myrrdin?" Padraeg asked. His voice shook, and pain shot through Leon's heart for the concern he showed. Had he begged for information about Leon like that? Had he mourned when each report came back with no new answers? "Your grandfather went bankrupt trying to find you, and Myrrdin's father hasn't been the same since you disappeared."

Shrugging, Ranon hummed before answering. "The ship sank a handful of miles off the coast of Sihia. Most of the crew drowned, but a few of us got to shore." He cracked an eye open, and the silvery sight turned Leon's stomach. "I wanted to go home, but we couldn't afford a new ship. Other paths were available, so those were what we took, even if they strayed too close to Dhuitholm for the taste of our hosts. Myrrdin stayed behind."

Leon's breath caught in his throat. Ranon had gone through the Fallow Lands. Right through the center of the Templesbane's power. Right by the ruins of Dhuitholm and the Brother's prison.

"That's impossible." Padraeg's hands tightened around the bars until his knuckles turned white. "No one's traveled through the Fallow Lands or the northern coast since Dhuitholm fell, and the mountains are impassable for most of the year."

"And yet, here I am." Ranon looked at Leon again, and his smile turned bitter. "It's a shame someone like you escaped when so many good people fell defending that glorious city. But then, there were so many refugees that I wonder if they bothered to put up a fight against the Templesbane at all."

For twenty years, Leon had been telling himself that he shouldn't have survived when everyone else died. He didn't need to hear it from Ranon.

"Did you know what you were transporting?" he asked in a low voice. "You had to know. You've been through there. You—"

His eyes weren't white, and the alchemy required to change eye color had disappeared when the temple of Reflection fell and their god was consumed. Even the Forge couldn't recreate that particular magic, and only a fool would enter Dhuitholm to reclaim it.

But what god granted silver eyes with a star-like sheen? Not the Sea or any god of the land, that was for certain.

Ranon let out a hollow laugh. "Did I know? I have no idea what was in the barrels I took from Mesley's men." His false, too-wide grin was back. "All I know is that a strange man tried stealing one of the barrels I'd been hired to deliver, and then I was attacked and found myself in a city jail. Perhaps it should be you answering that question."

Leon hadn't known about what was in the barrels until it was almost too late. Then he'd looked everywhere for more and paid for it with an aching head that threatened to knock him off his feet. Every part of him screamed to reach out once more, to feel the shape of Ranon's vows and figure out where he stood, but even the thought of doing so sent waves of agony rushing out through his whole body.

"Not until someone else figured it out," he said in a hollow voice. It wasn't a lie, but it wasn't the truth. The Knights Beyond had known, even if they hadn't outright told him, and Kelan had confirmed it. "But even if you didn't know, we still need you to tell the Truth priests everything."

"How long has this been going on?" Padraeg asked, stepping back from the bars. His face had settled into a cool indifference. If Leon hadn't seen it himself, he'd never have guessed that he'd been thrown by Ranon's survival at all.

Ranon looked up toward the ceiling and blew out his cheeks. "Oh, a month, perhaps two? You can check the gate logs and with my landlord at the Lauded Lord. The innkeeper is a servant of the Hearth, who knows me as Ran. I'm happy to tell the same to the servants of Truth."

Padraeg let out an explosive sigh and ran a hand through his already messy hair. "Ran. All right. I'll have someone double-check before we bring the Truth priests in. We'll be back."

"Oh?" Ranon jumped up and ran to the bars. "Leon, are you leaving me already? We just got started." He pressed his face against the bars and giggled. He'd always laughed like that whenever he got Leon or one of the other lower-born children into trouble. "Can't you spare a few more minutes for an old friend?"

That would require them being friends in the first place, but before Leon could stick his foot in his mouth by saying that, Padraeg spoke.

"We will confirm your story, and then we'll be back." Padraeg's eyes sharpened, and he stepped between Leon and Ranon. "Whether Leon will be here or not depends on what we find and how well your talk with the Truth priests goes."

Ranon's laughter followed them out of the cells and to the room where Kelan, Shea, and Bettany were waiting. Apparently, the years and the trauma hadn't changed him much.

"How'd it go?" Kelan asked. Then he caught sight of Padraeg's and Leon's faces and grimaced. "Not good?"

"We got his name," Padraeg mumbled. Sighing, he pulled the tie off his braid and unraveled it. "But he could, potentially, vouch for us that Mesley was behind the smuggling. From there . . . well, we'll cross that bridge when we come to it, but with luck, the other princes will authorize more extensive searches of Mesley's estates."

"Any orders, then?" Bettany had taken up position by the exit and crossed her arms. Her mouth was set in a hard frown that would've seemed harsh if it weren't for the constant, yet silent, tapping of her foot. She didn't like this any more than Leon did.

"Pull everyone back and don't arrest anyone else," Padraeg rumbled, combing through his hair with his fingers and then rebraiding it. "I'll send someone to confirm Ranon's story. We'll notify his family when we've cleared him of further involvement in this scheme. No one is to travel alone, not even to relieve themselves."

"Understood." Bettany made to leave and gestured for the others to follow. "We'll let Njeri know and reorganize things as needed."

They left the cells quickly. Bettany led their party, walking like she'd maim anyone who got in her way; Shea and Kelan went behind her, muttering to each other, and Padraeg and Leon pulled up the rear.

They walked in silence until they reached the yard. It was busier than before. The cart had disappeared, and a squad of fresh-faced recruits under the attentions of a plump and stern-faced sergeant was running drills where Leon and Kelan had left it.

Padraeg stopped at the threshold. The sun, which had just begun its daily journey down, still burned brightly overhead, searing Leon's eyes as surely as if they were being gouged out with a hot poker. By now, the others had reached the gate at the street and were saying their goodbyes. Bettany and Shea left to the mercenary guild, and Kelan stayed there, waiting for Leon.

Padraeg caught Leon's arm before he could go meet him. Leon turned, ready to ask what he needed, and stopped. Hesitation was written all over Padraeg's face. He inhaled deeply and then let it out. "Did you sense anything from him?" he asked in a low voice. "Anything . . . not right?"

Anything that could've been the husks or some other god not in favor with the higher aspects. He didn't need to say that for Leon to understand what he was really asking.

"No," Leon whispered. "I didn't, I—I couldn't." His headache had faded into the background from the shock but hadn't quite left him enough to use his senses.

Padraeg let out a relieved sigh. "So he's not one of them. I know his eyes are the wrong color, but I still worried. The Carricks have suffered enough. If he'd been a husk, I think it would've destroyed them. A few months of service in the halls of Justice, and he'll return to them."

Leon's stomach tightened. "No, I couldn't, I—" He hadn't told Padraeg about his headache earlier or that it was stopping him from using his abilities. Avoiding making the lecture worse and aggravating his headache had seemed like a good idea at the time. He also hadn't told him that Kelan knew Leon's secret. Of those two facts, only one felt like something Padraeg could eventually come to accept. He'd always wanted Leon to use his gifts as they were meant to be used. The one chance Leon had to actually do that . . . he couldn't. Because he'd overstretched himself, hadn't stopped when the pain started, and he hadn't asked the more experienced godsworn for advice. "I didn't," he finally finished. "I didn't find anything to show that he's a husk, but I would like to check again later. If there's some magic on him, it might have worn off by then."

By then Leon's headache might have died down enough for him to use his senses. If the Sister could hide the color of a husk's eyes, who's to say she couldn't also hide the nothingness from an inexperienced Knight Vigilant?

Padraeg's face darkened. "Are you sure? Any magic like that—"

Leon nodded and blinked back tears, grateful now that the sun had gone down far enough to hide them from Padraeg. "If anyone's capable of it, the Sister is. She has all the libraries and temples in Dhuitholm at her disposal, after all."

"Right." Padraeg sighed, relief stealing away the tension that had built up in his shoulders. "Then I'll let the jailer know you'll come back soon to talk with Ranon. We'll move him to one of the private cells in the meantime. Less chance for someone to recognize him that way."

"Of course," Leon said. A lie by omission was still a lie, but Padraeg had forgotten about their argument for the moment. He didn't want to restart it and risk making his headache even worse, so he forced down the ache it caused in his heart.

"You know," Padraeg said, staring down into the courtyard, "if this ends with the discovery that the Sister broke the treaty, things will change around here. Even the most cautious princes won't demand we follow the treaty if she won't."

Leon's heart sank deeper still, and he clasped his hands behind his back to hide the shaking. Looking away, he slowly counted the steps leading up to them from the yard. "We've had this argument before." More than a dozen times before he'd left home. Each time had ripped open old wounds that Leon didn't think would ever heal, even as they gradually changed sides in that debate. "If I reveal myself, the Sister won't rest until I'm dead, not even if I were locked in the safest room in Mezeldwelf with the entire city between me and them. You know that."

Padraeg had been the one to teach him that. When Leon was young and grieving and desperate for revenge, Padraeg had taken him in hand. He'd already lost Delke, the woman he loved beyond all reasoning, and Mael, one of the boys he'd hoped to raise alongside her. Losing Leon, his son in all but blood, would've broken him. That had been enough to keep Leon from announcing himself for a few years.

Then the weight of what Leon had lost had sunk in.

He was the last of his order. More than three thousand years of tradition and worship boiled down into one half-trained apprentice who hadn't had the sense to die when he should've, who couldn't even get the ghosts of those who came before to speak plainly to him, to teach him how to fight the way he was meant to. Delke, Mael, and all the other knights had died in Dhuitholm, and he'd been so eager to avenge them until he'd realized what that would cost.

"I know." Padraeg touched the end of his braid, tied off with a familiar and battered gray ribbon. "But things are different now. People are scared and tired, but they're willing to fight too. We could change things. You could change things."

Leon didn't answer. He stared into the yard, at the gate, and into the city beyond. Kelan was still waiting for him there. "I'm just one person. If the world wants to change things, it can do it without me." One day, if Death was kind, he would join the Knights Beyond. The last person who ever would. Then Death would take them all.

He wanted that day to be far in the future. Even if things changed here—if the merchant princes threw their entire support behind the Protectors and took up the sacred duty that Leon had abandoned—it wouldn't change enough for him to consider taking his place again.

With that hanging in the air between them, they separated. Padraeg went back into the keep, muttering something about a meeting he had to attend, and Leon went to his freedom. He squinted in the bright light, vainly wishing he knew where his cloak had ended up, and then set his shoulders and marched across the yard.

It was past time to go home. He wasn't any use like this. After some tea, rest, and ale, he'd be better prepared to go back to work.

***

"Leon! Leon, wake up!"

Gasping awake, Leon pushed himself up. A glance out the window was useless—he'd had them covered before he'd passed out—and it took a moment for him to place the voice of the person shaking him.

"Jackie?" he finally said, his voice rough with sleep. He almost shoved his blankets aside and then thought better of it. Both because he was only wearing a sleep shirt and because it was freezing. He ought to have lit a fire before he went to sleep, but he'd forgotten, and now the air had enough bite to set all his hair on end. "What are you doing?"

Jackie shrugged and set her candle on the drawer beside Leon's bed. "Njeri and the others are downstairs. I said you were sleeping, and Njeri told me to get you. She said to tell you to hurry." She held up Leon's trousers and looked away from him.

He took them and shimmied into them without getting out from under his covers. Once he was clothed, he braced himself for the chill and pushed the blankets back.

"Did Njeri say why they were here?" he asked, swapping his sleep shirt for a tunic and his armor. It was too dark to dress easily, but at least his headache was gone. Light filtered in from the hallway, where he could hear multiple distant voices.

174

Shrugging again, Jackie wrapped her arms tight around herself and shivered. "Nope. Just that you needed to get downstairs in a hurry." There was too much tension in Jackie's shoulders. Whatever had driven the others here had rubbed off on her, and it'd take hours for her to calm down if it wasn't handled right away.

Snagging his cloak off the hook by the door, he ushered Jackie out. "Go to bed," he advised. "I'll send someone up with some milk. Njeri probably wants me to go on another patrol."

Jackie's eyes narrowed, but she went without complaint. Leon waited until she turned the corner before he made his way downstairs.

Njeri and Kelan were waiting in the front hall. "You're finally here," Njeri said, stopping in her tracks. Judging by the line of muddy footprints on the floor, she'd been pacing since she got here. "Where's Jackie?"

"I sent her back to bed." He glanced around the front hall as he went down the steps. Shea and Bettany emerged from the hall that led to the kitchen, each stuffing wrapped food into bags as they walked. "Should I not have?"

Njeri shook her head. "No, that's for the best. Padraeg wants you out of Mezeldwelf before the sun's up."

"Out of the—?" Leon's mind whirled. "Why? And how? I've still got the—"

"The princes have—or are about to—put out a warrant for your arrest." She took one of the food bags from Shea and thrust it at Leon. "I don't know why or what for, but Aoife wants you out of the city before the paperwork gets sorted. She said she knows a fisherman that will hide you until dawn and then take you out of the city."

Leon took the bag and slung it over his shoulder. "What about the sigil? It's not like Padraeg will be able to hide it when it lights his arm up like a torch." And he'd have to deal with the burns as it seared into his skin, which wouldn't be subtle either.

Kelan spoke for the first time since Leon appeared. "He said he'd handle it as soon as he could get alone."

Tension coiled in Leon's stomach like a snake waiting to strike. That didn't sound good. Breaking a sigil without a trial would see Padraeg thrown out of the guard and Aoife removed from the council if they thought she had ordered it. He opened his suddenly dry mouth to demand more answers and then snapped it shut again just as quickly, staring into the darkened hall behind Shea and Bettany.

A figure dressed in battered plate mail emerged from the shadows, the sickly light of unlife clinging to them. **Hurry,** they whispered, others like them appearing behind them. **It's not safe for you here anymore.** A dozen voices joined together in harmony, reverberating so loudly it felt like a miracle the others couldn't hear it. **The false prince knows who you are.**

Chapter 11
Light in the Darkness

Leon stumbled back, his heart in his throat. Mesley couldn't know. He couldn't—but even if it was a wild accusation to throw Aoife and Padraeg off balance, it could still kill Leon. The council would hold him until they could determine the truth of the matter, which wouldn't take long once the Truth priests got involved. Even if he could get out of Mezeldwelf and the sigil was broken, the husks would never stop hunting him.

"Let's go," Njeri insisted, tugging Leon forward by his cloak. "We have to hurry to get you out of here before the warrant comes into effect, otherwise we'll have to turn you over or be kicked out of the mercenary guild."

"Gods," he breathed, pulling free of Njeri for long enough to grab his axes from their place by the door. They needed to go. Now. Aoife and Padraeg had given him a chance, and if he stood here gaping for any longer, he'd waste it.

"That's what I said." Kelan's grim voice rang out in the hall. He sauntered across the hall and peeked outside. "But that message sounded serious, and I'm not about to let our best employer in years down by getting her nephew killed."

He likely meant it as a joke, but it fell out of his lips too harshly for that. His whole body was as rigid as stone, and his smile could've cut flesh to the bone, but it was his eyes that chilled Leon's blood. They glimmered and shone with light that came from nowhere. The longer they went like that, the more Kelan would change to suit. His nails would become claws, his teeth like knives, and his steps would be quieter than death itself.

He'd called upon the Moon to strengthen the gifts they'd given him to get Leon out of this. If he held them too long, his body would never return to how it had once been. It was a risk any godsworn took with using their abilities too much. Divine power was as dangerous to the one wielding it as the one it was being wielded against.

"Come on," Shea muttered, shoving past Leon to get to the door. "Let's get moving."

For once, Leon had nothing more to say. He fastened his axes to his belt, pulled his hood down to hide his face, slouched down as far as he could, and followed Shea out the door.

They rushed toward the wharf, sticking to back alleys and side routes that Shea had used as a boy. With the harvest festival less than a week away, folks had taken over every spare room and open porch. The taverns, Pleasure temples, and fighting houses were rarely so full as they were when Mezeldwelf prepared to celebrate the harvest.

Shea led the way, Kelan at his heels. Leon came after with Bettany and Njeri guarding the rear. Quinn Manor was close to the docks, but that didn't mean they had an easy run of it. The celebrations got wilder as they crept along, bolstered by hundreds of sailors eager to spend their coin while their employers argued over who sold their goods where. The crowds roared around them as they traveled, seeking in their tankards and plates the cheer that wouldn't come when winter came. Compassion had already run dry, and it'd be harder than ever when they learned that Charity would be in short supply as well.

Even the alleys thrived with life. Pleasure's priests saw good custom with lonely sailors, and an alley was as good for a tumble—or an inspired bout of storytelling and song—as any tavern back room or ship berth.

Still, they were better for quick travel than the main roads, and they made good time. Halfway there, Kelan's head whipped around, and his lips pressed into a tight line. He scowled as he stared into the crowd behind Leon. He whispered something to Shea, something that Leon couldn't hear over a nearby chorus of drunks belting out a Falten drinking song.

Shea nodded and ducked into a tavern. Leon and the others followed him inside, out the back, and through two backstreets before they emerged into a warehouse yard.

It wasn't far enough for Kelan, who now scanned the roofs with death in his eyes. Once more, they went on the move. Through taverns and shops, between buildings and over gates, farther and farther away from the docks. Even for a circular path, this was extreme.

Each time they paused, Kelan's disquiet became more and more obvious. Leon's hands crept to his axes, and they settled there with white-knuckled intensity. Bettany's grumbles and the pounding of her spear onto the cobblestone echoed louder with each passing moment.

Leon didn't need to use his senses—didn't even dare for fear of triggering another headache like the one that disabled him that afternoon—to realize what had Kelan on edge.

They were being followed, and whoever was following them was getting closer. Despite Shea's best attempts, they got farther from the wharf with each step. The crowds were as thick here as they were in the market, but even hidden within them, they failed to shake their determined tail.

Their luck ran out in an alley near the Citadel.

Five members of the city guard blocked one end of the alley. Shea slowed to a stop, and his shoulders tightened as he brought his hammer into a defensible position. Leon turned, vainly hoping that there was still a way out, and his heart sank. Shouts and swearing from the main street grew louder and louder as more of the guard appeared and blocked the other end as well.

He turned back, heart like lead, and squeezed his axes. There were too many to fight without causing a panic, but that might be their only option.

A woman stepped forward. She wore a fine yellow tunic and a large cockatrice medallion around her neck. Mesley's steward, if Leon had to make a guess. She was ghostlike in appearance, so pale and silent that Leon might have mistaken her for a member of the Knights Beyond if it weren't for the solidity of her movement.

"Going somewhere, Mr. Quinn?" she asked pleasantly. In one hand, she held a halberd with well-worn grips on the handle. Leon didn't doubt she knew how to use it; the corded muscle of her arms and the set of her feet spoke well of that already. "Prince Mesley figured the guard-captain might try to spirit you away before you could face judgment, and sent us to ensure that didn't happen. Pity he was right, I always respected your father."

"We're out for a walk," Kelan said before Leon could answer, hooking his thumbs into his belt. His nails snagged on the material of his trousers, already longer and sharper than they'd been when they left.

"Let us by," Njeri's voice rang through the alley with all the authority of one of the merchant princes themselves. She stepped forward, resting her hand on the hilt of her sword. "You have no right to stop us."

The steward chortled, and her fellow servants echoed her. "Oh, but we do. You're trying to smuggle a fugitive out of the city." She leered at Leon, who tightened his grip around his axes. "Pity about that. I'd have thought the son of the guard-captain would've known better than to try running away while under parole." Her leer turned sour and she spat. "Especially as someone who already broke his parole once."

She raised a hand and the guards stepped forward, their every movement weighed down with armor beneath their tunics and their belts with weapons Padraeg had ensured they knew how to use.

Leon glanced around and met Njeri's eyes. She had to be doing the same mental calculations he was and coming to the same conclusions.

Roughly thirty guards and Mesley's steward versus the five of them.

It would be a hard fight, but theoretically, they'd be able to win. They were experienced mercenaries with years of fighting under their belts, while the guards mostly fought against drunks or in sparring sessions. What's more, Kelan had his god's gifts, Shea wielded his hammer with the strength of a former Forge priest, Bettany had been killing people longer than Leon had been alive, and Njeri had trained for years to take her father's position as head of the guard in her hometown. They were all very good at what they did and very familiar with killing people.

But even so, it *would* be a hard fight, and one they wouldn't be able to win without casualties. The revelers on the street would notice, and it would cause a panic. Aoife would face punishment for bringing in mercenaries that attacked the guard while they were trying to bring in a criminal under warrant. The Band would be declared bandits and outlaws.

It wouldn't be worth it, not even for Leon's freedom.

"What do you want?" he asked, lifting his hands above his head. Njeri shifted, and her foot dug into his, but he continued on without changing his expression. Bluffing was a long shot, but better than fighting. "I've got nothing to hide. My parole conditions allow me to travel the city after dark."

It didn't allow him to leave the city, but Mesley's guards had no proof that was what he had planned. Even Mezeldwelf wasn't entirely safe after dark, especially as more of the greater aspects were consumed, so it made sense to travel armed and in groups.

The steward frowned but gestured again, and the guards lowered their weapons. "Oh? It didn't look that way to me. You've been running from us for a long time. Someone with nothing to hide would've faced us."

Kelan stiffened, and his lips dropped into a deep frown, but Shea beat him to speech.

"Anyone would run when cutpurses or worse pursue them," he growled. He pulled himself as tall as he could and twirled his hammer in a quick circle. The head slammed into the ground with a thunderous boom. "And I've yet to see proof you're not either of those. Anyone could impersonate the guard."

The steward's hands tightened around the haft of her halberd, and for a moment, Leon thought she might hit Shea, but she scoffed instead. "I'm the steward of House Mesley," she snapped, "and these are members of the guard assigned to the Citadel district. We have the authority in the Citadel district, not you lowly mercenaries."

"We're well within our rights to be here." Njeri stalked up to the steward, eyes blazing. "You're blocking our way. Unless you have a warrant or cause to arrest us, leave us be."

The steward leaned in, staring at Njeri like a cat with a mouse in her sight. "It just so happens," she said, practically purring, "that we do. The princes want him"—she pointed at Leon as she pulled a scroll from the bag at her hip and waved it around—"locked up in the Citadel until the harvest festival. Since you're trying to stop us, then I guess we'll have to take you too."

Njeri stiffened, and Leon caught her arm before it could complete its journey to her hilt. "Njeri," he said in a low voice, "it'll be fine. Go back to the others and get out of town fast. Aoife will send you your pay." Raising his voice to a normal level, he slung an arm over her shoulder and smiled broadly. He wasn't sure what the effect was when his hood still covered most of his face, but it was better than nothing. "I'm sure we'll get this all cleared up before tomorrow."

"Leon . . ." She breathed in through her nose and let it out her mouth. Her arm relaxed and he dropped it, to the noticeable disappointment of Mesley's steward. "Let me see that."

She snatched the scroll so harshly Leon thought she meant to tear it in two, but instead, she unrolled it and held it out so Leon could read it too. It was hard to make any of it out as there was only one streetlamp in this particular alley, but he could see enough.

That was his name written there, signed and stamped by one of Justice's clerks. As official as it could be.

Njeri growled. "We're going with him," she announced, rolling the scroll back up and thrusting it at the steward. "I don't trust you further than I could throw you, so I'd rather keep my man where I can see him."

The steward laughed. "Fine by me. *I'd* rather keep you mercenaries where we can see you." She picked up her halberd and pointed it at Leon. "You, you're going right in front of me. If you run, I'll rearrange your guts for you."

The others all caught Leon's eye as they walked. Shea and Bettany for support, Njeri for worry, and Kelan for genuine fear. His eyes no longer glowed, but he still walked with an unnatural grace. Without even speaking, he begged Leon to run, to take whatever chance he could to get away, but Leon couldn't. For one, the steward didn't lie. Her halberd dug into his spine with each step. For another, running would just end up with the others hurt. If Njeri and the others were killed, the Band would have no leadership and would likely be forced to dissolve. Everything he'd worked for since he'd left Mezeldwelf, everyone he'd come to care about would be ruined if he ran.

But Kelan wasn't the only one asking for things the others couldn't hear. As they walked, ghosts appeared out of the crowds. They matched Leon step for step, never lifting their eyes from the pavement. Their voices swirled around him, a broken chorus calling for a hundred different things.

Run, survive, fight, claim his place, remember his oaths, defend the weak, hold the strong to account, rebuild what had been broken—on it went, never more than distracting, but loud enough that Leon couldn't ignore them if he tried.

Mesley's steward led them deep into the Citadel, to a waiting room near the council chamber on the third floor. The Knights Beyond crowded around them, eyes fixed on the ground, and silently ushered Leon forward. Two city guards stood outside a thick oaken door. They kept their eyes averted from Leon as Mesley's steward handed Leon and the others over.

Leon lagged behind the others, and he caught a glimpse of the steward's smug smile as she left him to his fate. Taking a deep breath, he held his head high and went inside.

The room he found himself in was large enough that those inside weren't sitting on top of one another, but small enough that they couldn't escape each other either. A fire burned merrily in the far-right corner with a couch and two armchairs placed in front of it. On the other side of the room, two padded benches were pushed against the wall, where two whispering people were huddled around something between them.

But it was someone else entirely who caught Leon's attention.

Charity sat precariously on the small windowsill opposite the door. Their eyes shone like a candle, and they smiled brilliantly when he set foot inside. Their broken and mismatched grin offered kindness he wouldn't find anywhere else, and what little of their skin was visible underneath the dirt and grime was the same color as a peach. Today, their hair was as gray as Leon's eyes, and they wore a tattered, blue cloak with a familiar owl crest embroidered on the breast.

Leon had worn a cloak just like that when he escaped Mezeldwelf. Padraeg and Aoife had hidden it away for his own protection while he'd been recovering, and he hadn't seen it since. The memory made his heart ache. What had happened to it?

The door shut behind him with a pointed thud. That the sound of the key turning in the lock failed to follow, it gave Leon a hollow sense of comfort. At least the knights had stayed outside, even if he could still hear their voices.

Leon averted his eyes from Charity and shuffled forward. The others had long since settled onto chairs around the fireplace, very diligently not staring at the divine incarnation sitting less than ten feet away and smiling at Leon.

It was then that Leon finally recognized the other people in the room. Padraeg, still dressed in the ceremonial armor he'd had on the last time Leon saw him, and Aoife, wearing a red and blue dress that must be part of her council robes, waited on one of the padded benches with a very familiar figure that had been previously hidden by Padraeg's bulk, chattering away between them.

"Jackie?" Leon's jaw dropped, and his mouth opened and shut three times before he could speak again. "What're you doing here?"

Jackie smiled innocently and tossed a nut into her mouth. She held up a bag of nuts and offered a handful to Padraeg and Aoife, who took one each. "I came to see Papa Padraeg," she announced. "You and the others left before I could get my cloak, so I was worried I'd have to go on my own, but then Charity offered to take me!"

Leon shot a glare at Charity before he could think better of it. Charity, for their part, just smiled at Leon. "You should've waited at the manor," he said in as low and even a tone as he could manage. "Aoife, why didn't you send her home?"

Snorting, Aoife took a nut from Jackie's bag. "I tried, but she refused to leave unless Padraeg or I took her, and we couldn't risk not being here if any news came in." She pointedly did not look at Njeri or the others, who also avoided Leon's gaze. "I'd hoped you'd miss all this, but it looks like Mesley was better prepared than we thought, and well, it's better to have her here than at home by herself, don't you think?"

"He realized we were closing in on him," Padraeg muttered. His hands closed into fists and his face darkened. "As soon as I started my report on the guard rotations, he revealed——" He looked down at Jackie and swallowed. "Well, he wants the princes to question you about——his accusations. We were worried he'd send someone to the manor."

As much as he didn't like it, Leon understood. Mesley had already crossed lines that no merchant prince should, and Leon doubted he'd care if Jackie got caught in between them.

Jackie cocked her head. "What's he accusing Leon of?" Her eyes narrowed, and she ate another nut. For a moment, she reminded Leon of nothing less than a squirrel facing down a wolf. "It's not about that fight, is it? Because that's my fault. I wasn't supposed to be there, and he hit that man to protect me."

Padraeg let out an explosive sigh and seemed to collapse in on himself. He looked older than he had when Leon left him that afternoon. The neat braid and immaculately trimmed facial hair failed to hide the deep bags under his eyes or the grayish tint to his skin. His hands, covered in small liver spots, shook nearly imperceptibly in his lap.

He was old now. Instead of enjoying his waning years with his family in a well-earned retirement, he was forced to wait helplessly while people he'd known his whole life decided the fate of his son. If they decided to turn Leon over to the Templesbane, Padraeg would lose him and be forced to go into exile for harboring him in the first place.

"No," Padraeg whispered, ruffling Jackie's hair. "It's not your fault. It's something I did a long time ago."

Leon's heart panged, and he looked away. It was his fault, not Padraeg's. If he hadn't come back, then Padraeg and Aoife wouldn't be in this mess.

Everyone knew Leon hadn't been to Mezeldwelf since the treaty was signed, and anyone associated with the Knights Vigilant was banned from the city. If he'd never come home, then Mesley wouldn't have anything on Padraeg and Aoife. The treaty wasn't retroactive. "What did he say about why he wanted me arrested?" he managed to ask around the lump in his throat. "I need to know, I . . ."

He didn't need to know, but it succeeded in taking Jackie's attention away from the previous topic. Rolling her eyes, she closed her bag of nuts, slid off the bench, and ran over to the others. She hated listening to anything that could be described as politics, and this, unfortunately, counted.

Padraeg let out a harsh laugh as he watched her go. "He said Ranon discovered what you were while he was traveling through the Fallow Lands, in some ledger he recovered from an old Knight Vigilant watchtower. He brought the evidence to Mesley, who waited to report it until he'd 'verified its accuracy.'" His eyes closed, and he took a deep breath. His shaking hands closed into fists, the only physical sign of the emotions that must be tearing through him. "He turned it in when he realized we were targeting him for looking into your background."

Aoife set a hand on her brother's arm and squeezed. "It's politics," she said, her lips turning down in a sneer. "The wharf is one of the more profitable districts, and I've controlled it for years. The others want a bite of that fish more than they want to look closely at what Mesley is saying."

They could always reexamine the evidence later, when Aoife had been cut down to size and reduced to managing the bakers' guild—if she managed to retain her title at all. Mesley might get a slap on the wrist or have to pay a blood fee to the Quinn household, but by then, Leon would be long gone. Consumed the way the other knights had been. Forced to serve the very evil he'd sworn to fight when he was a boy.

After all, turning an alleged Knight Vigilant over to the Templesbane was their civic duty. It would save the city, even if Leon hadn't been exactly what they were accusing him of. Better to sacrifice one man than an entire city.

Leon sank into the bench. His knees bumped into Aoife's, and she pressed back, a solid and comforting presence. He closed his eyes and breathed deeply, staving off the edges of panic skirting the corners of his mind. He'd get out of here before the harvest festival. The Band wouldn't leave Leon to die, and Padraeg might be able to convince some of the guard to look the other direction. He'd get out of this.

He'd have to.

An indeterminate time later, a warm body settled on Leon's other side. He opened his eyes to see Kelan smiling at him.

"I thought I'd check on what you were doing." His voice never rose louder than a whisper in deference to the tight quarters. Even Bettany, currently telling a Falten folk story to Jackie, never went louder than a normal speaking voice. His finger—tipped in a long and sharp claw that was quickly turning black—traced a silencing sigil on the bench beside them. Leon's skin prickled as power flowed into it, and their voices were deadened to all who weren't in this circle. "The others are keeping Jackie distracted, and I decided someone ought to check on the guests of honor."

Leon grunted. "How's Njeri holding up?" he asked in lieu of answering properly.

Kelan shrugged. "Oh, you know how it is. We gossiped for a bit, she put forth one theory about the supposed proof Mesley has, Shea put forth another, and Bettany thinks he's going to point to your eyes and your height." Chuckling, he shook his head. "Jackie is enthralled with the idea that you're a knight and that you're going to break us all out of here on some manner of enchanted steed, but other than that, she's holding up well."

"He's not a knight," Aoife and Padraeg said simultaneously.

Rolling his eyes, Kelan picked up his legs so he could sit cross-legged on the bench. "You haven't told them I know?"

Leon flushed but didn't duck his head. Kelan's eyes were easier to meet than Aoife's and Padraeg's. Their glares were currently digging into his skull like ice picks. "It didn't come up."

"Tell us you know what?" Aoife said, her words dangerously close to cutting.

Padraeg growled. "If you so much as breathe another word, I'll kill you myself."

Kelan smiled at Aoife and glared at Padraeg and Leon in turn. "I've sworn an oath," he said pointedly. "To the Moon themself. I could no more break that oath than you could shortchange one of your fishers, and I cast a silencing spell when I sat down. No one else can hear us."

"It's all right," Leon said, setting a hand over Padraeg's before he could do anything either of them might regret. "He figured it out the other day, when we first found the husks."

Padraeg didn't look soothed, but he did turn his rage to Leon instead of Kelan, so Leon was willing to call that a victory. "How'd he find out? None of the lunar orders can tell what god someone is sworn to by sight alone."

Kelan laughed. "No, I figured it out myself. To tell the truth, most of the Band has suspected Leon was godsworn since before I joined. He's not exactly . . . subtle."

Leon wanted to protest—he could be very subtle if the situation called for it—but couldn't, since the only reason Kelan knew was that he'd gotten into an argument with a bunch of ghosts while they were on patrol together. He had not been at his best since he got to Mezeldwelf.

Aoife snorted and crossed her ankles. The fine fabric of her dress wrinkled under the pressure. He'd never seen her in something so fine, and it suited her. It hurt to realize that supporting him might cause her to lose everything she'd worked for.

"He's never been good at subtle," she said dryly. "How many of the others know?"

What she really meant, and made no particular attempt to hide, was how many people would she have to bribe or do worse to keep this secret. Her smile was too sharp to be anything other than a threat, and her pockets were deep enough to make good on that threat even if she lost her position.

Kelan was intelligent enough to read between the lines and answered without delay. "Shea and Bettany both think he's godsworn of some sort—although Shea figures he swore himself to Fidelity, and Bettany assumes he's a follower of Justice—and Njeri thinks he's a household guard who left because one too many people reported him to the merchant princes and Protectors for the crime of being a tall man with gray eyes." Kelan pulled a flask out of a hidden pocket and took a swig. He offered it to the others and didn't bat an eye when Aoife took it and downed half in one go. "They've kept it quiet, though, as it's none of their business what he's running from. He's far from the only member of the Band with a past they'd rather keep hidden."

"He's telling the truth, you know. I can see my sibling's power in him."

If Leon had said he didn't jump when a pint-sized deity appeared in front of him, he'd have been lying. The others handled it much better. Aoife smiled, Padraeg stood and bowed, and Kelan landed somewhere between the two, although he actually managed to speak.

"Your Grace," he said smoothly, bowing as well as he could while neither uncrossing his legs or standing up. It was almost impressive. "I'd wondered if we might be blessed with your conversation tonight."

Charity inclined their head in acknowledgement of the others, then fixed their attention on Leon. "I heard your father's prayers. I came to offer what aid I can."

Leon bowed his head. "I thank you for your support, Your Grace." His voice cracked and he swallowed painfully. He hadn't had anything to drink since he got back to the manor that afternoon. It was a marvel it was only bothering him now. "I didn't think one such as you would bother with something like this." Criminals warranted some level of Charity, but it was rare that they brought the attention of the being themself.

Charity smiled again, softer this time. "Your order is very dear to me," they said in a low voice. "Your brethren helped keep people out of my flock. Their loss is the world's loss."

"Your Grace . . ." Leon began. The words dried up on his tongue before he could get any further. He sighed. "You know that I can't stop what's going to happen to you, don't you? Not even if you convince the princes to exile me instead of turning me over."

The husks would come. They'd take Charity and whoever passed for their head priest, and Charity would be consumed. Leaving him with the backbreaking weight of another failure.

Charity shrugged. "If I limited my grace to those that could return the favor, then none would know me." Their cloak ruffled in nonexistent wind, and Leon glimpsed countless people, in Mezeldwelf and beyond, who needed Charity before the world lost them hidden between each fold. His face was not among them. "But I won't refuse those who wish to extend it to others."

Kelan nudged Leon. "Listen to the god," he said, his smile brittle despite his apparent ease. "They're your best shot at getting out of here."

But it wasn't only Leon's best shot, even if Kelan didn't mean it like that.

Even though they couldn't hear what was being said in this corner, the others were aware that Charity had come to speak to Leon. The outcome of this conversation would change their lives for better or worse.

By coming with him, Njeri and the others had put themselves at risk. If they'd let the guard take him without a fight, they could've claimed ignorance and walked out of Mezeldwelf with their pockets full. But no. They'd thrown their lot in with him, and that would taint them for better or worse, no matter how this ended. If Charity vouched for them, they could still get out of here, reputation intact.

They could leave. Charity might even be able to convince the merchant princes to look kindly on Padraeg and Aoife for sheltering Leon while he was here.

"What do you want?" he asked quietly, the words escaping before he'd even realized he was going to speak. The bench dug into his legs, and the cold stone of the wall behind him bit into his back. They were calming, grounding, and desperately needed. He would help Charity if it saved the people he cared about.

Nine pairs of eyes weighed down on him, and Charity's were not the heaviest. He didn't look up or away, didn't acknowledge Aoife stiffening next to him or Padraeg's gentle gasp. He just stared at Charity and at the people he caught glimpses of each time wind sent their cloak dancing.

Charity's face darkened, and tears fell from their starry eyes. Their cloak came to a stop, hiding everything that weighed them down. "There is someone here who needs my blessings," they whispered. "But no god can act by themself without disrupting the world's flow. Without aid, without believers, most of us have no more power than the wind."

Whispers erupted from everywhere and nowhere, a thousand voices as familiar to Leon as his own face but as foreign as distant Sihia.

"Listen to them." Charity's voice grew, bouncing off stone, wood, and flesh alike to hit Leon like a hammer blow. "Listen and follow them to the one I need you to help."

Down, the voices whispered, each overlapping the ones before it until it barely counted as speech. *Stretch your senses, you will know them.*

Leon did as he was bid. He closed his eyes and let loose the power that had disabled him that morning. Out he stretched, following the lines the voices drew in the stone and carpet. Down stairs, through halls, and past exhausted guards and harried clerks, to a locked door in the farthest part of the dungeon.

Beyond that door was an emptiness. A hollowness with something, someone screaming underneath it. Drowning under the nothingness but fighting to stay afloat with every breath.

"They're below us," he whispered, his eyes fluttering halfway open. "They've almost given up. We need to hurry."

Someone grabbed his shoulder and shook him, but it was like a fly hammering against a stone wall. If they spoke, he no more heard it than he heard the clouds drift across the sky.

"Then we will go to them," Charity said. Their voice echoed a dozen times over without growing any louder than a whisper as their form shifted and changed. What was once an urchin became a child cloaked in majesty, their cloak the color of the dawn with stars lining the hem, their hair as fiery as the sun. "No one will hold me from one who needs my help."

The others were talking, yelling, begging for his attention. Padraeg's voice alone was loud enough to deafen, but Leon barely heard it. What he did hear didn't matter. Charity would help if he did this for them. The chanting from the hall outside pounded in his ears, and for once he gave in to the urge to listen.

Charity walked to the door, and it opened without a sound. The guards on the other side dropped to their knees under the weight of Charity's burden. They shook, trembling with awe and fear, and Charity walked past without care. Leon followed, entranced by the voices and the distant figure holding back the nothingness that wanted to consume them entirely.

The knights of old stood on either side of the hall, leading the way to the cells like an invisible honor guard. Their voices rang in discord with the ones coming off Charity, a harmony that did and didn't belong together. **The Vigilant will return,** they cried. **The barriers will fall.**

He should have protested. He wasn't taking up his duties, and this wasn't a noble effort. It was the last attempt of a doomed man to save his friends and family.

It will be enough, whispered the voices that weren't the Knights Beyond. Unseen hands caressed Leon, pushing him ever forward.

These voices weren't the only ones trying to direct Leon. Guards, nobles, clerks, and friends alike tried to redirect him, to demand answers, but all were brushed aside. Leon's eyes were fixed on Charity, and his senses on the one he knew waited for him at the end of this journey.

They came to the private cells. Distantly, Leon was aware of the crowd that now followed him, armed but silent. They'd stopped trying to hold him back, trusting Charity the way they wouldn't trust him.

The cell opened for Charity, who turned to face Leon. Their face, still childlike in its innocence, brimmed with ancient knowledge. Then they bowed and gestured for Leon to enter without them.

Ranon waited inside, curled against the far wall, as far from the door as he could get.

No, it wasn't Ranon. It was the nothingness inside him. The nothingness Leon hadn't been able to sense earlier, that he hadn't looked for because Ranon's eyes were the wrong color. The nothingness that turned him into a shell, a husk of who he used to be.

The thing that wasn't Ranon snarled. "I was wondering when you would crawl out of your hole," the nothingness hissed. It warped Ranon's voice, too harsh and too ancient for human tongues to truly speak. "But you're too late. Nothing will stop what's coming."

You must grab hold of him, the knights commanded, crowding into the cell. Ranon's eyes, still silver after all this, darted back and forth like the nothingness could see them. **We will help you, but you must take the first step.**

The whispers urged him forward, quieter in here, away from Charity.

Ranon saved him the effort by charging, racing toward the cell door and screaming that Leon was going to kill him. Leon's body moved without his permission, years of training taking over where his conscious mind failed.

Ranon hit the wall with a hollow thud, one of Leon's hands around his neck and the other wrapped in his shirt. The nothingness inside Ranon surged, pushing against Leon's senses, burning everything it touched.

It hurt, breaking and ripping and shattering. It took a moment for Leon to realize that the pain wasn't just in his mind, but his body as well.

Ranon howled, and his hands clawed against Leon's arms, his nails drawing blood everywhere he could reach. The nothingness was afraid, Leon realized between one moment and the next. If it lost Ranon, then others would know that it could still be beaten. If it couldn't keep Ranon in its grasp, it would kill him.

And Charity—Leon—couldn't allow that.

The Knights Beyond laid their hands on Leon, pushing a thousand generations of knowledge into him. With power he didn't understand, he fought back, armoring his mind against the nothingness's assault and waiting for his chance to strike.

The silver of Ranon's eyes brightened as the magic hiding their true color dissipated under Leon's assault. They were now whiter than snow and stared at Leon with all the hate in the world.

"You can't save them," the nothingness growled in Ranon's voice. "The gods will fall, and we will wipe out your wretched order once and for all."

It wants you to respond, whispered the voices who weren't the Knights Beyond. *If you answer, it will ensnare you the way it ensnared those who came before you.*

The way it claimed the city of the gods.

The way it trapped the Knights Vigilant.

It wouldn't. Leon wouldn't let it. He would do this, and he'd go back to the others. They'd leave, and the merchant council could handle the aftermath of all this.

A hundred Vigilant Generals tightened their grip on Leon and showed him what to do, what paths to take. They had known how to bring someone back from the grip of the Templesbane in life, and while they couldn't do it in death, they would lend their knowledge to one who could, just this once, with the power of a god to aid them.

Reach out, they demanded.

Grab hold, the other voices whispered.

Together, they called out to their gods, and Leon joined his voice to theirs. To Charity, to the Watchful Peace, to any god that would listen and take pity on Ranon.

Leon reached out to the young man screaming under the nothingness, the one that had wanted to return to his family and home even if it meant creeping under the watchful gaze of an ancient evil. The one that even now fought to claw his way back to control.

He grabbed hold. He channeled magic not through his limbs or his weapons, but through his senses, and pulled with all his strength.

The nothingness screamed, clutching Ranon's spirit like a miser clutched each coin in their hoard, but found no grip.

Onward the knights pressed, chasing down each scrap of nothingness, each loathsome miasma that still sought shelter in the deepest crevasses of Ranon's mind, body, and soul. While Leon cradled Ranon's soul, they directed each strike and defense against the nothingness. They pushed, bringing light and warmth and safety to someone who'd almost forgotten what that felt like. They pulled, Leon pulled, and the nothingness let out a scream.

Ranon's body stilled. Letting out a shaky breath, Leon stumbled back and dropped Ranon from nerveless fingers before he fell to his knees. Each limb and muscle shook. The voices and the Knights Beyond were gone, and the world he'd ignored came back in a torrent of sound and light.

When he caught his breath, when he looked up again, Ranon was staring at him.

His eyes were brown.

Chapter 12
End Over End

"Leon?" Ranon whispered, his entire body shaking. He threw himself forward and wrapped his arms around Leon. "Thank the gods, I thought—I didn't—I—" But he dissolved into shaking sobs before he could say anything coherent.

Leon froze. Ranon lay awkwardly on top of him, curled in his lap. This was not the man Leon had known, the one that delighted in tormenting anyone less fortunate than he. This man . . . he was broken. Shudders wracked his entire body; sobs tore out of some deep part of him that had been buried in nothingness and emptiness and pain for gods knew how long.

Leon laid his hand on Ranon's shoulder and gasped at what he felt. He hadn't realized it before, but there was no meat under his hand, only bone that felt so fragile he worried it would shatter under his gentle touch. When was the last time the Sister let Ranon eat? Did she even realize her followers needed food?

"You did it." Charity's voice echoed through the chamber, a hundred distinct sounds slowly fading back to one that was more than one, and Leon's head jerked up. The memory of getting to the cells was blurred and filled with dead and distant voices. Charity had led him here, and he'd followed without thinking. "I wasn't sure . . . The Watchful Peace has been so quiet since the Knights Vigilant fell. Most of their strength is locked behind walls that have only recently begun to fade. I wasn't sure I had the strength to take their place."

"Can you help my friends now?" he whispered. "Can you persuade the princes to let them go?" His other arm came up to wrap around Ranon, unconsciously offering comfort to a man who would've killed him that morning if he were given a chance. The thing inside him, the nothingness that was the Templesbane, had done its best to do just that not that long ago.

Leon ached because of it. Even as he sat here, his body cried with a thousand pains that had no physical cause. Each muscle screamed like he'd held it tensed for an hour, and for all he knew, he had. He'd made an offering to Charity, after all, and their work was never easy and rarely quick. It was up to them to decide what they did with his offering.

Charity entered the cell, their cloak—now blue again and still eerily reminiscent of the one Leon had when he was young—floated behind them. The images hidden in its folds were softer now, like this single action had wiped clean the agonies of a hundred thousand needy souls. "I was always going to help." Their form shifted, the majesty and glory that he only half comprehended quieting and fading away until a small Alkan child in tattered white rags and a blue cloak stood in front of Leon.

"I don't need to do anything else," they whispered, running a hand down Ranon's back. "You did it yourself when you helped me." They looked up, and their smile was caught halfway between despair and exultation. "You may come to hate me for it, but the princes cannot deny what's at stake now. Too many witnessed what you've done."

Leon's breath caught in his chest. "Witnessed?" he rasped. "But—"

He hadn't been subtle about it. Twenty years, and he'd thrown it all away because he hadn't wanted those he loved to bear the weight of his sins. Because he'd begged a god for help and forgotten how even the kind ones could be cruel.

He'd followed Charity down here, followed voices of the dead and those in Charity's flock, and found the sole heir to a fallen merchant house. They'd pushed past guards and servants, ignored everyone who tried to make them stop, and then he'd purified the stain on Ranon's soul where everyone could see him.

He knew what waited for him outside Ranon's cell. Dozens who had seen him and dozens more who had run to spread the news of the last Knight Vigilant as soon as they heard he was here. "Help me," he pleaded, painfully aware of the irony of asking for help from the god that had put him in this situation. For a moment, he thought Ranon's shaking was getting worse, but no, it was him. His breath came in short bursts. His hands refused to settle, and he doubted his legs would support him even if he found the strength to stand. "Help me get away from all this."

The Great Treaty was broken. Ranon was proof of that. If he remembered anything of his time as a husk, then the princes would have no choice but to act. Even if he didn't, Charity would vouch that Ranon's soul was his own once more. Unless Leon could get away, the princes would push him to the forefront of the fight with the Sister. All he wanted was to help the ones he loved escape what was coming. He didn't want to be a martyr; he didn't want to be a figurehead. He just wanted to help his friends.

Charity shook their head, and their curls danced the way their cloak did. "The consequences are out of my hands now," they said, eyes glimmering in the darkness. "Fate has decreed that you would help me and that others would see you doing so. What happens now is between you and them."

They reached down, took Ranon from him, and then laid a hand on Ranon's forehead. Slowly, Ranon's tears dried and the shaking stopped. He inhaled and pushed away, sitting back on his heels. The light flickering in from the hallway, marred by countless shadows, lit the tear stains on his cheeks like candles.

"That's right," Charity whispered, pulling their hand back and drawing their cloak around them. "Deep breaths. There's work for you yet."

Ranon nodded, stood, and pulled his shoulders back. From Leon's position on the ground, he looked like some ancient knight heading out to battle. His ragged clothes and battered body were proof of the battles he'd won and the one he had yet to win.

Then Ranon left. Gasps and loud exclamations came in through the open door like a flood, and each hit Leon with the force of a physical blow. Ranon's voice echoed, demanding for guards to take him before the princes and promising news of what Leon had done.

"He'll tell the princes what he knows." Charity stared at the door, a weight to their gaze and their words. "I'm keeping the ones waiting to speak with you away for the moment, but I can't hold them off forever. The city needs you. If Mezeldwelf falls, Hyderia will fall with it."

And if Hyderia fell, the world would descend into a darkness such as hadn't been seen since before the first Vigilant General thrust her sword into the Sister's heart and freed the gods from her wretched gullet. The gods would be consumed, the people would drown in nothingness, and Leon would be to blame.

"I don't want this," he whispered, curling his shaking hands into fists. The stone floor bit into his knees, and even that chill couldn't distract him. "I couldn't even help Ranon on my own. That was all the Knights Beyond, I didn't do anything."

Charity shook their head. Their feet glided over the ground as they crossed the room to lift Leon's chin with one small hand. "You did what you must."

"If I'd known this was what you wanted, I wouldn't have done it," he said halfheartedly. It was a lie. Even if he told himself that he'd been mesmerized by Charity or that he hadn't had full control over his actions, it was a lie. He'd have done whatever it took to save the ones he loved. "This city doesn't want my help. It doesn't even want the Knights Vigilant back. You know what they wanted to do to me."

One shouldn't lie to the gods, but he couldn't help it. He'd told himself that he didn't care about what happened to this city every day since Mezeldwelf started handing over the gods instead of fighting to protect their world and culture. The merchant princes had a choice back then, and they'd chosen comfort and temporary peace over hardship and something that could've lasted.

If they had acted differently all those years ago, maybe Leon never would've left. Maybe he'd have announced himself by now and joined with the Protectors. Maybe he'd still believe in the oaths he swore on the day his world ended.

But they hadn't. They'd signed that godsdamned treaty. If they weren't willing to put themselves on the line to protect the world, why should he?

You promised, came a voice from the corner of the cell.

Leon's heavy eyes turned that direction and then widened.

An Alkan woman emerged from the shadows. Her white locs were tied back in a knot at the base of her neck, and her battered armor shone with the light of unlife. Leon had known her once, had stared at that armor in the dining hall every day for two years. In her youth, she patrolled the borders of the Fallow Lands, driving off husk incursions and bringing aid to any who needed it. In her old age, she'd run an orphanage in Dhuitholm where two little boys mourned a father lost to plague and a mother lost to the Sea, before they were taken in by a knight.

Leon had always admired her, even if he'd long since forgotten her name. She'd died three days before Dhuitholm fell. They hadn't had a chance to bury her.

You swore to keep the watch, to remain vigilant, she said, her voice barely more than a whisper on the breeze. **The life you've lived since then kept you safe until the time came to honor the oaths you made.**

The voices outside were growing louder. Guards, servants, and nobles alike wondered if they should go in or whether the last member of an extinct order wanted to consult with the gods for a bit longer. Charity was a solid presence at Leon's back, offering silent support even as they kept the others away.

Leon's laugh was sharp and bitter. His knees ached, but he couldn't find the strength to move. "I was a child."

You were a squire, eager to join your master and your brother in our ranks. Her eyes softened, and a ghostly hand passed through Leon's cheek, a motherly touch from a being who hadn't had hands to touch anyone in years. **You were chosen for this because you chose to take the oaths instead of fleeing with the others your age.**

"Chose me? Chose me for what?" He scoffed and pushed himself to his feet on shaky legs. "The senior knights anointed any squire past their first three years of training. We didn't even have time to choose mounts before Dhuitholm fell."

If they'd chosen him for this, he wanted nothing to do with it. Watching his city and newfound family fall, spending years struggling under the knowledge that even if he had been fully trained, he had no chance against the armies of the Templesbane, and now on the precipice of watching it all happen again—

You were strong, she uttered with all the fire of every Forge priest combined. **Strong and braver than you know. Delke believes in you. That is why you were sent away.**

Sent? No. He hadn't been sent away. He'd taken the first opportunity after the holy oil dried to grab his axes and a plow nag and run before the husks could break down the gates.

A hand reached up to card through Leon's hair, and he wished it could've actually touched him.

You need to help this city, she whispered. **Even if you run again afterward, even if you fail, you must do that.**

"And you'll all leave me be once that's done?" he whispered. "You let me go?"

He wasn't even sure what he meant by that. Only the Watchful Peace could release him from his oaths, and they had been silent since their city fell.

He was so tired of running.

Her lips turned down in a deep frown, and she pulled back. **When the city is saved . . .** Her voice dropped, fading from a whisper on the breeze to a memory of things once spoken, and her form faded with it. **We will speak again.**

And she was gone. Leon and Charity were alone.

***

Charity saved him once more. They led him through the crowd of whispering people, the ones that scarcely seemed to believe their own eyes as he passed. He had no doubt that if he'd been on his own, they'd have swarmed him as soon as he left Ranon's old cell. He kept his eyes fixed on Charity, desperate to block out the world around him, but it was hard not to hear since they all said the same things.

He was a Knight Vigilant. He'd purified a husk. He was the savior of Hyderia, the one who would drive back the Templesbane, reclaim Dhuitholm, and bring back the gods.

A tall order for anyone. Taller still for one who had every intention of spending whatever was left of his life getting as drunk as possible in a tavern in some far-off corner of Hyderia, where he never had to think about what he'd lost getting there ever again.

Charity left him with the guards at the council chamber, who held his newfound followers back. Lacking an escape route, he went in, and those following him muttered excitedly, their whispers gaining strength with each passing moment. The heavy door closed behind him, muffling the sound, and the lock turned with a solid thump.

As if in a trance, Leon walked forward, down the hall and into the council chamber proper. The torchlight flickered on the walls, and he found himself watching the flames dance as he went. His limbs still shook, his throat burned, and his stomach was beginning to ache. His senses, which had threatened to drive Leon to his knees only that afternoon, flit about without his permission. Reaching for something, stretching far beyond what he'd been able to do before tonight.

Oddly, that was the only part of him that didn't hurt. The magic raced through him without his conscious control, like a dam had been knocked down and the river it held back was free to flow how it wished.

Angry voices washed over him when he left the hall, and he found himself at the back of the council chamber.

He paused at the threshold, taking in the room that was the true center of power in Mezeldwelf. He'd only been here a handful of times since he first came to the city, but it hadn't changed at all in that time.

The vaulted ceiling, made of the same red stone as the city walls, stood thirty feet high and was lit by six massive chandeliers for the original six sections of the city. Four rows of raised benches covered each wall, and forty boxes made of dark wood—none higher than the one that sat next to it—stood in front of those benches. In the boxes sat the forty merchants who ran the city.

Or rather, thirty-nine of the merchants who ran the city. The box at the front of the room, right in front of the darkened rose window that looked out over the harbor, where the prince in charge of the treasury usually sat, was empty.

No one noticed Leon creeping in, because all the princes were yelling to be heard over each other. Ranon stood in the middle of the raised seats, his hands bound in front of him with a chain threaded through a loop in the floor. Beside him sat a familiar figure in bright yellow robes.

"You must listen," Ranon yelled, raising his hands, like that would convince people far too used to others hanging on to their every word to quiet themselves. "Please, I wasn't the only one here. There are hundreds of husks below the city, digging tunnels and weakening defenses, and there were more on the way. If you hurry, if you call out the guard, you can stop them."

Leon edged around the corner and settled onto a bench that gave him a good view of the proceedings. His legs gave way underneath him on his way down, but the bench held his weight without much complaint. A seat was a seat, and he wanted to sit until he could find a quiet way out of here. Pulling his hood down low over his eyes, he scanned the room for familiar faces and settled back against the wall.

Most of the other princes were strangers to him, but they also didn't matter very much. They might blow hot air about and fuss about the proper way of doing things, but they couldn't deny the truth now. It was just a question of how long it would take for them to pull their heads out of their rear ends.

Aoife sat in the box to the left of the rose window, and Padraeg stood at her shoulder. Together, they presented a united front that the rest of the princes couldn't hope to match. Padraeg's armor gleamed in the lamplight, shining like a knight of legend, and Aoife had added a white cape to her ensemble to match his.

A small smile crossed Leon's lips when Padraeg leaned down to whisper in Aoife's ear. They were in control here. Mesley himself had accused Leon of being a Knight Vigilant, and too many had seen him purify Ranon for the other princes to deny it. What had seemed foolishness or pride an hour ago now looked like prudence and foresight with Ranon's testimony about Mesley's allegiances.

Once they were finished here, they'd be able to help Leon get out of the Citadel without being swarmed. That was the most important part.

Still, his eyes did catch on the one other prince he knew. Or rather, the former prince he supposed. At this angle, he had an excellent view of whatever was going on.

Artur Mesley had been old when Leon was a teenager, and was now far into his ninth decade. In his youth, he'd been a strong and tall man, capable of hoisting barrels and throwing troublemaking youth into the harbor with ease. He'd managed his family's warehouses for thirty years and then took over management again when Myrrdin's older sister left to join the Protectors. He'd always stood tall and strong in Leon's memories, the unconquerable and kind master of the Mesley trading houses and de facto leader of the merchant princes.

Now, sitting in the middle of the council seats and staring up at the people who'd been his peers not even an hour ago, he drowned in the robes that had once fit him well. Wisps of snow-white hair covered his head, and his wrinkled skin looked as delicate as parchment. His hands, covered in a web of veins and wrinkles, clutched the cane between his legs like it was the only thing keeping him upright. The guards hadn't even bothered to bind him.

But the glare he shot at Ranon could've frozen the heart of a lesser man. If his limbs remembered their old strength or Vengeance answered his call, Leon had no doubt that Mesley would've cut Ranon down where he stood.

"Enough," Aoife yelled, banging her gavel on her table. It succeeded in little more than muffling the meeker princes. "Shouting won't solve anything. Ranon Carrick has brought proof before us. Prince Mesley has broken our laws and invited the Sister into the city."

"Prince Mesley denies these charges," one of the princes shouted, leaping to her feet. She pointed dramatically at Ranon, like he was the Brother himself come to be judged. "I say that this is a trick. Guard-Captain Quinn's own reports say there was no evidence that Ranon Carrick was a husk prior to Charity and Leon Quinn allegedly purifying him."

That, at least, quieted the shouting. The other princes muttered back and forth to each other while Aoife rubbed her eyes.

"The Sister has access to alchemical wonders beyond your imagining," Ranon yelled. His chains clanked against each other as he took a step closer to the accusing prince, but no farther. "While I don't know why Sir Leon didn't cure me before, the fact remains he was able to do it now, which restored my eyes and my mind. Ask him or Charity if you must, but we have to act now, before the Sister sends her husks to attack. She's been gathering her forces for months—"

The prince snorted and gathered her blue and green robes to sit primly, as if on a throne. "It's a trick. If Leon Quinn is a

Knight Vigilant, after all, why didn't he announce himself after Dhuitholm fell? Why hasn't he been rebuilding the order or wiping out the husks?"

"An excellent question," Mesley said, pushing himself to his feet. His robes, bright yellow with cockatrices embroidered all over them, were nearly his end as they caught under his cane. "And one we must have an answer to. Perhaps we ought to ask him, hmm?"

He lifted his cane with trembling arms and pointed at Leon. His face contorted into a sneer, and his voice dropped into a growl more suited for a wolf.

"What does the man, the *mercenary*, who already lied to our gate guards and just so happened to return home right before the harvest festival, when Charity was to give themself to the Templesbane, have to say about these accusations, hm?" He snarled and spat. "He's the one who called the Sister down on us. All I did was try to bring the festival delegation in quietly, as is my duty."

Leon arched an eyebrow and crossed his arms. "You're asking me? About what I think of you trying to sneak husks into the city?"

He ought to be enraged. Even if he weren't a Knight Vigilant, the husks and the Templesbane had destroyed his life. There wasn't a merchant or noble in the city that didn't know Padraeg Quinn took in a Dhuitholm refugee after the city fell. Leon had spent years on the border, seen firsthand what life was like for people there, and now returned to the only safe place he'd ever known, only to find that one of the people who was supposed to be protecting it was smuggling in agents of the beings that wanted to destroy the gods and remake the world in their own image.

It was a horrible thing to ask, and he should be enraged, but he wasn't. Tension was wound up in his chest, and his limbs ached, and he couldn't stop sensing things, but he was so tired. It would be dawn in a few hours, he hadn't eaten, he couldn't remember when he'd last drunk anything, and he wanted to go back to bed. This shouldn't be a fight.

"Yes," one of the princes said, a man in a white robe with blue accents. He nodded vigorously and gestured for Leon to come to the floor. "Charity has left us, but you were there. You, allegedly, were the one to cure Mr. Carrick of his affliction, and you are *supposedly* the only member of the Knights Vigilant to survive the fall of Dhuitholm. You're the only one who can answer these questions."

Leon settled into his seat, spreading his legs and silently daring the prince to pull him to the floor himself. His hood slipped down, revealing his whole face to the waiting crowd. "I think that the council knows the punishment for a prince whose actions cause the city to suffer. You don't need me to give you proof." It was a veiled threat and they all knew it. The princes fell so silent he could've dropped a pin and listened to it echo for hours.

A prince mismanaging or neglecting their sector would see their wealth claimed to repair the damage. If the damage was great enough, they might lose their title or be exiled. But a prince who intentionally brought ruin or destruction onto the city, no matter how little damage it actually caused . . . their lives, their houses, and even their names were forfeit. Everyone would know what they had done and what had been done to them in turn.

If the guard discovered Ranon was telling the truth, any prince that stood in his way would face that judgment.

When the other princes seemed contrite enough, Leon spoke again. "Send the guard to investigate the places Ranon claimed the husks were digging. If you still doubt him, call for a priest of Truth. They might charge more for being dragged out of bed at this hour, but if it convinces you to call out the guard, then I'm sure Prince Quinn will shoulder the cost."

The silence continued for another minute. Aoife's face was neutral, but Padraeg made no effort to hide or dull his proud smile. Then Mesley scoffed.

"Fine then, call a priest of Truth. I have nothing to hide. My dealings with the people of this city have always been honest."

"Aye," Padraeg said, the pride in his face dropping into a cold rage. "That's why you tried to convince the council to turn my son over to the Templesbane."

"Indeed," Aoife said. She reached down into her box and pulled a thick ledger out. "Which is why we will be going over what the Band of Broken Blades and the city guard discovered while investigating smuggling on vessels *your family* sponsored while Guard-Captain Quinn and Sir Leon fetch a priest of Truth." Her blank expression broke, and she smiled. There was nothing kind there, only teeth and a sense of vindication so vicious it may as well have been an act of war. "Mr. Carrick can fill in anything they missed."

The way Mesley sank back into his chair, his face pale, was something that would stay with Leon for a long time.

Smirking, Leon stood. Padraeg was already moving and managed to meet Leon before he could go down the hall.

"Not that way," he said in a low voice, tugging Leon underneath the raised benches. "There's a secret door this way. The guard uses it to get prisoners in and out without being seen."

Leon followed without question. Perhaps Padraeg would let him sleep in his office or one of the private cells. He'd done that a few times when Leon was young and terrified of letting Padraeg out of his sight. It was probably too much to ask that he be allowed to go home.

The halls were busy for the hour. Everywhere Leon looked, he saw guards rushing back and forth and squires carrying armor and weapons. Every lamp was lit, and every bench, table, and flat surface had gear laid out on top with a squire inspecting it for flaws.

"Did the princes allow you to raise the guard?" he asked, slipping behind Padraeg to take up less space in the hall.

Padraeg snorted. "I'm the guard-captain. I don't need their permission when there's an army hiding somewhere in the city. I sent runners to bring everyone to the Citadel the moment Charity led you out."

"You were that confident?" Leon's stomach twisted, and he couldn't tell if it was pride or caution. "You didn't even know what they were going to ask me to do."

Tugging a small door open, Padraeg let out a soft laugh. "Leon, your eyes were glowing. You kept talking about an emptiness below us and the oaths you had sworn before making a beeline for the cells. I made an educated guess, and now we can have the guards out searching for the husks in an hour instead of waiting until dawn." He ushered Leon through and followed after him. When he shut the door, the only light came from a small lamp hanging on the opposite wall. Padraeg took it and held it in front of him like a shield. "Come on, we're almost there."

In the distance, Leon could hear rushing water. They must have been closer to the port than he'd realized.

It was good that Padraeg had done that, Leon supposed as he followed Padraeg down the hall and then down a narrow staircase. It was a little alarming to hear how things had looked from someone else's point of view, but at least the guard had been alerted. He hoped the others hadn't been—

"Where'd the others go?" he asked, adrenaline flooding through his limbs. "Did they—"

They had to have seen. Jackie might've been too young to know what was happening, but the others weren't. They'd have followed him, and they'd have seen what he did, and they would know what it meant and that he'd lied to them the entire time they'd known each other. Why hadn't he realized it before now and—

"Leon," Padraeg snapped, waving a hand in front of his face. "Breathe, son. They're fine. Aoife sent them to take Jackie home before any of the witnesses could realize they were with you."

"But they saw what happened?" he rasped. Gods, he needed a drink. The rushing water was even louder now, and that only made his throat feel dryer by comparison. "Did they realize . . . ?"

Padraeg's eyes softened, and he let out a great sigh. "Yes," he admitted, turning around. "They saw. That Forge priest of yours was the first to realize what it all meant, and he told the others. He . . . wasn't happy about it." He stopped once more and slammed a hand against his head. "Gods, I'm an idiot." And he pulled a waterskin from underneath his cloak. "Here. You sound like you've been drinking sawdust."

Leon took it without question, uncorked the skin, and tilted it up. Tepid water flooded into his mouth, but it may as well have been divine ambrosia. He drained half the skin before he even paused for breath, and the other half as soon as he had air again. "Thank you," he said, handing the skin back to Padraeg while wiping his mouth with the back of his hand. The world felt less awful now that he wasn't parched, but all the water in the world couldn't take his questions away. "But the others, what did they—what did Njeri do? Is she angry? Is . . . Jackie angry with me?"

They'd had to leave the Band because the husks had sensed Leon. The husks had latched on to Jackie as a scare tactic, to frighten Njeri into giving them what they wanted, and because of that, Jackie and Leon had to leave them behind. She'd gotten hurt because he'd hidden instead of fought them.

She loved hearing about the Knights Vigilant. What must she think of them now that she knew the truth about him? Leon was many things, but he was far from one of the great knights of legend.

"I should've done that when I first saw you skulk in." Padraeg squirreled the skin away and resumed walking. Out of the darkness ahead of them emerged a metal gate. Through it, Leon could hear the rushing of a river. "I think it's best you talk with them instead of hearing it from me. They ought to be waiting for you at the manor. I told them I'd send you that way as soon as Aoife and I could free you from the Citadel."

"They—good." And Leon wished that he had another skin, this time full of wine. He didn't want to face this conversation sober, or at all, but he'd no more be able to avoid it than he could avoid the sunrise. "I'll head that way, then."

Padraeg hung the lantern off a hook and then pulled a heavy set of keys from his belt. "This culvert will lead you to a guard station on the harbor. I've sent word, and someone will meet you there with a new cloak and guard tunic. Throw that over your gear and wear a helmet, and you should be able to get home without anyone questioning you."

He pulled the gate open, and the hinges squealed. The change from Citadel hall to culvert couldn't have been more severe. On one side of the gate, there was chiseled stone and light, and on the other was a river five feet across with a tiny mud path on either side.

Padraeg turned back to Leon, and a myriad of emotions crossed his face before settling into careful neutrality. He stepped forward and laid a hand on Leon's shoulder. "I know this couldn't have been easy, but you did the right thing. Revealing yourself . . . it'll do more good than you realize. Even if you go back into hiding after this, people know you're out there. It'll give them something to hope for again."

Leon's heart jumped into his throat, and one hand crept up to grab Padraeg's wrist. "I didn't do it because I wanted to give people hope," he said numbly. "I did it because it was the only way Charity would agree to vouch for you and the others. I wanted to keep you safe. I'm not—I'm not a knight, Padraeg. I'm a mercenary, and this time my fee was you, Aoife, and my friends."

Padraeg and the princes and everyone who had seen what he and Charity did were building this into something it wasn't. Building *him* into something he wasn't. He wasn't some great hero, here to save the day and ride off into legend on a winged horse with a motley collection of allies at his side. If they built him up into that, they'd be crushed when the veneer was wiped away and they saw the truth hidden underneath.

"I know," Padraeg whispered. He squeezed, and the pressure wasn't demanding or harsh. It was soft. Comforting. "I was there for that, too, Leon. But no matter why you did it, why you followed Charity and revealed yourself, things will change now. People will realize the Protectors were right, that there's still hope left, and that someone, somewhere, is capable of defeating the Templesbane."

"But I'm not—" He sighed. What more could he say? Even if he spelled it out, Padraeg wouldn't understand. "I should get going. The harbor's a long way from the Citadel."

Pushing Padraeg's hand off, Leon rushed into the tunnel. The dirt gave way as soon as his foot hit it, and he stumbled back, flailing for the gate, for the wall, for anything to catch himself instead of falling in the murky water.

Strong hands caught him before he went down. "Careful," Padraeg chided. "The ground is soft here, and carrying a lantern all the way to the wharf is just begging for people to realize where you're coming from. It might be safer to walk in the water."

"I realize that," Leon snapped, pulling his now-sodden boots from the mud and settling them onto the firmer ground next to the gate. "I'm fine."

Padraeg let out a huff of air and smiled. "Sure you are," he said in a low voice. "You've got this handled."

"I have, in fact," Leon said gruffly, fighting back the blush currently turning his cheeks rosy red. Thankfully, it was too dark for Padraeg to see; otherwise he'd never hear the end of it. "You can go back to the princes. Let Aoife know I'll be fine. I'll send a message when I get back to the manor." Deciding his boots were already coated in mud and worse, so there was no point trying to stay out of the water, he tromped back into the river and silently cursed every decision he'd made today, starting with getting out of bed in the morning.

Padraeg called for him before he got more than ten feet down the tunnel. "I am proud of you, you know. For everything. Not just this. Not just tonight."

Leon paused, and the water rushed around him.

"I know," he said finally, the sound of the water stealing most of his words away. "I know."

Then he started walking again, and if Padraeg called after him, the water absorbed that too.

Chapter 13
Secrets and Lies

By the time Leon reached the harbor, he was soaking wet and sore in addition to exhausted and overwhelmed. He'd tripped over hidden rocks and holes, paying for his clumsiness with a face full of foul water and mud so many times he lost count.

The guards at the outpost near where the tunnel let out looked at Leon with awe in their eyes. The news about Leon's true identity must have already reached them. They offered him not only a guard tunic, cloak, and helmet, but also a dry change of clothes and a fresh pair of boots that almost fit. Neither was older than twenty. One, a man with pockmarked skin, gasped when Leon turned around to change. The other hadn't been able to take their eyes off Leon's arms since his shirt came off.

Leon made a mental note to report them to Padraeg before he left Mezeldwelf. It was one thing to admire someone; it was another to look at them like a piece of meat while they were relying on you to keep a watch. *Especially* when they were relying on you to keep watch.

But he was tempted to let it slide, since they also offered him a bag to hold his armor. Wet leather was an unpleasant smell at the best of times, and the thought of wearing it home while it was soaking wet and covered in all manner of filth made him want to vomit.

With a word of thanks, he settled the helmet on his head, pulled his hood up over it, and slung the bag over his shoulder to begin the long walk to the manor.

This late, most of the taverns had closed, and even the most dedicated of Pleasure's servants had found their way back to their temples or into a devotee's bed. The beggars and orphans had retreated to the shelters and temples they called home, and the only people Leon crossed paths with were bleary-eyed taverngoers stumbling home and bakers heading to work.

That, and guards. Leon's senses followed them without his control, reaching deeper into the city than he'd ever gone before. Into sewers and basements and old smugglers' tunnels he doubted existed on any city map. And in them, there was nothingness so intense it made his head spin.

As he walked, his limbs trembling with exhaustion and his mind buzzing with anxiety, he kept a careful watch on the nothingness. It wasn't hard, since it was all around him. He knew the exact moment that the guards found the husks because the nothingness seized, screamed so loud he was shocked it wasn't audible on the surface, and then vanished as those it controlled were cut down. Ranon had been telling the truth, and Prince Mesley, if he were wise, would have to confess everything he'd done in service to the Templesbane.

So lost was Leon in his thoughts, in the nothingness dwindling far below his feet, that he didn't realize he'd arrived at Quinn Manor until he walked into the gate.

A servant met him at the door. She took one look at him, took the bag and his cloak from him, and demanded he march straight to the washing room. From the way her nose crinkled and how she kept herself out of arm's reach, he figured that his wet leathers weren't the only things that smelled.

But he didn't complain. The others were waiting for him, and he didn't have the slightest clue about what he was going to say to them. On the way out of the tunnels, he'd been too focused on not falling again to consider it. While walking back, he'd been distracted by the battle going on below his feet. Now that he was here, with the prospect of their angry glares waiting for him, he faltered.

If he took long enough, perhaps they'd leave or fall asleep. It was late, after all. The servants would prepare them rooms, and he could use this time to figure out how to answer the questions they were sure to throw at him. In the morning, things wouldn't look as bad. Aoife, Padraeg, and Kelan could help him explain why he'd never told any of them who he was.

Yes, that would work. They'd all approach this much more rationally on a full stomach and with a night's rest behind them.

It was a good plan. Only, he didn't count on the washroom door bursting open with a thunderous crash and Njeri charging through, an inferno lit behind her dark eyes, minutes after he sank into the warm water.

"Leon Quinn," she thundered, charging to the edge of the tub. "What the hell were you thinking?"

Leon's heart froze. "Does this have to happen now?" he muttered, sinking deeper into the water. The tub wasn't big enough to cover all of him, but at least Njeri wouldn't be able to see anything important through the suds. Thank the gods he'd been able to rinse off before he got in; otherwise he'd have been stuck in dirty water for who knew how long. "I smell like a sewer, in case you didn't notice."

"And you're lucky I don't throw you into one, you insufferable—" She let loose a long string of Alkan curse words that made Leon wish the servants hadn't taken his clothes away to be laundered. He might have to make a run for it.

"Njeri—"

"No, you don't get to do that," she said, stabbing a finger into Leon's bare chest. "You don't get to 'Njeri' me when *apparently* you're some mythical lost knight, and you didn't even give me the courtesy of telling me you were godsworn."

"It's not—Njeri, it's not like that. I didn't mean to keep it from you." Even as the words left his mouth, he knew they were a mistake, but if he'd somehow been thick enough to miss that, the lethal glare she shot at him would've clued him in.

"Didn't mean to keep it from me?" Her voice dropped dangerously low, and Leon gripped the sides of the tub in case he needed to make a quick exit. He'd only ever seen her lose her temper three times in the years he'd known her, and each time, someone had ended up bleeding. "You—one of my most loyal officers, the only one beside Bettany who's been at my side since damn near the beginning—didn't mean to keep it from me?"

"I . . ." He swallowed and forced himself to relax. It wouldn't help him if Njeri thought he was preparing to run. She always waited until they ran. "It's complicated. The only ones who knew were Padraeg and Aoife."

Aoife had figured it out like Kelan had. She'd been smart enough to keep it quiet, even back then. In the first few years after Mezeldwelf fell, unscrupulous people had kidnapped gray-eyed folks, dressed them up as knights, and presented them before whatever noble or desperate village that could scrape together the coin for a little protection from the Templesbane and the husks. There was a reason gray eyes were so rare outside of Falte these days.

Njeri scoffed. "And yet, you still didn't tell me, even when it became obvious we were dealing with husks. Damn it, Leon. I'd have gotten you out of the city no matter what it took if I'd known that. Do you have any idea how much danger—"

This time it was Leon's glare that shut Njeri up.

"Believe me," he said darkly, taking the soap and rag the servants left beside the tub and dunking both in the water, "I know better than anyone how dangerous it is to travel with someone like me." The water turned brown around him as he scrubbed. All the mud, dust, and gods alone knew what else that hadn't washed off when he'd rinsed earlier were finally cleared away, and he kept scrubbing until his skin turned bright red.

He kept his eyes fixed on what he was doing. He'd wanted to wait for this conversation for a reason. Sure, he could've sent word to the others that he was going to wash first, but he couldn't—he hadn't—

Today had been very long, and all he wanted to do was sleep. Failing that, he wanted ten minutes alone with his thoughts. But Njeri was here, and he wouldn't be able to avoid talking to her forever.

"I'm sorry," she whispered, sitting heavily on the counter. She looked smaller there, like all the fight had gone out of her at once. "I didn't mean it like that."

Leon sighed. "I know."

If their situations had been reversed, if Njeri were the last Knight Vigilant and he were the mercenary leader, he'd have reacted the same way. It wasn't right that he'd kept this from her, not when having him in the Band put the rest of them in danger.

He considered the water as the minutes ticked by. It was too dirty for his hair and barely clean enough to get the rest of the filth off. He'd need to drain it to rinse, but that would require leaving the tub, and he wasn't ready to be naked in front of Njeri again. For more reasons than just her anger.

"If you're not going to talk and you're not going to leave, could you get me a bucket of water?" he asked carefully. "The pump is by the wall. I need to wash my hair, and then I can go see the others with you."

She let out a huff of laughter but did as he asked. "What, are you worried about the cold, or did you regrow some noble sensibilities while you've been here? It's nothing I haven't seen before."

He let out a choked-off laugh. "We're next to the kitchen. I don't think the cold is something I have to worry about." He stretched to take the bucket from her, but she pulled back before he could.

Instead, she grabbed a second bucket, turned it over, and kicked it behind Leon before sitting down. "Here, let me help."

He turned halfway, limited by the water level and his own desire to keep certain bits of his anatomy hidden. "You're sure? I can do this on my own."

She snorted and pulled a ladle from the bucket. "Relax. Just because my hair's a different texture doesn't mean I've never washed hair like yours before."

"I wasn't—" He cut himself off before he could say something stupid and picked up the soap. "Thank you."

As quickly as he could, he worked the lather through his hair, and Njeri dumped ladlefuls of cold water over him whenever she deemed it necessary. It was a good system. One where they didn't have to talk. That didn't last long though.

"Why didn't you trust me?" she asked, scooping more water over his head.

"It wasn't about trust," he muttered, spitting out the soapy water that had made its way into his mouth. If it were, he'd have told her years ago. She'd more than earned his trust, both before and after they'd tried to make things work between them. It was just . . . letting anyone know the truth about him was about more than trust.

It was hard enough to keep a secret when only three people knew. If he had told her, how long before he would've wanted to tell the others? How long before he would've gotten lax or too at ease discussing it and the wrong person found out?

"It was safer to keep it from everyone. The only reason Aoife figured it out was because she met my master and my brother the last time they came to Mezeldwelf." She'd said Leon looked like Mael's twin apart from his eyes.

It had broken Leon's heart the day he turned sixteen and realized he was older than Mael would ever get to be.

"I realize that, but . . ." She sighed, then dropped the ladle in the bucket with an audible splash. "I'm still upset. For ten years I watched your back, hoping that one day you'd trust me enough to tell me why you always ran when the Protectors came looking, or what kind of monsters you'd seen to wake up screaming more often than you slept through the night. I wanted you to trust me the way I trusted you."

The water was cold now. Leon stared into its murky depths and let out a long sigh.

How many times had Njeri had to cover for him while he hid from the Protectors? How many times had she looked the other way when he moved a little too fast, hit an enemy a bit too hard? She'd supported him for years, told him things about her past and the family she'd lost to the Templesbane that she'd never told anyone before. In return he'd put her in danger because he couldn't bear to be alone but couldn't face the truth about himself either.

"I wanted that too," he whispered. They dropped into silence again, each lost in their thoughts, before Leon spoke again. "I'm sorry you found out like this. If I'd known what Charity had wanted me to do, I'd have told you all the truth beforehand. You should've heard it from me."

He got a faceful of cold water and a bucket dropped over his head for his honesty.

"Njeri," he yelped, forgetting himself for long enough to jump halfway out of the tub. A towel hit him across the back, accompanied by Njeri's sharp laughter. He turned, nearly upending the tub, in time to see her wipe something off her cheek.

"Come on, you're clean enough." She spun around, gesturing for him to follow her. "Get dressed. I'll wake the others. If you try to hide again, I'll send Shea after you."

***

Once Leon had rinsed and dressed again, he'd made his way to the dining hall. Despite the late hour, someone had laid out a tray of salted pork and bread as well as three bottles of wine, all of which had been claimed.

Whatever heart he'd managed to regain while talking with Njeri in the washroom disappeared, and he hovered at the threshold, trying to talk himself out of running away again.

But that choice was taken from him when Njeri looked up and waved him in. She and Bettany had claimed one of the wine bottles and were passing it back and forth between them while they ate. They'd set up camp about halfway down the table, near the food. Kelan sat opposite them with the second bottle. Jackie was asleep on the bench beside him, her head pillowed on his lap.

Shea sat at the far end of the table, nursing the last of the bottles. The glare he shot at Leon was so full of loathing it was a wonder he didn't follow it up by throwing the bottle at Leon's head.

"So he finally joins us," Shea said, snarling. He raised his bottle, already half-empty, in a mock toast and then swallowed a good portion of what was left. There was a noticeable slur to his words. Somehow, Leon doubted this was his first drink of the evening. "The mighty knight emerges from his castle and blesses us mere mortals with his presence."

"Be quiet, Shea," Njeri snapped, setting her bottle down with a loud thunk. "If you let him talk, he'll explain himself."

"Of course he will. Whatever he told you when you went off together, he's gonna tell us." Shea leaned forward and shot a glare at Leon that could've terrified a husk. His eyes were glassy and red, and his knuckles were white where they were clutched around the bottle. "I'm sure he had an excellent reason for hiding all these years and another one for how many people he left to suffer while he drank his life away in the borderlands."

Leon's hands itched to curl into fists, but he forced them flat against his leg. Shea had a right to be angry—considering his god had been consumed because Leon had stayed hidden—and there was no doubt in Leon's mind that once the amazement of having a Knight Vigilant back wore off, Shea wouldn't be the only one acting like this. "I apologize for keeping this from you all," he said. "It wasn't safe for me to reveal myself while I lived in Mezeldwelf. The Sister was looking for surviving Knights Vigilant, and it was best for everyone if she didn't know I was alive."

It might actually have ended up worse if he had revealed himself. The Sister wouldn't have stopped until he was captured or dead, no matter what or who stood in her path. Without Mezeldwelf's support and without the army the Protectors had been building since the Great Treaty was signed, he was as good as dead. Even with them, he'd still be as good as dead if he let those things persuade him to confront the Sister.

Bettany snorted and snagged the bottle from Njeri. "I always knew there was something strange about you, but I thought you were sworn to some minor god or from some noble's house guard, like Njeri. Maybe both."

Shea snorted and finished his bottle. "It'd be better if he were," he slurred, stumbling to his feet. He met Leon's eyes and sneered. The bottle flew past Leon's head and somehow didn't shatter when it hit the ground. Shea stumbled closer, and his wine-thick breath made Leon's eyes water. "But no. He's a coward and a drunk, hiding from the world while the gods give their lives for him."

For one wretched moment, Leon wanted to hit Shea, but all that would've done was start a fight and wake Jackie, assuming she wasn't awake already and hiding it. He might be a coward, but revealing himself wouldn't have saved the gods. All it would've done was put a target on Leon's back while hundreds of people died defending their gods and he lost the ones he cared about. At least this way the Sister wasn't actively campaigning against the people of Sihia, Hyderia, or Falte. She was too focused on finding him.

"Sit down," Njeri snapped, tugging Shea back to the table. "If you get up again, I'm assigning you first watch for a month. Bettany, keep him there." She glanced up at Leon, and her glare was so icy it felt like they hadn't talked at all. "And you should sit down. It feels weird to have you looming over the rest of us like that."

So much for whatever peace they'd reached in the washroom.

With ever-growing trepidation, Leon slid onto the bench next to Kelan, who held a finger up to his lips.

"Let's all remember that there's a sleeping child on me," he said in a voice hardly louder than a whisper. "One we all know won't stop until she's asked Leon every question she can come up with, so everyone should keep their voices down if we want to finish this before sunrise."

Leon smiled gratefully at him and folded his hands on the table. At the very least, that hid how they shook. "I know you all have questions, and I'm trapped here for the time being unless

Padraeg and Aoife figure out a way to smuggle me back to the Citadel, so . . . ask. I'll answer honestly."

"How'd you escape Dhuitholm?" Bettany snagged the wine bottle and drank. Wiping her mouth with the back of her hand, she continued, "The refugees said the Knights Vigilant pulled back to defend the pantheon temples and the keep when they told the townsfolk to evacuate. You should've been with them."

Right. Bettany had never been one to pull her punches. He sighed, then reached for the bottle in front of Kelan. Of the two left, it was the only one mostly untouched, and he didn't want to think about that night while sober.

Shea lunged across the table before he could grab it, scattering the food as he went. "No, you don't get to drink this away," he snapped, clutching the bottle tight to his chest. "You've done enough of that."

Leon shot him a withering glare and opened his mouth to argue, but Njeri raised a hand to cut him off before he could get a word out.

Grinding his teeth together, Leon inhaled deeply. "Fine, then. I left out one of the side gates after the senior knights called everyone back to the keep."

To call his memories of that day shaky would've been an understatement. Some things he remembered as if they were still happening before him—the smell of the holy oil as Delke and the Vigilant General anointed him, the bloodstains on Mael's armor, the feeling of his axes in his hands as he killed his first husk, and the all-consuming *nothingness* that broke down the gates and marched on his home—but most of that day existed as little more than fragments.

The actual escape was one of those things. He remembered the earthy tunnel, hands helping him mount a horse rescued from a burning stable, an unfamiliar voice telling him to hide until the time came—and then nothing. The next thing he remembered was standing on a hill three miles from Dhuitholm, watching green flames burst through the keep's windows. Had he said goodbye to Delke and Mael before he left, or had they spent the last hours of their lives looking for his face among the dead?

Kelan's hand on Leon's arm broke him from that spiral before it consumed him.

He swallowed, wishing for wine. "I made my way to Mezeldwelf. A patrol found me and brought me to Padraeg."

"Did he know what you were?" Njeri asked, resting her elbows on the table. Shea listed to one side when she removed her support.

Leon nodded. "He knew my master. They were—he was going to join the order before he was made guard-captain. To be with her. They were close."

That was another understatement. Once, while deep in his cups, Padraeg had told Leon the truth of things. He'd loved Delke fiercely, wildly, and beyond reason. She'd come to Mezeldwelf to mediate a conflict between two warring princes. He'd been the guard assigned to escort her around the city. By the time the negotiations finished up and several corrupt officials were punished, he was ready to leave everything he'd ever known behind and follow her to Dhuitholm.

Then he'd been forced into the position of guard-captain when his predecessor was arrested. Unable to leave while the city was still in turmoil, he promised to follow when he'd found a suitable successor, and Delke returned without him. Over the next few years, she took in two orphan boys and settled into a position managing the stables. Neither had forgotten the other.

"And you spent the next ten years as a wealthy merchant's brat." Shea snorted and drank most of the bottle. By now, his

230

wine breath carried across the table. "Gods, did you even try to honor your oaths, or did you just leave?"

"Shut it," Kelan snapped. One hand settled on Jackie's head, over her exposed ear. "He was a kid. Imagine how you'd have felt if the Forge was consumed and Mezeldwelf fell apart around you when you were fucking thirteen."

Shea stared at Kelan, his eyes narrowed. A thought visibly worked its way from one side of his brain to the other. His head twisted back and forth between Leon and Kelan once, twice, then a third time. His eyes widened. "You knew," he hissed, his voice never rising above a whisper. "You knew about *him!*" He pointed straight at Leon the way one might point at a particularly repugnant dead rat and glared at Kelan like he'd been the one to drop it at his feet. "How long have you known?"

Kelan, for his part, didn't even flinch. "The Order of the Risen Moon has always been good at sniffing out secrets. I knew he was godsworn on the day we met," he said, running a hand through Jackie's hair. "But it wasn't until I saw how he reacted whenever we ran into husks that I put two and two together."

And he'd overheard Leon arguing with the dead knights who followed him around. Leon appreciated that Kelan was keeping that to himself. It had been hard enough for Padraeg to accept that the Knights Beyond were more than a colorful legend about the Knights Vigilant. Shea and the others would never believe it.

"What do you mean?" Njeri asked. Her face was calm and neutral. The lip on the scarred side of her face twitched periodically, the only sign that she was affected by this revelation at all, but Leon knew better than to believe that meant she felt as little as she showed. He'd known her for years, and right now he'd have known she was furious even if he'd been blinded, deafened, and half-dead with fever. It was bad enough he'd kept this from her, but hearing that Kelan had known before she did would've been like a knife to the heart. "You didn't think to tell me?"

Kelan shrugged. "I'd assumed you already knew. Failing that, I'm not the first godsworn to join the Band. When you meet enough of us, it's easy to tell when someone has taken an oath. Someone would've slipped eventually." He glanced at Leon, entirely unimpressed. "Frankly, I'm surprised he wasn't figured out sooner. Most of them must have thought as I did, which is the only reason I can think of that he's gotten away with this pretense for so long."

Leon wanted to argue, but he couldn't without revealing how his own stupidity and panic had confirmed Kelan's suspicions. Instead, he grabbed a chunk of salted pork Shea hadn't knocked off the table, and chewed it morosely.

"What do you plan to do after this?" Bettany asked, finally breaking the silence the room had fallen into. "I mean, you can't stay with the Band, and—while the princes would love to keep you here to sniff out husks—I'm sure the Protectors would blind their seers if it meant having you on their side."

Considering how many seers Leon had seen killed over the years while chasing him—including the one they found at the crossroads outside Amberbrook—that wasn't an exaggeration. The Protectors considered themselves the last hope for a free Hyderia and for the people and gods that called it home. Leon had run into more than one who were more than willing to risk their lives for the chance to add someone who might be the last Knight Vigilant to their ranks. Their trauma, their despair, and their stark willingness to do whatever it took to drive the Templesbane back shaped them into a terrible force to be reckoned with. One that terrified Leon almost as much as the Templesbane.

One couldn't argue with grief that had sharpened to a killing point.

"I'm not . . . I don't intend on joining the Protectors after this," he admitted. He rubbed the sigil still burned onto his arm, and frowned. He'd have to talk to Padraeg about removing it in the morning. The last thing he wanted was for some overzealous clerk to lead Protector sympathizers right to him. "And I don't want to stay in the city either."

Even if the guard found and killed all the husks in the city, the Great Treaty was broken, and the protection it offered was gone. The Sister would make a beeline for Mezeldwelf, and if she found him here, she wouldn't hesitate to cut down anyone and anything standing between them. It was safer if he left. It was late in the season, but he might be able to find a boat heading to Falte or even Alke. If he went far enough, maybe the Sister would leave Mezeldwelf alone while she chased after him.

It was a foolish daydream, but still something pleasant to think about.

Shea's eyes widened and he set his pilfered bottle down. "You're actually going to fight them? That's a suicide mission." He sounded reluctantly impressed. And, perhaps, a little upset.

Leon shook his head. "Of course not," he said, far harsher than he intended. "I'm not—" He rubbed his face. Gods, there wasn't any way to put this that didn't make him look like a selfish coward. He'd done what Charity and the Knights Beyond had asked him, and now everyone expected things from him that he couldn't provide. "Not that," he finally said. "Leaving will get the Sister's attention off Mezeldwelf, which will give the princes time to get in contact with the Protectors. They'll be able to send someone to help with the evacuations."

That was closer to the truth but still gave him too much credit. There was pride in Njeri's eyes and something close to respect on Shea's face, and even Bettany looked impressed. Leon couldn't stand it.

"Don't look at me like that," he snapped. "It's not . . . I can't be the knight everyone expects me to be." There was a wine stain on the table. He'd never noticed it before, but right now examining its every dip and curve was preferable to looking any of his friends in the eye. They wanted him to be a hero, expected it of him. But he couldn't be what they wanted. He hadn't been able to when he left Dhuitholm, and he couldn't be that now. "I never finished my training, and I never learned how to use my god's gifts. Today wasn't—it was the exception to what I can do, not the rule." He took a deep breath and let it out again. "I'm not even sure I could do that again."

It wouldn't have been possible without the Knights Beyond and Charity's help. The kind of magic it took to purge someone of the Templesbane's touch by himself was beyond him. Even if it weren't, if he could purify husks and save gods, he—he couldn't. If he had to face what had become of the other knights or look the Sister in the eye, it would destroy him. Even if Charity or another god helped him, if they took the place of the Watchful Peace, it would overwhelm him. Their power wouldn't be enough.

He couldn't do that. He couldn't ask another god to give themself up like that when he knew it would end in failure.

Silence fell around the table. Leon stared harder at the wine stain. Looking up would mean meeting someone's eyes, and he wasn't sure he'd be able to keep his resolve if he did that. He didn't want to be anyone's martyr, and he wouldn't let himself be convinced otherwise.

"So you're going to go back into hiding?" Bettany asked, her voice hollow and brittle. It was fundamentally wrong and made Leon's head jerk up. The look in her eyes threatened to break

Leon. Anger and sadness and grief and despair and a dozen more emotions just as wild and chaotic. "The entire city—gods, the entire world is counting on you. You're the only one who can fight the Templesbane and have a shot in hell at winning. Even if purifying that man was a fluke, it's something you are capable of and could get better at." She gripped the edge of the table and inhaled harshly. "You can't abandon them, not when you've given people the first shred of hope they've had in years."

Leon didn't have anything to say to that. No, that was wrong. He didn't want to think about that, not when those same thoughts had occupied him for years. Every time he'd asked himself whether he was doing the right thing by hiding, every time he saw people mourning life and land taken by the Templesbane, he'd had to face down the truth of his cowardice. And every time, he'd landed on the same answer. Fighting bandits and minor lords' squabbles was one thing. Facing down beings that consumed gods was another.

"And if it kills me?" he asked in a hollow voice. His chest ached. With a sincerity he hadn't felt in ages, he prayed for this to end. He wanted a drink, he wanted to sleep, and most importantly, he wanted all this to have been a nightmare because at least then he had a hope of waking up.

Shea snorted and drained the rest of his bottle. "I should've known." His lips twisted into a sneer, and he stood. "It would've been better if you'd died with the rest of your order."

"What would you expect me to do?" Leon asked, jumping to his feet. His knees caught on the edge of the table, pushing it back with a loud squeal. Njeri made a sound, but Leon plowed on. This whole situation was out of his worst nightmare. He couldn't escape what was coming, not if everyone he knew and loved kept pushing him into the fire. "If I fight them here, the Sister will bring the full force of her power down on Mezeldwelf to get me. If I join the Protectors, they'll drag me straight to the Templesbane themselves in some fool effort to reclaim Dhuitholm." His breath caught in his chest, and he let out a hysterical laugh. "I don't even have the benefit of my god, because the Watchful Peace hasn't answered a single prayer or even fucking whispered to me since Dhuitholm fell. I am the last of the Knights Vigilant, and the order will die with me."

It shouldn't hurt this much. He'd accepted that he'd never hear his god again, that he was the last of his kind, and Death's sentinels would take his soul beyond the edge of the void for oath breaking. He'd never see an afterlife, never find his loved ones in the darkness beyond life. He'd accepted that, and yet his heart wanted to scream. He deserved a chance at happiness, a chance for one day when he wasn't looking over his shoulder, terrified the wrong person would see his eyes or that the husks would find him or that the Protectors would take him and send him to his death.

None of this was fair. He'd been a child when he'd sworn his life away, and he'd paid for his brashness every day since.

He stood there, breathing deeply and blinking back tears. None of the others spoke. Kelan was looking at him with pity, the only one here that had left his order and god behind but still kept to his oaths, like Leon. Even Shea seemed to realize, for the first time, that Leon hadn't hidden himself out of some cruel desire to see the people of Hyderia suffer.

Njeri was quiet. This time, she was the one who refused to meet Leon's eyes. Why wouldn't she look at him? She'd forced this on him, on all the others. If she'd let him wait until tomorrow, maybe he'd have found a way to explain that didn't end with Shea angry, with Bettany disappointed, and with Kelan staring at him with that horrible understanding in his eyes.

The impasse stretched on. And on. Leon's legs shook, and his breath came faster and faster, and when had his cheeks gotten so wet? All this was too much, and he wanted to drink, and he wanted to sleep, and he wanted to be anywhere else but here, but especially in Padraeg's study with a book and something to eat, far away from the world until things made sense again. None of this was right, none of it was fair, and he just wanted to sleep.

Then, miraculously, marvelously, it was broken.

Jackie sat up, rubbing her eyes. "Leon?" she asked, a yawn splitting his name in two. "Is that you?"

His attention turned to her, and some of the tension knotted up in his shoulders bled away despite the weight of the others' eyes upon him. Here was his chance to escape, to hide away until tomorrow, when everything would still be awful, but at least he'd be well rested. "Yes," he whispered. His voice was watery and weak. He took a deep breath and tried to make it firm. "It's late. You should be in bed."

"Noooo," Jackie whined, pushing up from Kelan's lap. She tried and failed to rub the sleep from her eyes. "No, I'm not sleepy. I wanna talk to you."

"In the morning," he promised her. Kelan obligingly moved away so Leon could take her by the hand.

He didn't look anyone in the eye as he led a stumbling Jackie from the dining hall and upstairs to her room. She fell asleep again as soon as her head hit her pillow, and Leon stole away to his room, pretending he didn't hear the raised voices downstairs.

Chapter 14
Legends Revisited

The sun had long since risen by the time Leon dragged himself out of bed. Someone had left a loaf of bread, a canteen of water, and a bottle of wine on a large, green chest outside his door. None of that had been there when he'd fallen into bed last night, but he didn't question it. He left the chest there but took the tray inside. He picked at the bread, sipped the water, and drank far more of the wine than he ought to as he debated his options for today.

He could search the others out. In a one-on-one conversation, he might be able to explain things the way he couldn't last night. Njeri may have offered inconsistent support then, but they'd all been tired. If he could make her understand, then she could help him handle the others. Gods, he wished he'd gone to bed the second he got home. She might have been more reluctant to wake him with Kelan there to explain why that was a bad idea.

But no, he'd decided to bathe and then do the noble thing of facing the comrades he'd lied to for as long he'd known them. They had said some things, he had said things back, and now he was sitting alone in his room, drinking wine on an empty stomach.

No, he didn't want to face them yet. If they wanted to talk, they'd be able to find him.

Since the Band was out, he'd have to look somewhere else for occupation.

Aoife and Padraeg would no doubt have things for him to do if he asked them. Padraeg would want his help looking for the husks, and Aoife would want him to stand threateningly behind her in the council chamber in case any of the other princes tried to start something. That would be easiest, as even the most stubborn prince couldn't deny that the Sister had broken the treaty first. Helping Padraeg would be more work but likely more rewarding.

However, like finding the others, that would require him leaving the house. And worse still, it would require him to go to the Citadel. Since the entire bloody city had to know the true identity of Padraeg Quinn's delinquent son by now, it wasn't like he'd be able to avoid scrutiny at their sides either. Gossip in Mezeldwelf spread like wildfire in the best of times, and considering how many people had seen Leon and Charity purify Ranon and how many guards would've been involved in the sweeps, any hopes Leon had of keeping a low profile were dashed before they'd even had the time to form.

That being said, he'd probably go mad if he was stuck in here all day, no matter how good the wine was. Maybe he could slip out the back. The guard uniform he'd borrowed last night should be clean by now. It should be enough to get out of here. Perhaps even enough to get to the Citadel, assuming he could sneak in with some of the patrolling guards.

When he was there he could . . . what? Helping with the patrols would exhaust him. Helping with the council would drive him out of his mind. Even if he hid away somewhere, he could only do that for so long. Someone would find him, and he'd be dragged into helping with the defensive effort.

No. He was already too mixed in with everything that had happened. Anything more, and there'd be too many eyes on him when he needed to slip away. Maybe going to find the others would be best, after all. At least Kelan would be willing to get drunk with him.

The slow spinning cycle of his thoughts continued in that vein for a long time as he stared at the blank ceiling. The sounds outside grew louder. Too loud for this time of day. Gods, he hoped there weren't people outside waiting for him to make an appearance like he was some famous beauty or bard.

The sun inched its way across the ceiling, and he hadn't decided anything. He ought to get up. He ought to eat or drink something that wasn't wine or the bread he'd been picking at. He ought to do something, but right now everything felt like too much work.

The bottle was empty and sitting uneasily in his stomach when he realized he hadn't seen Jackie today. That meant someone—likely Aoife or Padraeg—had convinced her to leave him alone. The green chest he'd left outside his room when he'd poked his head out to get breakfast suggested Padraeg. Leon had seen one just like it in the corner of Padraeg's room years ago that he hadn't been allowed to touch. There was a note on top, but he hadn't been able to work up the energy to read it, nor did he care to look inside the chest.

He should find her. He'd promised to talk to her today, after all. It might even be easier to talk to her than it had been to talk to the others, since she didn't harbor the same level of resentment or expectations that they did. She might even forgive him for keeping the truth from her.

With a course set in mind, Leon pushed himself off his mattress. The world spun, graying at the edges, and he shook his head to clear his vision. He should stop by the kitchen to get something more substantial in his stomach first. Yes, now that he was up, that sounded like a splendid idea.

Leon tucked the mostly untouched loaf of bread under his arm and stumbled out his door, immediately ramming his foot into the chest outside. He let out a loud string of curses and made a rude gesture in its direction. Limping only a bit, he managed to reach the kitchen, which was blissfully empty, without further injuring himself and went back upstairs with a hunk of cheese, a bag of nuts, and three apples to supplement his loaf of bread. It was a lot, but this way he'd have something to share with Jackie.

Now he just had to find her, which was proving more difficult than he'd anticipated. Checking her room, which used to be his, yielded no results. Mildly perplexed, he pulled the door shut and realized for the first time that he had no idea what Jackie did during the day while she was here. Was she even at the manor? He'd assumed so, since she wasn't supposed to leave by herself, but he hadn't seen any of the servants since he emerged either. Maybe they'd gone to the market and taken her with them, or they'd taken her to one of the public shows that took over the public squares in the weeks before the harvest festival.

Or, perhaps, she'd been angrier than he'd thought. Maybe she'd left Quinn Manor with the others. Maybe the others had decided it wasn't safe to keep her around him anymore now that the truth was out. Maybe they'd never let him see her again.

No—Njeri wouldn't do that. She wouldn't be that cruel, not when Aoife and Padraeg both cared for Jackie. They would keep Jackie safe even if being around Leon was dangerous. Njeri would at least let him say goodbye.

His steps quickened until he was running. Juggling the food and his frantic thoughts, he tore downstairs. The dining hall was empty, as were the kitchen, the pantry, and the washroom. The sitting room, the front hall, and the drying room, even the hall to the servants' quarters—all as empty as the halls of Dhuitholm.

He called for her over and over again only to be greeted with the lingering ringing of his own voice through empty rooms and halls.

With the downstairs searched and Leon's thoughts racing like a thoroughbred, he turned to the upstairs. There wasn't much up there. Most of it was off limits to children—as he'd repeatedly been informed as a curious and bored teenager trying to get into the attic or Aoife's and Padraeg's rooms—but she could've snuck past him. Maybe she was upstairs looking for him the way he was down here looking for her.

It was a sound idea and plausible enough to calm Leon's panicked breathing. Upstairs he went, tracing his steps back. She wasn't in her room and wasn't waiting in his. She wasn't hiding in the linen closets or in the music room. She wasn't—she wasn't here. She'd left. Gods, he had to talk to her. He'd promised he'd talk to her. He was the reason the husks had targeted her, the reason she'd broken her leg; he had to apologize. Surely Njeri would allow that?

His breath came faster and faster, and his fingers clutched the food still in his arms. The world spun, and he wanted to vomit, and gods please let this be a dream, and—

And the door to Padraeg's study was cracked open. Leon's breath caught in his chest, and he found himself whispering prayers under his breath, offering words of worship to gods that had never answered him and promising sacrifices in exchange for their answers. To Absolution, he offered an honest conversation with those he'd lied to in exchange for Jackie's forgiveness. To Justice, a vow to be their hand for those too weak to defend themselves as penance for leaving her. To Kinship, a solemn oath that he'd rebuild the relationships he'd shattered if he regained Jackie's trust. Please, just let her be here.

Give him one chance to fix things before he had to leave Mezeldwelf forever.

The door opened easily and silently at his hand. The food dropped from Leon's nerveless fingers. He sucked in air like a drowning man breaking the surface of the ocean and let out a hollow laugh.

Jackie blinked up at him from an armchair she'd dragged close to the fire. "Leon?" she whispered, rubbing the sleep from her eyes. A thin book slid from her lap and tumbled to the ground. Her eyes widened, and a grin spread across her face. "Leon! You're finally up! I've been waiting for you all day. Papa Padraeg said he'd left you a message and you'd come find me when you got up." She eyed the food that now lay scattered over the study floor, and smiled. "Is that for me?"

Wordlessly, he nodded. She was still here. She didn't hate him. Gods, she looked happy to see him.

She uncurled from the armchair, galvanizing him into movement.

"Ah, sorry," he managed to say, dropping to his knees to gather the spilled food. "I didn't mean to drop it—"

Jackie snatched up one of the now-bruised apples before Leon could grab it. "Food is food," she said, shrugging. "A little dirt isn't gonna stop me from eating it."

Without his conscious permission, Leon let out a sharp laugh. "Is that so?"

Jackie nodded and went back to her armchair. She examined her prize and wiped it on her shirt before taking a large bite. "Yep," she said through her mouthful. "Besides, I'm pretty sure we could eat soup off this floor. This place is so clean that I haven't even seen any mice."

His laugh this time was more generous, albeit still weak. He gathered all the food in one arm and used the other to pull the

243

other armchair closer to the fire. There weren't any small tables or convenient stools to use as a table, and despite Jackie's wonder at the state of Quinn Manor, he'd rather not eat off the ground, so the other armchair would have to be their feasting table today.

He sat on the floor next to Jackie's armchair and broke the loaf of bread in two. Passing one half to Jackie, he attacked his portion with more enthusiasm than he'd shown it this morning.

"What were you reading?" he asked shakily between bites. "It looks . . . enthralling."

That wasn't why he was here, but now that she was in front of him, he was reluctant to bring up last night before she asked about it. She was happy to see him right now. Even if it was only because he had brought food, he didn't want to lose that feeling.

He'd need to talk about it before he left, but for now . . . where was the harm in waiting to see if she brought it up first?

Jackie scrunched her nose. "It's a rule book," she mumbled around her apple. "I asked Papa Padraeg to get it for me this morning. I wanted to—" Whatever she wanted was lost when her voice dropped to an unintelligible level.

"A rule book? For what?" Leon smiled softly before tossing a handful of nuts into his mouth. "Is Padraeg trying to teach you one of his strategy games? Those are rigged, you know."

Leon had played dozens of those games with Padraeg. He rarely understood the rules until the third round or so and lost more games than he won, but they had been a constant when he lived in Mezeldwelf.

Jackie swallowed and then took another quick bite. When she took a third without answering, Leon arched an eyebrow.

"There's not much of that apple left," he teased. "Did the servants leave before giving you breakfast?"

244

Jackie shook her head and then tossed the core into the fireplace. She considered the bread in her hand and took a large bite. "No. They gave me lots of food. I'm just—I'm kind of hungry, and anyway, they all went to see the guards about boring stuff, so it's been just me this morning. I tried to read that book, but it uses so many words I don't understand, and the writing is all weird."

"Oh? Maybe I can help." He reached for the book, which was still lying on the ground in front of Jackie's armchair, but she scooped it up before he could.

"No," she yelped. "It's fine. I'll ask Papa Padraeg to help when he gets back. He said he knew it really well and—"

"Jackie," Leon said, crossing his arms over his chest and leveling his best stern look at her. It was less effective than it ought to be, since he was still on the ground, but it did make Jackie look away. "Did Padraeg give you that book, or did you take it from somewhere?"

"He gave it to me," she mumbled. "You were sleeping, and I wanted to know . . ."

His heart sank. He craned his head to see the cover, and then his stomach followed his heart out his body and deep into the ground. He knew that book. He'd taken it from Dhuitholm before he ran, and he'd traced the owl embossed on the cover countless times. He'd reread it over and over again until Padraeg had to take it to get the binding repaired. Padraeg shouldn't have kept it. Up until last night, having it was treason under the terms of the Great Treaty.

"Why do you have that?" he asked in a hollow voice. His promises from earlier swirled in his mind. He'd wanted to talk to her, but with that book in her hands— "Why do you have a copy of *The Knights' Oath*?"

It was a fairy tale, a history lesson, and a stark reminder of the role the Knights Vigilant had played in the world.

The Knights' Oath was as much an ancient story about the Knights Vigilant as it was a breakdown of their code. The first story about them, actually. About how they'd sworn themselves to a minor aspect of Vigilance in exchange for the ability to protect the world from an unspeakable evil. On the last page was the oath they swore to their god, the oath he'd imprinted on his soul the day Dhuitholm fell.

It was an excellent story, but a story nonetheless.

Jackie fidgeted with the hem of her shirt. "I wanted to know about you," she mumbled. "But Papa Padraeg said I should let you sleep. He sent the others away this morning because they wanted to talk to you again, but he let me stay, as long as I waited to find you until you woke up." She shrunk into her chair, the book still clutched to her chest. "When I asked him for stories about your—about the Knights Vigilant, he gave me this. It was in a chest he left in front of your room."

Of course he had. Leon inhaled through his nose and let it out again, repeating the exercise several times.

"Are you mad at me?" she whispered. "I didn't mean to make you mad, but I thought that I could help you if I knew what you promised the Watchful Peace. I've got gray eyes like you, and you said that meant they had plans for me."

No. No, no, no, no. "That's not—" He hadn't meant it like that. It wasn't even how things worked, but Jackie looked so happy to think that she was meant for this. Like having to spend the rest of her life running and living with the ghosts of long-dead knights chasing after her was something to aspire to. "You could've asked me."

She shrugged but relaxed a bit when he made no move to take the book from her. "You were sleeping." She ducked her head, and a blush spread across her cheeks and the tips of her ears. "And I heard all of you fighting last night, even if I pretended to be sleeping. I know you're the last Knight Vigilant, which is why you don't want to fight the Templesbane, so I decided to help you. I'm going to be your squire, and then we can fight them together!"

Fuck.

"You want to help me?" he echoed. "To be my—" He couldn't even say it.

She nodded.

Gods damn it. "That's not—I can't have a squire." He stopped and took a deep breath. Stumbling over this wouldn't help Jackie understand why it was a terrible idea to try to help him or stay at his side now that his secret was out in the world.

All that aside, he couldn't take a squire. Even if he wanted to drag her into the battlefield that his life was about to become, it wasn't possible. He couldn't give the oaths.

"Do you know why I'm the last Knight Vigilant?" he said in a low voice. "Why I can't anoint Padraeg or Kelan or Shea so we can all go fight the Templesbane together?"

Jackie shook her head. She leaned forward, a look in her eyes that was half interest and half apprehension.

"It's because it's impossible," he said hollowly. "The Knights Vigilant—we're different from other godsworn. Most chivalric orders allow any member to knight someone they deem worthy or who has gone through the proper training, but we can't. It takes more than the ability to swing a weapon or sing a song to join us. We need to—" He let out a ragged sigh. "It's hard to explain. There are tools and potions I'd need to anoint a new knight. All of those were lost when Dhuitholm fell."

"Make new ones, then," Jackie said. Snorting, she crossed her arms and slumped into her chair. "The Watchful Peace is still alive. Otherwise your eyes wouldn't still be gray and you wouldn't have your god's gifts. I'm sure they don't care that you don't know the right words, especially not if making new ones means fighting off the Templesbane."

If only it were that easy. But life had never been easy, not for Jackie, not for Leon, and not for anyone with the misfortune to live in this time. They didn't have the luxury of time, or wisdom, or innocence.

"Do you know why we're called the Knights Vigilant?"

It was cruel to rob her of her heroes like this, but it needed to be done. Right now, Jackie viewed the knights through the eyes of a child, seeing only the glory and the strength legends had ascribed to them. Stories like *The Knights' Oath* painted a pretty picture about the first knights that covered up the blood they'd shed and everything they'd lost to get there. Too many people had forgotten how they began or hidden it away because it was inconvenient.

He took a deep breath and set his hands on his knees when she shook her head. "It's—it starts at the beginning, as most stories do."

Delke had been the first one to tell him the true story of the Knights Vigilant, and she'd started it like this. Even then, only scholars of ancient history, gods, and the Knights Vigilant themselves had known the truth. He'd been about Jackie's age then, and even now the truth sat uneasily upon his heart. There was a reason the world had done its best to forget what happened.

"Do you know why the Knights Vigilant honor the Watchful Peace and not, say, Vigilance itself?"

Jackie snorted and rolled her eyes. "Duh, Vigilance is gone." She pulled a bag of dried berries out of her pocket and popped a handful into her mouth. "The Templesbane consumed them ages ago, and there's nothing left."

Leon nodded. One hand curled in the fabric of his trousers, and he forced it flat before the fabric tore. "Yes. Many scholars believe that Vigilance was the first god the Templesbane consumed, and no one, not even the first Vigilant General—who many consider the most powerful of our order—was able to restore them." He paused and his stomach swirled. Gods, he should've had something more to eat. "But the knights knew that the truth was more complicated than that. Vigilance isn't gone, even if we follow the Watchful Peace now. They weren't even entirely consumed. In fact, Vigilance was the last—and first—victim of the beings who became the Templesbane."

Jackie stopped chewing. "Wait, really?" she asked, bits of berries spewing everywhere. She swallowed and wiped her mouth before speaking again. "But then why don't they—and what does this have to do with anything?"

Leon continued like she hadn't spoken, staring at the back of Jackie's armchair in lieu of looking at her. It was easier that way.

"The Knights Vigilant were an ancient and honorable order. The only order, in fact, that survived the first war with the Templesbane." The fire crackled and popped, casting ash and dust onto the hearth in front of it. Padraeg used the same wood Delke had favored, a pine that burned brightly and let off a pleasing smell. The smell filled Leon's nostrils, casting him back to the first time he'd heard this story. "Without them," he said in a low voice, "Hyderia would've been lost to the Templesbane, and the world would've crumbled in the aftermath."

The Knights Vigilant had hidden in their temple as the other knights and armies fought and fell against an evil no one understood. They'd stayed away from the battles and watched as countless orders full of soldiers they'd trained died. The first wave of warriors went for glory, the second for their gods, and any who lived through the first two attacks fought for the lands they called home and the souls struggling to survive in a land that had gone fallow.

Jackie rolled her eyes. "I know," she said, crossing her arms and pouting. "I already read a lot of the book even if I didn't know all the words. Next you're gonna say that the Watchful Peace told the knights to wait until the Templesbane came to their temple so they could trap them. I already know that."

Leon let out a huff of air. "Then you should listen well, because almost everything in that book is a lie."

Not a lie. The world's attempt to forget what its protection cost.

Jackie's jaw dropped. "No way!" she yelled. "Padraeg gave that to me, and—and he said it was yours." Her mouth closed with a snap. Shaking her head, she clutched the book close to her chest. "You're making fun of me. You wouldn't keep this around if it was a lie."

"No." He closed his eyes and took a deep breath before opening them again. His hands were shaking, and he closed them into fists. "The Knights Vigilant weren't brave soldiers waiting for the right time to strike. They weren't listening to the sage advice of a god, they were—they were cowards."

When the first rumors came from the kingdom that would become the Fallow Lands about a darkness that consumed gods, land, and people alike, the old knights kept watch. When it escaped past the World's Bones Mountains and the Lyrien River that had protected that land for generations, they'd been the only ones who hadn't sent any troops to fight against it. God after god fell to the appetites of the beings that became the Templesbane. Even the great Sea ceded some of their territory

250

to those voracious appetites. When priests, kings, and generals came begging for whatever help they could offer, the knights of old refused. That wasn't their purpose, they claimed. They were teachers and guardians, not warriors.

"The knights of old didn't yet worship the Watchful Peace. That came later, toward the end of the first war with the Templesbane." He swallowed and took a deep breath. Gods, he wished he had water. Or better yet, ale. Even after such a short time, his head was already clearing of this morning's wine. "The old knights were teachers and priests, followers of Vigilance. They trained the scions of a hundred orders and had their pick of students to carry on their traditions. Vigilance themself took human form and worked among them, passing on their knowledge and gifts to worthy students."

Delke had paused here, filling the gap with ideas, techniques, and traditions the old Knights Vigilant had learned at Vigilance's knee. History was best taught when linked with its impacts on the present, or so she liked to say.

But he wasn't Delke, and Jackie wasn't a squire, so he pressed on.

"However, Vigilance was as dangerous to their followers as they were to their enemies. After all, when one searches for danger for long enough, soon that's all they can see." Some days, it felt like that was all Leon saw. That was when he found as many wineskins as he could carry and drank until he couldn't stand, far from everyone else. "So it was for two siblings who came to the old knights for training and protection."

Jackie's eyes widened. "The Brother and the Sister? But, they're—"

"Gods? No. Something close, but they used to be human, or so the legend goes." He let out a harsh laugh. He'd had a similar reaction when Delke had reached this part of the story. It didn't make sense that humans would want to destroy the gods. If one wished to take power from them, all they had to do was withhold worship. Killing them, consuming them, was more personal than that, something only kin could do. "They weren't the first students to fall, but none had advanced so quickly through their training as they had. They should've been strong enough to withstand Vigilance's darker aspects."

Paranoia, Panic, and Fear were formidable when working alone. Together, they could turn even a hardened commander into a gibbering wreck who saw her death in every stranger and harsh word or rip every ounce of kindness from a soldier's heart. When a student gave in to them, they made the darker aspects stronger, a plague that infected everyone around them.

"According to legend, Vigilance asked the man who became the Brother and the woman who became the Sister to follow them out to a hidden cave in the World's Bones Mountains, where Vigilance promised to help purge the influence of their darker aspects from the siblings." He half expected the shadows and the smoke to take shape, for the Knights Beyond to reveal themselves now to fill in anything Leon might have forgotten. He felt oddly bereft when nothing more came of the smoke besides marks on the chimney. "Vigilance promised to return in three days' time to assist the old knights with researching how their darker aspects had infected the siblings, to make preparations so it could never happen again."

"Did it work?" Jackie asked, leaning forward in anticipation. Then she frowned and shook her head. "No, it couldn't have. Otherwise the husks wouldn't be here."

He shrugged. "We don't know what happened. Vigilance hasn't been seen on this plane or the divine one since, even though the gods know they still live. What we do know, however, is that Vigilance never returned to their temple, and then, minor gods started disappearing, followed by small farms and villages. With each passing year, more vanished, and the land they lived on went fallow. The knights had, by then, realized that something was wrong with Vigilance. They no longer answered prayers or summons. Their students abandoned them as many believed their god had, for what use is a temple or a priesthood without a god?"

"But Vigilance didn't abandon them," Jackie protested. She let out a harsh huff of air and waved a hand as if that would make Leon unspeak his words. "The knights still had their gifts. It's why they could defeat the Templesbane."

"Hush," Leon gently admonished, the way Delke had. "Otherwise we'll be here forever." She wasn't wrong, though. Even through that war, the knights never lost their gifts. Vigilance had still touched them.

Shaking his head to drive the distraction away, Leon continued. "The knights wished to help, but before they could, they received visitors at their temple, the first in years."

Jackie made a sound like she wanted to interrupt, but a stern look put a stop to that.

"Their lost students had returned, and they carried with them fragments of Vigilance, broken down and buried deep within themselves, twisted through the gifts Vigilance had given them." His heart ached, screaming with a pain that wasn't his own, like the agony of the ancient knights that witnessed their god brought low still resided in his soul today. "They said they were Vigilance given new form, that they would destroy all that was wrong with this world and reshape it without the stain of the gods and their impact on humanity. When the knights refused to help them, the Brother and the Sister used their stolen power to bind the knights to their temple on pain of a fate far worse than death. To save themselves and any chance they had of recovering Vigilance, the knights were forced to watch the slow death of the world."

He paused. The fire crackled and popped, and he and Jackie stared at each other without blinking.

"That was how things stood until the Watchful Peace came to the knights. They were a minor aspect, a child almost, of Vigilance and Duty. They knew what had been done to Vigilance and despised it. Yet, like all gods, there was little they could do on their own. Without prayer, without followers, they were as helpless as the knights in the face of the siblings' wrath. Despite knowing this, they came to the knights with a plan. A way to break Vigilance's hold on their order and free the shattered god. The knights, desperate for salvation, agreed."

This was the part the world tried to forget. More than the truth that the Templesbane had once followed Vigilance, more than how the knights had stayed away while the Templesbane slaughtered the gods, the world wished to forget that knights had gained the power to defeat the Templesbane by becoming like them.

By consuming a god.

"The Watchful Peace broke themself into pieces," he said, his voice shaking and sharp, "and the knights took those pieces into themselves. So it was that the knights of Vigilance became the Knights Vigilant and gained the power to fight the beings that destroyed their old master."

That was why no Knight Vigilant could leave their order and why no god would allow one of their followers to join the order. No god could accept the allegiance of another, and they recognized the scraps of their kin within each Knight Vigilant.

"Do you understand now?" he asked bitterly. "There can be no new knights without the Watchful Peace there to join with them. They are bound to the Knights Vigilant, and we are bound to them until the original contract is fulfilled. Until Vigilance is freed or given over to Death's sentinels."

The Templesbane had known the instant the Knights Vigilant left their temple. The Brother and the Sister had attacked a thousand times, separately and together, and were driven back each time by the sheer force of the power that the Watchful Peace had given the knights. The first Vigilant General had used it to drive the Templesbane back, to purify the lands and reclaim the gods. The ones that followed used it to keep the Templesbane contained as much as they were able while searching for any sign of Vigilance. Leon—the last, lost, fallen knight that he was—used it to stay away from the Templesbane.

Jackie stared at Leon, tears glimmering in her eyes, and he stared at her. Her limbs trembled and shook, but she never looked away.

Gods willing, this would be enough. She would understand why she couldn't follow Leon, why it was safer to follow the others.

"That's one hell of a story." The voice, as familiar to Leon as his own, came from behind him.

A chill ran down Leon's spine, and he pushed himself to his feet. His legs were numb, but he wasn't going to have this conversation sitting down.

"Shea. Dare I ask why you're here? Last time I saw you, I'm pretty sure you'd have taken a knife to me if you saw an opportunity."

Jackie shoved past him and threw herself at Shea, wrapping her arms around his waist much like a spider clinging to its web. "You're here! Leon's saying stupid stuff. You should tell him he's wrong."

Shea shrugged and hugged Jackie back. His long, dark hair, normally tied back like anyone with respect for the forge would have it, had long since escaped its tie and hung loose around his shoulders. He raised his head and nodded at Leon. "Njeri sent me."

"Threatened to kick your ass, did she?" Leon asked, walking over to Padraeg's desk. It was a little short for him to lean on, but it was better than continuing this conversation on the ground or standing straight, which might very well send him back to the ground.

"A bit." He let out a harsh laugh as he detached himself from Jackie, who satisfied herself by clinging to his cloak, and leaned on the doorframe. "A lot, actually. Once I sobered up, she got as many of us together as she could and explained things. Then we helped the guard and your father with searching the sewers for more husks. Most of the city is currently tearing down walls in their basements to see if any of them escaped, which your father was rather annoyed about, to be honest, and the folks that aren't doing that are currently camped outside the Citadel, waiting for details of the evacuation, or this house, hoping to get a glimpse of you."

Leon snorted and crossed his arms. "Sounds like you had a busy day, then. What does Njeri want?" He kept his voice even and measured. It did nothing to slow his heart rate, but at least it made him look calm. Njeri had sent Shea instead of coming herself, which sent a variety of mixed messages Leon wasn't sure how to decipher. Either she was still angry at him, or she was unable to pull herself away from her work and Shea was the only one available. Both answers sat poorly with Leon.

"She wants to ask you how you planned on separating from the Band." His lips curled down, although Leon couldn't tell if it was from disappointment or disgust. "Your contract isn't up for another year, but she's willing to view this as a mitigating circumstance. She even offered to pay you your full cut of this job."

A sharp pain arched through Leon's chest, and he inhaled. "I see." So she was still angry with him. Ten years together meant little when it came out that one party had been lying to the other the entire time. It was understandable, but it hurt all the same. "She couldn't come herself?"

"No. The Band has been conscripted into the defensive effort. She's too busy to come drag you out of your—"

A familiar voice cut him off, its echoes nearly shaking the ceiling beams.

"Leon! Leon, where are you?" Aoife's voice bordered on frantic, a far cry from the orderly figure she tried to present herself as before others. "Leon, answer me, gods damn it."

"I'm in the study," Leon shouted back, gathering up the food and depositing it on Padraeg's desk. Aoife would kill him if there were stains.

Just in time too, because no sooner had the last scrap of bread been set down than Aoife charged into the study, shoving past Shea like he wasn't even there.

"Oh good, you're still here." She let out a relieved sigh, then strode across the study, grabbed Leon by the collar, and hauled him off the desk. "Come on, we need you back at the Citadel. We—" She let out a sharp gasp when she saw Jackie. "Oh sweetheart, what are you still doing here? The children are supposed to go to the temples to be evacuated, it's not safe."

"What are you talking about?" Jackie asked, clinging even tighter to Shea. "I've been here all day."

Aoife blanched as several emotions crossed her face simultaneously. Fear, grief, despair, and anger all fought for dominance, but nothing won. Finally, she dropped her grip on Leon and wrapped her arms around herself.

"It's the Sister," she whispered, glancing out the window toward the harbor like that would summon them. "A group of hunters just came in, raving about an army to the west. We only have a few days before they arrive."

Chapter 15
Blades Broken

Leon sprinted toward the Citadel, his heart pounding in his ears. Aoife ran alongside him, taking two steps for every one of his but still keeping pace. He'd run out of the manor so fast he'd barely bothered to grab his boots, let alone his cloak or a hood. Periodic cheers greeted him as he passed and people figured out who the gray-eyed giant running beside Prince Quinn was. Thankfully though, no one tried to stop them.

The city was just as busy as it had been before the husks were discovered, but the energy was directed in a different direction. Toward escape instead of deterrence. Somehow, the Sister had managed to hide an entire army marching out of Dhuitholm, and the knowledge must have swept through the city like a tidal wave. According to Aoife, not even Ranon knew how the Sister had kept the march a secret until now. It made Leon grind his teeth, and he ached to help the preparations, but he didn't dare stop moving to consider it.

They should've had more time. Yes, the treaty was broken, but they'd caught the husks in the city off guard and eradicated them before they could finish the tunnels that would've let the husk army flood into the city. The harvest festival wasn't for another week—that was the earliest the husks would've arrived in a normal year. But no, the evacuations that were supposed to take place over a week now had to be crammed into two days.

"Go see Padraeg," Aoife ordered when they passed through the Citadel gates. She gasped for each breath but never broke stride. It was two miles from Quinn Manor to the Citadel, and she'd spent more time behind a desk than she'd spent helping at her warehouses since she became a merchant prince. "He's conscripted all the mercenary guilds in the city, and he's speaking with the captains. When you're done there, find the princes. We'll have things for you to do after Padraeg's done."

"Understood." He picked up his pace, leaving Aoife behind him, and dodged around the frantic guards racing from one place to another.

The Citadel halls were packed, but not with petitioners or merchants seeking to meet with the princes. No, what looked like the entire guard, most of the reserves, and a good portion of the mercenaries in the city were running around, shouting at the top of their lungs and getting in Leon's way. He slowed once inside. He should've asked Aoife where Padraeg was before they'd parted, but she was already long gone.

It took almost as long for Leon to find someone who'd stop to talk to him as it did to get to the Citadel in the first place, and even then, it was a struggle to find someone who knew the information he needed. None of the mercenaries cared, none of the reserves in ill-fitting uniforms and awkwardly holding their weapons knew, and the guards were all busy directing the others. It wasn't until Leon snagged a guard-lieutenant who recognized him that he was directed toward the feasting hall in the rear of the Citadel.

Muttering unkind things toward Chaos and Panic, Leon shoved his way past the crowds and finally reached the feasting hall. Padraeg's voice thundered into the foyer outside, underwritten by the voices of those he was speaking with. Leon entered the hall to see Padraeg standing behind the head table, a large crowd of mercenaries in eclectic dress around him. There were Faltens in heavy winter furs, Sihianese in battered silks and scaled armor, Alkans both bare-chested and in thick plate, and

Hyderians who wore the gamut. Njeri stood right next to Padraeg.

Leon involuntarily let out a quiet curse when he saw her. Her mouth was drawn tight, and she had a white-knuckled grip on her sword. Gods, had she even slept or taken the time to eat? Leon was almost certain she'd been wearing the same thing when Mesley's servants found them.

Padraeg's booming voice soon drew Leon's attention back where it needed to be, and he crept forward, joining with the crowd.

"The Great Company and the Company of the Rose will assist the priests with dismantling and desanctifying the temples. The Children of Alke, the Band of Broken Blades, and Cearl's Roustabouts will assist with unloading anything that isn't provisions from every ship in the port, while the Gods' Own will assist a squad of the city guard with evacuating the towns around Mezeldwelf. The villages and farms between us and Dhuitholm will be prioritized. If there is any evidence of husk activity, we are to assume the entire village has fallen and move on."

He continued without pausing for breath as Leon worked his way forward. The more Padraeg said, the more Leon's stomach sank. Every ship in the harbor and any that would come in were to be loaded with children, priests with their altars, and those too sick to fight or flee on foot, and taken to Falte in the northeast. Wagons, carts, carriages, and all animals that could be hitched to the above had been requisitioned to carry people and provisions the same way. Most of the mercenary companies would be sent with those traveling on land, to defend them until they reached Falte. It'd be a hard journey on foot with winter coming on, and they'd have to cross the Castorious Mountains to even get into Falte. For Padraeg to be considering all this . . .

He wasn't planning for an invasion, and he didn't expect to return. He expected the Sister to take the city. This wasn't about defending Mezeldwelf. It was about making things as difficult as possible for their attackers for as long as possible. Any who stayed behind would fight and would likely die in defense of the city. They wouldn't be able to go over land, and even if, by some miracle, the winds were favorable, the seas were calm, and the ships were able to return, they would have to contend with the husks while trying to escape. They would need to watch Mezeldwelf fall while they retreated.

The world fell away under Leon's feet, and he sucked in a ragged breath. This wasn't right. If they'd had the full week or more ships or more gods, maybe they could've managed it, but instead, no matter how they put it, the city would fall, and its defenders would have to choose between letting the Sister have it and destroying it themselves.

"Sir Leon—" Padraeg's voice, suddenly directed at him, had Leon's head snapping up so fast his neck cracked. "I need you to work with the guard. Go into each of the tunnels and search for any husks that may have escaped or any weak point we might have missed. We can't afford to lose you to the Sister, so we'll keep a ship back for you that you will take when the preparations are complete." His eyes drilled into Leon's, less to impress importance and more to make sure Leon knew this wasn't something he could argue against. "If the worst comes to worst, you'll be given the fastest horse in the city and a group of bodyguards that will escort you to the Castorious Mountains."

A part of Leon wanted to protest, but he bit it back down. Now was not the time to argue. He'd get out of the city no matter what happened. No matter how the thought of leaving it to burn under the Sister made his soul scream. No matter how the Sister would chase the refugees until the Castorious Mountains and beyond if it meant catching him.

Without Leon, the only hope the refugees had was the grace of the Falten jarls and the slim protection offered by the fjords and seas. The only hope left for Hyderia was if Leon escaped, and to do that, he'd need to doom the city that had taken him in.

Gods damn it all.

"Understood." He met Padraeg's harsh glare with one that matched it. "What next?"

***

"Leon, wait up!" Njeri's voice boomed over that of the other mercenaries as the crowd shuffled out of the hall, Leon and Padraeg caught up somewhere in the middle of all that. "I need to talk to you."

Padraeg had kept them another hour, detailing the finer points of where Leon would strike, what exactly the mercenaries were expected to do, and what they would get in return. Assuming they got the refugees to Falte, the mercenaries would be given decent pay for this involuntary job. Unlike them, Leon wouldn't have a nice sack of gold waiting for him. If he was lucky, he'd escape his minders without too much trouble and disappear into the Castorious Mountains before the Protectors got their claws into him.

Njeri called again, and Leon decided he couldn't pretend he hadn't heard her. Slowing, he gestured for Padraeg to go on without him. They were both supposed to meet with the merchant princes before heading out with the guard, and Padraeg would catch Leon up on anything he missed.

Padraeg made an understanding face and disappeared into the crowd.

Sighing, Leon stepped to the side of the hall. He couldn't avoid Njeri forever, and he wasn't sure he wanted to. Before they separated, they needed to finish their talk and air out the last of the dirty laundry Leon had kept hidden away. Once the Band left the city, it was highly likely that they would never see each other again.

"Thank the gods," Njeri muttered, sliding to a stop by Leon, "I was hoping I'd see you again before we left, but—well, you know."

Leon snorted. He did, in fact, know how things had been going. Shrugging, he cast his eye onto the dwindling crowd so he didn't have to look at Njeri. "Aren't you supposed to be helping with the wharf evacuations?"

She let out a huff of air that wasn't a laugh and wasn't a sigh. "We are. And when all that's done, we've been assigned a collection of priests to escort to Falte. The jarls aren't as religious as the princes, but even they suffer when the gods are consumed."

Leon hummed. The crowds had thinned to the point that calling the few stragglers left a crowd was disingenuous. In another minute, even they were gone, and Leon and Njeri were left alone.

"Are you feeling better?" she asked, nudging Leon with her elbow. "Shea wasn't too rough on you, was he? I wasn't sure what to think when he volunteered to find you, but everyone else was so busy—"

"He was fine." Sighing, Leon finally turned back to Njeri. "He said you had questions about my contract. I suppose we ought to deal with that. This will probably be the last time we speak." She flinched, and Leon nearly regretted his words. Nearly. It was time they faced the truth of the situation. "If it's fine by you, I want to end my contract. I'll speak with Aoife, get an advancement on my pay. That should be enough to support me while I'm on the run."

Njeri nodded silently, her bright eyes darkening. "I see," she said quietly. "And there's no changing your mind?"

"Change my—" Leon gaped. He pulled himself straight and narrowly avoided slamming his head on a support beam in his rush to do so. "You can't be serious," he sputtered. "What's there to change? Padraeg and my own fucking conscience made it clear that I don't have a choice in what I do or where I go until the Sister is on the fucking city threshold. Even then, my options are to flee by sea or flee by land. You and the Band will be long gone by then, and even the strongest winds won't bring you back in time to save the city."

She didn't expect him to stay with the Band, did she? To sneak out like he had twenty years ago, abandoning a city that needed him? He might be a coward who planned on running as soon as he left, but he wouldn't leave Mezeldwelf like that. He didn't want his last memories of Padraeg, Aoife, and this city to be like his last memories of Delke, Mael, and Dhuitholm. He was better than that. He'd help as much as he could, and then he'd get out of here long before the husks attacked.

Njeri glared at him. "Everyone has a choice," she said, her calm tone a remarkable contrast to the anger in her eyes. "Even you. And especially the Band."

He crossed his arms and met her glare with one of his own. "And what, pray tell, are my choices?" he asked, a sharp growl underlining his words. He leaned down, covering her in his shadow. "What exactly am I supposed to do that isn't follow the path Padraeg laid out for me?" His voice dropped into a harsh whisper. "He's done everything he can to guarantee I have an escape route after all this is done. He's even convinced the princes to let me off the ship before we reach Falte. I can't—I can't abandon that, even if it would give me a day or two head start on everyone that's going to want me as their martyr."

Njeri's fist slammed into his shoulder. "If you'd let me speak," she snapped, baring her teeth like a stray dog, "then I'd tell you that you don't have to run. The Band, we're—"

"You're what? Joining the Protectors once you get to Falte?" He scoffed, and his hands curled into fists. "What life would that be? I may as well face off against the Sister here. At least then I know I'd die doing something that makes sense instead of trying to reclaim a ruin."

It was hollow. So incredibly hollow. His choices dwindled with each passing moment. Once Mezeldwelf fell, his options would be slim to none. The small villages and towns that dotted the plains would empty, their inhabitants fleeing the borderlands as fast as they could. The ones that stayed would hear of him and come to hate him in time. Every pseudonym he'd ever used, every contact he'd built over the years would be exposed. Time, the Templesbane, and the Protectors would whittle him down until the only choice he had was how many husks he'd take out with him when he went.

Njeri knew it. He knew it. Padraeg, Aoife, and anyone with any godsdamned sense in their heads knew it. Leon's time was running out, and by the gods, he'd claw, scratch, and bite for every second he could.

Leon heaved for air, the last echoes of his outburst still fading down the hall, and Njeri—she just looked at him. The anger and the disappointment faded away, and Leon wanted to scream. Why wouldn't she go? Now was the time to leave the conversation while she still had some fond feelings toward Leon and before he could sour every positive moment they'd spent together. Before she realized what a selfish coward he was.

She needed to go because Leon was going to hold on to every moment with her and the Band until the day he died. Every job, every argument, every dinner, every prank. If she didn't leave and take any chance Leon had of staying with the Band with her, then Leon would never have the strength to leave her side.

Her mouth narrowed into a grim line, and Leon steeled himself for her sharp goodbye. A bitter ending was better than nothing at all.

"Follow me," she said darkly, pushing past Leon. She marched down the hall like she expected Leon to be at her heel.

The worst thing about it was that she wasn't wrong.

"Where, exactly, are we going?" he argued, matching her step for step. "I'm supposed to be in a meeting with the merchant princes, in case you forgot."

"Shut up," Njeri snapped. "We're going to speak with the others. Bettany is updating the Band's records. If you're set on running for the rest of your life, we'll need to strike you from them."

Despite it being exactly what Leon wanted, it tore his heart in two. A mercenary lived and died by their reputation, which was backed up by the records each company kept. If Njeri had let him dissolve his contract or he'd died, they'd have noted his last date of service and left it at that. Striking him from the records was as good as saying they no longer recognized his service with them. It would be like the past ten years hadn't happened at all. He ducked his head, wishing he'd thought to say more than a quick farewell to Jackie before he left Quinn Manor.

Gods, he wanted a drink.

Njeri led him away from the feasting hall and the council chamber. The halls still bustled with guards, mercenaries, and servants, but even those who recognized Leon took one look at Njeri and thought better of speaking with him.

Finally, they came to one of the winter training rooms, the one closest to the private cells.

"In," Njeri said shortly, pulling the door open. She grabbed his arm and pushed him in like his legs weren't already headed that direction. At another time and in another place, he'd have made a joke about that. "Now."

Once Leon was through, the room fell silent. Two hundred mercenaries watched Leon with something close to awe. Njeri pulled the door closed behind them.

"Now," she said, loud enough that there was no doubt the others heard it, "Bettany's over there. We'll discuss your final pay, strike you from the records, and then you can be on your way."

It took a tremendous force of will to not shrink under the intense scrutiny. "Here?" he asked quietly. "Can't we do this somewhere else? Somewhere less . . . crowded?"

Njeri shook her head harshly. "No. Bettany's busy enough updating the records. I won't put more on her plate just because you don't want to deal with people."

Leon's complaints died in his throat. He nodded, set his shoulders, and followed Njeri to the back of the room, where Bettany had set up court with a thick book and two stacks of paper. The crowd around her cleared as they approached. Leon kept his eyes on Njeri, unwilling to risk meeting the eyes of any of his soon-to-be former comrades.

"If you've made your decision, put your paperwork in the appropriate file," Bettany said without looking up from the book. "I'll update the records appropriately." Her quill scratched loudly over the paper, and Leon doubted she'd even realized everyone else had stopped talking.

"He's not here about that," Njeri snapped. "Leon's decided to leave us. He doesn't anticipate he'll be able to assist with the refugees either. As his actions are unbefitting a member of the

Band of Broken Blades, we've decided to strike him from the records. He'll receive his final pay, and then we'll part ways."

We.

As if Leon had any part in deciding to strike his service from the records. As if there was any other choice for him.

Bettany's quill stopped, and she raised her eyes to meet Njeri's for a handful of seconds. Then they dropped back down to her work, and her quill resumed its rapid journey over the paper. "I see." For all the emotion she showed about it, she might as well have been discussing the next cooking rotation. "I assume this is a permanent estrangement, then?"

"Yes," Leon and Njeri said simultaneously. They exchanged a glance, and the anger sharpening her glare until it felt like a knife driven into his chest forced him to look away again.

His throat suddenly felt dryer than an Alkan desert. "Yes," he repeated, swallowing with some difficulty. "I don't anticipate I'll return."

He couldn't. Once the Band was gone, that was it. He'd be left in Mezeldwelf, and then he'd spend the rest of his short life running. Staying close to them would only bring the husks down on them.

Bettany hummed and made a note. "Right. I'll make some calculations for your final pay. I'll send you a messenger with your money when I'm done." She gestured for Leon and Njeri to move, and Leon deflated. "Now go somewhere else, please. You're not the only one with things to do before the evacuations start."

That was it? Leon had seen more ceremony from Bettany while burying a summer soldier or saying goodbye to the ones that made it to fall.

"Go," Bettany repeated. "I'm sure the princes are waiting for you. I've got things to do. I've added you to the list."

Njeri stared at him, eyes lit up with something that couldn't be triumph. She wasn't that cruel. She wasn't.

That look faded and fell as she and Leon stared at each other. The triumph became confusion and then horror. Leon didn't care to figure out why. It wasn't his business anymore.

He turned. He left. He did not run out of that room, even with the heavy eyes of warriors he'd fought alongside for years pressing down on him like a millstone around his neck. He walked like a great thunderstorm followed in his tracks, out into the hall, and left that chapter of his life behind.

Chapter 16
Bonds Reforged

He wasn't sure how long he'd been walking. The walls and people all looked the same, and no one tried to stop him.

It shouldn't have been that easy to walk away. Ten years of his life, gone. Reduced to little more than scribbles crossed out among the deeds of other fighters and a bag of gold that he wouldn't be able to spend before he died. Even though it was what Leon had wanted to happen, it still hurt.

So he walked. Past rooms, up stairs, and away from the Band. Each step felt lighter than the one before, lighter and disconnected from what was happening around him. His chest ached, and he realized belatedly that his breathing didn't seem to be helping, but he didn't dare stop moving.

His world, the one he'd worked so hard to build, had come crashing down overnight. His relationship with everyone in the Band—except perhaps Kelan—was destroyed. Shea hated him for hiding, Njeri for lying, and Jackie would hate him for running. Padraeg and Aoife might try to hide it, but Leon knew they were disappointed in him too. Padraeg had always wanted to see Leon take his place in the world as a Knight Vigilant, for him to stop running and hiding, and this might actually be enough to convince him that Leon would never be able to do that. He'd give up on Leon, too, and that'd be the end of it.

It wasn't until his legs were screaming and he realized that he hadn't seen anyone in a while that he finally stopped. He looked around, his gaze sliding over the familiar stained glass, patterned tile, and colorful tapestries. Somehow, he'd wandered all the way up from the winter training halls to the guard offices. Specifically, right to Padraeg's office.

An office which should be empty. Padraeg was managing the evacuation, and everyone else who worked in this area was off helping with that. Even if they weren't, they knew better than to go inside without permission, something Padraeg had always promised Leon. It'd be safe and quiet, and he'd be able to catch his breath before he faced others again.

Before he could think better of it, Leon pushed the door open and darted inside. When it clicked shut behind him, he let out a shaky breath and leaned against it, eyes closed.

"Aren't you supposed to be helping Papa Padraeg and Aunt Aoife?" Somehow, Jackie's presence wasn't as much of a surprise as it should have been. She'd always had a knack for being where Leon least expected her.

"Aren't you supposed to be at the temples with the other children?" he shot back, too drained to do more than open his eyes.

Jackie shrugged. "The manor was boring, since everyone was gone, so I decided to come find you all." Padraeg's chair dwarfed her small frame, casting shadows in the late afternoon light that almost looked like the man himself was looming behind her. A large bag of nuts and *The Knights' Oath* lay in front of her, blocking out the paperwork Padraeg had been working on before that fateful council meeting. "One of the guards found me and said I should wait in Papa Padraeg's office for him to get done with his meetings."

Letting out a hollow laugh, Leon sank to the floor. Of course they would. People paid attention to random children that appeared in the homes of merchant princes, especially when they were attached to the last Knight Vigilant. "I see." *The Knights'*

Oath taunted him from its spot on the desk. "Are you still reading that?"

Jackie nodded. "It's a good story. Better than the one *you* told me." Her nose scrunched up, and she stuck out her tongue. "I asked the guard who took me here, and they said they'd never heard it that way."

Of course not. Delke always said people didn't like remembering what actually happened. Better to imagine the knights of old as divine warriors blessed by the gods than the humans they'd actually been. Better to forget the cost of their victory than remember how closely they walked the line of becoming the exact thing they fought against.

"I'm not surprised," he said finally. "Most of the people that knew the real story died in Dhuitholm." The stone was cold underneath him as he stretched out on the ground, reveling in the relative silence and the lack of eyes judging his every movement.

For a blissful few minutes, the only sound in the office was that of Jackie chewing nuts and flipping pages. Then Jackie spoke again. "Are you going to stay with the Band?"

Gods.

"No," he said, letting out a heavy sigh. "Njeri and I decided it would be better if we went our separate ways." A stabbing pain arched through his chest, and his throat tightened around the lump that had lodged there. "It's not safe for me to stay with them."

"Oh," Jackie whispered. Then, "You're going to leave?"

"Yes." He didn't want to. He had to. It was the only way to keep the Band safe. The Sister would never stop hunting him, especially now that he'd proved he could purify things. Staying would make things worse.

"Oh," she repeated, voice wavering. She sniffled and rubbed her eyes. "Are we ever going to see you again?"

Leon looked away before he could see her crying. "I . . ." No. He should say no. After he left the city, he'd never see the Band again. Giving Jackie false hope would be cruel, but he couldn't make himself tell her the truth. He couldn't make himself be honest with her, because then he'd have to be honest with himself.

He didn't want to leave the Band. He didn't want to leave Padraeg and Aoife. He'd already lost two families, and losing the one he'd found against all odds would destroy him in ways the Sister couldn't even be able to imagine.

But if he didn't leave . . . if he stayed and fought alongside them, he'd doom them all the same. At least if he left, they'd have a chance of surviving what was to come, and he wouldn't have to watch them die.

He didn't want to watch them die. He didn't want to have to see them hurt for him, because he was a coward who'd put them in danger if he stayed with them.

"I'll let Padraeg know you're here," he said finally, pushing himself to his feet. "He'll want to know where you are." Jackie's gaze dug into the back of his head as he pushed the door open, but she didn't try to stop him.

Stifled cries followed him into the hall, and he rushed off before they could convince him to go comfort her. The cries got louder as he walked away, whimpers becoming gasps becoming sobs. His steps got faster and faster until he was running through the halls, pushing past guards and squires and servants. He couldn't stop. If he stopped, reality would catch up to him, and he'd be crushed by the weight.

It wasn't until his lungs were screaming and his legs were shaking so hard they threatened to give way beneath him, that he stopped. Even then, it was less of a stop and more of a collapse. The cool stone, uneven from age and wear, dug into his knees and palms.

Gasping for air, he swung his head around, examining the darkened hall he found himself in. It was a dead end with the only light coming in through the window at the end of the hall.

An unused storeroom, perhaps? He didn't recognize it, but the barrel ceiling, musty smell, and stacks of damaged furniture all around him, blocking most of the stone walls from view, suggested that was likely. He didn't recognize it, but there'd been little cause to explore this part of the Citadel when he was a boy, and as a man . . . Well, he'd been busy enough in the past few days. He didn't have time to wander his old home.

Letting out a harsh laugh, Leon dragged himself to a bench that had been broken in half and left to rot down here until someone remembered to repair it. The shattered middle had been propped up on a crate, which creaked under his weight, and he resolved not to think about that. He had enough on his mind right now without worrying about being dropped onto the ground.

In what felt like the only bright spot today, he'd be alone down here. Padraeg's office had failed to provide the solitude he'd wanted, but based on the dust on the floor and the limited light, this particular area wasn't well trafficked. He could hide down here until he worked up the energy to find his way to the princes.

"Is this where you'd go whenever you and Padraeg would fight?" Njeri's voice echoed across the stone ceiling. He groaned without looking up. Her steps were nearly silent, a skill he'd admired before now. First Jackie and now her. How had she even found him?

"Gods, what do you want now?" he said, but there wasn't any heat to it. "I'm not part of the Band anymore, so unless Aoife assigned you to be my bodyguard—"

She raised her hands in mock surrender. "Some of the Band were concerned about how you stormed out of there. I wanted to check if you were all right."

He scoffed. "Am I all right?" Did she even hear herself? She'd just kicked him out of the Band—and in possibly the cruelest way she could—immediately after the secret he'd kept for twenty years was spilled in front of the most important people in Mezeldwelf. Even if much of the blame for that could be pinned squarely on him, she was smart enough to figure out how his mental and emotional state would be right now. "Well, as you can see, I'm fine. You've asked, so go back and leave me alone."

She arched an eyebrow and crossed her arms. "I can see that," she said dryly. Her lips turned down, and Leon felt inordinately like a child throwing a tantrum. "So you don't want to talk?"

Of course he wanted to talk, but it wasn't like he had anyone to talk to. Njeri had made her position clear, and Kelan was the only one of his former comrades that might still be interested in hearing his point of view, but Leon hadn't seen him since yesterday. "No. Not after—" He took a deep breath and turned away so she couldn't see the myriad of emotions on his face. "Just go. If Padraeg or Aoife comes looking for me, tell them I'll be up soon. And—Jackie's in Padraeg's office. Someone should check on her."

He rubbed his eyes again and stared out the window, ignoring the sharp pricks in the corner of his eyes. It got dark so early these days. Before long, it would be blacker than night in here. He ought to get a move on. He'd already kept Padraeg and the princes waiting, and there were still so many duties he had to attend to. It was a miracle no one had come looking for him before now.

"No."

Leon jolted up when Njeri spoke, and then stiffened when she sat on the bench beside him. They were so close their shoulders brushed. He let out a hollow laugh and pressed the bridge of his nose.

"You're not even going to give me the dignity of privacy?" His heart ached, and he wished for nothing more than to rip it from his chest. "The past ten years may not have meant anything to you, but I'd still like to mourn them before I return to my duties."

The bench creaked again, and Leon spared a thought for the integrity of the crate currently supporting their weight.

Njeri sighed and leaned forward to rest her elbows on her knees. "I shouldn't have spoken the way I did earlier," she said in a low voice. Her eyes were fixed on the wall opposite them, and she hardly seemed to blink. "I was . . . hurt when the truth came out, and I let the opinions of others get the best of me. It's made me inconsistent, which is unbecoming of someone in my position."

Leon mirrored her position. "That's one way to put it." Not that he blamed her. Yesterday—gods, had it only been a day?— he'd more than understood how she felt. Kicking him out of the Band was harsh, but understandable. Even if it hurt. "If I were in your position, I'd have been a lot angrier that this was hidden from me. I should've told you I was godsworn at least."

Had he told her that before he got out of the bath? No. He'd thought it, but there'd been so much whirling between them when she confronted him in the washroom that it had fallen by the wayside.

Then Shea had taken over the conversation in the dining hall. Njeri had been upset that Kelan knew before her and that Leon didn't want to join the fight against the Templesbane, but she'd let him leave with Jackie. She hadn't stopped him, and then she'd sent Shea instead of coming herself.

No. He hadn't told her that he understood before now. There simply hadn't been time.

Njeri made a noise that could've been a scoff, and leaned back. Leon followed her with his eyes, drinking in the way the dim light lingered on her scars and in the beads in her hair, like he'd done in front of countless fires before now. The gods alone only knew if he'd have the chance to do this again, and he'd already wasted so much of their limited time together wrestling with the secrets that tore them apart.

"Are you still planning on leaving after the city is evacuated?" she asked in a low voice, pressing her shoulder into his. "I mean, I know you don't like the Protectors, but the city guard and most of the merchants and mercenaries voted to join them. With Padraeg on your side, you'd be much safer with them than if you were on your own."

"Yes."

It didn't need more explanation. As guard-captain of Mezeldwelf with decades of experience, Padraeg would naturally be given a position of authority with the Protectors, but that didn't guarantee he could protect Leon from the machinations of the more established generals that had been running a hopeless resistance since before the Great Treaty was signed. Before long, even the merchant princes would start to weigh the costs of pushing forward at great risk to Leon's life or imprisoning him until the last possible moment to use as a sacrificial lamb.

Going back to Dhuitholm was a suicide mission. Even if Leon had other gods on his side that could help him, even if he had all the armies of the Protectors at his side, it would just end in tragedy. The only way to fight the Templesbane was with the blessing of the Watchful Peace.

She let out a huff of air and shifted until her knee brushed his, but still her eyes stayed focused on the wall opposite. "There's no convincing you, then?"

He shot her a dark look that made her look away.

"Right," she mumbled, rubbing a hand over the back of her neck. "I should've known better than to ask that. You've always made your feelings on the Protectors clear."

They lapsed into silence that grew more awkward with each passing second. Njeri's knee never moved, nor did she ever look up to meet Leon's eyes. He tried not to think about how he didn't move either.

Finally, he sighed and pushed up. "The princes are expecting me. I should be going."

He should've been gone ages ago, and now he didn't even have peace of mind to show for his delay.

"Leon—wait." Njeri's hand caught his sleeve before he got more than three steps away.

He stopped. Even though he wasn't a member of the Band anymore, ten years of instinct and trusting someone with his life didn't vanish in an instant.

"I'm sorry. I didn't say it before, but I am." She took a deep breath, and her hand clenched Leon's sleeve tighter. "You've been given a shit hand, and the way I've been acting hasn't helped any."

He tugged his sleeve away and took a step back. "It's all right. I already said I understood."

"But do you?" She pulled herself to her full height and still barely reached Leon's shoulders. She might be tall for a woman, but he was head and shoulders taller than most men. "Do you understand why Padraeg, Aoife, and—and I keep pushing you about this?"

"I have a good idea," he said dully, hands curling into fists.

Because they wanted him to live up to everything they'd heard about the Knights Vigilant. Because they couldn't imagine not doing everything they could to fight the Templesbane. Because at the end of the day, they hadn't lived the life he had or come as close to death at the Templesbane's hands as he had. Because they didn't understand what he'd already lost fighting them.

"Do you? Because it seems to me like you keep putting words in people's mouths." She stepped forward and rammed a finger into Leon's chest. "I know for a fact that whenever we've discussed your plans, you always assume that we want you to go charging headfirst into the husks' ranks. Aoife said you refused a place in the Mezeldwelf city guard because you were terrified someone would find you out."

Leon wanted to protest, but his tongue felt like it was weighed down with millstones. Njeri was asking foolish questions, ones she'd know the answer to if she would just stop and think for a moment.

Why else would anyone want him to reveal himself? Why else would Padraeg insist Leon stay at his side, even when it became illegal for him to even be in Mezeldwelf? They wanted to use him. The Templesbane threatened everyone, and a battle couldn't be won if those fighting it left their best weapons at home. It was inevitable that those who knew the truth about him would want to use him.

Her voice broke, and any words Leon had managed to gather crumbled into dust. "Is it so hard to believe that we want to help keep you safe? That we don't want you to spend the rest of your life hiding yourself away?"

Those weren't her words. She may have shared the emotion, but she hadn't been the first to bring them to light. He'd heard them before, from Padraeg and Aoife. It hadn't mattered then, just like it didn't matter now, because it didn't change anything. Fate had wrapped their hands around Leon's throat twenty years ago and been squeezing ever since. He knew what they had planned for cowards like him. He couldn't run from them forever, no matter how hard he tried.

"You don't think I know that?" he whispered, the words that had been so hard for him to gather just seconds before now spilling out of his mouth without his permission. "I've known what everyone wants from and for me since I was thirteen." His voice rose in pitch and volume as he spoke. "Padraeg, Aoife, even the fucking Knights Beyond—they might want what's best for me, but they've never bothered asking me what I think that is."

"And what do you want?" Njeri asked, taking another step forward. The echoes of his outburst hadn't even faded yet, and she was so close they were breathing the same air. "If it weren't for the Templesbane and the Protectors and all the rest of the shit you've had to deal with, what would you want to do?"

"That's not—I can't—" And once more, his tongue failed him, leaving him to sputter and gape like a fool. "I can't," he repeated, stumbling back into the far wall, as far from Njeri as he could go. "It's not a matter of what I want, that's how it's always been." When he'd wanted to fight, Padraeg had held him back, forcing him to hide until he was older. When he'd decided to hide instead, Padraeg, the Protectors, and the Knights Beyond

281

had pushed him to reveal himself, to fight a hopeless war without his god or anyone like him.

Njeri stepped in front of him, and one scarred hand came up to rest on his cheek. "It's not, though," she whispered. "You clearly don't want to leave. Even last night—you were more upset while justifying yourself to us than you were when the guards caught us."

She paused, and Leon wanted to yell, scream, anything to take that look off her face. He'd hurt her and the others by lying all this time and by not being what they expected him to be. Leaving them was some divine punishment for fleeing Dhuitholm when the Templesbane attacked.

"Would it be so bad if you let yourself want something? If you just . . . stopped running for a while?"

Yes. Of course it would be. If he stopped, if he faltered for even a moment, the Sister would find him, destroy everything he loved again, and then drag him back to Dhuitholm, where she and the Brother would kill him. Everything he'd fought for, everything he'd built would be for naught.

"Come with us. You've got so many people on your side now. Padraeg, Aoife, the guard, and . . ." She paused. Tears glimmered in her eyes but refused to fall. "And you have me and the rest of the Band. If you'll put a stop to this, if you stop running away, you wouldn't have to face them alone."

He let out a choked gasp but didn't move away this time. His eyes slid shut, and he took in a shaky breath.

She didn't understand. That was his only option. Everyone would leave him one day. The most he'd been able to hope for since he was thirteen was the slightest chance that he'd see the ones he loved again. He'd been wrong about that more often than he'd been right. This—the hell on earth that she was asking of him—would be no different.

If he followed the Band to the Protectors, he'd have to bear the weight of thousands of people's expectations. Their hopes, their fears, and eventually, their anger that he hadn't stopped all of this before the Sister destroyed Mezeldwelf. When they realized that he wouldn't be able to save them the next time either, they would turn on him.

But here, in a dark and little-traveled hallway, with Njeri's hand on his cheek and an entire city waiting with bated breath to see what his next move was, he wanted to believe her. He wanted to believe that he could stop running, that the people he fought beside wouldn't turn their back on him when he failed to live up to their expectations and wouldn't throw him to the wolves. Gods above, below, and beside him, he wanted to be selfish, to keep the relationships he had forged through blood, sweat, and tears and to believe that they had a fighting chance against the evil that still haunted his dreams.

He wanted so much, and if there was even the slightest possibility he could have any of it, he'd grab onto it with both hands and hold so tight that not even Death's sentinels would be able to pry it from his fingers. A year, a month, a week, or even a day longer with the ones he loved would mean so much more than a decade spent wandering the woods by himself. He was so tired of running.

"Okay," he whispered, his voice tiny and broken.

Njeri stiffened, and his hand shot up to catch hers before she could pull it away.

"Okay," he repeated. Tears slid down his cheeks, and he wasn't sure if they were sad or happy or some horrible mix finally breaking past the walls he'd been building up since they found the husks, but he couldn't stop them. "I'll do it. I'll join the Protectors with you."

And, gods willing, maybe they might be able to hold the Templesbane off just a little bit longer together than he could by running for the rest of his life.

Chapter 17
Charity in Times of War

"The evacuations are proceeding on schedule." Padraeg's steady rumble didn't echo, but it did reach every corner of the council chamber. Even if Leon hadn't been at his shoulder in Artur Mesley's old box, he'd have been able to hear him as clearly as if Padraeg were speaking three inches from his ear. "The last of the caravans left last night, and my guards have swept every house, alley, and sewer in the city to find any stragglers."

It was difficult to pay attention to anything Padraeg said, though, because Leon's new clothes itched.

Even in the haste of the evacuation, Aoife had insisted he dress to match his reclaimed station—to inspire hope in others, or so she said. She'd been ecstatic, possibly more than Padraeg, to hear that Leon would join the Band and the city guard in pledging their service to the Protectors. He wasn't sure where she'd pulled these clothes from, but they were finer than anything he'd ever owned, and she'd presented them with all the acclaim of one of the senior knights awarding a squire with their first blessed weapon. What's more, it might have been a while since he'd seen any, but the outfit looked like the uniforms the senior knights wore at high feasts.

The quality was just one of many things that made wearing them uncomfortable. Between the heavy wool and the misty-eyed way it made the older princes look at him, he wanted to rip them off here and now.

"Has there been any sign of the ships that are supposed to come back?" Aoife asked. She bit back a jaw-cracking yawn before she continued. She'd volunteered to stay back to oversee the evacuations over Leon and Padraeg's strenuous protests, and she'd barely slept in the last two days. Most of the other princes had left with the refugees fleeing on foot. The handful that remained, less than a fifth of the full council, were those overseeing the destruction of city infrastructure so the Sister couldn't use it to lure in passing ships. "The latest reports say the husks will be upon us tomorrow afternoon, and I want to start loading supplies as soon as possible."

"None," said the prince to her left, a mousy-haired man with thick spectacles named Toren. He'd abandoned his formal robes yesterday and wore a practical beige traveling outfit instead. "There are a handful of fishing vessels left as well as two pleasure ships the Ardan family donated, but those won't even hold a quarter of the defenders when the time comes for them to evacuate. We'll have to pray the Sea is kind."

The defenders would need to hold the husks' attention for at least two days to give the caravans time to escape. The ships held more of the population than Leon had anticipated, but most of the city was on foot, and there was only so much the mercenaries could do to hide their passage. If the Sky and the Storm were kind, the heavens would open and obscure the caravan tracks, but the autumn rains were holding off on their bounty thus far.

"Prince Hume, how go your efforts with the barricades?" Padraeg asked, scratching at the new growth on his chin. His goatee had gone from neat to wild in the past few days as shaving took a seat behind urgency. He'd even abandoned his fancy ceremonial plate on the second day of the evacuations for a more practical set from his earlier days on the guard.

Leon's attendance at these meetings was more a formality now, so he let his attention wander while Hume reported on the tunnels they'd collapsed since the last meeting. If there was anything that required his attention, someone would let him know.

He'd already scouted the city twice with Kelan and any godsworn that could be convinced to stay behind. Leon's senses still fluctuated randomly, and even without the pressing crush of minds around him, he'd been fighting off a headache all day. They hadn't found any signs of the husks either time, but that didn't mean their searches had been unproductive.

Battered boats, logs and barrels that could be turned into supply rafts, and more had been found and turned over to the guard for use in the evacuations. An Alkan woman sworn to the Hunt had even found a few smugglers' tunnels the guard had missed on their initial sweep, and gleefully helped in their destruction.

Once the meeting was over, he'd be sent to patrol somewhere in the city, then report back to the Citadel for dinner. After a few hours' sleep, he'd be packed onto one of the Aldan family's pleasure ships with the last of the princes, Padraeg, and the Band to ensure he, at least, survived the oncoming bloodbath.

Or at least, that's what Padraeg had said. A part of Leon wondered if he just didn't want to let Leon out of his sight now that he knew Leon would be coming with them to Falte instead of splintering off to lead the Sister away from the refugees as soon as they were far enough from Mezeldwelf.

He couldn't know for sure though. They hadn't had a chance to speak about it since Leon made his decision, despite all the time they spent together. Between work, eating, and snatching what sleep they could, there hadn't been many opportunities to have a heart-to-heart conversation. They hadn't even been able to remove Leon's parole sigil, because the evacuations took priority, and among his other crimes, Mesley had confessed to destroying the tools needed to remove a sigil without a trial. The few Justice priests left had been frantically trying to recreate them, but it wasn't a process done overnight.

It was especially odd, considering he'd had ample opportunity to speak with Njeri and the rest of the Band. After he'd made his decision, she'd dragged him back to their waiting room so they could tell the others, only to find that Bettany hadn't even bothered working out his pay or striking him from the record, since she figured he'd come to his senses and then she'd have to undo everything she'd done.

Then the next morning, in front of all of the princes, guards, and Padraeg, Njeri had pledged her service and the service of all in her company to the last of the Knights Vigilant in whatever he decided to do. Those who wished to leave, to hold off from swearing themselves to a single cause like that, were welcome to do so, but those that remained would fight at Leon's side. If he wanted to fight beside the Protectors, they would follow. If he wanted to stay in Falte and help with the refugees, they would offer what aid they could. If he wanted to face down the Templesbane themselves, they might grumble, complain, and ask for higher pay, but they would be there.

Only a handful, newcomers for the most part, had refused the call. The rest, nearly two hundred souls, had sworn themselves to their new cause. To Leon.

Just like that, Leon had an army of his own. Even Shea, morose but strangely excited for the chance to strike back against the Templesbane, had sworn to follow Leon or kick his ass as was appropriate.

Leon had ridden that peculiar high for the rest of the day, until he met up with Aoife and set off the sequence of events that led to where he was now. His new clothing and the old blue cloak that sat strangely on his shoulders were only one small part of that.

He tried not to think about the elaborately embroidered owl crests all over his clothing and especially not about how the cloak looked and felt much older than the rest of what he wore, as well as being a bit too short and broad for him, like it had been made for someone about Padraeg's size. It had been two decades since he'd worn the colors of the Knights Vigilant, and thinking too hard about it thrust him back into dark places he'd rather stay far out of right now.

"Artur Mesley hasn't spoken since his confession." Aoife's voice shook Leon out of his reverie. She had a stack of papers in front of her that was almost a foot tall, and was examining them through a pair of half-moon glasses. "And Ranon Carrick swore he had nothing more to give." She looked over the edge of her glasses, and her frown could've cut diamond. "I'm inclined to believe him on that part. Even without the Truth priests, he's remarkably eager to spill everything he remembers from his time as a husk."

Hume snorted and ran a hand through their close-cropped hair. Like the rest of their peers, they'd abandoned their robes for more practical—but still expensive—clothing. Unlike the rest of their peers, the clothing they chose was fashioned from at least seven different-colored fabrics, each tailored to hide some parts of their physique and emphasize parts they didn't have. "It's a marvel he remembered as much as he did. Considering what he went through, I can't believe that Guard-Captain Quinn had to force him to join the refugees instead of staying here to fight." Their face fell, and they pinched the bridge of their nose before sighing. "And I don't understand why Artur Mesley was left behind instead of sent with the other prisoners for judgment."

"Ranon didn't want to leave," Aoife said, shuffling through her papers. "He wanted to help hold off the husks until the refugee caravans were too far for them to capture—a penance he called it. My brother was able to convince him he'd be better suited to serving that penance by helping the refugees." She plucked one paper from her pile and examined it closely. Frowning, she shuffled it back into the stack. "Artur Mesley asked to stay, so we've locked him in the cells with some supplies. Considering his options, I'm not surprised he wants to throw his lot in with the Sister."

When Mesley realized there was no way to deny what he'd done and allowed to be done, he confessed to everything. From helping the Sister sneak soldiers into the city to hiding what he'd done with forgery and lies, he talked until the list of his crimes was longer than Leon was tall. On the one occasion Leon had seen him since the evacuations started, he looked older than he had during his trial and less than a shell of his former self. He'd looked like a dead man waiting for Death's sentinels to find him.

Scoffing, Hume leaned back in their seat and looked very like they wished Mesley was in front of their fist at that moment. "He's probably hoping the Sister will let him see Myrrdin before she turns him into a husk, but what she'd want with a ragged, old man like him is beyond me."

That was the other—unspoken—reason Ranon hadn't wanted to leave. Despite the miracle that had been his purging, Ranon desperately wanted to save his oldest friend. Somehow, he believed Leon would be able to purge Myrrdin, too, if only they could be captured.

But even then, Myrrdin Mesley would have their own sins to confront if they were purified.

They were the center of too many tangled webs to unravel, not the least of which was the situation currently facing

Mezeldwelf. When they were a young adult, their desire to succeed had fostered a hollow confidence and a drive to prove themself against anyone they deemed competition. Their desperation to prove themself to their father had driven them to seek the old sea routes to Sihia, even though the Sea around Dhuitholm had been impassable since the city fell. The Sea might be too large to be fully consumed, but they were a fickle god in their entirety and more than willing to kill their worshippers if it meant spiting the Templesbane. Myrrdin's ship had paid the price for passing too close to those shores.

When the Sihianese refused to repair or replace their ship, Myrrdin had been the one to suggest they return to Mezeldwelf by the land route. And because of their actions, Myrrdin had doomed themself and everyone they convinced to travel with them to the Templesbane.

At least, that was what Ranon said, and the Truth priests had found no lie in his words. The Sister might be evil, but she was smart. She wanted Mezeldwelf's gods and knew she couldn't get them while the Brother was trapped. She sent Ranon back to Mezeldwelf to barter with Artur Mesley, to dangle the possibility of regaining his youngest child in front of him like a worm on a line. He'd fallen for it like a child fooled by a bard's tricks.

Whether Myrrdin was still alive and even whether the Sister would've been able to remove her taint from them were questions Mesley hadn't bothered to ask. Ranon was alive, and that was proof enough for him that Myrrdin might be recovered one day.

"Mesley has made his choice," Padraeg said. His face was hidden from Leon at this angle, but the tension that appeared in his shoulders was as obvious as the sun. "Over and over again. If he wishes to face the Sister in lieu of the court, that is his decision, but we have too much work to do to bother with him."

The rest of the meeting went quickly. The remaining duties were laid out as evenly as possible. Aoife was to manage the collection of provisions, Hume and Toren to direct the mercenaries in building defenses, and Padraeg and Leon to patrol the temple district one last time, searching for any gods, altars, or holy items that might have been left behind. Laid out like that, it felt like too much to accomplish before the Sister arrived, yet Leon knew it would only occupy a handful of hours.

The major work had been done during the evacuation. Civilians on the way out of town had piled furniture in major thoroughfares; alchemists had rigged explosives in key buildings; and the nobles had opened their armories and their larders to the defenders. They would be well armed, well fed, and well rested before the battle began.

All that was left was to watch and wait, whittling down the hours until the eagle-eyed scouts reported the husks were in sight. The mood in the Citadel, which had been determined and cautiously optimistic during the evacuation, had faded to quiet despair. Those who stayed behind had all volunteered knowing they likely wouldn't survive, but it was one thing to hear that and another to face the quiet hours before the battle.

Leon, to his relief and grief, could do nothing to alleviate that burden. When the husks arrived, he'd be long gone and out of their reach, with the hope of the Mezeldwelf defenders on his shoulders. His time here was almost up, and he would leave all this behind, never to return.

The only bright spot in all of that was that Aoife and Padraeg would be coming with him when he left. Padraeg had fought, but Aoife had taken him by the ear and told him in no uncertain terms that if the princes would need to live to maintain the peace among the refugees, the guard-captain would be needed as well.

The only thing she would allow him to do was patrol his city one last time before the end.

***

"Still nothing?" Padraeg asked, peering into the darkened interior of a Harvest temple. He and Leon were walking through the eerily silent temple district, searching for any lingering gods or priests.

"Still nothing," Leon confirmed, massaging his temples. He hadn't used his gift to sense any divine force beyond the husks in ages, and it hurt in new and interesting ways, like how stubbing your toe felt different than twisting your ankle. It wasn't even the intended use of his senses, but it was one the old knights had used often when searching for abandoned temples and lost gods after the first war with the Templesbane. "I'm not even getting the lingering echoes we got yesterday."

In the temple district, that was unnerving. Normally, even those who weren't godsworn could feel the heavy power radiating from the temples. Hundreds of thousands of faithful came every day to pray, offer sacrifice, and worship their gods. That was why there were so many aspects in the city. Without them, their altars and worshippers, and the sheer amount of power they exuded on a daily basis, this district felt like a crypt. It was too quiet and too grand for normal life. Even the leaves blowing across the street and the strays wandering in and out of alleys felt less like part of the city and more like bits of the wild reclaiming land that once belonged to them.

"Good." Padraeg hummed and closed the door with a loud thunk. "Then we can head back to the Citadel. Aoife wanted someone to do one last check of the warehouses, and I want to join your band while they search."

"I know, I was there."

She'd made it very plain that she was concerned someone might have stayed behind, either looking to loot the goods that had been abandoned or to seek some advantage over a rival. Even in the face of a threat like the husks, there were some who would let their greed overwhelm them, and Aoife wanted to give them a fighting chance. Njeri had volunteered to lead a group of people to search for any stragglers that decided wealth meant more than their lives and to arm them so they could die fighting at the very least.

He was grumbling, but he felt he was excused. He was exhausted, and he'd much rather have worn his battered, old leathers and the chain mail he'd paid an arm and a leg for in Beldown instead of the festival clothes Aoife had pushed on him.

How she expected him to search the warehouses dressed like this was beyond him. The tunic and trousers were too fine for dirty work, and the cloak hung oddly on his shoulders. They'd be filthy before the day was out, and Njeri would mock him for it.

But at the very least, searching the wharf warehouses would give Njeri another chance to examine the ship they'd escape on. She'd sent most of the Band with the refugees, but between the remaining Band members, the princes, Padraeg, and the guards he'd hand selected to protect Leon, they'd need to cram over a hundred people on board, and she wanted to know every inch of that vessel from stem to stern.

Padraeg and Leon chatted comfortably—or at least, as comfortably as they could, knowing the evil that was coming closer and closer with each passing day. Despite everything lingering between them, they kept their conversation to surface level. How had the other slept, were they getting enough to eat—things that broke the silence but didn't address anything serious.

Like how Padraeg felt about Leon joining the Protectors after all this time, about the risks Leon would have to undertake in his new role, or about Padraeg's role in defending the people of Mezeldwelf once they reached Falte. Things that would clear the air, even if they hurt on their way out.

But, if Padraeg wanted to focus on Mezeldwelf before he left it for the last time, then Leon would let him. They'd have weeks on the ship together, and he'd seen enough of it to know how small it was. They would have time to talk.

They were passing one of the temple gardens when he stopped in his tracks. Padraeg went three more steps before he realized Leon wasn't following. He turned back, a question on his lips, and then followed Leon's gaze.

A small figure, dressed in rags, sat on one of the garden benches, admiring a dry fountain. They looked up and smiled, and that smile contained the fears of a hundred souls. A young man, terrified of what was to come but determined to hold out long enough for his family to escape; a woman praying to any god that could hear her that she'd live to hold her beloved once more; a prince knowing that they would never see their home again but willing to die to preserve its memory.

Leon's heart dropped from his chest, and he bit back the urge to swear. "Charity?" he whispered. And then again, louder this time as the sharp wind cutting through his clothes confirmed all this was real. "Your Grace, what are you doing here? You were supposed to leave with the priests."

Charity shrugged and pulled the rags of their cloak tighter around them. The visions that had been flooding Leon's brain quieted from a roar to a dull murmur. "I have a flock in this city," they announced casually, as if commenting on the weather instead of justifying why they stayed around with an army of husks on their doorstep. "You wouldn't expect me to leave those who need my care, would you?"

"I would, actually," Padraeg countered, stepping forward. "The ones who left need Charity more than those that stay. Those here would be better served knowing their sacrifice kept a god from the Templesbane."

They shrugged and pushed off the bench. Their cloak billowed around them, all at once a king's robe and a beggar's rags as they settled onto the ground. "I left a smaller aspect with the refugees, one that will encourage them to aid each other as they travel, but most of me is needed here, to care for those who might be lost."

"But no one here is lost. We all chose to be here," Padraeg shot back, pulling himself to his full height, like that would mean anything to a god. "And, once more, those behind wish to see you safe to help those society forgot rather than feeding the hunger of the Templesbane."

Charity shrugged. "My flock is my own. I will tend them as long as they need me in the manner that suits me best." A sharp wind cut down the street but didn't so much as disturb the inky ringlets on Charity's head or the edges of their cloak.

Leon let out a choked-off noise. "So you're going to stay here, then?" he asked, pinching the bridge of his nose. "The husks will find you, no matter where you hide." They couldn't force Charity to come with them. If Charity wanted to stay behind, no mortal could make them move, not even Leon. If they did decide to come, Padraeg and Aoife would need to incorporate them into their escape plan. As small as Charity's physical form may be, it still took up some of their limited space.

Charity nodded. "For now at least," they said, smiling. "Fate hasn't revealed their web to me, but they said I needed to be here, to remind you and the others that there are opportunities to serve others even when the worst has happened."

"But—" Leon took a deep breath and tugged his cloak around himself to fend off the chill. "Will you at least wait at the Citadel? The patrols would appreciate your support and guidance while you're here."

"Of course," they said, taking Padraeg by the hand. They pulled him forward, tugging him down the empty street as easily as if he were a doll on a string. "I came here to say goodbye to the temples. Many of my flock have left me by virtue of my siblings' aid in these past few weeks. It will be some time before I can claim to have so few followers again. I'll return to the divine realm long before the city falls."

"I see." Leon's stomach twisted and roiled. "I hope we can get this settled enough for you to leave, Your Grace."

"Things aren't as they seem, Leon Quinn," they called over their shoulder. Padraeg's hand was still in theirs, and he was nearly doubled over trying to keep up with them. "You will see that before you meet the Sister."

***

"Gods," Aoife breathed, pinching the bridge of her nose. "As if this whole situation couldn't get worse."

Charity had led Padraeg and Leon right to Aoife and the prince she'd been talking with in the Citadel courtyard. They'd then left them behind and went off to speak with some of the defenders.

Padraeg huffed. "Don't you dare say that. That's inviting the gods to test us."

"They're testing us already," she grumbled, shouldering a heavy bag, "and I, for one, don't actually see how me reminding them of that could make it worse."

Rolling his eyes, Padraeg set a hand on her shoulder and pulled her close into something that could have generously been called a hug. "It's nothing that hasn't been asked of humanity before. Things will get bad when they ask something new of us."

Aoife elbowed his ribs. "Get off. I have to go to the wharf to see if we can even make more room for them. Everyone will need to take turns sleeping on the deck as is."

Rubbing his side like Aoife's elbow had managed to penetrate his plate and the cloth below it, Padraeg laughed. It was bright despite the exhaustion weighing it down. "I'll send Leon down after you," he yelled at her retreating back. "With luck, by then we'll have convinced Charity to leave with us."

Leon let out an involuntary snort. Charity couldn't be coerced. It wasn't in their nature. Every action had to be willing.

"You be quiet," Padraeg snapped with no heat. Nonetheless, his face fell as he turned back to the Citadel. "You know as well as I do that we can't let Charity stay here."

"I didn't say anything," Leon protested, taking two quick steps to catch up with Padraeg, "and I agree, but I don't know what you can say that will convince them to leave with us or on their own."

The warmth of the Citadel called them like a siren. Inside, Leon would be able to grab a quick meal and figure out where Njeri and the others were before he went to the docks. He could already taste the creamy vegetable soup one of the defenders— a tavern cook before they'd volunteered to stay behind—had promised for today. There ought to be some bread left too. The bakers' guild had dropped off the loaves that wouldn't keep before they left, and it would be sinful to leave them uneaten.

Unfortunately, this wasn't meant to be.

"Guard-Captain Quinn, Sir Leon!" A high-pitched voice came from behind them and echoed off the marble and stone.

They turned, hands on their weapons, to see a disheveled man dressed in new-looking leathers sprinting up to them.

"What's wrong?" Padraeg asked immediately, leaping down the stairs; Leon followed, a heartbeat behind. Food and warmth would have to wait. "What news from the walls?"

The man skidded to a halt and almost tripped over his own feet. Setting his hands on his knees, he struggled to get each word out between his gasping breaths. "It's—the scouts on the walls—the husks, they're here. Call the princes, call everyone."

The air in Leon's lungs solidified into one giant lump of terror. He couldn't even take his hands off his axes or convince his legs to stumble away. They were supposed to have more time. They hadn't even—the boats weren't back yet. The defenders wouldn't last long enough to escape.

"Already?" Padraeg whispered, the color draining from his face until his skin was the same shade as his hair. "But this is too early, they weren't supposed to arrive until tomorrow."

The scout nodded, and his shaggy hair fell over his eyes. "It's true. The woman in the tower is sworn to the Hunt, sir. She can see for miles. We've got a few hours at most and then—" His voice broke, and all of sudden he looked like a child thrust into his father's armor. "They'll be on us before we know it, sirs. We have to hurry."

Even as the last words faded into silence, distant bells began ringing. Too quiet—gods, why hadn't they staffed all the towers? They should've had more time. If he and Padraeg hadn't been out here and the messenger hadn't been sent, the alarm would've been missed. They needed to move, but Leon's legs were frozen and he couldn't breathe and—

"Fuck," Padraeg snarled, turning on his heel. His cloak billowed out behind him like some hero of legend as he raced into the Citadel. "To arms, to arms!"

And Leon's legs remembered how to move. His lungs remembered how to breathe. He tore after Padraeg, voice raised alongside his. Now was not the time to let his fear consume him. They had work to do.

Chapter 18
An Ancient Enmity Renewed

The Citadel great hall was buzzing with life. The remaining princes, Padraeg, and Leon stood on the dais that would've held the head table in happier situations. A large map of Mezeldwelf and the surrounding countryside had been pulled out of storage and was covered in figurines.

Padraeg stood at the exact center, Leon and Aoife on either side of him. "At this point, we need to assume that anyone from outside the city is a husk, whoever they are." His voice boomed, filling every corner of the great hall. Despite the fear and chaos that the husks' sighting had caused, he was in his element and he was in control. "The husks moved far faster than we anticipated, but as long as the gates hold, we have the advantage."

Njeri stood at the front of the crowd, Kelan and Shea just behind her. Bettany and Jackie were long gone with one of the last refugee caravans and half the Band. Jackie hadn't wanted to leave without Leon and the others—especially after Leon assured her that he wasn't leaving the Band, after all—but when Leon threatened to lock her in a chest until the caravans were too far to return and Padraeg made it clear he would allow it, she'd gone quietly enough. If the gods were kind, they would meet again in the Falten capital or wherever the refugees were shunted once they crossed the border. Jackie would probably have a list of Falten delicacies a mile long that she'd want everyone to try.

That thought alone bolstered Leon more than he could say.

Aoife nodded. "They can't get through any of the gates. All of them, from the smallest side passage to the great southern gate, have been locked or otherwise rendered impassable. They'd need the power of the Sister herself to break through those without alchemy or a traitor inside the walls." Her face was as white as chalk, but she hadn't let her fear hold her back. She had a job to do and a city to abandon.

Leon wanted to speak, to match their bravery, but the swirling emotions in his gut held his tongue hostage. His worst enemy, the one that had haunted his nightmares for two decades, was getting closer and closer with every moment. It made his knees weak and stole the strength from his limbs, but he couldn't show that. Instead, he stood tall and tried to look braver and more commanding than he felt. Aoife had directed him here because she wanted the others to take courage from his presence, and he wouldn't disappoint her.

Except the horrible nothingness, the absence that drowned out everything but itself, was as loud as a temple bell ringing right in his ears. It had begun not long after the alarm sounded, and was growing louder and louder with each passing moment. He dreaded the cacophony that would assault him when the husks were at the walls.

He took a deep breath and stepped forward. "The important thing to know is that the husks have no thoughts of their own." At least he wasn't alone now. Others that knew he was a knight and still stood by his side. They'd escape this, together. "They will not try to strategize or plan in a group of this size. They'll march forward, taking the path of least resistance, and attempt to overwhelm us with sheer numbers." He pointed at the western gate on the map. "They're approaching from the west, so this is where they'll strike. When they can't breach this gate, they will go around the city, trying their luck at each gate in turn."

The defenders—guards, mercenaries, and volunteers alike—would need to divide themselves even further. It would do no good to defend the western gate if the eastern one fell because they were occupied with throwing stones at the husks that hadn't wandered off yet.

Padraeg took over now. "No matter who you see among their numbers, you must remember that they are not the ones you love. The Templesbane has them, heart and soul, and Sir Leon cannot purge them all on his own."

There was no blame or anger in Padraeg's tone or words, but shame cut into Leon's heart all the same. The only reason he'd been able to purify Ranon was that Charity had given him power and the Knights Beyond had lent him their experience. While Charity was still here, he hadn't seen the Knights Beyond since right after he purified Ranon. He was on his own. He knew it. The princes and godsworn knew it, and the defenders vaguely understood it. The weight of their eyes and their glares pulled at him as surely as his cloak pulled on his shoulders. They blamed him for his weakness. Why had he even decided to stay if he couldn't turn the Sister's soldiers against her? Why hadn't he left and drawn them off long before now?

Padraeg plowed on without care for the murmuring and reactions coming from the crowd.

"The seawalls extend too far into the water for them to dare breach them. Even a glance at the waves is enough to show that the Sea knows what's coming, and the husks won't risk it. If they are kind, the Sea will guide the other ships to us quickly, and everyone will be able to escape."

But the Sea hated the Templesbane to an unholy degree, far more than they loved any of their worshippers. If the Sea were able, they would flood the world and drown everyone, husk and human alike, if it meant purging the world of the stain of the

Templesbane. There was no negotiating with the Sea. They just had to pray that Mercy would temper their rage long enough for Leon and the others to escape.

"They will focus their attention next on the southern gate. Those based there will have the hardest time escaping due to its distance from the port, but the barricades and blockades there are piled as high as we could make them." Padraeg's face wasn't visible at this angle, but his voice was steady and sure, like he'd planned this battle a thousand times before. For all Leon knew, he had. The Great Treaty had always been a pause in hostilities, not a resolution. Only a fool wouldn't have prepared some sort of countermeasure against it breaking. "The alchemists marked their explosives. If the western gate is—" And he stopped, briefly overcome with an emotion that seemed somewhere between despairing and determined. "If the western gate is breached, the mercenaries will retreat and set off as many of the explosives as possible. With luck, that will delay the husks long enough for the defenders to reach the port and the ships that will take them away."

A woman dressed in furs and thick leather armor called out from the crowd. Her voice was lyrical and so thickly Falten it was nearly indecipherable. "And what if we cannot get away, eh? If the ships do not arrive, will we be abandoned to those godless husks?"

Leon wanted to yell at her, to demand what she thought Padraeg should do. She and whatever company she was part of had volunteered to stay behind. They knew the risks and the costs. They shouldn't try to back out now that death was staring them in the face.

The only thing that held him back was the little voice deep inside him that asked him what right he had to ask that sacrifice of them. He and the princes would be gone by then—they'd leave as soon as this meeting finished. The people here, the ones who had volunteered to defend the city long enough for the refugees to get away, wouldn't have that option. The ships that were supposed to ferry them away wouldn't return for another day at the earliest.

They deserved their rage in the moments when they realized that even the slim chance of rescue they'd hoped for wouldn't come.

Padraeg's face softened, and he met the woman's eyes head-on. "Then you will either die or join the husks." It was harsh, it was brutal, and it was true. The room emptied of air as every person in it inhaled as one. "This was asked of you. If you are unable to offer this, if you would run in exchange for your life, there is still time. The eastern gate is barricaded, but a ladder will be let down from a window above. Gods willing, the husks will not notice your footsteps."

"What if we gave them what they wanted?" This time it was a man in fine silks, not a prince but dressed as extravagantly as one. No doubt he'd thought this battle would be a fine feather in his cap and he'd be back with the upper crust of Mezeldwelf before long. "Why should we have to die when we have a Knight Vigilant and a god?"

A dozen voices rose in agreement, and were snuffed out almost immediately by their more intelligent peers.

Fire raged through Leon, and only the sight of a junior member of the Band slamming a fist into the speaker's stomach kept him from marching down there to do it himself.

Padraeg stood tall, and where his voice had boomed before, it now thundered. His face was a storm, a harkening back to the dark days when the gods viewed the earth as their playground and fought viciously over it. "What, are you a coward, and a foolish one at that? The Sister has no intention of honoring the treaty, and there is no option that ends with the city safe and the inhabitants at home." His hand moved to the hilt of his sword, and Aoife's firm grip on his wrist was all that kept it in its sheath. "She means to take the city, and anyone who thinks otherwise is welcome to go meet the husks and offer them that deal themselves."

"And Leon is one of us." Njeri's voice rang high above the crowd, as sharp and dangerous as her sword. "He swore the mercenary's oath and bound himself to my company. Anyone who suggests turning him over to the Templesbane is welcome to bring the matter before me and my blades."

The man from before, now surrounded by members of the Band and pinned under Padraeg's glare, wisely shrunk back under the attention.

But Padraeg didn't settle. "If there are no more complaints, I will go over our positions. Sir Leon, the Band of Broken Blades, and the princes will retreat to the wharf. They will hold their position as long as necessary to get everyone on board. The Great Company, the Gods' Own, and fifty of the city guard will go directly to the western gate. When the husks are within a hundred paces of the city, they'll sound the alarm. There should be plenty of crossbows and ammunition for every hand."

He pointed again at the map, this time at the southern gate. "The Company of the Rose, the Children of Alke, and whatever is left of the guard will space themselves out on the walls between the western and southern gates. Again, shoot to kill. Any husk we can stop before they throw themselves at the gate is one we don't have to worry about coming to kill us later."

He paused, and his hands curled into fists at his side. "Cearl's Roustabouts will retreat to the wharf. They are responsible for holding the barricades when the defenders at the gates retreat." His voice caught in his throat, and he had to clear it before he could continue. "You are responsible for the last line of defense. When you fall, you must make sure to blow the wharf so any ships that haven't heard about the evacuation can't dock."

Leon gasped, a sound echoed by everyone in the great hall. Without the wharf, Mezeldwelf would be crippled if—*when*, he had to think in *when*; the Templesbane would not hold the world forever—the refugees returned to rebuild. Mezeldwelf was the center of trade and culture in northern Hyderia for centuries, and the wharf was the reason it had become so. Padraeg couldn't have hammered in what was at risk better than if he'd slit half of the defenders' throats right now.

Padraeg nodded and took a step back. "Everyone is dismissed. Grab some food if you can. I doubt you'll get another chance."

***

Leon dashed down the dock, dodging around the mercenaries and princes doing the same, to grab Aoife's arm. She stood in between two long gangplanks leading up onto one of the ships allocated for those who would escape before the husks attacked, and held a wooden board with stacks of paper on it in one hand. "Have you seen Padraeg?" he asked in a hushed voice. "I tried to grab him after the meeting, but he ran out before I could."

Aoife clicked her tongue and made a check on her list as a woman dressed in blue silks, presumably another prince, rushed on board. "No," she said sourly. "But the damned fool better be here soon. Most of the passengers are already on board, and I'll kill him myself if he misses the ship because he's chasing glory on the walls."

"He's not with the mercenaries defending the wharf." Leon squinted into the distance like that would make Padraeg's familiar white head appear out of the crowd. "I checked."

Aoife swore yet didn't miss a single person. Hume, her match on the other side of the dock, looked appalled at the language but, notably, also didn't miss a mark. Say what you would about the princes, but they valued efficiency while dealing with personal crises. "Gods' sake, do you mind checking again? We don't leave for another fifteen minutes, but the tools to break your sigil are finally done, and I want to get that done before we get going. I give you my full permission to drag him out of the defenders by the end of his godsdamned braid if necessary."

Leon nodded and swallowed around the anxiety making war with the frantic screaming of the nothingness in his head. The husks had to be at the city walls by now. Even from the wharf, the nothingness was as obvious as the dawn, and the Sea was getting rougher with each passing moment. The real battle would begin soon, and despite how torn he felt about leaving the defenders behind, he couldn't help feeling tremendous relief that he wouldn't be here to deal with the coming battle.

Shaking his head, he started down the dock again. Padraeg would be there. He was a smart man, and he knew what was at stake. He'd grumble at Leon and Aoife for teasing him about how close he came to getting left behind, but he'd be there.

Leon passed groups of grim-faced mercenaries sitting behind barricades crafted from pikes, barrels, and shattered furniture. Farther down the wharf, other groups were focused on ensuring the explosives were set up properly, that they'd take out as much of the docks as possible without damaging the warehouses, stores, or houses in the wharf district.

Kelan and Shea, each carrying a heavy-looking barrel over their shoulders, caught his eye as he ran, and nodded. He let out a relieved sigh as he pushed past them. As far as he knew, they were the last of the Band to board. Njeri was already ordering the princes around and shuffling the little luggage they'd been allowed to maximize occupancy. Aoife would join her as soon as her list was cleared. The only one Leon had to worry about was Padraeg.

His pace picked up and with it, his anxiety. Scanning each group revealed half-familiar faces of people he'd planned with and eaten beside since the evacuation started, but no familiar braid or battered armor. Padraeg couldn't be far, but by the gods, he was making it hard to find him.

Leon reached the end of the docks and made it a good way down the main road before he finally caught sight of his quarry and could breathe again.

"Gods, were you waiting for a personal invitation?" he called, slowing to a stop.

Padraeg grunted. "They're at the gate," he said grimly, marching by Leon. A small group of equally grim-faced guards accompanied him and took up positions along the street. Beyond here, each side street and back entrance to the wharf had been blocked off. "And still moving faster than we anticipated."

Leon turned and matched Padraeg step for step. "Are they already attacking?" The alarm bells hadn't sounded yet, but that didn't mean much in times like this.

Padraeg shook his head, but it failed to ease Leon's worries. "No. They've stopped in front of the gate, but out of bow range. We hailed them as a stalling tactic, but the messenger I was speaking with said they haven't been answering."

As if punctuating his sentence, the alarm bells started singing their terrible song. Padraeg swore and broke into a dead run. "Is everyone on board?"

Leon nodded, his long strides more than matching Padraeg's. "Everyone except you and me by now." If they'd been thinking logically, Leon wouldn't have been the one going after Padraeg, but he'd be damned before he sent someone else to go fetch his father. "Even Charity. Aoife said they decided to accompany us, after all, and made themself comfortable in the hold."

"Good—" And if Padraeg had intended to say something else, Leon didn't hear it, because the next thing he knew, the quiet was shattered with a tremendous boom that shook the ground under his feet.

"What's going—" The first explosion was followed by a second and a third in quick succession, and Leon's heart sank deeper and deeper with each passing second, chilling his blood as it went. He flung out a hand and latched onto Padraeg's arm, both for balance and because Aoife would kill him if Padraeg raced back into the city to figure out what went wrong. "What's happening?"

The explosions were only supposed to go off if the husks got through the gate. If they went off too early, they could blow the barricades or open one of the tunnels they'd spent the last three days sealing. If they went off because they were supposed to . . .

That would mean the husks were in the city. That all their defenses hadn't even lasted a full hour. That anyone who wasn't on a ship before the husks reached the port was doomed. He reached out, and the sharp spike of fear that stabbed through him nearly sent him to the ground. Gods. The nothingness was too large, as big as Mezeldwelf itself, and too loud for him to tell if it was inside the city yet.

Padraeg shook his head and took three trembling steps backward. "I don't know," he whispered. Smoke was rising over the rooftops in front of them in three different sections of the city. His lips turned down in a severe frown. "Tell Aoife—" Fire started licking distant roofs, and he swore. "Gods damn it, run. Run!"

Leon didn't need to be told twice. Without dropping his hold on Padraeg, he sprinted down the road, past the barricade, and along the wharf. Padraeg ran beside him, barely keeping up with Leon's longer strides, but he was there. They would get to the ship. Leon wouldn't have to leave anyone he loved behind again.

There weren't any more explosions as they ran, but the alarm bells picked up speed and volume, which sent panic-fueled adrenaline pumping down Leon's legs. Even if the explosions were accidental, something had gone wrong.

Gods, where were the Knights Beyond? They'd been quiet for days, but they always showed up when Leon had a near brush with the husks, and this was far more than a brush. The army outside Mezeldwelf right now might actually be larger than the one that had attacked Dhuitholm, and the knights were as silent as a graveyard.

But Leon didn't have long to wonder at the fickleness of the dead. As they skidded past the last building and onto the docks, he realized with terrible certainty that things were much worse than he could've anticipated. The defenders at the barricades, who shouldn't have had to worry about doing their duty until long after the western gate fell, were fighting too many people to count, people who reeked of nothingness. Leon stumbled to a stop and let loose an oath.

"They're husks," he whispered, pulling his axes from their sheathes with trembling hands. "Gods, how'd they get around us?"

He wanted to be wrong. He wanted these to be peasants who'd somehow escaped the husks and the patrols, ordinary people trying to escape the oncoming hoard. But they couldn't be. Their bodies were hollow, emptied of everything that they had been, and stank of corruption and the depths of the abyss.

He charged forward, limbs moving automatically and mind racing over every possible answer for this impossible question in front of him. Had the explosions been a distraction, or had a tunnel been missed during the searches? There were too many husks for them to have hidden from Leon when he searched the city. He might still be struggling to control his abilities after purging Ranon, but his range had never been broader.

At least . . . he thought it had never been broader. If he'd broken something while purifying Ranon, he'd have no way to tell he'd done so. If that were the case, if he'd allowed himself to be lulled into a false sense of security—

No. No, this was not the time. The husks pushed toward the barricades, on the verge of overwhelming the defenders with sheer numbers, and the defenders had been caught off guard. The cries of battle were already rising like a hurricane all along the wharf, even before he crashed into the writhing horde of bodies.

His axes cut into flesh like a hot knife through butter, a terrible dance as familiar to him as the oaths he'd sworn. The husks would turn their attention toward him soon enough, and even though the husks were attacking, the thought of killing them made him sick. No kind god would call this a fair fight. The sigil flared and burned in turns, as if the magic couldn't decide whether this fight qualified as something that put Leon's life in danger or not.

Some of the husks had weapons—axes, spears, or farming equipment turned to a darker harvest—but most only fought with their bare hands. The Sister must have taken these poor people straight off the fields or out of their workshops. Not even one in ten wore armor thicker than a wool coat, and even those that did wore little more than rags underneath.

The Sister had torn these people from their lives and thrust them into battle without any thought for how they could fulfill their orders. They would die in service to beings who considered them less than the dirt beneath their feet, and there was nothing they could do about it. How long had they been under the Sister's control? Was that wear recent, the product of a harsh life on the border and forced march, or old damage caused by life lived with the bare minimum to survive?

Leon's mind screamed at him as he fought, removing a woman's arm with one strike before she could bring her sword down on Padraeg. Her face, her eyes morphed from the careful blankness of a husk into some semblance of self for a single moment before his other axe removed her head from her shoulders. A voice inside him that sounded too much like a scared child screamed that he should run to the ships, but Leon pushed back against it. They had to stand, had to fight. Padraeg was counting on him. Running now, even if it got him past the barricade, would leave Padraeg to the mercy of the husks, and Leon would fall on his axes before he did that.

He'd already lost one family. He wasn't about to lose another.

Padraeg's back pushed up against his, which only silenced that voice inside Leon further. They would get through this, together. The defenders beyond the barricade wouldn't leave them here long. They needed to slim the numbers a bit, hollow things down until they could get past—

"Leon!" cried a familiar voice, one that made Leon freeze midswing. Only a quick strike from Padraeg saved him from a knife to the gut.

He spun, thanking any god out there that Knights Vigilant were so tall, and scanned the battle.

"Leon," the voice cried again, and Leon's heart leaped to his throat.

Jackie was sprinting out of an alley, racing toward the dock like Death's sentinels were on her heels. A group of five husks was on her tail and rapidly gaining ground. Blood covered her face and the dagger in her hand, but he'd know her anywhere.

"Jackie!"

"Move," Padraeg thundered, ramming into Leon like a one-man army. "Hurry, there's an opening." He pushed Leon's unwilling body behind the barricade, and Leon fought with each step.

"Padraeg, it's Jackie, she's here, she's over there—" They couldn't leave her there. She wasn't supposed to be here. If she was here, then her caravan had been caught, and all the gods could damn him, but he wouldn't let the Sister keep her. He'd purify her no matter what it took.

"It's too late to save her," Padraeg insisted. "We have to hurry—"

"Leon, help me!" Her sharp cry was louder, breaking through the chaotic sounds of fighting, the distant alarm bells, and the shouts behind them.

This time it was Padraeg whose head snapped up, whose face whitened like he'd just seen Aoife on the other end of his sword.

"Gods," he whispered, dropping his grip on Leon like he'd been burned. "Gods," he said again, louder this time. "It's a trap, Leon, you can't—"

Leon was already running.

He didn't care that this was definitely a trap or that he was risking his life. Jackie was in danger, and Padraeg was safe now, behind the barricade. The defenders would hold the line, even against the husks that were congregating around this dock. If

Leon moved fast enough, he could grab Jackie and bring her back before Padraeg had a heart attack.

He sprinted forward, shoving through the crowd of husks, who didn't seem to care about Leon now that he was running into their arms rather than away. Jackie had fallen to the ground, and husks were practically on top of her. One had his hand on her ankle and was dragging her back, deeper into the smoke and rising flames of the city.

Magic rose in Leon's limbs, and he channeled every ounce into speed. His axes hummed in his hands, instruments of death that he'd inflict on all those in his path if it meant saving Jackie.

He struck them like a bull, knocking the unarmored husk prone. His axes flashed, slicing through flesh and bone alike, and before he knew it or was even aware of what he'd done, four were dead at his feet. The fifth, a man dressed like he'd been a noble once, had both hands on Jackie's ankle and was dragging her away like the deaths of his comrades meant nothing. His white eyes stared vacantly in the distance, and his expression stayed the same, no matter how often Jackie screamed or slashed at him with her dagger.

Leon rushed him, taking him to the ground and away from her.

They rolled around, the husk staring blankly at Leon even as he tried to wrap his hands around Leon's throat. Blood—thick and hot—trickled from the wounds Jackie made, covering Leon as they rolled around, mingling with the blood already staining his clothes. Like this, on the ground, it was even harder to get a disabling or lethal blow on the husk. Most men would at least wince when hit between the legs or when fingers dug into injuries, but husks felt nothing. They were empty shells piloted by the vague inclinations of a faraway being and wouldn't stop while they still drew breath.

"Leon," Jackie yelled, scrambling away from the wrestling men, "Leon, get him!"

"That's what I'm trying to do," he yelled back, twisting his legs around the husk in an effort to flip them again while slamming a free fist into his face. "Run back to the—to the barricades! Padraeg knows you're here."

The husk flew through the air like a sack of flour and hit the ground with a harsh thump. He met his end with Leon's axe in his throat, a last gurgling gasp of air as loud as thunder in Leon's ears. The look in his eyes, the terror as the white faded to green, made Leon want to vomit.

He stumbled up, breathing hard, and spun toward Jackie, who hadn't moved despite his orders. "Gods damn it, Jackie," he yelled, darting to her and grabbing her hand to tug her after his. He'd lost one of his axes in the tussle, but he could still defend her with just one. "What the hell are you doing here? You're supposed to be with Bettany." She was supposed to be gone, safely away.

Jackie stared up at Leon, her eyes wonderfully gray, a bloody dagger clutched in one shaking hand. "I didn't—" Her voice trembled and broke. "I ran away," she whispered. "I snuck away from the caravan because I'm gonna be your squire, and I'm supposed to be with you, but I couldn't find you. There was an open gate near the temple district, and an old man yelled at me to go away—"

They didn't have time for this, Leon decided abruptly. "Never mind, explain later. We have to go. Get on my back." The husks were thinning out, and he could see Padraeg fighting to keep it that way. If the husks from the rest of the wharf got the idea to help . . . well, Leon didn't fancy trying to swim to the ship when the water was this rough.

316

But an opening was an opening, and wasting time considering what-ifs would get him killed.

Once more, he sprinted for the dock, this time with Jackie hanging from his back and a single axe in his bloodstained hand. Padraeg was waiting for them, surrounded by the corpses of dead husks. They were almost there. The ships were ready to leave, and if he could just get beyond the barricade, they would be free.

They only were ten feet away when something Leon could only describe as a living wave of hate, of destruction, of *nothingness* slammed into him. It held him in place, nailing his feet to the dock and somehow pulling him back. He stumbled, his axe dropping from nerveless fingers. His senses screamed at him to turn around, to confront the nothingness, because he recognized it. He'd felt it once twenty years ago, and it had terrified him so much he'd been running like a dog with his tail between his legs ever since.

He stopped, his legs leaden and soul screaming. Jackie's voice in his ear sounded like it was coming from a thousand miles away. Hands too big to be hers caught him, pulling, yanking, pleading with him to come, but he couldn't. He couldn't.

When he turned, he'd have screamed if he had air in his lungs.

A woman with glowing white eyes, graying black hair, and an unholy smile stared back at him. The nothingness that came from her was total—absolute. A chasm. A void. An eternal gulf that screamed from the absence of anything to fill it. If there had ever been something more to her, it had been consumed long ago.

And yet—and yet, there was more. Beneath the all-consuming void, hundreds of thousands of voices screamed in terror. The nothingness branched out of her like sickly arms, reaching, reaching, reaching, into oblivion, begging for someone to pull them out.

The Sister's smile grew larger still, and her laugh chilled the very marrow in Leon's bones.

Chapter 19
A Barricade Falls

Leon stumbled back, the heavy weight of Jackie hanging around his shoulders and waist the only thing keeping him remotely grounded. The hands that had previously been tugging him back fell away as he passed the battered walls of the barricade.

Padraeg was beside him, equally slack-jawed as he stared at the impossibility before them. Did he understand that this was the Sister? Did he understand what was happening? He couldn't; otherwise he'd have run the second he figured it out. The way Leon wanted desperately to run, but his legs refused to listen to him.

"You . . ." Leon whispered. "You can't be here."

Because the Sister couldn't be that far from the Brother. That was the only reason she hadn't taken over Hyderia. The only reason that Leon had lived for this long. She and the Brother were trapped in Dhuitholm thanks to the senior knights and whatever magic they'd cast to trap the Brother there.

But she was here now, twenty feet away from Leon, and smiling at him.

"Goodness, I wondered which one of you traitors had escaped that horrid barrier the knights put up." Her voice was sickly sweet, like strawberries on a heady summer day, and as rotten as three-week-old fish. She stepped closer, and the husks shrunk back, away from the docks. The nothingness inside them twisted and swirled, tightening around them until Leon thought they would snap. The Sister's smile only grew as she stepped forward, closer, heedless of the bodies in her path. "I don't remember your face, but then, I killed so many of you before you stole my brother from me that you all blend together."

"You can't be here," he said again. It had to be a trick. She was projecting herself into that poor woman while her real body was back in Dhuitholm. The sheer weight of her presence forcing itself down on him was—it had to be fake. All of this would have been for nothing if she was here.

If Leon's legs could move, he would've run. If his lungs could breathe, he would've screamed. But no. He could barely stand. The hands had come back, and Padraeg was trying to make him run, but he couldn't run. None of them could. She would take the city and then take the world. But first, she'd take Leon.

"Oh—" The Sister chuckled, wagging a finger like Leon was an unruly child she'd been charged with straightening out. "You'll find that I can. My brother lent me some of his power so I could get away and take care of you rats. He felt so bad that his mistake has kept me at his side."

Padraeg stiffened at Leon's side and let loose an oath. Whether that was a prayer or a curse was unclear. Neither would help here.

An arrow whistled past Leon and narrowly missed the Sister. "Stay back!" a shaky voice called from behind them. Whoever was back there was equal parts brave and foolish. "We'll kill you if you take another step forward."

This time Leon was the one who wanted to laugh. Didn't they know the Sister couldn't be killed with any weapons forged by human hands? Only a weapon blessed by the Watchful Peace and borne by a Knight Vigilant could pierce that hide. She was here, and Leon wouldn't be able to get away. Jackie's weight slid off his back, and her tiny hand snuck into his. He didn't have to look down to know she'd also grabbed Padraeg.

320

"Let's go," she whispered, her impossibly small voice a whisper on the wind. "We're past the barricade. The ship is right there. Let's just—let's go. Please." Her voice dissolved into tears. She didn't know. None of them did. All they saw was Leon frozen on the edge of safety while an old woman approached.

Safety she could still reach. The Sister might command the husks to attack, but if Jackie was on the ship, the Sea would keep the Sister away.

"Go," he whispered, barely moving his lips. "I'll catch up—" His throat seized again. He didn't want to lie to Jackie. Choking, he squeezed her hand. "Take Padraeg and go. Tell them to pull up the planks. I'll be along."

Padraeg inhaled sharply but didn't speak. He didn't try to fight, to whisper that Leon should go, too, which made Leon more grateful than words could say.

As long as Jackie got to the ship, he could focus. If Padraeg went, even unwillingly, he'd be safe too. Aoife would keep them there. Jackie would pass on Leon's message and—gods, it hurt to consider—Njeri would believe that he would follow. Right up until the Sister ripped out his heart.

He would die here. Death had been two decades coming, but it was finally here. The Sea or the Sister would kill him. It was just a matter of what happened to his soul when all was said and done. Would Death's sentinels take him to whatever fate that would befall the Knights Beyond now that their last link to this world was gone? Would he be trapped in the same hell the knights he'd known as a boy were? Would—

Yes, run, a hundred thousand voices whispered, heavy with hate. **We left, hoping to draw her away. We are sorry. Run while you still can.**

Leon's breath caught in his chest, and tears pricked at his eyes. The Knights Beyond had come. They hadn't left him, and he wouldn't die alone. But that relief quickly turned to anger.

They were sorry? *Them?* Gods, they'd left him to face an army of husks and the bloody Sister after forcing him to reveal himself to the entire city. They'd gone, and now—and now what did they plan on doing? He tore his eyes from the Sister for a bare moment to glare at the nearest dead knight.

The Sister's grin grew wider still, and she clapped joyfully. "Oh, you've brought the dead to join us. I had wondered when they would come to add themselves to my collection. How long has it been?"

The defenders clutched their weapons, unsure of what to do or what the Sister meant. Some held bows and crossbows close to their chests; others held tight to halberds, swords, and axes. Leon's gaze swept over them in a detached sort of way. With the dead hanging over them, unseen but felt for the first time in millennia, they seemed to forget their fear.

Long enough to hate. The knights still spoke as one, and their voices boomed louder than the alarm bells and distant fighting, louder than the waves crashing onto the shore, and louder than the screaming in Leon's heart. **Leave or we will make you.**

"Leave?" She threw her head back and roared with laughter. "Why would I leave? Even that coward, Death, can't give you leave to touch the living realm, and their sentinels fear me too much to take the souls left behind. My ranks will swell with the lifeblood of this town and its gods." Her head tilted sideways to an unnatural degree as she took another step forward. "I think I'll take him," she purred. "If I spill enough of his blood on the threshold, do you think the barriers will fall? The rest of his order has worked so hard to keep me out while they torture my poor

322

brother. To see their faces when I slit his throat will be . . . delicious."

A presence pushed into Leon's back and spilled courage and strength into his limbs. **Be strong,** whispered a single voice, separate and distinct from all the others. **Have faith, the Watchful Peace hasn't abandoned you.**

He'd known that voice once. It belonged to someone who had bandaged his scraped knees, cradled him while he screamed for arms that would never hold him again, and took his hand when Delke came to meet him and Mael.

His hand tightened once more around Jackie's, and he nodded. "Get ready to run when I say so," he whispered through clenched teeth. He didn't care who heard him. The defenders had another barricade farther down the dock, less than twenty feet from the plank. It would have to be enough. They could jump into the water if it came down to it. Perhaps the Sea would feel generous today. "I can distract her." It wouldn't be him, but it was close enough. Whatever magic the Knights Beyond could use from the other side of the deathly veil would have to work.

The Sister took one more step forward, and the Knights Beyond bristled. Ten thousand dead knights drew ghostly weapons, and their faded forms solidified, casting shadows down below them to the terror of the defenders. Jackie clung to Leon, and he rested a hand on her back.

Then, the Sister contorted. Her limbs stretched and cracked, growing three times longer than her body was tall. Her eyes gleamed like stars ripped from the heavens, and the nothingness crawled across the dock like a spider crawled across its web.

Coming straight for them.

Run, the knights roared, their voices too loud and real to be entirely beyond Death's veil, and this time Leon listened. Everyone listened.

He spun, yelling as loud as he could as he scooped Jackie up. "To the other barricade, hurry!" He'd never seen someone become corrupted, become a husk, but he knew enough to know that if the nothingness touched them, it would be too late. They would become the Sister's playthings.

The Sister's infuriated screams followed them down the dock. Jackie covered her ears, trying desperately to block out the sound of things that weren't flesh hitting things that weren't steel. Ancient prayers and cursed oaths split the evening when waves began crashing on the dock. Three of the defenders were swept away, unnatural currents taking them out to sea.

Leon ran, Padraeg beside him and Jackie in his arms. Salt water soaked them, wind battered them, and the sky above them was turning dark as the Sea rose up in anger. The world narrowed to what was in front of him, to Jackie clinging to him, and to the horrible sounds coming from behind them. They reached the second barricades and the defenders, most whispering prayers through sobbing breaths, prepared to do their duty.

Aoife was waving them on, Shea and Kelan beside her, ready to yank the plank up as soon as they boarded. The other ship had already left, the current taking them farther away with each second as the water pulled back. The Sea would not let the Sister have them if they could prevent it.

They were almost there when a scream shook Leon's bones, and the dock exploded under his feet. Fire and pain erupted in equal measure as the dock disintegrated underneath him, and he desperately threw himself forward, thrusting Jackie away from him. If he was going to fall, let her be on the far side of the dock. Let him crash into the waves, dashed on the support walls or swept out to sea while the weight of his armor and clothes dragged him down. Let the Sea be a barrier between Jackie and the Sister.

But he didn't fall all the way. He stopped with a teeth-rattling jolt, his arm held tightly in an unknown hand keeping him from the roiling waters thirty feet below, the stone pillars that supported the dock, and the broken wood pointing up through the waves. Terror and relief flooded him, and his head snapped up to find his savior.

"I've got you," Padraeg hissed, clinging to a broken board on the wrong side of the gulf in the dock. A chunk of wood, a remnant of the shattered dock, stuck out of his shoulder, and blood dripped down his sleeve, slicking his hand and Leon's arm. "I've got you," he repeated through gritted teeth. His face contorted in agony, and Leon wanted to throw up.

He was hurt. He was bleeding and in pain, but he'd still saved Leon.

"Let me go," Leon yelled, tearing at Padraeg's fingers with his free hand. "I'm not hurt, I'll be fine. The water will catch me. You—"

"Hang that," Padraeg said, snarling. He glared at Leon like he'd suggested surrendering to the Sister. "I'm not letting you go. I just got you back, and the Sea can go rot if they think I'm losing you again."

But that wasn't—he wasn't worth that, Leon wanted to yell back. Sea spray and wind cut into him, chilling him down to his marrow, and he bit back pain that wasn't physical. He was the reason the Sister was here, why the husks had pushed so fast to get here. He'd purified Ranon, led the guard to the husks in Mezeldwelf, and in doing so revealed himself to the Templesbane. If it weren't for him, Padraeg would've gotten away.

If Padraeg dropped him, yes, he might get hurt, but Padraeg was already injured. He wouldn't be able to swim like that, and his grip was slipping even now. If he let Leon go, he might be able to save himself. He'd find a way across the gap, to Aoife and Jackie and everyone depending on him. Leon would be fine. He would be fine, because otherwise Padraeg would kill himself trying to save Leon.

He opened his mouth to tell Padraeg that, but unfamiliar voices interrupted him before he could. Two defenders, vaguely familiar mercenaries carrying rope, appeared over the edge. They grabbed Padraeg's arm, and one dropped the rope down for Leon to latch on to.

Despite himself, despite his willingness to submit to the water, Leon was glad to see them. Padraeg wouldn't drop Leon, and he couldn't pull him up with a shoulder like that. It was a miracle he'd been able to hold Leon this long. If they'd hung there any longer, they would've both fallen.

So Leon took the rope and used it to climb out, each laborious movement bringing each ache and pain he'd ignored to fiery life. Sharp wood jabbed into his legs, and sharper fingers dug into his back and shoulders before abandoning him to help Padraeg the same way.

Then Leon saw, for the first time, what the Knights Beyond were holding off with prayer, magic, and Death's own luck. The Sister, grown to monstrous size and form, with limbs bent at unnatural angles and thick branches of nothingness—like holes in reality—swirling around her as visible as the ocean itself. The knights charged, hacking at the nothingness that shouldn't be seen, beating it back. Leon felt the agony that swept through them when the nothingness made contact. Each blow and strike ripped the corporeality from them, wiping away the magic that ground them here. Consuming them.

It was as clear as the sunset. The knights were losing, and soon the defenders would have to take their place.

And Leon and Padraeg were still on the wrong side of the dock.

"Leon, Padraeg!" Jackie's scream, relieved and shaken all at once, reached Leon's ears like a divine chorus as he scrambled to his feet.

His head spun so fast his neck cracked. The relief beat down the terror, and he could've wept. She'd made it to the other side. He'd fallen, but she would make it. "Get to the ship," he roared, helping Padraeg up.

Padraeg's injury was worse this close. Even with the wood still lodged inside, he was bleeding a lot. Without healing, he might never use that arm—his sword arm—again.

Behind him, the Sister still fought the Knights Beyond, but the nothingness was winning.

Jackie hesitated, fear written all over her face. "Go," Leon yelled again. "We'll be fine, we'll—" He scanned the dock, desperate for some way to get Padraeg across, something he could use to save him if nothing else. The dock was destroyed. The explosives had gone off too early—whether some trickery by the Sister or unknown plan of the Sea—and cut Leon and Padraeg off from the other side. There weren't even any pieces long enough to use as a plank.

"We'll be fine," he repeated, smiling in a way he hoped looked confident. His words were hollow, and Jackie knew it, too, judging by the crestfallen face and the tears she couldn't hide. Setting her shoulders, she turned and ran, sliding across the soaking dock toward the ship and straight into Aoife's waiting arms.

"She'll be fine," Padraeg said in a low voice, panting for each breath. He held his injured arm close to his chest, and his face was turning gray. His sword wasn't at his side, likely lost to the waves below. "Now we have to get you across."

"Both of us," Leon snapped, readjusting his grip on Padraeg. "Come on. Let's hurry."

He wouldn't leave Padraeg behind.

Chancing a look back, Leon blanched and yanked Padraeg aside as the Sister sent a massive wave of nothingness hurtling toward them.

"Once knight," the Sister roared, her voice echoing through the air, the water, and the otherworldly plane the Knights Beyond and gods without forms spoke through. She thrust an arm out, and great towers of nothingness ripped through the ground, arching high into the sky. The husks, standing motionlessly behind her, fell to the ground as if she tore their very souls from them. "Traitor knight. You who left your brethren to fall at my hands. Face me."

Leon took a trembling step back. The gulf beckoned behind them. The Sister waited in front of them. The odds were not good in either direction.

"Fuck off," he shouted, far braver than he felt.

The Sister sneered, her lips pulled back to reveal black teeth dripping with the same nonexistence she wielded as a weapon. The Knights Beyond were gone. They were out of time.

The air froze in Leon's lungs as the towers came crashing down. The few defenders left, the ones that hadn't fallen off the dock or succumbed to the Sister, screamed and sobbed as their souls were torn from them.

Leon was about to die. The death he'd been outrunning since he was thirteen had finally caught up, and he would find out what the Templesbane had done to the other knights in Dhuitholm that day. And yet—and yet, it was only now that Leon found it in himself to pray.

Gods above, below, and around, he cried out from a place deep in his heart, where he'd locked away the boy who'd watched his home and family fall apart around him. Padraeg's weight hanging off his shoulder was a painful reminder of his last failure, but nonetheless, Leon clutched his hand like he'd done as a boy terrified of what he saw in his dreams. *Please let the ships get away. Please don't let this all have been for nothing.*

The refugees would escape. They'd go to Falte, and one of the gods there would remind the world of what the Knights Beyond had done to gain their power. A new order under a different god would be born, and the Knights Vigilant would be relegated to history, where they belonged.

As long as the ships got away, it would all be worth it.

The world slowed. The sound of waves, of distant explosions and fighting faded to nothing. Color bled away and feeling followed. Even the Sister herself froze like a statue.

"Risen knight," a voice whispered in Leon's ear, smaller than a breath across a butterfly's wings. "Found knight and vigilant knight. You cannot die here."

He didn't really have a choice. Whatever magic this was, whatever god had spared Leon for however many desperate seconds more, it wouldn't stop what was coming. There was no escape. The hourglass of Leon's life was running out, and all the tricks he'd used to pour even the smallest amount of sand in there wouldn't help here.

The voice chuckled, and the sound bolstered Leon's flagging limbs. He was as gray, as lifeless as everything else.

"Delke chose well," the voice whispered approvingly. "You have survived where others would not."

He hadn't. He'd always relied on others. On Padraeg and Aoife at first, and then, later on, Njeri and the Band. He'd hidden away the truth of himself until it was too late to reverse course.

"You did as ordered," the voice said sharply, "and you did well."

If Leon had been able to move, he'd have laughed. What did the voice know? Whatever god this was, they hadn't been there that day. Leon had chosen to run. To leave everyone he knew behind. This god, if indeed it was a god and not some deranged final attempt of Leon's mind to make peace with his past, may have given Leon a few moments to plan or maybe just froze the Sister until the ships got away, but that was it.

"We can do more," the voice interjected, somewhere between amused and disappointed. "If you ask me by name. I'm peculiar among my siblings that way."

Their name? How was Leon supposed to know their name? There were as many gods as there were fragmented parts of reality. He wouldn't even know where to begin.

"You do know me," the voice whispered, a feeling like fingers dragging through Leon's tangled hair accompanying it. "But the magic made you forget my touch, kept me from reaching out to you while you were under the protection of my kin. There are cracks in the walls of the old defenses, and it's past time for you to remember my voice."

And Leon did. Like a floodgate, a thousand memories crashed through a wall he hadn't even realized was there.

Praying before a tiny altar in the armory before he was anointed. The Vigilant General looking down at him with pity. Mael hugging him, begging him to stay safe until they could see each other again. Delke's hand leading him to the stable and down a tunnel. This voice, stronger then, commanding him to leave before the spell was cast, before the wall went up and the Templesbane realized they were walking into a trap. The trembling of the nag beneath him as he urged her ever faster away from the city before it was too late.

Then, sitting on a lookout point outside the city, watching green light spill from the keep when the spell that would require

330

every other member of the order to sustain was cast. The spell that would drain the Brother of every god and soul he'd ever consumed, down to Vigilance themself, that would separate Leon from everyone he'd ever known or loved. Feeling his memories slipping away to keep the secret of his own role in what was to come, even from himself, and the protections the other gods promised him sliding into place.

He hadn't run. He hadn't—he wasn't a coward.

"Ask me," the voice whispered, winding around each limb and deep into Leon's soul. "Ask me the way the knights of old asked for help freeing my greater aspect. Ask me like one who bears part of my essence."

And Leon found his tongue.

"Help me," he whispered, his voice no louder than that of the Watchful Peace, broken and small after years of holding back a far greater foe. They were different here, in the grayness, in the same way a god was different from their worshippers. "Help me save the ones I love." Padraeg, Aoife, Jackie, the Band, and even the knights and normal people that hadn't been able to escape Dhuitholm, the ones still trapped there behind a barrier no one could pierce. "Help me fulfill my oaths and my orders. Give me strength, oh god of the Watchful Peace."

The voice shivered, and the world snapped back into color, into movement, into sound. But this time, Leon wasn't alone. This time, Leon could fight as only a Knight Vigilant could.

Raising a hand, Leon whispered, and the words that came out were not of this world. The magic that burst from the spaces between his fingers was not meant for mortal souls to wield. The fires burning through him were not of him, and yet could never be separated from him.

The magic hit the falling towers and scattered them, what should've been divided between a thousand knights condensed into one man. The nothingness vanished when fragments of reality and power shared willingly, instead of taken by trickery, slammed into them. A hundred souls burst forth from the collision, darting back into the city, into the Fallow Lands, and beyond, seeking the beings they'd been torn from or the safety of Death's sentinels.

The Sister screamed in agony and doubled over in pain. "Traitor," she said, snarling through clenched teeth. "You had a chance to help us purge this world of your infernal kin, and you threw it away."

"Foul demon," the Watchful Peace thundered through Leon's mouth. His throat burned under the stress, under the power of giving a god a voice. **"Destroyer of gods and bane of temples. You will not take this man. You will not take these people."**

Leon took a step forward, and the Sister screamed once more. The waves around him settled, the dock reformed, and the defenders watched in awe as divine light poured from every inch of Leon's exposed skin, cleansing the taint of the Sister's presence from the world and repairing the damage she'd wrought to the city. Padraeg arched away, stumbling back, but Leon hardly noticed. The Watchful Peace would not abide chaos. They would not allow the Sister to escape this unharmed, and they would restore what she had destroyed, no matter what it took.

The Sister gave way under the assault. With each step, her attacks grew more wild, more scattered. Vigilance was a powerful god indeed, but their strength was still unwillingly divided between the Sister, the Brother, and whatever scraps of themselves they still possessed. The Watchful Peace could, for now, focus its strength on Leon, on each attack.

Before Leon knew it, he had his hand around her throat. Her skin burned like acid against him, and only the presence of his god kept Leon from dropping her.

"You have taken enough under the guise of peace, under the guise of *Vigilance.*"

Leon could feel each soul, each divinity buried deep inside her, giving her strength as the Watchful Peace raged. The gods held souls clustered near themselves, holding off the Sister's strength and keeping them from being wholly consumed. From completely giving in to the corruption that used their bodies like toys. They were entwined, as close to each other as one breath was from the next.

Charity and the Knights Beyond had helped him pull a single soul free of the quagmire. One soul who had left his touch on the ones around him, on the god that had sheltered him.

Ranon was the unknowing key to undoing some of the damage wrought by the Templesbane.

Just as Leon had done with Ranon, as the Knights Beyond and Charity had shown him, Leon latched on to the god that had sheltered Ranon's soul, and pulled. The power of the Watchful Peace burned through him, holding tight to their long-lost sibling and giving Leon the strength to pull a god free from the void.

Together, Leon and the Watchful Peace pulled and purified, shining a light where there had only been darkness for millennia beyond counting.

The Sister writhed, pulling all her strength back, clawing for every soul, but it wasn't enough. Each soul and god required their own scrap of power to keep under her control, and she dared not loosen her grip on even the smallest child for fear of losing them entirely. Partial effort wasn't enough to withstand the full force of the Watchful Peace.

A strange sensation filled Leon; a wound he hadn't even realized he'd been favoring suddenly made whole. And, far away, near Amberbrook, a lake that had been dark and stagnant returned to life. A thousand people that had been husks breathed free for the first time in years when their souls returned home.

It wasn't enough. The Sister still thrashed under Leon's grip, striking at him, clawing at his hands and face.

So Leon dove again, latching on to another god, larger this time, and tugged. The void bled where he'd previously struck, a weakness that rippled through it and spread to each surrounding soul.

He pulled, ignoring the blood pouring from his nose and the stabbing pain in his chest. The Sister had done enough damage, and the Watchful Peace was prepared to do whatever it took to regain the ones she had consumed.

Leon's senses burned, stretched far beyond his mortal ken. The wounds the Templesbane had dealt the world were as clear to him as her wretched face before him. When gods swallowed whole were retrieved, the salvation and healing that spewed forth were as bright as the dawn.

Families were reunited, souls freed, and life found its way back into places that had been barren for centuries. Fields burst into flower, rivers flowed anew, and Compassion warmed the hearts of people who had forgotten their touch.

Again and again he struck, each blow stealing as much strength from him as the Sister. His breath grew shallow, and his legs struggled to support him, but still he refused to let up the attack.

Voices reached Leon. Deeper, more sturdy ones that he never thought he'd hear again. Knights that had given their unlife, the strange force keeping them bound to the world and to Leon, to hold the Sister off. They, too, had been freed.

You must stop, they whispered, dancing around Leon like the wind. They were weaker, their voices the only thing they could manifest. **You can't save everyone. It will kill you.**

It was already killing him. Leon could feel the blood pouring down his nose, the strength leaving his limbs, and the agony tearing through his innermost self. The power of the gods was not meant to be wielded by humans like this, not even one who shared in their essence. It would destroy him, but in doing so he could free all the people trapped by the Sister. The Watchful Peace had awakened after twenty years and wouldn't be reined in that easily.

Gods, where had the others gone? Had the defenders run? Had Padraeg managed to get to the ship? How long had Leon been standing here? He had no answers. The world had narrowed to Leon, to the Watchful Peace, and to a battle happening that no one else could see.

They will listen to you. You are the order's last hope. They pushed into Leon, resting against the hand that clutched the Sister's throat. **Let go. You have done enough.**

Just one more, he argued, the warmth of the god reaching for him, strengthening the cracks in Leon's resolve. One more, and he would retreat. Dozens still remained, but the Sister was wounded—this had to be enough.

But this god was so heavy. A greater aspect that hadn't expected to be freed so soon. They'd taken many souls from their weaker siblings to shield them from the strain and refused to leave any behind.

We will help, the knights whispered, their voices fading even as they spoke. **But then we must rest.**

A familiar strength traveled down Leon's arm. The faint impression of hands grabbed onto him, bolstering him for what lay ahead.

The god saw them, and their joy flooded through Leon like the blazing fires of a forge. Their strength doubled. They inched free and then——

Leon fell, the connection broken. He dropped like a stone, far farther than he should have if he'd just been standing. He hit the dock with a loud smack, and agony untold arched through him, lighting every nerve on fire. Gods, even his hair hurt. Scrambling attempts to put together a coherent thought sent the world spinning.

Biting back a whimper, Leon forced himself onto his knees and squinted into the smoke and the fog. His vision blurred, and each breath knocked against something in his chest that made it go white. He could barely make out the vague forms of the defenders in the crowd and then breathed out an agonizing sigh when he saw that they still moved.

The Sister was the only thing that he could see clearly, and she was in no better position than he was. She cowered against the shattered remnants of the first barricade, older and smaller than before. A broken pike stuck through her stomach, sending black blood spilling down her tunic. She hissed through broken teeth and spat poison. "You—you stole something that belongs to me. You let those filth back into the world."

If he'd had the air and strength to speak, Leon would've protested. He hadn't stolen anything. He'd just taken back the souls and gods the Sister had stolen for herself.

But the Sister wasn't one to care about semantics like that. With a sickening squelch, she pulled the pike through her stomach, and a wave of nothingness emerged to stopper the wound.

Leon watched this proceed with a detached sort of interest. He ought to move, but even stringing two thoughts together was beyond him when the world spun like this.

Someone was yelling behind him, but they were very far away. And standing in a tunnel, apparently. He'd only ever heard echoes like that in tunnels and caves. They sounded scared, though.

"You haven't won yet." She looked at the pike and smiled before hefting it in her scrawny arms. "Your god can't help you now."

It shouldn't have flown that fast. Leon could barely stand, and she'd gone through the same thing he had, but in reverse. Besides, her arms were so scrawny. She shouldn't have been able to lift that pike, let alone throw it.

A blurry figure in battered steel armor leaped in front of Leon. A white braid, falling apart and covered in blood, dangled in front of Leon like a worm on a hook, and the world reorientated itself with a horrific twist.

Sound came back with a pop, and Leon let loose a scream that nearly took it from him again. He surged to his feet, heedless of the stabbing pain in his chest and the way his legs threatened to collapse beneath him.

The Sister cackled, and the nothingness, quieter but just as violent as always, swirled around her. Leon hardly noticed because Padraeg fell to his knees, the pike sticking straight through his chest.

Leon caught him before he could fall any farther, and pressed his hand to the wound. Blood poured out around the pike, and Padraeg let loose a pained gurgle.

"Gods, Padraeg," Leon cried. Tears spilled down his cheeks and fell on Padraeg's bloodless face. "We'll get you help, gods, why did you get in the way? I—I—" He couldn't even finish, his words dissolving into sobs.

Padraeg gurgled again but didn't answer.

"Sir Leon, you have to go," one of the defenders insisted, tugging Leon's arm. "The husks are regrouping and the barricades are gone, you need to leave."

"No," Leon snapped. "Help me with him. There are bandages on the—on the ship. We can't leave him, we can't—"

Gods, he couldn't lose Padraeg. He couldn't. Not when he'd just relearned his purpose. Padraeg could see Delke and Mael again. They could all be a family once Dhuitholm was freed, once the barrier came down and the Brother and the Sister were destroyed. Once Leon fulfilled his purpose.

A hand, coated in blood, reached up to brush the tears from Leon's cheeks. "G—go—go," Padraeg whispered. "Lea—leave me. I'm too—too hurt."

"No," Leon whispered, grabbing tight to Padraeg's hand and squeezing. "No, no, no, no. I'm not leaving, not without you."

"G—go," Padraeg repeated, holding tight to Leon's hand for a fraction of a second before he lost all strength. "Ta—take him, please. I'm so sorry."

Hands grabbed Leon under his arms. Familiar hands. Strong hands. They pulled him back, away from Padraeg, and he howled like a wolf, like a wild thing, fighting with all his strength.

"Stop," he roared, drawing the attention of every defender and husk on the wharf. "No, not without him, I'm not leaving."

But they didn't stop, and Leon, weak and injured, couldn't fight them off. He howled and thrashed and fought, each move bringing the abyss closer and closer to him, but he didn't dare stop. They couldn't leave Padraeg behind.

As Leon's vision clouded, a tall and familiar shadow tore past him and picked up Padraeg.

The relief that flooded Leon's body was too much for him to stand. This time, he welcomed the blackness.

Chapter 20
The First Goodbye

The sailors had scrounged up a length of white canvas. It might have been meant as a sail, but now it would never snap in the sea breeze. Now it was put to a darker, more somber purpose.

Leon knelt beside it and the form it covered, staring into the empty air. His tears had long since dried, and the ache in his knees was starting to overpower the lingering pain from his broken ribs, the collection of hastily stitched wounds that covered his arms and face, and the sigil seared into his arm. But he didn't move. Couldn't move. Moving would mean acknowledging that he was ready to let go, burn the herbs, and say his last goodbyes.

Shea, his eyes burning like the Forge's fires, had gotten Padraeg on board as the Sister sent her few remaining husks shambling toward the dock. Leon's memories were shaky, but he'd seen it happen. Padraeg had been alive and talking when Kelan and Njeri had pulled Leon away. He remembered that much at least.

Leon had regained consciousness to the distant sounds of explosions and a burning, searing pain from his arm as the sigil that they hadn't had time to remove burned itself into his flesh, tying him forever to a man who was dead now. Black smoke had drifted overhead as the only home he'd known in twenty years burned for the sins of another.

Aoife's was the only face he'd recognized then, his vision still blurry with pain and each breath a struggle. While other hands stitched him, she'd cradled his head, whispered nonsense, and assured him that everyone was fine. That Jackie was fine. That Padraeg would be fine.

He'd trusted her enough to drink the potion someone offered him, the one that sent him deep into sleep. When he woke up, he realized that Aoife had lied to him.

Because Padraeg never woke up. They'd been put into one of the smaller cabins, a makeshift sickroom, and Leon refused all offers to move. He wanted to be there when Padraeg woke up. Once he was awake, they'd talk, really talk, and Leon would rib Padraeg about taking a blow meant for Leon. They'd plan for future battles, and Padraeg would be at Leon's side when the Protectors finally drove the Templesbane from Dhuitholm. He'd see Delke and Mael again when Leon freed the Knights Vigilant from their self-made prison. Things would be fine when Padraeg woke up. As long as he kept breathing, as long as the fire that burned under his skin stayed low, Padraeg would be all right.

That was what Leon told himself, the denial he'd practiced for two decades hiding the truth from him.

The others came to try to woo Leon away. They knew what was coming, the facts that Leon ignored. They promised food, ale, conversation, and more if only Leon would leave, would stray from Padraeg's side for a minute and acknowledge what was to come. Only Shea, who lit the lamps with a flame that burst from his fingers and listened to Leon's words with ears as pointed as a blade, didn't try to argue. He brought Leon food and whispered news, keeping Jackie away from the sickroom.

All while Leon waited for Padraeg to wake. He hoped, prayed to the Watchful Peace and any other god listening. None of the godsworn on board had healing abilities. If they had, perhaps things would've been different. Even Charity, who sometimes visited to hold Leon's hand while he wept, lacked the power to heal damage of that scope.

After the third day, when Padraeg's skin burned and he started mumbling nonsense in his fever dreams, Aoife joined Leon's vigil. Before that, she'd wandered in and out, trusting her brother's care to Leon and Charity while she wrangled the other princes, the crew, and the mercenaries. But with the writing on the wall and growing evidence even Leon struggled to deny, she'd passed her duties on and waited at her brother's side. They'd each held one of Padraeg's hands when he finally took his last rasping breath on the fifth night out of Mezeldwelf.

And now, Leon was alone, sitting in front of the body that wasn't Padraeg anymore. He hadn't moved since Aoife went to prepare for the ceremony. When she came back, they would burn the herbs and offerings to Death and then give Padraeg's body to the Sea. They would offer token prayers and bite back their grief, and then everyone would move on.

The Quinn family had a mausoleum in Mezeldwelf. Most of the tombs were empty, as should be expected for a family that had been devoted to sailing and trade for generations, but Padraeg had a spot there. He'd shown Leon once, during a macabre mourning ritual Leon had insisted on throwing for the Knights Vigilant. Padraeg had expected to lie there one day, and now he never would. Instead, his body would be entrusted to the Sea, the way so many of his ancestors had been.

The door creaked open, and the sunlight, too bright and cheery for so dark a day, lit up the room. Leon didn't turn to see who entered. He knew who it would be and that denying them wouldn't stop what they came to do, but he couldn't face them. That would make it real.

Figures in dark cloaks, their hoods drawn and faces covered, passed him, litter in hand. Leon watched, fresh tears running down his cheeks, as they moved Padraeg's covered body onto the litter.

Sailors were a superstitious bunch. They had to be, serving a master like the Sea. A jealous and angry god that didn't tolerate any of their siblings poking fingers where they didn't belong. The things on the surface and the things deep below the waves belonged to them, and even Death had to ask permission to collect their due.

So when someone died on board a ship, the sailors—those sworn to the Sea—drew straws. The two unlucky souls that lost would act as Death's sentinels. They had prepared Padraeg, and they were the ones who would offer his body to the Sea while Leon and Aoife burned their offerings so Death could find his soul.

"It's time to go," Aoife whispered, her voice as rough as sandpaper. "I've prepared everything."

Leon rose on wooden legs. His limbs burned, his knees screamed, and his broken ribs ached. Each was a physical reminder that Leon wasn't dreaming. They were really about to do this.

Absentmindedly, he offered Aoife his arm. She took it and led them out of the cabin and above deck, where all the passengers and crew waited with heavy hearts and damp cheeks. There wasn't a soul born of Mezeldwelf that didn't know of Padraeg Quinn and all he'd done for the city he loved. The refugees would mourn when they heard of his death. The way those here mourned now.

Njeri stood by the stairs leading to the upper deck. Jackie, eyes already swollen and red from crying, held her hand. Njeri pressed a hand to her heart and bowed, an old Alkan mourning sign. Leon passed without acknowledging it.

The princes formed a narrow walkway leading to the port side, and the two sailors acting as Death's sentinels carried Padraeg's litter past them, stopping at the edge of the ship.

Hume, dressed in an excessively ornate mourning robe, held the herbs in a simple copper bowl. Toren, the mousy-haired prince, stood opposite them, sheltering a small candle from the winds with his hands.

Aoife led him right toward them, and Leon wanted to scream, to make it all stop. He bit the urge back and took the small bundle of herbs Aoife offered him. Ritual words spilled from Leon's mouth, things he'd said a hundred times before when burying members of the Band who'd fallen to blade or sickness.

He dropped the herbs back into the copper bowl, and Aoife repeated what he'd done. From her mouth, the ritual words were harsh and unnatural, as if she, too, struggled to comprehend how someone as strong as Padraeg needed them to be said. When her words and her goodbyes were finished, she dropped a tiny cloth bundle cut from Padraeg's clothes and tied around a lock of his hair alongside the herbs.

The wind battered Leon, and the waves crashed over them as Leon took the candle. Aoife's hand covered his, and she made an expression that could've been a smile if it weren't for the tears. Together, they lowered it into the bowl. The herbs caught first and then the cloth. As the flames burned, the sentinels tilted the litter, and Padraeg Quinn went to his final resting place.

***

Leon wasn't sure how long he'd been sitting there. Once the ceremony finished, Aoife pulled him below deck and led him to her cabin. It was large for one person, especially with the cramped quarters the rest had to deal with, but she wasn't supposed to be here alone.

She'd plopped him down on the bench and sat beside him. They'd fallen into silence, each staring into nothing and mourning separately a life they should be mourning together.

Finally, she drew in a shaky breath, and her hand darted to her braid, where a familiar gray tie held her hair together.

That was what broke Leon. "I'm sorry," he mumbled, wrapping a hand in her skirts like a child seeking comfort from their mother. "I'm sorry I couldn't—" There shouldn't be any tears left. The gaping hole in his chest had to close or empty at some point. "I should've saved him," he gasped out. "I should've stopped the Sister, but I—" He'd failed. He hadn't been strong enough even with the full force of the Watchful Peace bolstering him. He'd failed, and Padraeg had paid the price.

Aoife's hand came to rest on Leon's head and tangled in his hair, freshly washed and combed for the funeral, the first time Leon had paid attention to his grooming since they left Mezeldwelf. Her voice was hoarse, brittle, and stretched thin. "It's all right," she whispered. "Padraeg would've—" She let out a choked gasp and blinked back tears. "He'd have done anything to keep you safe."

If she meant it to help, it didn't. Each word stabbed into Leon's heart like a dagger. As much as he wanted to jump and snap that it hadn't been his fault, that he hadn't asked Padraeg to sacrifice himself like that, he made himself stay still and silent.

It was all his fault.

He deserved whatever blame Aoife leveled upon him. If he'd managed to stay out of Mezeldwelf, if he'd kept Jackie safe and healthy enough to find Quinn Manor without him, the Sister never would've come. The Band would've found the husks, and Padraeg would've made the ships without worrying about Leon.

They settled into a silence that gaped between them like the abyss between life and death. There were no words that could breach it, no gesture that could soothe the agony that struck both of them down. It merely existed, a wound that tore them from their loved ones long before their time.

"He left something for you," Aoife whispered. Her hand clenched the end of her braid, around the hair tie that had been Padraeg's and Delke's before him. "A letter. He left it with his things." She reached into her pocket and pulled out an envelope, creased and battered from its time there. "Here—I found it when I was getting ready."

Leon bit back a sob and took the proffered envelope before either of them started crying again.

It made his stomach twist to look at it, to see his name written in Padraeg's careful script across the front. It was heavy in his hand, too heavy to just be paper inside.

A part of him wasn't ready. Reading Padraeg's final words would destroy him. Opening that envelope would mean he'd have to read whatever Padraeg had written and deal with the contents. Good or ill, encouragement or scolding.

He didn't want anything to do with it. He wanted nothing less than to rip it open right now, to tear off the bandage and drown himself in the last thing Padraeg had ever written to him.

Aoife's gaze weighed on him, making the decision he couldn't bring himself to make.

He used his thumb to break the seal and pulled out the thin scrap of parchment inside. The envelope fell to the table as he devoured Padraeg's words.

Leon,

I know this isn't how you intended to reveal yourself when you were young. Charity forced your hand, and the princes won't let you leave quietly. It's a bad hand all around and not, I imagine, what you wanted when you brought Jackie here.

But . . . I can't help thinking that perhaps this was better. Without Charity and without your sacrifice, we'd never have been able to convince the princes that Mesley had betrayed us. Without you, the city and its people would have fallen into the hands of the Sister. For that alone, I will never be able to thank you enough.

I hope you know that I consider raising you, watching you grow from boy to man, to be one of the greatest privileges of my life. I know we've had our differences, but I always knew you'd wind up on the right path, whatever that may look like for you. Even if that path looked nothing like the one I wanted for you. Even if it took you away from me for a while.

I am immensely proud of you. As a man, as a mercenary, and as a knight. I am honored to fight at your side, and I will gladly follow you into oblivion itself.

With that in mind, I had this made for you by the Forge priests when you were sixteen. I had to guess on your measurements, but the Citadel forgemaster told me that the Forge took personal interest in the project, so it should fit, even if it looks a bit big to me. I figured you could use it no matter where life took you, and who knows, it might protect you when I can't. I look forward to seeing you wear it when next we meet.

With the deepest affection, your father,

Padraeg Quinn

Leon's hand shook and each breath hitched. Tears dripped down his face and onto the letter, smearing the ink when he went to wipe them away, but he couldn't stop them from falling. His hands shook as he folded the parchment and pushed it into his pocket. Fumbling for the envelope, he swallowed around the lump in his throat. There'd been weight in there. A small thing, but whatever was in there was better than nothing. He hadn't even thought to save a scrap of Padraeg's cloak before he went to the waves.

The envelope gave up its last treasure, a large bronze key meant for a chest.

His head snapped up, mouth open to ask a question he couldn't even form, and chastised himself for even thinking. His heart screamed, and he couldn't stop his face from falling. There was no way Aoife had brought whatever the key unlocked. They had barely had room for provisions, let alone—

"It's here," her voice rasped. She stood and scurried over to her bed, where she dropped to the floor. "He didn't tell me why, but it's one of the only things he brought."

There were cupboards built into her bed, Leon realized with a jolt. He stood and hurried to her side as she tugged a large and familiar green chest out from under her bed. A copper lock, the decorations a match for the ones at the end of the key, glittered in the lamplight.

Aoife may as well have not existed, for all he noticed her as he sank to his knees. Reaching out with trembling hands, he pushed the key inside. It turned ever so slowly before unlatching with a thunk that shouldn't have been that loud in such small quarters.

The hinges creaked and groaned. Too many years left unattended in a port town had aged them beyond belief. Leon held his breath as he forced them open, and then gasped when a fresh wave of agony tore through him like lightning. Aoife echoed it, her hands clapped over her mouth and fresh tears staining her cheeks.

Padraeg's final gift to Leon, the thing he hoped would protect Leon when he wouldn't, was armor. Chain mail, plate armor, and a thick, blue gambeson to go below it all. It was a gift worthy of the Vigilant General, one made with the blessing of the Forge and the skill of the Citadel forgemaster.

Leon couldn't breathe. It was too much for a poor mercenary. Too much for the disgraced son of the guard-captain of Mezeldwelf. This was something that the senior knights would've given squires when they first took their oaths.

The forgemaster had made it perfectly. Everything—from the style of the helmet to the owl with its wings spread wide that was embossed on the breastplate, to the regimented style in which it was laid out in the chest—was exactly as it would've been for a new knight. The only thing missing was the formal cloak that was currently hanging from a hook by the door, washed and restored by Aoife's command.

Padraeg had always known Leon would end up here. He'd kept that armor for years, waiting until Leon was ready for it, and now he would never get to see Leon wear it.

He stared at the armor, at the owl on the breastplate, and found he couldn't breathe. He lurched to his feet, gasping for breath, and spun around. He needed air. Without even bothering to tie his laces or grab the cloak that meant so much more now, he shook off Aoife's worried cries and darted out of the cabin like the Templesbane was on his heels.

Once he was above deck, the world felt bigger again, and he could breathe. The wind blew against his face, its chill cooling and comforting. The sun had long since gone down, and the deck was covered in people that hadn't been fortunate enough to win a place below deck for the night. Thank the gods, Aoife hadn't followed him.

He dodged around sleeping people and stumbled to the railing. The wood was sturdy under his fingers, if a little too low for him to rest on comfortably.

He gasped for air and reveled in the bite and the chill. It made thinking easier, soothed the whirling cacophony that was his thoughts into something resembling order.

Standing in silence, watching the stars pass by overhead, he could almost pretend this was some dream that had stretched on long past its original purpose. The darkness pressed in on him like a blanket, broken only by the stars and the shimmering glow of the winter lights.

It was peaceful, and gods knew Leon could do with some peace right now, even if it was only in these stolen moments under the stars.

"So, are you going to make for the shore?" Njeri asked, coming up to stand by Leon. She was so close the heat of her body burned against him like a furnace. "Or are you still going to Falte?" She paused, and her hand delicately curled around Leon's smallest finger. "The Band is ready to follow you."

They would follow him. Right into oblivion, like Padraeg had, if he asked them to. Leon shivered and blinked back the tears that kept threatening to fall.

He pressed his hand back against hers, a silent assurance that she was still here, even now. The Band, Aoife, and everyone on this ship would follow him no matter what he did. Even if Padraeg was gone, Leon wasn't alone in this.

"No," Leon said grimly, staring into the horizon. The winter lights lit up the sky, brighter than he'd ever seen before. From the northernmost Falten islands, they were supposedly visible all year. "I'm not leaving."

He'd always heard that sailors believed that traveling under the winter lights was a sign of luck, that the Sea would guide them safely to their destination. He didn't feel lucky now, standing beneath them with dozens of sleeping mercenaries lying huddled under their cloaks and blankets. Right now, he wanted to sleep alongside them, to forget that he had a warm cabin as befit his station, that he'd revealed himself and the whole world had expectations for him now.

But he couldn't. The people on this ship, the refugees on land, and the woman below deck staring at the last gift her brother had ever given someone, all expected things of him. He'd spent so long running, but he was done with that now. The time had come to face what he was running from.

"We're going to Falte." His hand dipped into his pocket and curled around the parchment buried there. Padraeg had believed in him, even when Leon made it clear he intended for the Knights Vigilant to die with him. Padraeg might not be here anymore, but he'd still believed in Leon, and Leon would do whatever it took to make sure that belief was not ill placed. "It's time the Protectors and I planned the march on Dhuitholm."

The End

ABOUT THE AUTHOR

Ceril N Domace is an accountant, animal lover, and a dedicated dungeon master.

As a lover of fiction works great and small, Ceril has been reading age-inappropriate stories since her father failed to pull *The Silmarillion* from her grubby little fingers at age five. As a grown-up accountant, her spreadsheet compiling gives her plenty of time to make plans for a fantastic world that isn't plagued by balance sheets . . . and also has dragons.

On the rare occasions she manages to free herself from an ever-growing and complex web of TTRPG, Ceril enjoys taking walks and griping that all her hobbies are work in disguise.

Made in the USA
Monee, IL
06 November 2024

68753100R00203